S0-BZS-556

"Brisk . . . candid"
—*Time*

"Full . . . lively"
—*The New Yorker*

"JACK LONDON LIVES AGAIN
IN THIS BOOK"
—*Books*

"A vivid and exciting history of a
vivid and exciting personality"
—*Times Literary Supplement*

"Jack London would have applauded the
skill and honesty with which his biog-
rapher has portrayed him. This is a
portrait in full relief, a biography as brave
as the life of the man"
—*The New York Times*

∅ SIGNET

(0451)

Great Reading from Irving Stone and SIGNET

- [ ] THE ORIGIN (133080—$4.95)*
- [ ] ADVERSARY IN THE HOUSE (111656—$3.50)
- [ ] THE AGONY AND THE ECSTASY (146921—$4.95)*
- [ ] CLARENCE DARROW FOR THE DEFENSE (134524—$4.95)
- [ ] DEAR THEO: AN AUTOBIOGRAPHY OF VINCENT VAN GOGH

 (140982—$4.95)*
- [ ] THE GREEK TREASURE (134575—$4.50)*
- [ ] IMMORTAL WIFE (111729—$3.95)
- [ ] JACK LONDON—SAILOR ON HORSEBACK (148320—$3.95)*
- [ ] LOVE IS ETERNAL (145402—$4.95)*
- [ ] PASSIONS OF THE MIND (134567—$4.95)
- [ ] THE PRESIDENT'S LADY (139909—$3.95)*
- [ ] THOSE WHO LOVE (134508—$4.95)

*Prices slightly higher in Canada

Buy them at your local bookstore or use this convenient coupon for ordering.

NEW AMERICAN LIBRARY,
P.O. Box 999, Bergenfield, New Jersey 07621

Please send me the books I have checked above. I am enclosing $_____
(please add $1.00 to this order to cover postage and handling). Send check
or money order—no cash or C.O.D.'s. Prices and numbers subject to change
without notice.

Name_____

Address_____

City_____State_____Zip Code_____
Allow 4-6 weeks for delivery.
This offer is subject to withdrawal without notice.

JACK LONDON,
Sailor on Horseback

A Biographical Novel by
IRVING STONE

A SIGNET BOOK

NEW AMERICAN LIBRARY

COPYRIGHT, 1938, BY IRVING STONE
COPYRIGHT RENEWED 1965 BY IRVING STONE

All rights reserved, including the right to reproduce this book
or parts thereof in any form. For information address
Doubleday & Company, Inc., 245 Park Avenue,
New York, New York 10167.

This is an authorized reprint of a hardcover edition
published by Doubleday & Company, Inc.

 SIGNET TRADEMARK REG. U.S. PAT. OFF. AND FOREIGN COUNTRIES
REGISTERED TRADEMARK—MARCA REGISTRADA
HECHO EN CHICAGO, U.S.A.

SIGNET, SIGNET CLASSIC, MENTOR, PLUME, MERIDIAN and NAL
BOOKS are published by New American Library,
1633 Broadway, New York, New York 10019

FIRST SIGNET PRINTING, JULY, 1969

9   10   11   12   13   14   15   16

PRINTED IN THE UNITED STATES OF AMERICA

To

JEAN

(Who Collaborates)

"If you suppress truth, if you hide truth, if you do not rise up and speak out in meeting, if you speak out in meeting without speaking the whole truth, then you are less true than truth."

"Let me glimpse the face of truth. Tell me what the face of truth looks like."

JACK LONDON.

1

ON A morning in early June of the year 1875 the people of San Francisco awakened to read a horrifying story in the *Chronicle*. A woman had shot herself in the temple because her husband had 'driven her from home for refusing to destroy her unborn infant—a chapter of heartlessness and domestic misery.' The woman was Flora Wellman, black sheep of the pioneer Wellman family of Massillon, Ohio; the man was Professor W. H. Chaney, itinerant Irish astrologer; the unborn child was to become known to millions the world over as Jack London.

The *Chronicle* article, though admitting in its last line that the story was Flora's as filtered through her friends, is solid invective against Chaney. He is accused of having been confined in the Tombs prison; of having laid several former wives to rest, 'at their heads a green grass turf, at their heels a stone'; of having forced Flora to drudge at the washtubs and take care of other people's children for hire; of having sold the furniture for which she had helped to pay; of ordering her out of the house, and abandoning her when she refused to go. There is as little truth in these accusations as there is in the heading of the *Chronicle* article: 'A Discarded Wife'; for Flora Wellman was never married to Professor Chaney.

Flora had but slight intention of suicide. She inflicted upon herself only a flesh wound. The bullet did far more injury to Chaney than it did to Flora, for the story was reproduced in newspapers all over the country, and the remainder of Chaney's life was spent in bitterness and disgrace. He disappeared from San Francisco shortly after. Jack London never set eyes upon his father.

At the time the *Chronicle* article appeared Flora Wellman was about thirty. She was a small, homely, wiry woman who

wore spectacles and a wig of black curls because a bout with
typhoid had cost her a good part of her eyesight and hair.
She had a big nose, big ears, a sallow complexion, and was
without taste in dress. Flora came of good Welsh stock, her
grandmother, Mrs. Joel Wellman, having guided her four
children across the Allegheny Mountains in midwinter, just
after 1800, from Canandaigua, New York, to Wayne County,
Ohio, a journey which demanded energy, self-reliance, and
courage.

Mrs. Joel Wellman's two sons, Hiram and Marshall, grandfather of Jack London, inherited these traits. While on a visit
to Cleveland they went by boat in the late fall to an island in
Put-In Bay. The boat failed to stop on its return and last trip
for the year and the two boys were abandoned on the desolate island without food or shelter, and winter about to set in.
With only such tools as they could make out of rocks and
driftwood they constructed a raft of sufficient strength to
carry them not only to the mainland, but all the way to
Cleveland.

Marshall Wellman settled in Massillon, Ohio, where he
built canals, patented inventions, chief among which is the
Wellman coal grate, accumulated considerable wealth, and
built one of the most beautiful homes in Massillon, in which
his daugher Flora was born.

Flora Wellman had all the advantages of her times. She
was trained in music, educated at a finishing school, was well
read, used good English, and had polished manners. As the
daughter of the wealthy Wellman family she could have
taken her choice of husbands and settled down, as did her
brothers and sisters, to a prosperous and solid life. But somewhere the machinery slipped a cog; clever inventor that he
was, Marshall Wellman could not think up a device to keep
his daughter in line. She was said by her friends to be a
clever and intelligent woman but a neurotic, a woman of
unstable emotions who had difficulty in holding herself to any
given discipline or direction. The attack of typhus she
suffered at the age of twenty is said to have left her mind in a
disorderly state.

At the age of twenty-five Flora put her belongings in a
suitcase and left Massillon, an unprecedented thing for a
young unmarried girl to do. To the end of her days she never
communicated with her parents, nor her parents with her.
That there was a row is indisputable, but the exact cause of
the trouble can only be surmised. The inventive *Chronicle* reporter suggested that 'she came to this coast about the time
the Professor took the journey overland through the romantic

sagebrush'; but Flora did not meet Chaney until three years later, in Seattle. We would give a great deal to be able to follow her trail during those three obscured years in which she traveled from city to city earning her living by giving piano lessons; from the evidence one is led to believe that it would not be a pretty tale.

Professor Chaney writes, 'Flora was known as my wife in the same lodging-house where she had passed as the wife of Lee Smith. It was a very respectable place, and one day when I came home I found all the lodgers moving away and great excitement throughout the house. As soon as I entered the room Flora locked the door, fell on her knees before me, and between sobs begged me to forgive her. I said I had nothing to forgive. Finally, after much delay and pleading she confessed about Lee Smith and said the lodgers were leaving on account of her being known as Miss Wellman, Mrs. Smith, and Mrs. Chaney all at nearly the same time. Had I followed my first impression I should have left her then, and it would have saved years of misery. But my own life had been a broken one, and on reflection I forgave her.'

Chaney first met Flora Wellman in the home of Mayor Yesler of Seattle, who came from Ohio and knew the Wellman family. Flora was stopping with Mayor and Mrs. Yesler; they confided to Chaney that she came from very respectable people, but that she had done something wrong. This undisclosed something wrong had probably been the cause of Flora's leaving home. Chaney was intimate with the Yeslers; he came often to their house; and when he later encountered Flora in San Francisco they met as old friends.

What kind of man was Jack London's father? Of his antecedents we know little, except that he was a full-blooded Irishman, and was born in a log cabin in Maine. He spent many years of his youth at sea. He was a short, powerfully built man who at the age of sixty was able to knock downstairs a bully who had been sent to beat him up. He spent his life writing, editing magazines, lecturing, teaching, and drawing up astrological nativities. He assembled a comprehensive library on philosophy, mathematics, astronomy, and occult subjects. He was a linguist, an able student of history and the Bible. Among his friends, students, and followers he was known as a remarkable man; among astrologers he was acknowledged to be one of the best. As an old man in Chicago he is said to have devoted his great energies, some sixteen hours a day, to the cause of astrology, in which he had a passionate and genuine belief. He considered it to be an exact science, like chemistry and mathematics, one which could raise humanity from the mire.

Chaney's greatest weakness was women. When reproached by his friends for moral delinquency he would point to his horoscope and cry, 'Alas! It is in my nativity.' He could quickly be aroused to anger, was not easy to get along with, for he had always to be the headman, the leader, the teacher. He spent most of his life in poverty because he was impractical with money, taught for nothing when his pupils were too poor to pay, and was constantly giving away what little means he had.

His students testify that his lectures always commanded close attention, for he had something to say and said it in a pleasing manner. Yet few were his match in sarcasm and irony. He gave his friends plenty to think about if they were capable of thinking, and if they were not, they did not remain his friends long. In Portland, Oregon, his weekly lectures were popular. The audience sat before a two-foot horoscope on a blackboard while Chaney stood before it with a pointer indicating the various configurations and calling on the class to explain their significance. After an hour-and-a-half lecture he entertained them with amusing stories, for he had a lusty Irish humor.

One of his followers, Joe Trounson of Healdsburg, later a brother socialist of Jack London's, wrote in 1909, 'One charm of his conversation was his habit of saying, "Ah, that gives me an idea!" and then he would proceed to elaborate a beautiful truth or what appeared to be a fact in nature heretofore overlooked. In mathematics and astrology he was wonderful; he taught me the method by which the ancient writings were deciphered. He was a thorough grammarian, was profound, scholarly, had a wonderful memory, and could write for sixteen hours a day without fatigue. He often lectured just as our socialists do in these more modern times; he spoke of the rich getting richer and the poor getting poorer, and the causes and cures of poverty. He taught me more than all the others put together, and was very versatile. One day he said to me, "I will teach you to calculate an eclipse or any science you wish to learn." In short, whenever I wanted to know anything I wended my way to Professor Chaney's.'

Trounson does not neglect to mention Chaney's failings. He was idiotic in music; he hated the champions of woman suffrage; he was an unrelenting enemy as well as a true friend, and could hardly give the devil his due after a quarrel; he accepted money from the Freethinkers to lecture against orthodoxy . . . and could not stay away from young widows.

Having joined forces with Flora Wellman, Chaney set up house on what was then First Avenue, between Mission and Valencia Streets. He joined the staff of *Common Sense* magazine, which advertised itself as the only Free Thought magazine west of the Rockies, wrote articles, delivered a series of sociological lectures for the Philomathean Society, and gave private readings in horoscopes.

'The Professor has located permanently in San Francisco for the practice of ASTROLOGY. He will also teach the science to such as may desire to obtain a knowledge of this celestial art, which includes among its pupils and admirers such minds as Galileo and Sir Isaac Newton.—In the long lists of persons advertised in this city under the head of Astrologers, there is not one who knows anything of the science. Those calling themselves Astrologers are simply fortune-tellers who divine through a teacup or pack of cards, and by their charlatanism have done much toward bringing genuine Astrology into disrepute.—Office hours from 10 to 12 a.m. and from 2 to 4 p.m. Receptions for the evenings may be secured by special arrangement.'

Chaney was no quack. That he was not consciously racketeering off the gullible is evidenced by the fact that the greater part of his life was spent in teaching, writing, and lecturing for the cause without pay. A few anecdotes will illuminate the position he held in his field.

'At one time a house burned down. It was evidently incendiary. The owner consulted Professor Chaney. Chaney said there were three engaged in it and described them so accurately that the owner went to them and said Chaney said they did it. They confessed at once. If Chaney said it, it was useless to deny it.

'A middle-aged woman who had apparently not lived too rigorously correct a life went to Chaney to have her horoscope read. In the middle of the reading she jumped up and fled, exclaiming, "That man can read God's mind!" '

On Sunday nights Chaney gave lectures on astrology in the Charter Oak Hall, where Flora sold tickets at the door for ten cents each. For a time these lectures were well attended, though a portion of the audience came to scoff and amuse itself.

The best record of Chaney's mind and work to come down to us is contained in the articles he published in *Common Sense:* 'The Causes and Cure of Poverty,' and 'What Is to Be Done with the Criminal?'—subjects on which his son Jack would be writing heatedly some twenty years later. In 'Man Should Be Able to Predict the Future' he writes, 'A false education had taught us that the future belongs to God, and that it is blasphemous for man to even attempt to pry into it. Trained from earliest infancy in this belief, probably nine tenths of the people of the United States are disposed to doubt when they hear it asserted that the future can be predicted. They occupy a position similar to the people before the time of Galileo. Educated in the doctrine that this earth was flat, they looked with abhorrence upon all who maintained that it was a sphere, and when Galileo was imprisoned by the Pope and Cardinals for maintaining that it moved in an orbit, the common people felt that this early martyr to science was properly punished.'

A study of Chaney's articles reveals a clear, forceful, and pleasing literary style, an authentic erudition, courage to speak his mind, a sympathy for the mass of humanity, and a desire to teach them to better themselves. His point of view is modern and progressive; in his article on criminology he writes that the certainty rather than the severity of the punishment is what deters criminals, and in another article proposes that the Philomatheans organize a Brotherhood and Sisterhood of men, women, and children to hold weekly meetings in which the adults will write and discuss theses, and the children will practise music, composition, and criticism so that they may continue to improve the race until in a few generations vice and crime will almost entirely disappear.

At many points the writing, the attack, the attitudes, the enthusiasms, the very turning of a phrase is so similar to the writings of Jack London that the reader rubs his eyes in amazement.

Flora was not only an astrologer, but an ardent spiritualist as well. She held séances in which the public was invited to communicate with the dead, to send messages to former loved ones, and because of the vantage point of the dead, to receive advice from them on how to conduct their businesses and love affairs, how to settle quarrels and control their husbands or wives. Spiritualism was very much in vogue in the 1870's; dozens of séances were being conducted all over San Francisco, and the believers went so far as to consult the spirits for approval before they would engage a housekeeper.

Flora and Chaney spent a number of happy months together in San Francisco, Flora keeping house, giving piano lessons, conducting séances, lecturing on spiritualism, and taking tickets at the door of the sawdust-floored tent where Chaney was lecturing on chemistry, astronomy, and occultism. They had friends among the astrologers, were well thought of, occupied a position of leadership in their cult. Flora seems to have loved Chaney, and was eager to be married to him, but Chaney was too busy lecturing to the Philomatheans on 'The Phenomena of Physical, Intellectual, Moral, and Spiritual Life' to be bothered with anything so mundane as marriage.

When Jack London was twenty-one years old he wrote to Chaney to ask if he was his father. On June 4, 1899, twenty-four years to the day after the appearance of the *Chronicle* article, Chaney replies to his inquiry, addresses him as 'Dear Sir,' agrees to 'comply with his wish to observe silence and secrecy,' and gives his own version of the happenings leading to Flora's attempted suicide. 'I was never married to Flora Wellman,' writes Chaney, 'but she lived with me from June 11, 1874, until June 3, 1875. I was impotent at that time, the result of hardship, privation, and too much brain work. Therefore I cannot be your father, nor am I sure who your father is.'

Acceding to Jack's plea to help him determine who his father was, Chaney repeats the gossip that linked Flora's name with two other men in the spring of 1875, but readily admits that he 'knows nothing of his own knowledge.' He then pens one of the most heartbreaking pages ever written. 'There was a time when I had a very tender affection for Flora; but there came a time when I hated her with all the intensity of my intense nature, and even thought of killing her and myself, as many a man has under similar circumstances. Time, however, has healed the wounds and I feel no unkindness toward her, while for you I feel a warm sympathy, for I can imagine what my emotions would be were I in your place. . . . The *Chronicle* published that I turned her out of doors because she would not submit to an abortion. This was copied and sent broadcast over the country. My sisters in Maine read it and two of them became my enemies. One died believing I was in the wrong. All others of my kindred, except one sister in Portland, Oregon, are still my enemies and denounce me as a disgrace to them. I published a pamphlet at the time containing a report from a detective given me by the Chief of Police, showing that many of the slanders against me were false, but neither the *Chronicle* nor any of the papers that defamed me would correct the false statement. Then I gave up defending myself, and for years life was a burden. But reaction finally came, and now I have a few friends who think me respectable. I am past seventy-six, and quite poor.'

Unsatisfied, Jack London sent another urgent demand for

information. Chaney, still denying that he was Jack's father, wrote one last letter.

'The cause of our separation began when Flora one day said to me, "You know that motherhood is the great desire of my life, and as you are too old—now some time when I find a good, nice man are you not willing for me to have a child by him?"

'I said yes, only he must support her. No, she must always live with me and be the wife of Professor Chaney. A month or so later she said she was pregnant by me. I thought she was only trying me and did not think she was pregnant. So I made a great fuss thinking to warn her not to make the attempt. This brought on a wrangle that lasted all day and night. After daylight I got up and told her she could never be a wife to me again. She was humbled in a moment, for she knew I was in earnest. She crawled on her knees to me, sobbing, and begged my forgiveness. But I would not forgive her, although I still thought she was merely pretending to be in a family way. But her temper was a great trial, and I had often thought before that time that I must leave her on account of it.

'When she left she went to Doctor Ruttley's house; went out to the back yard, soon returned, a pistol in one hand and a box of cartridges in the other, a wound in the left side of her forehead and the blood running over her face. In reply to Mrs. Ruttley, Flora said, "This little woman has been trying to kill herself and made a bad job of it."

'A great excitement followed. A mob of a hundred and fifty gathered, swearing to hang me to the nearest lamp-post.'

Although all the copies of the defense pamphlet Chaney published have disappeared, its existence has been verified by people who read it at the time. The detective reported that the pistol was second-hand and had not been discharged since being oiled; that it smelled of oil and not of gunpowder; that a carpenter working within twenty feet of Flora at the time had heard no report of a pistol; that her face would have been filled with powder had she shot as she had said, but there was no mark of powder about her.

What is remarkable about Chaney's effort to prove that Flora was only shamming is that he made no attempt to look at Flora's wound to see if it were real or imaginary, nor did he bring up this point in the defense pamphlet. And for good reason: that Flora carried the wound on her temple has been attested by her stepdaughter, Eliza London Shepard, and by her stepgrandson, John Miller. Chaney was apparently trying to establish that if Flora had wounded herself at all, it was with some instrument far less lethal than a gun—for example, a jagged piece of metal—but even if he had proved his point, he would have been no better off.

This same type of omission is what makes Chaney's denial of paternity unacceptable. If he had wanted to confound Flora's charge that she was pregnant by him, and he had been truly impotent, all he would have had to say was, 'Flora, you and I have had no sexual relations, so how can I be the father of your child?' And if he were impotent, would Flora have been so foolish as to claim that she was pregnant by him? Chaney, with all his education, simply got his words twisted; he meant to tell Jack that he was sterile, and could not create life; for nowhere does he deny that Flora was in point of fact a wife to him.

Why did Chaney deny that he was Jack London's father? Since his denial seems sincere there is reason to believe that he had genuinely thought himself sterile, and was convinced that Flora had been with another man during that critical month. But even if he were not convinced, he was now past seventy and too tired to begin a father-and-son relationship at the very end of his life. He had suffered greatly because of his union with Flora Wellman, and he had no mind to plunge all over again into an affair that had embittered him for so long. Jack London was a stranger to him, an unknown name. All Chaney wanted, in relation to Flora and Jack London, was to be let alone.

It was futile for Chaney to have denied his fatherhood. His writing of the name Jack London on the envelopes of the letters he sent to Jack cannot be distinguished from Jack's own signature. Jack inherited from his father his strong, handsome Irish face, his light hair, high forehead, deep-set mystical eyes, sensuous mouth, powerful chin, and short, husky torso. Doctor Hall, who attended Flora during her pregnancy, testifies that sixteen years later he saw a handsome, heavy-set young boy walk on the ferryboat who was so much the spit and image of Professor Chaney that he knew even before asking his name that it could be none other than Chaney's son. But more important, Jack inherited Chaney's brain and character; never were there a father and son more completely alike in temperament and tenor of thought.

After the attempted suicide Flora was taken into the home of William H. Slocumb, a writer on the *Chronicle* and the publisher of *Common Sense*, where she was befriended until the birth of Jack. After his failure to clear himself, Chaney joined the one sister in Portland who had not lost faith in him. Here he lived for many years, collected a fine library, published pamphlets and an astrological almanac, acquired students and followers. Later he went to New Orleans where he published an occult magazine and tutored two young boys for his board and lodging. His last move was to Chicago, where he finally married, named himself principal of the College of Astronomy, and eked out a living by giving oral nativities for one dollar each. Before the end of the century he passed on, fulfilling to the letter, according to one of his students, a prediction that he would die on a given day and be buried in a blizzard.

Flora Wellman gave public lectures on spiritualism and was active in séances up to the day her son was born. San Franciscans remember her standing on the platform, weirdly dressed, the false black curls reaching her shoulders, crouched over as though there were a hump in her back, her baby sticking straight out in front of her. They were sorry for this frail unmarried woman who was alone in the world; several times collections were taken up to help her.

On the fourteenth of January, 1876, the *Chronicle* once again prints the name of Chaney, but this time more kindly: 'Chaney.—In this city, January 12, the wife of W. H. Chaney, a son.' The boy was known as John Chaney for only eight months; then Flora married John London.

John London was born in Pennsylvania, of English extraction. He went to country school, and was fond of quoting. At nineteen, when boss of a section of the Pennsylvania-Erie Railroad, he married Ann Jane Cavett. The couple had ten children, and lived together happily. London left the railroad and became a farmer. When the Civil War broke out he fought for the North until an attack of typhus destroyed one lung. After the war he took up a section of government land near Moscow, Iowa, where he farmed, was sheriff, worked as a carpenter and builder. He was a deacon of the Methodist Church, and on Sundays after the sermon brought the parson home for Sunday dinner.

Not long after Ann Jane Cavett's death one of their sons was injured by being struck on the chest with a baseball. The doctor recommended that the boy be taken to California where the climate would help him recover. The doctor failed to mention that within its twelve hundred miles the state had several different kinds of weather. San Francisco being the only town in California that London knew about, he bundled his sick son and two youngest daughters onto a westbound train for that city. After ten days of San Francisco fogs the boy was dead.

London next sent to Iowa for a married couple to come to California and keep house for him and his two daughters. The couple took care of the children for a few months, then went upstate, where the man had been offered a job. Once again left alone with his two girls, London paid to have them kept in the Protestant Orphan Asylum on Haight Street.

John London was then in his mid-forties, a nice-looking man with a full-face beard, kindly, gentle, remembered by everyone as sweet. Still grieving over the loss of his wife and son, he was persuaded by a fellow worker to attend a spiritualist meeting. 'Come on, John, and see if you can't get a message from them.' Instead of getting a message from his old wife, London got himself a new one.

Whether London met Flora before or after the birth of her son is not a matter of record, but there can be little doubt that he knew Flora had not been married to Chaney. Flora told it herself in public meeting in Charter Oak Hall while in the process of giving the now absent Professor a thorough castigation. At the time most people wondered why London married Flora. Though not in robust health he was well set up, had a pleasant personality, and was liked by the women he took out, particularly the attractive actress who accompanied him on Saturday afternoons to visit his two daughters in the Orphan Asylum.

John London was alone in San Francisco, he was a homebody; he longed for a wife and hearth for himself, and for a home and mother for his daughters. Flora was convivial, she was a good talker, she played the piano for him and filled his lonesome hours. When he once again came down with typhus, she nursed him. Two weeks after John was confined to his bed Flora appeared at the Orphan Asylum during the Saturday afternoon visiting hours, told the girls that their father was ill and that she was to be their new mother. The girls refused to believe her.

On the seventh of September, 1876, Flora Wellman signed herself as Flora Chaney on the marriage license and took her eight-months-old son to live with John London in a small flat in the workingman's section south of Market Street. When the family was settled John went to the Asylum and brought home his two daughters, of whom the oldest was Eliza, a plain-featured, plain-spoken girl of eight, mature and self-reliant for her age. Eliza was shown through the house by her father and told that the baby was her brother. When she looked down at Jack for the first time she saw that there were flies on his face, for Flora had not thought to buy a piece of mosquito netting with which to cover the infant.

Eliza asked no questions; she made a fan out of a piece of paper and sat by the cradle keeping the flies off the baby. In that instant the practical-minded girl of eight adopted Jack as her own child, a trust she was to hold sacred to the day she buried Jack's ashes on a high hill overlooking the Valley of the Moon.

Flora had little liking for the job of mother. She was restless, temperamental, moody, too busy with her music and lectures and spiritualism to pay attention to the boy, who fell ill with bowel trouble. Upon advice of their doctor the London family moved from town to Bernal Heights, a district of farms, where Flora advertised for a wet nurse. Mrs. Jenny Prentiss, a negress who lived across the road and who had just lost her own baby, became Jack's wet nurse, foster mother, and life-long friend. Mammy Jenny was a tall, broad, deep-bosomed woman, black as coal, hard-working, religious, proud of her home and family and her respected position in the community. She took Jack on her spacious lap, sang him negro lullabies, squandered on him all the impetuous love she would have lavished on her own child had he lived. Between Eliza and Mammy Jenny, little Jack was now well cared for.

After a year the family moved back to the crowded workingman's section, 920 Natoma Street. By this time Jack was toddling and had a little red wagon that he pulled. Eliza would put her doll in it, and Jack would haul it up and down the sidewalk. One day when Eliza returned from school she found her doll had been smashed because Flora had given it to Jack but had neglected to tie it in the wagon.

The Londons lived in a long railroad flat in the three-story frame building for two years. Flora took in a boarder, whose rent money paid for a Chinese servant. John London worked as a carpenter and builder, but the depression of 1876 still had the West in its grip and work was scarce. He got a job opening crates for the IXL Emporium, and later canvassed for the Singer Sewing Machine Company, earning a modest living.

When an epidemic hit San Francisco, Jack and Eliza came down with diptheria. The two children, who were quarantined in the same bed, were dying. Eliza wakened out of her coma long enough to hear Flora ask, 'Can the two of them be buried in the same coffin, doctor, to save expenses?' While Jack's mother was thus arranging her son's funeral, his foster father was rushing about town to find a trained nurse and a doctor who might save the children. Hearing of a doctor in the city of Oakland, across the Bay, who was having marked success with diptheria cases, John took the first boat across and pleaded with him to come to San Francisco. The doctor came, burned the white cankers off the children's throats, poured sulphur down them . . . and the double funeral was averted.

As soon as Jack and Eliza had fully recovered, the family moved to Oakland, a sun-flooded, sleepy suburb of San Francisco which was trying to become a metropolis on its own. They rented a comfortable five-room cottage on Third Street. Flora was gone from home all day with get-rich-quick business schemes to supplement John London's sporadic earnings. Her chief scheme was selling gold leaf to saloonkeepers with which to gild the frames of the pictures over the bar. When the saloonkeeper refused to be convinced that the frames of his pictures would look better in gilt, Flora stood on the bar and gilded them herself.

Mammy Jenny was a little later to move to Oakland to be closer to her 'white child,' but in the meanwhile the mothering of Jack fell squarely upon Eliza's shoulders. She either had to stay home with the boy, or take him with her to school. When she explained to her teacher why she had to bring her little brother along, the teacher fixed a box on the platform as a desk for him and gave him picture books to pore over. Jack, then four years old, enjoyed playing in the yard with the other children, who would give Eliza an apple or allow her to wear their rings for the privilege of letting Jack sit with them.

John London next ventured to open a grocery store in the workingman's section of Oakland at Seventh and Peralta Streets. The family lived in the four rooms behind the store. It was here Jack received his first inkling that something was wrong in the family relationship, for in his hand-scrawled notes for an autobiography which he one day hoped to write under the title of *Sailor on Horseback*, he tells of a six-year-old boy overhearing a quarrel in the back of a grocery store, in which the father reproaches the mother for having a child out of wedlock, and the mother defends herself by crying, 'I was so young, and he promised me a bed of roses.'

The grocery store prospered. John London, who was an excellent judge of produce, traveled among the outlying farms to buy the best in fruits and vegetables, while Flora and Eliza waited on trade and Jack helped himself to candy and nuts every time he tripped through the store. Mammy Jenny settled in a cottage in Alameda, where Jack spent many hours of his day playing with her children, eating at her table, being watched over and nursed and cared for by the kindly woman to whom he was as much a son as her own blood. From her Jack received counsel and comfort; when he tired of playing in the back yard with the other children he would climb onto her lap to hear the lullabies of his baby days, or fairy stories which Mammy Jenny had inherited from her race.

It seems to have been a happy period for the family. Only Flora was discontented, for she did not feel they were going ahead rapidly enough. She introduced John to a man by the name of Stowell, to whom she persuaded her husband to sell a half interest in the store so they could expand and make money faster. Together the London and Stowell families rented a large, modern house on Sixteenth and Woods Streets in a solid residential neighborhood. The store was enlarged, and the business grew so big that John London had to spend all his time in the country buying merchandise. Stowell took charge of the store and the money that came in. London no longer knew what was going on. One day he returned from a trip to find his store stark empty: Stowell had sold out the entire stock and fixtures and absconded with the cash.

Broke once more, John London returned to his one and only love, farming. He leased the twenty-acre Davenport place in Alameda, where he raised corn and other vegetables for the market. Jack writes that it was a forlorn period of his childhood, for he had no playmates and was forced to turn inward on himself.

London was a skilled farmer and would have made a success of it, but Flora was not one to let well enough alone. Because she was supposed to be the smart member of the family John entrusted the business to her hands. He never could figure where she spent the money, for apparently she did not pay her bills. Flora prided herself on being a clever woman; she was always trying to make money out of new ventures, including lottery tickets and stocks. She meant well, but she was fly-by-night. In addition, she insisted that every detail in the running of the household be guided by departed spirits. In spite of the fact that London never went to another spiritualist meeting after his marriage, Flora invited groups of spiritualists to her house. During the séances six-year-old Jack would be laid on a table in the center of a dark room and seven pairs of hands would be placed on the edge of it. Jack and the table would then begin floating about.

As a result of these spooky sessions, of the frightening conversation he had overheard in the back of the Oakland grocery store, and of the emotional instability and lack of control he had inherited from both parents and the shattered nervous system bequeathed to him by Flora, the boy suffered from frequent nervousness and was occasionally on the verge of a breakdown.

Flora was a little thing—she could walk under her husband's outstretched arm—but the scenes she could create were out of all proportion to her size. Besides, she had a 'heart.' She would have heart attacks at the dinner table, and then the three children would have to help her to the couch and make a great fuss over her. The housework consequently fell upon the shoulders of Eliza, who by the age of thirteen was doing the cooking, cleaning, and washing.

There are numerous anecdotes told about Jack's childhood, but many of them are apocryphal, and one treads among them as on broken glass. Aside from his occasional nervous attacks he appears to have been a normal, wholesome child, good as gold, never malicious. He was blond and had curly hair, blue eyes, and a clear skin. At the least little thing his sensitive mouth would quiver. Here in Alameda he started school, but the better part of his time was spent in the fields paddling about with John London, who was his idol.

On Saturday nights the family went to the Tivoli Theater in Oakland, where beer and sandwiches were served while plays were given. John set Jack on the table so that he could see the comedy, and the boy would laugh and clap his hands. One weekday, playing in the kitchen where Eliza could keep an eye on him while she scrubbed the floor, he fell against a jagged hole in the sink and cut his forehead from the hairline to his nose. Eliza, remembering how her father had treated a cut on a horse's leg, filled the wound with cobwebs and covered it with tar. The first Saturday after the accident John put a bandage around Jack's head and took him to the theater as always, but the second Saturday Flora refused to take him with the bandage. She told Eliza she would either have to scrape the tar off the boy's head, or stay home with him. Eliza and Jack both wanted to see the show; standing in the middle of the kitchen she picked off the tar and the scab with it. Jack always carried that scar on his forehead.

The Londons now had a cow, plenty of vegetables, and a comfortable house. John culled all his produce, selling only the best to the market, and giving the less desirable vegetables to the poorer families about him. He established a reputation among the produce men for having first-rate goods, and he could have continued to earn a fair living on the Davenport place. Yet before long we find them giving up the farm and moving to San Mateo, a few miles down the coast from San Francisco. The family reports that the Londons moved because they wanted more space to raise horses. It is questionable whether John wanted to leave his farm; perhaps Flora agitated him with a get-rich-quick horse-breeding scheme, or perhaps she simply forgot to pay their bills, and they were forced off the land.

On his seventy-five acres along the fogbound coast John London planted potatoes, put his few horses to graze, and rented out pasture land. Jack attended school on top of a hill below Colma, with the one teacher and four or five grades all in the same room. In their free hours he and Eliza went to the beach to wade and gather clams and mussels. It was desolate, unbeautiful country, with a harsh coastline. Jack spent the dreariest year of his childhood here; he had no playmates, the farms were far apart, and the neighbors were either Italian or immigrant Irish for whose company Flora cared little. The only bright moments came when he and Eliza tramped to a neighboring farm to watch an Italian wedding or dance, or when he rode into San Francisco on the high wagon with his father when John was hauling potatoes to market.

Jack remembered this period as the hungriest of his life. He maintained he was so hungry for the taste of meat that he once stole a piece the size of his two fingers from a girl's lunch-basket, and that when his schoolmates threw chunks of meat to the ground because of surfeit, only pride prevented him from dragging them from the dirt and eating them.

When Jack was eight, John London put a down payment on an eighty-seven-acre ranch in Livermore, in the warm valley behind Oakland, and the family moved into an old farmhouse on the property. He planted a row of olive trees all about the ranch, put in vineyards and orchards, and cultivated his fields. This was the first time since he had been in California that he had bought, and he intended to make this his permanent home. Here Jack began doing the simple chores, hunting eggs, bringing in wood, drawing water from the well. Often he sat on the high seat alongside his father (Jack called him Father and loved him as a father even after he learned there was no blood relation between them) when John drove his produce to the Oakland market. London implanted in the boy's mind an enthusiasm not merely for farming, but for that scientific farming which brings forth only the finest produce from the earth and the finest animals from breeded stock. It was a devotion which Jack mistakenly thought was in his blood.

It was here too the boy discovered the authentic passion of his life, which was in truth passed down to him by Professor Chaney, the one talisman that never failed him, that brought him meaning and direction: the love of books. His teacher loaned him Irving's *Alhambra;* in the homes of neighbors, who possessed books only by accident, he stumbled upon a life of Garfield, Paul du Chaillu's *African Travels,* and most important of all a copy of Ouida's *Signa,* the lyrically written story of an illegitimate son of an Italian peasant girl and a wandering artist, who rose from poverty and hardship to become one of Italy's great composers, a story which in its essentials Jack was to duplicate. Jack writes that reading *Signa* pushed back his narrow hill-horizon, and all the world was made possible if he would dare it. Eliza reports him saying at this time, 'You know, Lize, I'm not going to get married until I'm forty years old. I'm going to have a big house, and one room is going to be filled with books.' By the time he was forty he had the big house, and several rooms filled with books. . . .

Though Jack enjoyed going into the fields with John, and reading with his sister Eliza, the two years spent in Livermore were also dismal ones. He was not too young to sense that there were several things wrong with his family; the home was rarely a pleasant one in which to live, dominated as it was by Flora's confusion of mind, her scenes and heart attacks and demands. Flora was not cruel to Jack, he loved her as any normal child will love its mother; she simply had no tenderness to bestow upon the boy, who turned to Eliza for affection. However, Flora arranged to board a middle-aged Civil War veteran by the name of Shepard, who had been widowed with three children. To her task of cooking and keeping house and mothering Jack, sixteen-year-old Eliza now had the added responsibility of mothering Shepard's three children, the oldest of whom was thirteen.

By the end of the first year John London had once again established himself in Oakand as a producer of fine vegetables, and there was always a market for his crop. The prospects for the future were so bright that the family bought Jack his first store-bought undershirt, which fairly transported the boy who had never known anything but the coarse homemade shifts. Then Flora, again not satisfied with their rate of progress, hatched a business scheme. She took John across the Bay to San Francisco on numerous trips, brought him into contact with the manager of one of the large hotels, negotiated an agreement whereby John was to start a chicken ranch and the hotel man was to buy all his chickens and eggs.

John London, who knew nothing about chickens, mortgaged his interest in the ranch to build enormous coops and steam-heated brooder houses. For a short time the San Fran-

cisco hotel man bought all his eggs and whatever chickens he
wanted to sell. Then three calamities hit him at once: Eliza,
who took care of the chickens, married Shepard and left the
ranch; an epidemic killed off a flock of the hens; and the remainder refused to lay. London's money being sunk in olive
trees, orchards, and brooder houses, when the interest on the
mortgage fell due he was unable to pay. The bank foreclosed.
Once again the Londons were out on the road, their belongings piled high in their potato wagon.

Jack London's mind was like a seismograph that recorded
every slight tremor about him . . . and tremors there were
aplenty, for the next thirteen years of the family's life were
spent in poverty and defeat. He often said that he had had no
childhood, that his first memories of life were pinched by
poverty, and that the pinch of poverty had been chronic.

Jack was ten years old when John London gave up forever
the farming he loved so well and went back to Oakland. Jack
was wiry, fair of face, with dark blue eyes, still suffering
keenly from the loss of Eliza. He was not a fighter, but at the
Garfield School there was the established California custom
that every boy fight every other boy, so he soon learned to
use his fists. He enjoyed most hunting ducks and fishing along
the Alameda sea wall with his father, who gave the boy his
own small gun and fishing rod. The constant failure and flight
of the family, the horrors of the spiritualist séances to which
he was exposed, the presentiment that there was something
askew in his paternity made him self-conscious, timid, unas-
suming. Between the older man and the boy, both suffering
from injuries inflicted upon them by Flora, each powerless to
right the wrong, there grew an ever-deepening sympathy.
They escaped together as often as they could to spend whole
days forlornly roaming the waterfront. They loved and
trusted each other completely, but it was a love touched by
sadness.

In Oakland the family rented a bay-window cottage on
East Seventeenth Street. Close by were the California Cotton
Mills, which had brought a number of girls over from Scot-
land to do their work. The manager asked London if he
wanted to board the girls. John was now fifty-five, crushed by
the knowledge that he would never again get back to the land
or be his own master; and there were not many jobs he was
still able to fill. He agreed to run the boarding-house.

Flora had brains, and at the beginning of each new cycle
she used them to advantage. She sent John, who knew good
produce and their prices, to do the marketing while she su-

pervised the cooking. The twenty young Scotch girls were satisfied, the mill management was pleased, and the Londons cleared such a substantial profit that at the end of a few months they were able to make a down payment on their cottage. When the mills imported another group of girls, Flora insisted that she and John buy the lot next door and build a second bungalow to house them.

For a time everything went well. The second bungalow brought them increased profits, for Flora was still managing carefully. Then the inherent emotional instability of her character overcame her. She lost interest; they were not making money fast enough, there was no excitement about a boarding-house . . . there were plenty of enterprises in which a woman as clever as she could make a fortune. She began spending—no one knew on what—and when the payments came due on the two mortgages, there was no cash with which to meet them. The bank took away both buildings, and with them John London's last steady means of earning a living.

While the London boarding-house had been prospering, young Jack had made a great discovery—the Oakland Public Library. During the five years he had been reading he had found but five genuine books; for the rest the barren countryside had afforded him only discarded dime novels and old newspapers. Dimly the child knew that there were other and even more beautiful books, but he had no conception of how to get to them. He had never dreamed that there was such a thing as a public library, a building that held thousands of books, all of them free for the asking. Jack dated his spiritual birth from the moment that he stood, cap in hand, in the doorway of the wooden building, his eyes wide with unbelieving that there could be so many books in the world. From that day on, though he would suffer much, though he would undergo agonies of the brain and soul, though he would be beaten and despised and cast out as a pariah, never again would he be alone. For Professor Chaney's son had come home.

In the public library he met for the first time an educated woman, one who was at home in the world of books. Miss Ina Coolbrith saw the light in his eye as he walked down the rows of books and ran his finger tips lovingly across the bindings. Before she came to his rescue he had stumbled across and read such mature books as Smollett's *Adventures of Peregrine Pickle*, and Wilkie Collins's *The New Magdalen*; Miss Coolbrith soon learned that his greatest desire was for books of adventure, of travel, of sea voyages and discoveries, and she supplied him bountifully. She was a cultivated woman, the poet laureate of California, and Jack came to love her. Each day he tried to read all the volumes she had given him so that he might see her again the next day when he returned them.

The boy gorged himself on the books for which he had been famished; he read in bed, at table, as he walked to and from school, during recess while the other boys played. Possessor of a volatile imagination and nervous system, his feelings were molten and could easily be poured. He enjoyed being able to soar to the heights in vicarious ecstasy, plunging to the depths of despair when the characters with whom he was identifying himself were unhappy or defeated. He consumed so many books in so short a time that he developed the jerks. To everybody he replied, 'Go away; you make me nervous.' From the tales of old travels and romantic voyages he gained the heady notion that Oakland was just a place to start from, that the world and its exciting adventures were awaiting him just as soon as he was able to escape.

John London was now out of work. The family moved to poorer quarters on San Pablo Avenue near Twenty-Second Street. Mammy Jenny lived not far away, and to her Jack went constantly to tell his troubles and pleasures, to be fed at her table, have his neck scrubbed and his hair combed at her sink, and be sent out into the world again with a reassuring pat on the shoulder. John London tried to find regular employment, but there was nothing available and it became the task of eleven-year-old Jack to furnish food for the family. He got up while it was still dark to call for his bundle of newspapers, which he delivered along a regular route; after school he delivered another route. The job paid twelve dollars a month, which he turned over intact to Flora. He also worked on an ice wagon on Saturdays, and set up pins in a bowling alley at nights and on Sundays. He had little time for reading, for he was learning about life at first hand now, fighting with the other newsboys, watching brawls in saloons, becoming acquainted with the colorful life on the Oakland Estuary, which was filled with whalers from the Arctic, curiohunters from the South Seas, opium-smugglers, Chinese junks, Yankee sailing ships, oyster pirates, Greek fishing boats, blackened freighters, houseboats, scows, sloops, and fish patrols. Just as he had escaped the London household by way of adventure books when he was ten, so would he escape it by way of the Estuary and the sea when he was thirteen.

John London at length found a job as night watchman at Davies Wharf, but this did not mean that Jack would have the spending of the money he earned. Since he was never permitted to buy such toys as a top or marbles or a knife, he traded his extra papers for the pictures given away with each package of cigarettes—Great Race Horses, Parisian Beauties, Champion Prize Fighters—and when he had completed a set he would swap it for the things he wanted so desperately and the other boys had the money to buy. He developed into a sharp trader, a faculty that was to come in handy when he was exchanging his stories for editors' cash. His sense of values became so acute that other boys called him in to sell their collections of rags, bottles, sacks, and oilcans to the junkman, paying him a commission.

Ina Coolbrith pictures him at this time as coming into the library with a bundle of newspapers under his arm, badly poised, looking poor, shabby, and uncared for, asking for something good to read, and wanting to consume every book that had an interesting title. Miss Coolbrith reports him as having confidence in himself, and feeling sure he would get what he wanted. Thus appears the first fundamental contradiction in Jack's nature: he was timid and shy because of the inferiority and uncertainty he felt over his illegitimate birth and chaotic home; he was confident and sure because he had inherited a forceful brain from Professor Chaney.

There is little to distinguish his years in the public schools. Frank Atherton, his chum from Cole School, reports that when Jack heard the Chinese were paying large sums for wildcat meat to make them strong for their tong wars, he and Frank made slingshots and went hunting wildcats in the Piedmont hills because Jack wanted to earn enough money to leave school and become an author, a typical instance of *after-the-fact* reminiscing. An anecdote that sounds more in character is that the two boys rented a boat on the Estuary to hunt mud hens: Jack's twenty-two-caliber revolver falling overboard, he demanded that Frank, who could swim, dive the five fathoms after it. When Frank refused, Jack threw both oars into the Estuary in a fit of temper, then had to float helplessly for several hours. At the Cole School, where they had community singing every morning, the teacher noticed that Jack remained silent. She asked him why. He replied that she did not know how to sing, that she would spoil his voice because she flatted. The teacher dispatched him to the principal to be punished. The principal sent him back with a note saying that he could be excused, but that he would have to write a composition each morning for the fifteen minutes of singing. Jack ascribed his ability to write a thousand words every morning to the habit formed in this class.

Along with his love for books the greatest love of his life was for the sea. He spent every spare minute around the Yacht Club on the Estuary, hoping for a chance to work on the boats and at the same time earn the additional money he had to bring home. The yacht-owners grew to like him because he was courageous, would crawl out on a boom in the roughest weather, and did not care how wet he got. They paid him small sums for scrubbing down decks and taught him what they knew about small boats. Before long he was able to reef a sail in a stiff breeze.

By the time he was thirteen he had managed to hoard two dollars in nickels and dimes which his conscience left him free from handing over to Flora. With this money he bought an old boat, ran it up and down the Estuary, and attempted short sails on the Bay. Short sails they had to be, for the boat had no centerboard and never stopped leaking. He was constantly swamping his craft, crashing into other boats on the Estuary, capsizing, but by trial and error he trained himself. He was happiest when he could feel the swell of waves beneath his boat, when he could taste the ocean salt on his lips, and cry, 'Hard a-lee!'—even though he was alone in the boat —when he wanted to practise the maneuver.

At thirteen he was graduated from the Cole School. He was named class historian, and was selected to give a speech at graduation, but since he owned no reputable-looking suit of clothes in which to appear he never even attended the exercises. There could be no thought of his going on to high school, for John's employment was becoming more and more fitful. Jack continued to carry his paper routes; he also sold papers on the Oakland streets at night, and took any kind of extra job he could find, such as sweeping out saloons at Idora and Weasel Parks after Sunday picnics. He was a shabbily dressed, hard-working kid with a beautiful flashing smile; a tough fighter, prone to outbursts of temper, and frightfully sensitive.

Over the course of a year, from special odd jobs about which he told Flora nothing, he scraped together the six dollars necessary to buy him freedom in the form of a second-hand skiff. When he had been able to accumulate a dollar and seventy-five cents he painted it a gay color; another month of odd jobs provided him with the two dollars for a sail; and when he finally put together a dollar and forty cents for a pair of oars, the world was wide open for him to explore. He took ever longer sails on San Francisco Bay, going out on ebb tide to Goat Island for rock cod, and coming in on the flood at evening; shipping water in the wake of ferry-boats; singing sailor chanties, 'Blow the Man Down' and 'Whiskey, Johnny, Whiskey' while the winds whitecapped the strong tides and splashed him with spray; and crossing the Bay in his open skiff in a roaring southwester, with the scow schooner sailors telling him he lied because it couldn't be done.

He was not only fearless, he was foolhardy; the worse the weather the greater chances he took, for he was not afraid of the sea. Floundering always in his mind to learn what he was, he liked to tell himself that he was a Viking, descendant of those mighty sailors who crossed the Atlantic in an open boat; that he was an Anglo-Saxon, a member of a fighting race, afraid of nothing. And because he was afraid of nothing, because he seemed to have an affinity for the sea, he became one of the most expert small-boat sailors on the treacherous Bay.

For a year, between selling papers and doing odd jobs, he managed to find an hour or two every day to spend in his beloved boat. But before he was fifteen John London was struck by a train and severely injured. The family lived in an old cottage on the Estuary in what is reported to have been squalor of an aggravated type. Many of the near-by shacks were built from wreckage or dismantled ships and old buildings. Jack's clothes were ragged, his house had no modern sanitation, he suffered from an ever-gnawing hunger of the belly and brain. He got a steady job in a cannery in an abandoned stable by the railroad tracks, at which he was paid ten cents an hour. The shortest day he ever worked was ten hours; on occasion he worked eighteen and twenty. There were weeks on end when he never knocked off earlier than eleven o'clock. Then he had a long walk home because he could not afford carfare. He was in bed at half-after midnight, and at half-past five there was Flora shaking him, trying to strip down the bedclothes to which the sleeping boy clung desperately. In a huddle, at the foot of the bed, he still remained covered. Then Flora braced herself and pulled the bedding to the floor. The boy followed the blankets in order to protect himself against the chill of the room. It seemed as though he would fall head-first to the floor, but consciousness fluttered up in him, he landed on his feet, and was awake.

He dressed in the darkness, went to the greasy sink in the kitchen, and washed himself with soap grim with dishwater and hard to lather. Then he dried himself on the damp, dirty, and ragged towel that left his face covered with shreds of lint, and sat down to the table to eat his bread and drink the hot muddy liquid the Londons called coffee. Outside it was clear and cold; he shivered at the first contact with the air. The stars had not yet begun to pale in the sky, and the city lay in blackness. As he entered the cannery gate he always glanced to the east, where across a ragged skyline of housetops a pale light was beginning to creep.

On January 1, 1891, he began a section in his notebook called 'Financial Receipts and Disbursements.' For cash on hand he lists fifteen cents. Between the first and the fourth of the month he spent five cents for limes and ten cents for milk and bread, and then could buy nothing more until he received his wage of ten dollars and a half, out of which he paid the rent of six dollars, and bought butter, coal oil, oysters, meats, nuts, ice, doughnuts, and twenty-five cents' worth of pills for Flora. A notation of fifty cents paid out for washing indicates that Flora was not exerting herself to make both ends meet.

As he trudged through the weary months, unable to find time to go to the library, too tired to keep his eyes open over a book at night, he asked himself if this were the meaning of life, to be a work-beast. He had Professor Chaney's short, husky torso, he could stand up to the work physically, but temperamentally he was unfitted for mechanical labor. A son of an intellectual, having inherited his father's active brain and fertile imagination, he found the work deadening, and he revolted against it. If he could have known that he was Professor Chaney's son he might not have tormented himself by demanding why he detested this work so bitterly when the other young boys and girls around him accepted their fate with a kind of heroic phlegm.

He remembered his skiff, lying idle and accumulating barnacles at the boat wharf; he remembered the wind that blew every day on the Bay, the sunrises and sunsets he never saw; the bite of the salt water on his flesh when he plunged overboard. There was only one way to escape the deadening toil, and still support his family—to go to sea. In his own words he was in the flower of his adolescence, athrill with romance and adventure, dreaming of wild life in the wild man-world.

On Sunday afternoons when he took his skiff for a sail, and hung around the waterfront, he became acquainted with the oyster pirates, a hard-drinking crew of adventurers who raided the privately owned oyster beds in Lower Bay, and sold their booty for good prices on the Oakland docks. Jack knew that they rarely made less than twenty-five dollars for a night's work, and that a man who owned his own boat could clear two hundred dollars on a single catch. When he overheard that French Frank, one of the older pirates, wanted to sell his sloop, the *Razzle Dazzle,* Jack's mind was made up. He would buy it! He who had inherited from his father the passionate desire to be quit of the brutish labor of the machines, also inherited from his mother the disregard for that discipline which to his working comrades dictated that they remain fast by their honest if bestial jobs.

But where was he to get three hundred dollars, he who had never known anything but poverty? Straight he ran to Mammy Jenny, who had been working as a nurse. Would she lend her white child the money? *Would she!* What Mammy Jenny had was his.

The following Sunday Jack rowed out to the *Razzle Dazzle,* joined a party that was going full blaze, and made his offer. On Monday morning he met French Frank in the Last Chance saloon, paying over Mammy Jenny's bright twenty-dollar gold pieces. No sooner was the deal wetted down with his first drink of whiskey than he ran all the way to the dock, broke out anchor, and filled away close-hauled on the three-mile beat to windward out into the Bay. The breeze blew its tang into his lungs and curled the waves in midchannel. Before it came the scow schooners, blowing their horns for the drawbridges to open. Red-stacked tugs tore by, rocking the *Razzle Dazzle* in their wake. A sugar bark was being towed from the bone yard to the sea. The sun-wash was on the water, and life was big. There it was, the smack and slap of the spirit of revolt, of adventure and romance.

Tomorrow he would be an oyster pirate, as free a freebooter as the century and the waters of San Francisco Bay would permit. He would outfit his grub and water in the morning, hoist the big mainsail, and beat his way out of the Estuary on the last of the ebb. Then he would slack sheets, and on the first of the flood run down the Bay to Asparagus Island and anchor offshore. And at last his dream would be realized: he would sleep upon the water.

2

TO HIS amazement Jack found that when he had purchased the *Razzle Dazzle* from French Frank for three hundred dollars he had also inherited Mamie, queen of the oyster pirates. She had been French Frank's girl, and had fallen in love with the handsome open-faced boy the day before when he had boarded the *Razzle Dazzle* to make the deal. Mamie was sixteen, a wild-spirited, good-looking waif. Jack said that she was warm and kind, and that she made him a real home in the little cabin of the *Razzle Dazzle*, the first congenial home he had ever known. Jack was the youngest skipper in the fleet, the only one who sailed with a woman on board. This caused a sensation and not only forced him to fight with several skippers to keep his girl, but nearly cost him his life at the hands of jealous French Frank.

That night Jack took part in his first raid on the oyster beds. A black-whiskered wharf rat by the name of Spider, who had been working on the *Razzle Dazzle*, agreed to stay with him as his crew. Big George, Young Scratch Nelson, Clam, Whiskey Bob, Nicky the Greek, and a dozen other men, big and unafraid, some of them ex-convicts assembled in sea boots and gear, revolvers strapped about their waists. Having laid their plans, the flotilla set out under cover of darkness. It was the big June run out of the full moon; the fleet lowered its small boats in the Lower Bay and rowed until they hit the soft mud. Jack nosed his skiff up on the shore side of a big shoal, opened his sack, and began picking. In no time the sack was full and he had to return to his boat for a new one. At dawn he raced back for the early morning market in Oakland, sold his oysters to the saloon- and innkeepers, and found that he had made as much in one night as he had by working for three months in the cannery. To the boy's mind it had been a glorious adventure. He paid

Mammy Jenny back part of her loan; the balance he turned over to Flora for the household.

As the weeks passed he won his spurs among the toughest of the oyster pirates. When French Frank tried to run him down with his schooner and get Mamie back, Jack stood on the deck of the *Razzle Dazzle*, a cocked shotgun in his hands as he steered with his feet and held her to the course, compelling his fifty-year-old adversary to put up his wheel and keep away. There was the proud morning that he brought the *Razzle Dazzle* in with a larger load than any other two-man craft; the time the fleet raided in the Lower Bay and Jack's was the only craft back at daylight to the anchorage off Asparagus Island; the Thursday night the entire fleet raced to market, and Jack brought the *Razzle Dazzle* in first, without a rudder, to skim the cream of the Friday morning trade.

When police officers came aboard, Jack opened his choice oysters, served them with squirts of pepper, and rushed the growler with a can for beer.

He was a convivial lad. He liked his friends among the pirates, he wanted them to like him. When they drank, he drank; when they got drunk, the fifteen-year-old boy, eager to prove that he was a man, got as drunk as the best of them. Since he had established himself as one of the smartest sailors in the crowd, strong, fearless in a fight, given to gales of gusty laughter, he was accepted as an equal and a pal. But in between raids, when he was tied up to the wharf, he walked to the Oakland Library where he had long talks with Miss Coolbrith, and selected an armful of books to take home to the *Razzle Dazzle*. He locked his cabin door so that his companions wouldn't catch him, lay on his back in his bunk, and lighted one book off the end of the other while he sucked on cannon balls or chewed taffy slabs.

Among the oyster fleet there was constant drinking, fighting, stabbing, and shooting; boats were stolen, sails burned; there were killings among the partners and crew. To Jack, who was still cramming himself with tales of buccaneers and sea rovers, sacks of cities and conflicts of armed men, all this was life raw and naked, wild and free. From the sandpits of the Oakland Estuary where the pirates settled their grievances, where knives flashed and sand was thrown into the eyes of opponents, the way led out to the vastness of adventure of all the world, where battles would be fought for high purposes and romantic ends.

For many months he sailed his *Razzle Dazzle*, repaid Mammy Jenny the rest of the three hundred dollars he had borrowed from her, supported his family, went on a hundred exciting and perilous adventures among the fisherfolk of the Bay, lived happily with Mamie in the cabin of his boat. Then he teamed up with Young Scratch Nelson, a twenty-year-old daredevil with the body of a Hercules. Jack adored the older boy because he was a blue-eyed, yellow-haired, rawboned Viking. During a drunken brawl in which the entire fleet of pirates participated, Young Scratch was shot through the hand and his boat, the *Reindeer*, beached and ripped open, while Jack got into a fist-fight with Spider, his crew, who set fire to the mainsail of the *Razzle Dazzle* and then deserted. Another crowd of enemy pirates boarded the *Razzle Dazzle* and scuttled, fired, and sank her. Jack and Young Scratch joined forces, repaired the *Reindeer*, borrowed money for an outfit of grub from Johnny Heinhold, proprietor of the Last Chance saloon, filled their water barrels, and sailed on the *Reindeer* for the oyster beds.

Young Scratch's greatest joy was to steer to miss destruction by an inch. Never to reef down was another of his manias, blow high or blow low. They barely missed death many times because Young Scratch dared what no one else would think of doing. Jack kept up with his reckless exploits, even attempted to surpass his master, for was he too not a Viking, a fearless one?

They roamed, pirated, and raided up and down the several hundred miles of waterways of the sloughs, straits, and rivers leading into the Bay, making as much as a hundred and eighty dollars for a night's work, but forever broke because the mad devil Young Scratch went on blind drinking bats the moment he reached shore to keep up the high level of excitement he was enjoying in his race with death and the penitentiary. Here too Jack felt that he had to keep up with his pal, drink along with him whiskey for whiskey, even though he had no innate taste for liquor, nor desire to get drunk.

After a while it was no longer difficult to swallow the vile-tasting raw whiskey. He began to be enamored of the effects of intoxication, the wild laughter and singing, fierce fighting and new friendships, and the maggots crawling in his brain that made him sound brilliant to himself. When times were dull he drank, he got drunk. Ever an extremist, his uncertain poise made him want to do everything better and more mightily than everybody around him. Just as it was necessary for him to become Prince of the Oyster Pirates, so he had to become Prince of the Drunkards. He deserted his hard-pressed family, spending in saloons the money they needed for food and rent. The old-timers around the waterfront, hard drinkers themselves, became disgusted with the fifteen-year-old roustabout who was drinking himself to death at an unprecedented rate of speed; they gave him a year to live.

One night, broke and thirsty, but with the drinker's faith in the unexpected drink, he sat in the Overland House with Young Scratch waiting for something to turn up. Joe Goose dashed in to tell them that there was free booze, as much as they wanted of it, at a political rally in Hayward. All they had to do was wear a red shirt and a helmet and carry a torch in a parade. After the parade the saloons were opened and the Oakland waterfront gang jammed six deep before the drink-drenched bars. Finding this method of securing drinks too slow, Jack and his pals pushed the bartenders aside and took the bottles from the shelves. They went into the street, knocked the necks off the bottles against the concrete curbs, and drank.

Joe Goose and Young Scratch had learned discretion with straight whiskey; Jack had not. He thought that since it was free he should drink all he could hold. During the course of the night he consumed more than two quarts. When it came time to go back to Oakland he was burning internally, in an agony of suffocation. On the train he broke a window with his torch to get air, but this precipitated a gang fight and he was knocked unconscious. He awakened seventeen hours later in a waterfront lodging-house where he had been dumped by Young Scratch, so close to death that he was within an inch of fulfilling the waterfront prediction that he would not last out the year.

Had Jack been like the other pirates he would have continued in his raiding and carousing until a bullet through his head laid him on the coroner's slab in Benicia as it did Young Scratch, or he had drowned or been stabbed to death as were his friends Clam and Whiskey Bob, or ended in San Quentin for greater crimes than oyster pirating, as did Spider and Nicky the Greek. But Professor Chaney's heritage was stirring in his brain, urging him to leave this wasteful life for nobler adventures in more exotic corners of the world. After each bout with Young Scratch he would creep into the cabin of the *Reindeer*, sick from the whiskey, lock the door behind him, and open his beloved books, to be made well again by the new, fresh copies of Kipling's *The Light That Failed*, Melville's *Typee*, Shaw's *An Unsocial Socialist*, and Zola's *Germinal*, which Ina Coolbrith had put away for him when they arrived, still smelling of wet ink, from the publishers in New York.

He was slowly groping toward a break when an accident befell him. He and Young Scratch had made a big haul, and been on a drunk for three weeks, with what Jack called but few intermittent spaces of partial sobriety. At one o'clock in the morning, dead drunk from a bout with a fishing crowd, he tried to stumble aboard his sloop at the Benicia pier, and fell in. The tides which sweep through Carquinez Straits as in a millrace bore him away. He said that the blues were heavy upon him; he decided that drowning would be a splendid culmination to his short but exciting career. The water was delicious, and this was a hero's way to die.

When he passed the Salano wharf, where there were lights and people, he cunningly kept quiet. Clear of interruption, he lifted his voice to the stars in his own dirge and quite enjoyed the thought of saying good-bye to the whole works. He lay on his back in the starlight watching the familiar wharf lights go by, red and green and white, bidding sad, sentimental farewells to each. However, the cold water sobered him; he decided that he didn't want to die, after all. He undressed and struck out, crossing the current at right angles. When daylight broke he found himself in the tiderips of Mare Island where the swift ebbs from Vallejo and Carquinez Straits were fighting each other. He was exhausted and numb with cold; the land breeze was washing waves into his mouth. A few moments more and such great novels as *The Call of the Wild, The Sea Wolf, Iron Heel, Martin Eden, Valley of the Moon, Burning Daylight, Star Rover*, and a hundred superb short stories would have drowned in the flood tide from San Pablo Bay. A Greek fisherman running in for Vallejo hauled him unconscious over the side of the boat. It was the end of his wild drinking for many years to come.

A few days later, while he and Young Scratch were running in a load of oysters at Benicia, they were hailed by a state officer who suggested that they give up the fugitive life of an oyster pirate and become deputies for the Fish Patrol. San Francisco Bay was infested with Chinese shrimp raiders and Greek salmon thieves who were violating the fish laws of the state. These men were not imprisoned when caught; they were fined. Jack was offered fifty per cent of the fines collected from the law violators he captured. Having played one half of the game of Cops and Robbers, he gleefully accepted the job as state officer and was appointed a deputy of the Patrol.

His first assignment was a raid on the Chinese shrimp catchers who put down nets of such fine mesh that not even the newly hatched fish could pass through. Jack, Young Scratch, and four other patrolmen left the Oakland docks in the *Reindeer* and a salmon boat. They ran down after dark, dropped anchor under the bluff of Point Pinole, and at dawn slanted across the Bay on the land breeze. The shrimp fleet lay spread out in a half-moon, the tips of the crescent three miles apart, each junk moored fast to the buoy of a shrimp net. The Chinese were asleep below.

Jack was ordered to throw Young Scratch and George, one of the patrolmen, each onto a junk, and make fast to a third himself. He ran up under the lee of a junk, shivered his mainsail into the wind, and glided past the stern so slowly that Young Scratch stepped lightly aboard. By now a conch shell was sounding the alarm. The decks were beginning to swarm with half-naked Chinese. Jack rounded the *Reindeer* alongside another junk for George to spring aboard. Then he threw out his mainsheet and drove down before the wind on a junk to the leeward. The boats came together with a crash, the two starboard sweeps of the junk crumbling. An evil-looking Chinaman with a yellow silk bandana tied around his pock-marked face let out a curdling yell of rage, planted a pike pole on the *Reindeer's* bow, and began shoving the en-tangled boats apart. Jack paused long enough to let go the jib halyards, and just as the *Reindeer* cleared he leapt aboard the junk with a line and made fast.

Alone, unarmed, he stood facing five threatening China-men, each of whom carried a long knife under his sash. They advanced upon him threateningly, but he stood his ground and put his hand on his hip pocket. The Chinamen retreated. He ordered them to drop anchor at the junk's bow. When they refused, he went forward, let go the anchor, and with his hand still on his empty hip pocket forced the Chinamen to board the *Reindeer*. He then sailed his boat to the junk on which he had left George, who herded his Chinamen on board at the point of a revolver.

The Chinaman wearing the yellow bandana brushed against Jack's hip pocket and felt that he had no revolver. He quickly incited his men, who prepared to rush the two patrol-men and throw them overboard. George, the deputy with the revolver, was in a funk and demanded that Jack put the Chi-namen ashore on the beach at Point Pedro. He refused. George turned his revolver on Jack and cried, 'Now will you head for the beach?'

Faced by a gun, and sixteen Chinamen with knives, Jack thought of the shame of losing his prisoners. He threw one hand into the air and brought his head down. The bullet went high. He then grabbed George's wrist. The Chinamen lunged at him. He swung George's body around to receive their im-pact, ripped the revolver from George's fingers, and flung him at Yellow Bandana, who stumbled and fell over him to the deck, giving Jack time to cover the prisoners with the gun.

His share of the fines amounted to nearly a hundred dollars.

The ensuing months proffered similar adventures. There was the time he had to run for his life down the Martinez wharf, pursued by a howling mob of fishermen because he had just caught two of their number red-handed and arrested them; the time he came upon two men with an illegal sturgeon line and chased them round and round a wheat ship; the time he was outsailed by two men who used a Chinese line to trap the sturgeon, but raised their line with over a thousand pounds of sturgeon on the hooks.

He worked for the Fish Patrol for nearly a year, living, fighting, and adventuring with hundreds of men: honest and courageous patrolmen, sailors, gamblers, fishermen, barkeeps, stevedores, navigators, men who had been to every port of the world, seen every sight, committed every kind of crime, loved every kind of woman, and engaged in every kind of adventure. Each time he took the *Reindeer* up or down the Bay he passed the Golden Gate Strait, which led out to the Pacific. Beyond that strait lay the exciting lands of the Orient, the colorful experiences and dramatic ports these men told him about, and that he read about in the pages of the Oakland Library books. He was seventeen now, big and strong and bold, with the feel and look of the man about him. He wanted to see the world, and there was only one way for him to reach it.

Becoming a deep-sea sailor had been implicit in his fate ever since the moment, four years before, when he had bought a leaky skiff for two dollars and sailed it down the Estuary. There were many ships tied up along the San Francisco docks among which he might choose: freighters, schooners, passenger ships. He chose the most romantic of the lot, one of the last sealing vessels to sail out of San Francisco Bay, headed for Korea, Japan, Siberia, and ninety days of harpooning seals—for had he not read over and over again Herman Melville's *Moby Dick?*

The *Sophie Sutherland* was an eighty-ton schooner, built for speed. She carried an enormous spread of canvas, over a hundred feet from the deck to the truck of the main-topmast. The forecastle into which Jack dropped his dunnage bag was lined on either side to a V point by bunks, while on the walls hung oilskins, sea boots, and lanterns.

Though he had never been out of the Golden Gate Strait, he had signed on as an able-bodied seaman because it carried a higher wage. The other sailors were men who had been at sea for years, and had paid with years of suffering to acquire their sea skill. They were mostly rawboned Scandinavians who as boys had served sailors, and as able-bodied seamen expected to be served by boys. They resented this youngster's being signed on as an equal. Unless Jack could prove that he knew his job he would be forced to suffer seven months of maltreatment such as one can only undergo in a sailing schooner from which there is no escape.

Because he had been around with sailors long enough to know their simple psychology, he resolved to do his work so well that no one would be called upon to do it for him. He never malingered when pulling on a rope, for he knew that the eyes of his forecastle mates were squinting for just such evidence of his inferiority; he made it a point to be among the first of the watch to go on deck, among the last to go below, never leaving a sheet or tackle uncoiled. He was always eager for the run aloft for the shifting of the topsail sheets, nor did it take him long to learn the names and uses of the few new ropes, to box the compass.

On the third day out the *Sophie Sutherland* ran into a storm. It was Jack's trick at the wheel. The captain questioned whether this seventeen-year-old boy could hold the ship on her course in the fierce wind and swift-running sea. After watching him for a few minutes the skipper nodded his approval and went below for his supper. Jack fought the storm while the wind whipped his hair into his eyes, exulting in keeping the vessel on her tack for an hour without another soul on deck, the entire crew leaving its fate in his hands. Nothing he ever was to accomplish made him prouder or gave him more pleasure than this feat.

When the storm had lifted and the *Sophie Sutherland* was once again racing along, Jack noticed that the resentment was gone from the faces of his mates. He had an occasional fight, for the forecastle was narrow and crowded, and his temper did not allow for anyone's trampling on his feet; but for the greater part the voyage was a happy one. After the storm there followed fifty-one days of fine sailing. At night as he lay stretched on his back on the prow, his head pillowed on his interlocked hands, the stars were so sharp and close they seemed strung on a tarpaulin. During the warm days he and his mates stripped on deck and threw buckets of sea water over each other. He made friends with Big Victor and Axel,

and for the rest of the cruise they were known as the Three
Sports.

He spent enjoyable hours listening to his comrades in the
forecastle spin yarns of storms at sea and gigantic catches;
when things seemed dull there he went aft to the steerage
where the hunters bunked, their guns on the walls, tall tales
in their mouths, and a thousand fights in their fists. At nights,
when he came off his trick at the wheel and the rest of the
forecastle was snoring lustily, he slipped smoothly into his
other life, even as he had when he was an oyster pirate, prop-
ping a book against the steel wall of the prow, a history of
the Orient, or sea tales by Melville and Jacobs that he had
bought out of his *Sophie Sutherland* advance, Flaubert's *Ma-
dame Bovary* and Tolstoi's *Anna Karenina,* which Miss Coolbrith had loaned him from her private collection, and holding
a lighted wick in a saucer in one hand, turned the pages with
the other and read the night out.

At length the *Sophie Sutherland* lifted the volcanic peaks
of the Bonin Islands, sailed in among the reefs to the land-
locked harbor, and dropped anchor among a score of sea
gypsies like herself. Aborigines in outrigger canoes and Japanese in sampans paddled about the bay. After ten years of
dreaming, ever since he had read *African Travels* at the age
of seven, Jack had won through to the other side of the
world; he would see all that he had read about in the books
come true. He was wild to get ashore, to climb a pathway
that disappeared up a green canyon, emerged on a bare lava
slope, and continued to climb among palms and flowers and
strange native villages. And at last he would fish from a sam-
pan!

The Three Sports went ashore. Jack was their pal and they
each had to buy him a drink, and he was their pal and he
had to buy them each a drink. At the bars they met mates
from the San Francisco waterfront, friends from other voyages, comrades from the days of oyster pirating. Every reunion meant another round of drinks, for what else had they
in the world but good fellowship?

Though the *Sophie Sutherland* remained in the bay of
Bonin Islands for ten days, Jack never climbed the path
among the flowers and native villages. Instead he made hundreds of friends among the whalers, heard endless yarns, got
drunk with his comrades, helped wreck the native village,
sang rollicking sea chanties under the stars, was rolled for his
money by runaway apprentices, and in general behaved like
an old tar.

Having filled her water casks, the *Sophie Sutherland* raced for the north. Jack, who was a boat-puller, spent many days binding the oars and oarlocks in leather and sennit so that they would make no noise when creeping up on the seals. Then one day the lookout raised the coast of Japan, and they picked up with the great seal herd. North they traveled with it, following as far as the coast of Siberia, ravaging and killing, flinging the naked carcasses to the sharks and salting down the skins. After Jack had rowed his hunter back to the ship he went to work with a butcher knife to skin the seals, working each day on decks covered with hides and bodies, slippery with fat and blood, the scuppers running red. It was brutal labor, but to Jack it went under the name of adventure. He loved every hour of it.

After three months, the seal herd having been dispatched, the *Sophie Sutherland* sailed south to Yokohama, a batch of skins in her salt, and a heavy payday coming. At Yokohama Jack drank shoulder to shoulder with the men with whom he had faced death and incredible hardship, smiling to himself when he remembered that only five months before they had thought him a boy who had no right to call himself a seaman.

Back in San Francisco he bought his mates one round of drinks, bade them farewell, and took the ferryboat home to Oakland.

He found his family in debt, trying to live off the few dollars that John London earned as a constable of Brooklyn township. From his *Sophie Sutherland* wages he paid the bills, bought himself a second-hand hat, coat, and vest, some forty-cent shirts, and two fifty-cent suits of underwear. What was left he turned over to Flora.

His infatuation with the Oakland waterfront was now quite dead; he had no more desire for vagrancy. For a few days he soaked himself in books at the library; then it was time to settle down.

He had chosen an unfortunate time to look for work. The financial panic of 1893 had thrown the country into a severe business depression; eight thousand business organizations had failed, many of them banks. All active enterprise had stopped; only the most necessary work was undertaken, and a large proportion of the workingmen were unemployed. The man with any kind of job was considered lucky. In Oakland ten cents an hour was all that could be earned by able-bodied men. This rate of pay caused strikes and lockouts, further decreasing employment.

The only job he could find was in a jute mill at ten cents an hour, one dollar for a ten-hour day. The mill was filled with long rows of machines, their bobbins revolving rapidly. The air was warm, moist, thick with flying lint, and the noise so terrific that he had to shout at the top of his lungs to be heard. At the machines were children from eight years of age up, some crippled, many consumptive, all undernourished and suffering from rickets, earning their two dollars for a sixty-hour week.

At this time he was developing what he liked to call troubling potencies and proclivities, a rather ponderous phrase to describe his interest in young girls. The seventeen-year-old boy who had had Mamie for wife on board the *Razzle Dazzle,* who had had other hardened women up and down San Francisco Bay, was so shy and self-conscious over his rough manners absorbed from rough company that he was in agony whenever he chanced to be in the company of a nice girl. He had been so busy being a man that he didn't know anything about girls.

Since he came from the wrong side of the railroad tracks he had little opportunity to meet the sweet and pretty ones in whom he was now interested. He became chums with Louis Shattuck, a blacksmith's apprentice, whom he describes as an innocently devilish young fellow quite convinced that he was a sophisticated townsboy. Louis became Jack's tutor. After work the boys went home for their supper, washed, put on a clean shirt, and met in a candy store where they bought cigarettes and candy red-hots. They had access to no girls' homes, and they couldn't go to public dances because they both had to pay board at home, and this left them with about seventy-five cents a week spending money. All they could do was stroll the streets in the early evenings. Louis tried to show him how to give a certain eloquent glance of the eye, a smile, a daring lift of his cap; then, hesitancies, giggles, a spoken word. But Jack was timid and bashful. Girls remained strange and wonderful to him, and he failed of the bold front and necessary forwardness when the crucial moment came.

After a time he did make a few friends; occasionally he would take a girl out to Blair's Park, twenty cents for carfare, bang, just like that, ice cream for two, thirty cents . . . and he was broke for the rest of the week. He had a penchant for Irish girls; in his notebook are listed the addresses of Nellie, Dollie, and Katie, factory girls who enjoyed his banter, his vigorous dancing and infectious laughter. Best of all he liked Lizzie Connellon, who worked with a hot fluting-iron in an Oakland laundry. Lizzie had a pretty face and was fast on the saucy comeback; she gave Jack her gold ring with a cameo insert to show that he was her feller.

But at last love came. Her name was Haydee. They sat side by side in a Salvation Army meeting. She was sixteen, wore a tam o'shanter, a skirt that reached her shoe tops, and had a slender oval face, beautiful brown eyes and hair, and a sweet-lipped mouth. For Jack it was love at first sight.

They arranged stolen half hours in which he came to know all the madness of boy and girl love. He knew it was not the biggest love in the world, but he dared to assert that it was the sweetest. He who had been hailed Prince of the Oyster Pirates, who could go anywhere in the world as a man among men, who could sail boats, lay aloft in black and storm, go into the toughest hangouts in sailor town and play his part in any roughhouse that started, or call all hands to the bar, he didn't know the first thing to say or do with this slender chit of a girl who was as abysmally ignorant of life as he thought himself profoundly wise. They never succeeded in managing more than a dozen meetings; and they kissed perhaps a dozen times, briefly and innocently, and wonderingly. They never went anywhere, not even to a matinée, but he always fondly believed that she loved him. He knew that he loved her. He dreamed day dreams of her for a year or more, and the memory of Haydee always remained very dear.

One evening Flora, who well remembered that Jack's father had been a writer, came to him with a copy of the San Francisco *Call* and urged him to write a composition for the contest the paper was holding. Jack hesitated for a moment, recalled a typhoon off the coast of Japan that the *Sophie Sutherland* had battled, sat down at the kitchen table, and began composing. He wrote quickly, smoothly, and painlessly. The following night he finished the story, polished it as best he could, and sent it to the editor of the *Call*. He was awarded the first prize of twenty-five dollars. Second and third prizes went to men connected with the University of California and Stanford University.

A reading of *Typhoon off the Coast of Japan* shows it to be fresh and vigorous after the passage of forty-five years. The imagery is vivid, the element of suspense is never lacking, the prose rolls onward with an authentic rhythm of the sea; and there is music in the sentences of the seventeen-year-old boy who had had only a grammar-school education. The *Call* wrote, 'The most striking thing is the largeness of grasp and steady force of expression that shows the young artist.' Prophetic words.

When the article appeared John London had his happiest moment since he left Moscow, Iowa; Flora chuckled silently at her secret joke; and Jack promptly sat down at the kitchen table to write another sea yarn. However, the editor of the *Call* was not running a fiction magazine, and sent the manuscript back. In his notebook Jack lists at this time an expenditure of thirty cents for stamps and paper wraps, which leads us to believe that he continued to write, and to send his manuscripts to magazines.

If Jack had continued to handle the 'Financial Receipts and Disbursements' as he had at the age of fourteen when he worked in the cannery, the family would have fared moderately well. However, he turned his wages over to Flora. Thomas E. Hill of Oakland, in whose sister's home both he and the Londons rented rooms, reports that Flora fell two months behind in her rent, and his sister was forced to ask the family to move.

The jute mill had promised to raise his wage to a dollar and a quarter a day, but after he had worked there for several months they refused to make good their promise. Jack quit. Having observed that manual labor would always keep him at the bottom of the trough, earning ten cents an hour, he decided to learn a trade. The new discovery called electricity looked as though it were going to have a future, so he decided to become a practical electrician. He went out to the power plant of the Oakland Street Railway, told the superintendent that he was not afraid of hard work and that he was willing to start at the bottom. The superintendent put him in the cellar shoveling coal for thirty dollars a month, one day off a month.

His job was to pass coal to the firemen, who fed it to the furnaces. He had to pass the coal for the day and night shifts, so that despite working through his lunch hour he rarely finished before nine at night, making it a thirteen-hour day. This brought his wage under eight cents an hour, less than he had earned at the cannery when he was fourteen. Dripping with sweat from the intense heat of the furnaces, he filled the iron wheelbarrow with coal, ran it to the scales, weighed the load, trundled it to the fire room, and dumped it on the plates before the fires. When he got a little ahead of the day firemen he had to pile the night coal higher and higher, buttressing the heap with stout planks.

Once again he became a work beast. When he reached home in the blackness of night he was too exhausted to eat; it was all he could do to wash and fall into bed. There was no time or energy for books, for nice girls, for anything that smacked of life, for he did not have even a Sunday off. He lost weight, navigated always in a nightmarish fog of coal dust and heat. Once again he could not understand why he suffered so much on this job, he who had worked at more difficult tasks among men older and stronger than himself. This time one of the firemen took pity on him and told him that there had always been two coal-passers, one for the day shift, one for the night. Each of these men had received forty dollars a month. When Jack had come along, young and eager to learn, the superintendent had fired the two coal-passers and put him in to handle both jobs. When he asked why he had not been told before, the fireman replied that the superintendent had threatened to give him his time if he let on.

A few days later the same fireman showed him an article in an Oakland newspaper which told how one of the former coal-passers, whose place Jack had unwittingly taken, and who had a wife and three children to feed, had killed himself because he could not find work. Jack flung aside his shovel.

The result of this work orgy was to sicken him with manual labor. Apparently a man had to be either a slave or a vagabond; there was no visible middle ground. He was young and strong and loved life. The call of adventure ran wild in his blood. Wasn't it better to royster and frolic over the world than break his fine young body on the wheel of other people's greed?

By the time he reached this conclusion, in April, 1894, the amount of unemployment in the United States had grown to staggering proportions. In Massillon, Ohio, Flora's birthplace, a man by the name of Coxey was organizing an army of unemployed men to march on Washington and demand that Congress issue five million dollars in greenbacks with which to put men to work on the building of public roads. The newspapers gave Coxey's Army of the Commonwealth so much space that detachments sprang up spontaneously in a number of American cities. In Oakland a man by the name of Kelly organized the unemployed into military companies and arranged with the railroads to provide his men with free transportation in boxcars.

When Jack heard of General Kelly's detachment he jumped at the chance to join the Army and go to Washington. Such an adventure was too good to resist. That he was walking out on Flora and John London, who were in sore need of his wages, did not deter him any more than it had deterred him when he quit the cannery for the dubious life and dubious income of an oyster pirate. Neither Flora Wellman nor Professor Chaney had ever been adepts at discipline or sacrifice, or sticklers for the fulfilment of moral obligations.

Kelly's Army was scheduled to leave Oakland on Friday, April 6. When Jack and his chum, Frank Davis, reached the freight yards that afternoon they found the Army had left early in the morning. Jack cried, 'Come on, Frank, I know all about this tramp business; we'll beat our way east on the freights until we catch up with Kelly's Army.' Within the hour he had found a train that was ready to pull out. He slid open the side door of an empty boxcar and climbed in behind Frank. He closed the door. The engine whistled. Jack was lying down, and in the darkness he smiled.

He had not been exaggerating when he told Frank Davis that he knew all about the tramp business, for this was not the first time he had gone on The Road. Three years before, when he had been fifteen, there had come a lull in oyster pirating; his boat lay at the end of Steamboat Wharf at Benicia and he sat on deck in the warm sun, the fresh breeze on his cheeks, the flood tide swirling past. He spat over the side to gauge the speed of the current, saw that he could run the flood nearly all the way to Sacramento, cast off his moorings, and hoisted sail.

At Sacramento he went swimming in the river, and fell in with a bunch of boys who were sunning themselves on the sandbar. They talked differently from the fellows he had been herding with. They were road-kids. The yarns they told had made Jack's oyster pirating look like thirty cents. A new world was calling to him in every word spoken, a world of rods and gunnels, blind baggages and side-door Pullmans, bulls, shacks, chewin's, pinches, getaways, strongarms, bindlestiffs, punks, and profesh. With every word they uttered the lure of The Road laid hold of him more imperiously. He joined the push, or crowd.

He was given the monica of Sailor Kid. The ringleader, Bob, took him in hand and turned him from a gay-cat or tenderfoot into a punk, or road-kid. They taught him how to batter the main stem for light pieces, that is, beg for money on the main street. They showed him how they rolled drunks, preyed upon bindlestiffs, and successfully taught him how to steal a five-dollar Stetson stiff-rim from the head of a prosperous Sacramento Valley Chinaman. Arrested in a whopping street fight, he had served three days in jail.

Jack had soon heard expounded the law of The Road, that no kid was a road-kid until he had ridden the blinds over the Sierra Nevadas. One night Jack and French Kid, who had just joined the push, waited in the darkness ahead of the Central Pacific Overland and when it went past nailed the blinds.

French Kid slipped, fell under the wheels, and had both legs amputated.

Bob had warned Jack to deck her, or ride the top of the car, until the train passed Roseville, where the constable was reputed to be 'horstyle,' and then to climb down to the blind behind the mail car. But Jack had held down the deck the whole night, clear across the Sierras, through snow sheds and tunnels and down to Truckee on the other side, in a funk over climbing down the swiftly moving express train. He never confessed his disgraceful conduct to the push, which welcomed him back to Sacramento, renamed him Frisco Kid, and made him a full-fledged road-kid.

After a few weeks he had tired of Sacramento and rode a freight back to Oakland. Now, three years later, he was once again 'mate to the wind that tramps the world.'

Jack and Frank Davis left their side-door Pullman at Sacramento, only to learn that the Army had departed for Ogden at four that afternoon. They caught the Overland Limited and held her down until Truckee, where they were ditched, or thrown off. That night they tried to take the Overland east; Frank made her out, but Jack was left behind. He caught a freight train instead, and slept so soundly in spite of the cold that he was sidetracked at Reno without waking. He spent the day in Reno watching the unemployed congregate on street corners as they made up a detachment to start east; all along the line he met hundreds of unemployed chasing the first detachment of the Industrial Army.

Intent on catching up with Frank, he left Reno before the company was formed, traveled all night and all day in a box-car, and at Wadsworth slept in an engine cab in the yards until four in the morning when the wipers routed him out. He caught an early morning freight and rode the blind, or space behind the coal car. A spark from the engine landed in his overcoat pocket and suddenly burst into flame. The train was going forty miles an hour, and it was difficult to put out the fire. His overcoat and coat were ruined and had to be thrown away.

That night in Winnemuka he caught up with Frank. They decided to wait for the Reno detachment and travel with it, but a freight train came through and the temptation was too great: they boarded her and rode east. Two days later Jack and Frank once again parted company. Jack notes in his boyish scrawl, 'The Road has no more charms for Frank. The romance and adventure are gone and nothing remains but the stern reality of the hardships to be endured. Though he has decided to turn west again I am sure the experience has done him good, broadened his thoughts, given him a better understanding of the low strata of society, and surely will have made him more charitable to the tramps he will meet hereafter when he is in better circumstances. He starts west and I start east tonight. I am going to break coal on the engine from here to Carlin.'

For Jack the greatest charm of tramp life was the absence of monotony. In Hobo Land the face of life was an ever-changing phantasmagoria where the impossible happened and the unexpected jumped out of the bushes at every turn. Each day was a day apart, with a record of swiftly moving pictures all its own. At nights he rode the freight and express trains, at meal times he 'threw his feet,' that is, begged at back doors for a handout, or panhandled along the main street. He encountered hundreds of hoboes with whom he beat the trains, pooled his money and tobacco, boiled up, cooked mulligan in the jungles, battered the main stem, played cards, swapped yarns, and fulfilled the dictates of the profesh, to keep going on the fastest trains.

Ditched in the Nevada Desert, he had to walk all night to a junction. It was early in the year, and cold in the upland pastures where snow lay on the mountains and a miserable wind blew; priding himself on being a blowed-in-the-glass tramp, he carried no blanket. Oftentimes he would 'throw his feet' for hours without getting a scrap of food at a back door, or land in a strange town at midnight without a penny in his pocket, and nothing to do but sit in the jungle by the tracks and shiver the night through. Other nights he spent on the pilot behind the engine, where he tried to doze off to the coughing of the engine, the screeching of the wheels, and the rain of hot cinders. Once when he was ravenously hungry he was given a big handout wrapped in newspaper. He ran to a near-by lot to devour the meal . . . and found it to be soggy cake which the people at the party the night before had refused to eat. He sat on the ground and wept.

It was while 'throwing his feet' that he developed the art of spontaneous story-telling, for upon his ability to tell a good story depends the success of the beggar. The instant a back door is opened he must size up his victim and tell a story that will appeal to the peculiar personality and temperament of that victim. In Reno a kindly, middle-aged mother opened her back door. Jack instantly became an innocent, unfortunate lad. He couldn't speak . . . never before in his life had he asked anyone for food . . . only the harsh pangs of hunger could compel him to do so degraded and ignoble a thing as beg. The good woman had to relieve his embarrassment by telling him that he was hungry and urging him to come into the kitchen for a set-down, the tramp's delight.

Later in Harrisburg, Pennsylvania, he knocked on a back door just as two maiden ladies were about to sit down to their breakfast. They invited him into the dining-room to share their buttered toast and eggs out of egg cups. The two maiden ladies had never looked upon the bright face of adventure; as the Tramp Royals would have it, they had worked all their lives on one same shift. Jack was hungry, he had been riding the blinds all night; while the servant brought him more and more eggs, and more and more toast and coffee, he thrilled the ladies with wild yarns, bringing into the sweet scents and narrow confines of their existence the large airs of the world, freighted with lusty smells of sweat and strife and danger. Jack never forgot that breakfast, and one is safe in assuming that the maiden ladies never forgot his hair-raising fiction stories.

When the going got too tough, when middle-class doors remained locked, when the big house on the hill refused him scoffings and he could no longer stand his hunger, he would go to the poor section of the town, to the shack with its broken window stuffed with rags and its tired-faced mother broken with labor. Here he could always find something to eat, for the poor never withheld from what they needed for themselves. From these experiences Jack later said that a bone to the dog is not charity; charity is the bone shared with the dog when you are just as hungry as the dog.

Best of all Jack liked the exciting and dangerous contests with the train crews, for he was out to prove that he was the greatest Tramp Royal on the Road, the Prince of Hoboes. He would run ahead of the crack Overland in the darkness before it left the depot and when the first blind came past jump on. The crew has seen him. The train is stopped. He jumps off and runs ahead into the darkness. This time the brakeman rides the blind, but there is no entrance to the train from the blind; before it is going very fast he must drop off and catch a rear car. Jack stays so far ahead of the train that the brakeman has dropped off the blind by the time it reaches him and he can safely jump on; safely, providing he doesn't slip and kill himself. He thinks he is secure, but in a few moments another brakeman who has ridden the engine comes after him. The train is stopped. Jack jumps off. He runs ahead. This time when the train comes past the brakeman is riding the first blind, so Jack jumps on the second one. The brakeman drops off the first and jumps on the second. Jack drops off the opposite side and sprints ahead for the first blind. The brakeman pursues him, but the train is picking up speed and the brakeman cannot catch up. Once again Jack thinks he is safe . . . until the fireman plays a stream of water on him . . . the train is stopped . . . he sprints ahead into the darkness . . .

He is mighty proud that he, a poor hobo, has four times stopped the Overland with its many passengers and coaches, its government mail, its two thousand steam horses straining in the engine. So the game goes on through the night; in order to escape the ever-pursuing brakemen he decks her, straddles the ends of two cars, goes underneath and rides the rods. By now he has the engineer, conductor, fireman, and two brakemen after him, but to the eighteen-year-old boy who prides himself on being at the top of the profesh, the fun of the game is enhanced by the terrible price he would pay if he lost.

He took incredible risks, jumped off trains that were going at full speed, at one time traveling so fast through the air that he knocked down and stunned an officer who was standing on a street corner watching the train go by. He rode the rods on bad lines, lines on which the brakemen were known to take a coupling pin and a length of bell cord to the platform in front of the car under which the tramp was riding, and let the coupling pin strike against the rails, beating the tramp to death. He was afraid of nothing; the greater the risk, the greater the fun. Was he not a Viking who had crossed San Francisco Bay in an open skiff in a howling southwester?

Routed out of a boxcar in the mountains during a snow storm, he gave up Lizzie Connellon's ring to a brakeman who was shaking him down for money. When the nights were too cold for travel he went to the roundhouse and slept in an engine cab, and several times went to the electric-light works where he slept on top of the boilers in the terrific heat. In the afternoons he would go to the town library to read; at night he always tried to catch the blind baggage of the express. With great delight he writes, 'I was determined to hold her down all night, and pursued by the train crew I rode the blinds, the tender of the engine, the cowcatchers, the pilots of the doubleheader, the decks and the platform in the middle of the train.' The nights were so cold and the days so hot that his face began to peel, and he describes himself as looking as though he had fallen into a fire.

All these details and a thousand others he writes meticulously in his notebook. The seventy-three-page diary of The Road reveals him to be a well-bred and gentle boy in spite of his rough background, nefarious activities, and cutthroat associates. The notebook is filled with character sketches of the men he met, stretches of dialogue he overheard, notes on individual stories of how they came to be tramps, railroad and tramp vocabularies, descriptions of towns and scenes and adventures. Though the diary was scrawled in pencil in boxcars, roundhouses, jungles, and saloons, the writing is literate and lyrical, the charming unstudied flow of a natural-born writer.

For the greater part the notebook is robust and joyous, the picturings of a vigorous young man in love with all the startlingly new and fascinating phenomena of life; but he cannot keep himself upon this high plane of evowal, sustain this eternal Yea! Suddenly his nerves are shattered, he becomes depressed; in his notebook he will scrawl a passage on the right to commit suicide which takes us back to the night four years before when he fell off the Benicia pier and decided that drowning was a hero's death. For him his own life always had a strong death appeal.

Caught in a blizzard at the summit of the Rockies, where he was freezing in an open blind, a friendly brakeman told him that on the opposite track was the Reno detachment of Kelly's Army. When Jack climbed into the boxcar he found eighty-four men stretched out, two feet of straw under them, keeping each other warm. Since there was no available straw upon which to step, he stepped on the men, who promptly put him through their threshing machine, bandying him from one end of the car to the other until he found an unoccupied bit of straw. Thus was he initiated into the Industrial Army.

They were a jolly crowd; some of them were unemployed who really thought they would get work from Congress, others were tramps just going along for the ride, and still others were young boys like himself out on the adventure trail. While the car rode through the blizzard they instituted a Scheherazade in which every one of the eighty-five men had to tell a good story. The penalty for failure was the threshing machine. Jack says that he never sat through such a marvelous story-telling debauch.

For twenty-four hours the Reno detachment rode out the storm, locked in their car without a bite of food. When they reached the plains of Nebraska they took up a collection and wired the authorities of Grand Island, which they would reach at noon, that eighty-five healthy, hungry men would arrive at meal time and wanted something to eat. When the freight train stopped at Grand Island the police and special reception committees marched the detachment to the hotels and restaurants, fed them, and marched them back to the train, which had been ordered to wait for its passengers.

When they arrived in Omaha at one in the morning they were met by a special platoon of policemen who guarded them until they were shipped across the river to Council Bluffs. Ordered to march in a torrential rain the five miles to Chautauqua Park where General Kelly was encamped, Jack and his new pal, Swede, a six-foot towhead mechanic, slipped through the police lines and sought shelter. They found a saloon propped on big timbers where Jack spent the most miserable night of his life. The building, perched in the air for the purpose of being moved, was exposed in a multitude of places through which the wind whistled. Soaked to the skin, Jack rolled under the bar, where he shivered and prayed for daylight. At five in the morning, blue with cold and half dead, he caught a freight back to Omaha and begged his breakfast. He saw the sights, then started out for Camp Kelly but was stopped at a toll bridge. A sympathizer gave him a quarter to ride all the way to Chautauqua Park. Arriving there he reported to General Kelly and was assigned to the last rank of the rear guard.

The railroads operating between Omaha and Chicago were hostile, afraid to give the Army free boxcar transportation for fear of setting a precedent. They filled their trains with armed Pinkerton detectives to ward off Kelly's men. For two days and nights Jack lay with the Army beside the railroad tracks, pelted by sleet, hail, and rain. Then two young ladies of Council Bluffs induced a boy to steal his father's engine, and a committee of Omaha sympathizers threw together a train of boxcars. When the train reached Kelly's encampment it was found to be too small to accommodate the Army, and was regretfully returned.

After a number of unsuccessful skirmishes General Kelly decided to walk his Army to Washington, where he would join General Coxey. Taking to the road with twelve wagons loaded with food and campstuffs donated by the people of Omaha and Council Bluffs, the Army made an imposing array with flags and banners and General Kelly at its head astride of a fine black horse presented by an enthusiastic Council Bluffs citizen. After two days the soles of Jack's shoes wore off, and he was walking on his socks. He went to the commissary, but they claimed they had no shoes for him. The next day he had such a crop of blisters that he could hardly walk; as a gesture of protest he walked in his bare feet . . . which promptly brought shoes from the commissary.

The state of Iowa was friendly and hospitable; when the

Army arrived at a town the entire population lined the main street with flags and banners. As soon as the men were encamped the crowds moved out there to have community sings, listen to political speeches, and watch the town nine play baseball against the Army team. Jack remarks in his notebook that the ladies mingled their sweet voices with those of the boys all hoarse from the cold weather. He also notes with pride that everybody expressed a good opinion of the Army, and many were surprised at the gentlemanly bearing and honest appearance of the boys.

Still a non-conformist, finding discipline intolerable, and with a desire to know everything about the country through which he was traveling, Jack ran the Army pickets every night to look the new town over. He again developed blisters and determined to ride the freights, but the marshals provided wagons to get the non-walkers out of town. Just before the Army reaches Des Moines the wagon rides ran out, and Jack vowed to go to jail rather than walk another step on his festering feet. He went down to the railroad station, and 'playing on the sympathy of the people, I raised a ticket.'

When the Army reached Des Moines the men swore their feet were sore and refused to walk any further. Stuck with two thousand itinerants, Des Moines put up the Army in an abandoned stove works and fed it six thousand meals a day, while the officials tried to persuade the railroads to carry it on to the next stop. The railroads declined. Jack rested, played baseball, caught up on his sleep and food. Then the town took up a subscription and the Army built rafts to float itself down the Des Moines River.

Sailor Jack and nine other men from his company, all of whom he termed hustlers, picked a good boat and went down the river on their own. They were always half a day to a day in advance of the Army. When they approached a small town they raised their American flag, called themselves the advance boat, and demanded to know what provision had been made for the Army. When the farmers brought forth the supplies, Sailor Jack and his pals took the cream: the tobacco, milk, butter, sugar, canned goods. They were not altogether heartless, they left for the Army the sacks of beans and flour and slaughtered steers, but as Jack remarked, they were living fine. They even disdained to use coffee boiled in water; they boiled it in milk. Jack admitted that this was hard on the Army, but then, the ten of them were individualists, they had initiative and enterprise, and ardently believed that grub was for the man who got there first.

General Kelly was outraged. He sent a light skiff to head

off the 'advance boat' and when this failed, sent out two men on horseback to warn the countryside. After that Jack and his comrades were met with 'the icy mitt,' and were forced to go back to the regular Army. In Quincy, Illinois, which someone told Jack was the richest town of its size in the United States, he 'threw his feet' for a whole day and returned with enough underwear, socks, shirts, shoes, hats, and suits to clothe half his company. He had told a thousand stories to the people of Quincy, and every story a good one. When he came to write for the magazines he regretted the fecundity of fiction he lavished that day.

However, that was the end of opulence for the Army. For thirty-six hours the farmers provided no free food. The sun came out hot and strong, spring was at hand, the scents in the air were intoxicating . . . and the Industrial Army began to desert by whole squads and platoons. Jack jotted in his notebook, 'Am going to pull out in the morning, can't stand starvation.' All nine of his boat comrades deserted with him. General Kelly pushed on and with a few men finally reached Washington, but by the time he got there he found General Coxey in jail. Coxey, who was a few administrations ahead of his time in demanding federal projects to create work for the unemployed, had been arrested by Capitol police for walking on the grass!

Jack rode the Cannonball into Jacksonville, the Kansas City passenger into Mason City, caught a cattle train, and rode it all night into Chicago. At the post office he found mail from home, with four one-dollar greenbacks from Eliza. He located the second-hand district where he bought shoes, a hat, pair of pants, shirt, and overcoat. That night he went to a theater, saw the sights, and slept in a fifteen-cent bed, the first he had lain in since leaving Oakland. The next day he took a boat across the lake to St. Joseph, Michigan, where Flora's sister, Mary Everhard, lived with her husband and children. Jack stayed for several weeks in the comfortable Everhard home, wrote many pages of notes, made up for lost meals, enjoyed being spoiled by his Aunt Mary, did a little farm work, and told the Everhards exciting stories of The Road.

By midsummer he had ridden the rails into New York City. He got into the habit of begging for food in the mornings, and spending the afternoons in the little park by the City Hall, where he could escape the sweltering heat. For a few cents each he bought current books that had been injured in the binding, and lay on the cool grass reading and drinking penny glasses of ice-cold milk.

One afternoon he joined the throng watching a group of youngsters playing pee-wee. Suddenly one of the boys yelled 'Chickey for the bulls!' and the crowd broke up. Jack was sauntering toward the park with a book under his arm when he saw an officer coming toward him. Jack paid him no attention. The policeman hit him over the head with a club and knocked him down. Dizzy and sick, he managed to scramble to his feet and run, for if he had not escaped it would have meant thirty days on Blackwell's Island for resisting an officer.

Two days later he rode into Niagara Falls in a boxcar, and headed straight for the Falls. Entranced by the spectacle, he remained all afternoon without eating. Eleven o'clock that night still found him watching the dark water under the moonlight. He then headed out into the country, climbed a fence, and slept in a field. At five o'clock he awakened and returned to the Falls. As he walked through the sleeping streets he saw three men coming toward him. The men on either side were hoboes, the one in the middle a fly-cop who demanded the name of the hotel at which he was staying. Unable to conjure up the name of a hotel, he was arrested as a vagrant and taken to the Niagara Falls jail. In the morning sixteen prisoners were brought into the dock. The judge, acting as his own clerk, called out the names of the vagrants and promptly sentenced each of them to thirty days at hard labor.

Jack was handcuffed to a tall negro, a steel chain was run through the links of the handcuffs, and the eight pairs of men were chained together and walked through the streets of Niagara Falls to the railroad station. On the train he shared his tobacco with the man behind him, who had been in many prisons and knew the ropes, and they became friends. They were taken to the Erie County Penitentiary, where Jack's head was shaved and he was put into prison stripes. Early the next morning he joined the lock-step and marched out to the yard to unload canal boats.

After two days of hard manual labor on bread and water —meat was served once a week, and then not until all the nutrition had been boiled out—Jack's friend from the train came to his rescue. The man had found former prison pals among the trusties, had been appointed a hall man, and in turn had secured Jack's appointment as a hall man. It was his duty to serve the prisoners their bread and water, to keep them in order. Jack bartered the pieces of bread that were left over for books and tobacco, or for suspenders and safety pins which he would swap with the long-timers for meat.

Once he had become a trustie the halls were open for him

to watch what went on. He saw prisoners throw fits, go mad; be whipped down eight tiers of stone steps; beaten to death; indescribable horrors in a torture chamber of helpless derelicts. He became friendly with other trusties, guards, short-timers, long-timers; he came to know hundreds of men, to hear their stories, record their dialects, grasp their philosophies, integrate their backgrounds. And all the time, in order to keep his job as a trustie, he stayed in solid with his pal. They spent many warm and comradely hours together planning the burglaries they were going to pull when they got out.

At the end of the thirty days the two men were released, begged pennies on the main drag of Buffalo, and went into a saloon for 'shupers' of beer. With the foaming beer in front of him, Jack excused himself from his crony, went to the rear of the saloon, jumped the fence, and ran all the way to the railroad station. A few minutes later he was on board a freight headed west.

It took him several months to beat his way across the three thousand miles of Canadian railroads. A number of times he kept himself out of jail only by his ability to invent tales which convinced the police that he was anything but a vagrant. Often he went hungry because he couldn't speak French, and the Canadian peasants were afraid of tramps. He rode nights in freezing boxcars and in the mornings was barely able to crawl out and beg his food. But he enjoyed his adventures, particularly the time he rode the same coal car for a thousand miles, begging his food in town each time the train stopped, returning to his coal-bed to eat it while he watched the Canadian countryside slip past. At last he reached Vancouver, signed on the *Umatilla* as a sailor, and worked his way back to San Francisco.

3

SEARCH the records as one may, one cannot find that Jack London thought a socialistic thought or uttered a socialistic sentiment prior to the year spent among what the sociologists termed the submerged tenth. He had been what he later learned to call a rampant individualist; an individualist who, with his nine cronies in the fastest boat of the fleet, victimized his comrades of Kelly's Army out of their food because 'we had initiative and ardently believed that grub was for the man who got there first'; an individualist who as hall man at the penitentiary had not distributed the surplus bread among the unfortunate prisoners, but had made them pay for it from their scant supply of tobacco, books, and meat. He had good health, hard muscles, and a stomach that could digest scrap iron; he exulted in his young life and was able to hold his own at work or fight. He saw himself raging through life without end, conquering by sheer superiority and strength. He was proud to be one of nature's strong-armed noblemen.

What changed his mind was the startling manner in which he found the submerged tenth had been recruited. Before going on the road he had imagined that the men who were tramps were tramps by choice, because they wanted to roam and adventure without responsibility, or because they were loafers, lunatics, dullards, or drunks. Though he realized that a certain portion of these men would be waste material under any economic order, he soon saw that the greater part of them had once been as good material as himself, just as blond-beastly: sailormen and laboring men wrenched and twisted out of shape by toil and hardship and accident, then cast adrift like so many old horses, tramps on the road without a blanket or spare shirt or meal to their names. As he battered the drag and slammed back gates with them, or shivered with them in boxcars and city parks, he listened to life stories that had begun under auspices as fair as his own, and which had ended in the shambles in the bottom of the social pit.

They were men who had been injured and maimed at unguarded machines, and abandoned by their bosses; men who had sickened because of fourteen hours a day of toil in airless factories, and been let out as useless; men who had grown old in the harness and been replaced by younger and stronger ones. They were men whose industries had been killed off by changing times, and who had been unable to find or adjust themselves to new ones, who had been supplanted by machines, who had been replaced by women and children at lower wages, who had been thrown out of work by depression and had never been re-employed. They were men who had not been sufficiently skilled to handle new technical equipment; migratory laborers whose very jobs forced them to be idle from a third to a half of each year; the inefficient, the mediocre, the discouraged workers; slag of competitive and uncontrolled industry who had chosen vagabondage in preference to the slums. They were men who had gone on strike against long hours and low pay, had had their jobs taken by scabs, and been blacklisted by employers.

Jack saw that in five, ten, twenty years he too would be replaced by a younger and stronger man, would perforce become part of the slums of the city or the slums of The Road. He learned two things, first that he would have to educate himself so that he could work with his brain instead of his easily replaceable brawn; and second, that there was something wrong with an economic system that took from a man the best years of his working life, then cast him on the junk heap to starve and rot, a tragedy for the individual and his family, brutalizing and wasteful for society.

By the time he got back to Oakland he knew his thinking and attitude toward life had changed, that he believed in something new. He was not quite certain what this something was. Professor Chaney's brain led him direct to the books to find out. From workers and wanderers on The Road, some of them educated and trained men, he had heard a good deal about trade unions, socialism and workers' solidarity, which provided a clue as to where to begin his search.

He learned at once that modern socialism was only about seventy years old, so contemporary that it had been born but a few years before his own mother; he had the feeling that he was amazingly fortunate to be alive at the very beginning of the movement, to be almost a charter member. The very timeliness lent an added zest to his discovery. His next step was to perceive that economic conditions and not men breed revolutions. France, the mother of modern socialism, had revolted against a corrupt and burdensome monarchy only to find an equally burdensome bourgeoisie strapped to her back. The coming of machine production brought long hours, low wages, and cyclical unemployment, and the condition of the mass of workers became worse than it ever had been under the profligacies of Louis XIV and Louis XV. Another revolution, economic in nature instead of political, was needed, and from this need arose the Utopian Socialists who were led to socialism by observing that the few were surfeited with riches while the many, who worked ceaselessly, lived in poverty.

He went to the work of Bebeuf, Saint-Simon, Fourier, and Proudhon, where he found the first recorded attacks on private property and the first differentiation of the economic classes; the insistence that the basis of private property was labor; the demand for the abolition of unearned income and inheritance of wealth; and the revolutionary conception that social reform was a function of government. Jack bought a five-cent brown paper tablet at the stationery store and in his undisciplined scrawl wrote down the aims of these pioneers who tried to visualize an industrial society wherein no man would live off the labor of his fellows, where every man had to work and work was guaranteed to all. He noted that although these men had broken ground for the revolution, they had not been able to provide a mechanism by means of which the socialist state was to be achieved; they had hoped that the masters would give the workers socialism out of the Christian goodness of their hearts.

A wandering philosopher of The Road had told him about a pamphlet called *The Communist Manifesto*. Jack secured a copy of *The Communist Manifesto*, and reading it avidly found that it was as though his own heart and brain had suddenly become magnificently articulate. He capitulated utterly to Karl Marx's reasoning, for here he found the method whereby man not only could achieve the socialist state, but under historical imperatives would be compelled by economic force to embrace it. In his notebook Jack jotted down, 'The whole history of mankind has been a history of contests between exploiting and exploited; a history of these class struggles shows the evolution of economic civilization just as Darwin's studies show the evolution of man; with the coming of industrialism and concentrated capital a stage has been reached whereby the exploited cannot attain its emancipation from the ruling class without once and for all emancipating society at large from all future exploitation, oppression, class distinctions and class struggles.'

Pushing onward in *The Communist Manifesto* Jack found scientific socialism demanding the abolition of private property in land; abolition of all rights of inheritance; factories, means of production, communication, and transportation to be owned by the state; and all wealth, except consumption goods, to be owned collectively. With his heavy pencil he underlined in the *Manifesto* the call of socialism to the workingmen of the world: *'The socialists disdain to conceal their aims and views. They openly declare their ends can be attained only by a forcible overthrow of all existing conditions. Let the ruling classes tremble at the socialisitc revolution. The proletarians have nothing to lose but their chains. They have a world to gain. Working men of all countries, unite!"*

It was not long before Jack was to proclaim that socialism was the greatest thing in the world.

Having decided that he would live by his brain rather than his brawn, Jack settled upon the kind of work he wanted to do. He had kept a notebook during his year on the road, and he knew for a certainty that his life could have meaning and he could be happy only as a writer of the stories that charged through his brain. For him to have reached this decision at so early an age is not difficult to understand; the thousands of astrological divinities Professor Chaney had written were short stories, pure creations of fiction. Jack came legitimately by his passion to spin yarns for a living.

He also settled upon the University of California in Berkeley, just a short streetcar ride from his home, as the place where he would derive the ultimate in education. However, he had never attended high school and had three years of routine work ahead of him before he might be admitted.

He was nineteen when he entered the freshman class of Oakland High in a much-worn, wrinkled, and ill-fitting dark blue suit and woolen shirt without a tie. He was strong and rugged looking, his face sunburned, his tawny hair disheveled as though he always ran his fingers through it. He was still chewing tobacco, a habit he picked up on The Road and continued when he returned to Oakland because it anesthetized the pain of the numerous cavities in his teeth. When Eliza offered to have the cavities filled and to replace the extracted teeth with false ones if he would give up chewing tobacco, he readily assented. Pleased with his shining new teeth, Jack invested in the first toothbrush he had ever owned.

He was slouchy in manner, a habit acquired during the months of begging, and leaned back at his desk with his feet stretched out in front of him, his hands in his pockets, looking off into space. He turned his head first one way, then the other; at short intervals a shadow would pass over his face, then he would pull himself together and the smile would come back. When called upon to recite he raised himself with apparent difficulty to a half-upright position, keeping both hands on his desk as though to steady himself. His recitation was always in a low voice, soft, almost inaudible, his answers as curt as possible. When finished he would sit down quickly and abruptly, as though exhausted.

The boys and girls around him were fourteen and fifteen years old; most of them came from protected homes, had never been farther away than San Francisco. To Jack they seemed babies. He had the feeling too that although education was the gateway to a better life, the lessons he had to go through in French, Roman history, and algebra were childish. He made no attempt to conceal from his classmates that he was bored, that he considered the work trivial, that he was interested in the world of maturity into which they had not yet been initiated.

He wanted to be one with his class, yet couldn't. He would stand by and listen eagerly to the general conversation, but if spoken to by one of the boys or girls would show irritability and leave abruptly. Once again was manifested the fundamental contradiction in his nature first noticed by Ina Coolbrith: his supreme self-confidence existing side by side with his strangulated shyness and sense of inferiority. To the students he seemed resentful about something, as a result of which he was often gruff when they wanted him to join their activities. They were sorely pressed to understand him. One of his classmates, Georgia Loring Bamford, reports that at times his face beamed and showed the character of a beautiful child, at other times he looked like a waterfront loafer and seemed proud of it. He kept his cap stuffed in his coat pocket and when school was over pulled it out, stuck it on his head, and dashed out of the building swinging his arms sailor fashion.

He would have had little time for social life even if Oakland High had accepted him. John London had found employment as a special depot guard during the railroad strike, but Jack still had to support himself. On Saturdays and Sundays he solicited odd jobs, mowed lawns, beat carpets, ran errands. From her modest income Eliza bought his supplies and books and provided him with a bicycle to ride to school. He was always pressed for cash. When the janitor of Oakland High needed an assistant, Eliza got her brother the job. After

school was over Jack remained to sweep the floors and scrub
the lavatories. Years later he proudly wrote his daughter that
he had washed every window in the building where she was
attending high school.

A group of girls, seeing him go into a saloon on Broadway
with a couple of tramps he had known on The Road, spread
the word that he associated with rough companions and was
accustomed to violence. With Jack becoming the school janitor the chasm between him and the other students became
even more unbridgeable.

However he had discovered the student literary magazine,
The Aegis, and when they accepted his article, 'Bonin Islands,' he decided that he was going to like the school after
all. The article, which ran in January and February of 1895,
is written with verve, with a freshness and vitality that keeps
it enjoyable even at this distance. The pictures of the whaling
fleet and the Islands are vivid, the characters are warmly
human and lovable, and above all the prose has a music of
words. Seeing his article in print taught Jack more about
writing than all the criticisms scrawled over his manuscripts
by the English teacher who abhorred his informal style, his
spontaneity, his gusts of eagerness and delight with nature. In
March *The Aegis* published 'Sakaicho Hona Asi and Haka-
daki,' then came two stories from his experiences on The
Road, called 'Frisco Kid' and 'And Frisco Kid Came Back,'
both rich in dialect and showing insight into the psychology
of road-kids.

The railroad strike was settled, John London lost his job,
and it was up to Jack to provide for the family. He had to
find more outside jobs, work harder. Since he could no longer
spend any money on himself his classmates noted that he became more and more shabby. He was always overworked, on
edge, going without sufficient food or sleep. Because he wrote
honestly about himself the students came to know that he
had been a sailor and a tramp. The girls would have nothing
to do with him. The fact that he was a writer not only did
not make his eccentricities acceptable, but made him the
more a creature apart. He enjoyed writing his stories in his
spare hours at night, he enjoyed the great number of books
he took out of the public library on the six family cards, but
there was little in his days to bring him personal happiness:
friendship, love, a place in the sun . . . he had none of these.
Then he joined the Henry Clay Debating Society.

The Henry Clay Debating Society was the one rallying
point for intellectuals in Oakland. To it belonged young
schoolteachers, doctors, lawyers, musicians, university stu-

dents, socialists, all interested in the world about them. More than any other group in Oakland they judged a man by the quality of his mind rather than the clothes on his back. Jack sat quietly during a meeting or two, then entered the discussions. The club appreciated the clear and logical manner in which his mind worked; they enjoyed his robust Irish humor, his lively stories of the sea and the road, thought him good fun and jolly company. They were moved by his burning passion for socialism and the fund of knowledge he had already acquired on the subject. But most important of all for Jack at this point, they liked him, they accepted him as an equal and a friend. In the warm glow of their acceptance Jack shed his ill poise, his moroseness, his self-consciousness; he kept his head up, expressed himself fully and with ease. He had found a place among his contemporaries.

Of all the members Jack liked best Edward Applegarth, a slim, brown-haired, brown-eyed boy who came from a cultivated English family that had settled in Oakland. Applegarth had a keen wit and an incisive habit of thinking. The two young men were of the same age; they stimulated each other to swift, sound thought. They began spending their spare hours together on long walks and friendly talks. To Applegarth Jack was not an ill-dressed, crude-mannered boy from the wrong side of the railroad tracks; he was an intelligent, roguish, well-traveled chap who happened to be poor at the moment, but who was on his way up.

Applegarth brought Jack into his home and introduced him to his sister Mabel. Jack had no more than crossed the threshold when he fell in love with all the speed and spontaneity of his forceful nature.

Mabel Applegarth was an ethereal creature with wide, spiritual blue eyes and a wealth of golden hair. Jack likened her to a pale gold flower upon a slender stem. She had a beautiful speaking voice and tinkling laughter which to him was the most musical sound in the world. Mabel was three years his senior, an honest woman without pretense or coquetry. She was a student at the University of California, taking special courses in English. Jack marveled at all the knowledge that was so neatly stored in her pretty head. Her manners were flawless; she had a profound sense of breeding; art and culture were her constant companions. Jack loved her as a goddess to be worshipped but not to be touched. To his delight she accepted him as an equal and a friend; had the boy only known it, she was as much drawn to his warm strength and crude manliness as he was to her delicacy.

Jack became a frequent visitor at the home of the Applegarths, who lived in a rambling house filled with books and paintings. They loaned him their books, their knowledge and training in fields he had not yet invaded; he watched them carefully, their gestures, their speech. Before long the rough words began to drop out of his vocabulary, the sailor's roll from his walk, the crudeness from his manners. He was invited to the homes of other members of the Henry Clay Society where he met other cultivated young ladies whose dresses reached the ground, and with whom he discussed poetry and art and nuances of grammar over cups of tea. His brusqueness dropped away and his handsome, flashing smile more and more adorned his clean-cut face. He gave himself to his new friends with a full and deep love. When it was enthusiastically reported back to the students of Oakland High that Jack London was a charming and remarkable young man who surely had a brilliant future, they glanced over at their badly dressed and bored classmate and wondered what had gone wrong with the judgment of their elders.

The members of the newly formed Socialist Party of Oakland, one of the first on the Pacific coast, invited Jack to join their Local. Here he met such men as Austin Lewis of the British Socialist-Labor Party, German Socialists who had been exiled from their Fatherland by the ban against socialists, mature and well-trained men who served as whetstones for the young boy to sharpen the tools of his mind. The Socialist Local in Oakland was more a cultural than an economic group; they met of evenings for music and a glass of beer and to study and orate on political economy. They were intellectuals, theoreticians not directly involved in the class struggle, for no workingmen had as yet joined the party. Grateful as he was for this company and training, Jack did not believe that socialism belonged to the intellectuals. He believed that it belonged to the workingmen and the unions that were destined by the processes of history to carry on the class war, fight the revolution, and establish the proletarian world state which Karl Marx had taught him was the next step in the development of civilization.

He began attending workingmen's meetings, talked about socialism at labor unions, listened to speeches in City Hall Park. One afternoon, feeling moved, he got up on a bench and told the large crowd of listeners that capitalism was a system of organized robbery which had the laborers by the throats and was choking the last dollar of labor out of them before flinging them aside. He had not been talking more than ten minutes when there was a clatter of horses' hooves on Broadway, a black patrol wagon drew up alongside the park, and two officers clapped him under arrest. They escorted him through the crowd to the patrol wagon, rode him behind locked steel doors through the Oakland streets, and threw him in jail. When Jack protested that this was America where they had free speech, and that socialism was no crime, the desk sergeant replied, 'Maybe not, but speaking without a license is.'

The Oakland papers ran the story under huge streamers, calling Jack 'The Boy Socialist,' a name that was to stick to him for years.

What made Jack London a socialist? He was raised in poverty, he knew hunger and deprivation, he had learned harrowing lessons about the fate of the laboring man. But hundreds of thousands of Americans of his time who had grown up in hunger and deprivation believed in the capitalist system and went out to corner their share of wealth. Just as he had been wise enough to understand that a certain number of the men on the road would be waste material under any civilization, he also realized that only a portion of the hardships of his youth were a result of the unsocial structure of American capitalism, that the major part of his hunger had been caused by his mother's unbalanced business schemes that had prevented John London from earning a living.

Professor Chaney was inherently a socialist before Jack was born. He had an intense though intellectual interest in the working class and a belief in the willingness of men to work hard and to work together. For many years he lectured and wrote articles on the causes and cures of poverty. This sympathy with and interest in the workers is, for those who are not workers themselves, a matter of temperament, tied up with a warm human nature, a sensitivity to the hardships of others, a personal liberality, and an imagination sufficiently vivid to project one's self into the sufferings of conscientious men whose wives and children are starving. Professor Chaney had all these attributes; they made him a socialist; he bequeathed them to his son, and they made his son a socialist.

Chaney was an Irishman; so was Jack. They both were endowed with the characteristics that go to make up the genius of the Irish: compassion for the sufferings of others; liberality with their own possessions; the love of a fight such as the Class War between capital and labor; and the courage to plow in with boths fists flying.

Would Jack London have been a socialist if Flora had kept her hands out of John London's affairs, and the family had prospered? The answer would seem to be yes, though he more likely would have developed into an intellectual or utopian socialist rather than a workingman's socialist, and would have been content to let socialism filter slowly through the centuries by means of the ballot, instead of rising up and demanding militantly that the workingmen Unite! Throw off their chains! Wipe out by force the ruling predatory class!

To Jack, socialism was a system of human, historical, and economic logic, as irrefutable as the multiplication table. Though he had as yet accumulated only a limited *content* of thought he had the apparatus for a scientific *method* of thought, the perseverance to follow a given line of reasoning, and the courage to accept its conclusions no matter how they might violate his preconceived notions.

Then too, he had an inexhaustible quarrel with the world: his illegitimacy. Since he could not fight with his mother about it, rectify the wrong that had been done him, nor bring it out into the light, it festered in the subterranean darkness of his unconscious. The only quarrel in the external world which had the epic proportions to match in magnitude his internal quarrel was the overthrowing of the predominant class of society by the subservient class, of which he was a member.

The Chamber of Commerce and a section of the established Oakland society were outraged at his preaching destruction of the existing order; and in the public City Hall Park! They agitated to have him sent to prison. When the case came up the judge recommended that Jack's youth be considered a mitigating circumstance, and let him off with a warning that if he ever did it again he would be sent away. After Jack's death Mayor Davies of Oakland dedicated an oak tree to him in City Hall Park on a spot not too far distant from where he had been arrested for this first fiery speech.

The position he had begun to establish for himself was shattered by the arrest and unfavorable publicity. The Socialist Local stuck by him, as did Edward and Mable Applegarth and a few of the other Henry Club debaters, though Jack complained at this time that really decent fellows who liked him very well drew the line at his appearing in public with their sisters. A number of the homes that had been opened to him through the Henry Clay Society were now closed. For the rest of Oakland he had merely strengthened the impression of being a none too savory character. He had been known to be an outlaw; in his pirating days he had been seen drunk along the waterfront and in questionable company; he had been a tramp; he came from a poverty-stricken, déclassé family living in the worst part of town. The people of Oakland believed that being a socialist not only proved that there was something wrong with a man's mind, but with his morals as well. So rare a phenomenon was a socialist that reporters were sent to interview him. When Jack boldly took a stand for the municipal ownership of public utilities he was branded a red-shirt, a dynamiter, and an anarchist. The interviews when published were pathological studies of a strange and abnormal specimen. Jack shuddered when he thought what the newspapers would have called him if he had admitted that he believed in the public ownership of all means of production.

Although Mabel Applegarth was shocked by Jack's arrest and was displeased at the derogatory newspaper interviews, the incident made no difference in their relationship. They were perfect complements, Jack robust, vital, crude; Mabel delicate, cultivated, and polished. They took bicycle rides together, ate picnic lunches in the deep golden poppy fields of the Berkeley hills overlooking the Bay, went for long sails in his skiff. One Sunday afternoon in early summer they were drifting down the Estuary with Mabel sitting primly in the prow in a fluffy white gown and picture hat. She was reading to him from Swinburne's poetic pessimism in such a soothing voice that Jack fell asleep. The tide went out and left them stranded. Because she knew how little rest he got, Mabel did not disturb him. When he awakened he had to roll his one good pair of trousers above his knees and carry her though the mud to shore. It was the closest he had as yet gotten to the young lady.

Jack had received a B average in his courses for his first semester. After working during the summer to help the family and to get a few dollars ahead for his school needs, he returned to Oakland High to continue his preparation for the University. *The Aegis* continued to publish his articles and stories, running ten in all. The short stories, such as 'One More Unfortunate' and 'Who Believes in Ghosts?' show an innate sense of story structure. 'One More Unfortunate' tells of a promising young musician who went forth to conquer the world, as did Ouida's Signa, learned over a period of difficult years that he had but a small talent, was overjoyed to find refuge as a fiddler in a cheap beer garden, and one night killed himself because he realized how far he had fallen from his childhood dreams.

In 'The Run Across,' taken from his sailing experiences on the whaler *Sophie Sutherland,* his eye exults because each moment new beauties appear: he follows the gulls, solemn and graceful, watches the glorious sunrises at sea, the schools of porpoises and a whale blowing to the leeward, at night the dim form of the helmsman and the sails lost to view in the black vault. To his ear nothing is harsh or discordant, everything harmonizes. The creaking of a block is music, the groan of the towering canvas, the dash of water from the dancing stem, the splutter of flying fish against the sails. He exults when nature is angry, when the sky is overcast with black storm clouds, the air is a howling unseen demon, and the decks are a flood of churning waters. The joy of combat sends his blood leaping when the bellying sails are overcome or the reluctant rope is forced to yield; and the chants of the seamen make sweet music in his ear as men conquer Mother Nature in the fierce struggle to subsist.

He loved Nature tenderly for all the beauties there were in her, but above all he loved her for her force, the terrific strength with which she dwarfed all mankind.

That the Oakland High School *Aegis* had a liberal editorial policy is evidenced by the fact that they published his socialist article, 'Optimism, Pessimism and Patriotism,' in which he accused the 'powers that be' of keeping the masses from education because education would make them revolt against their slavery. He charged capitalism with long hours, sweat systems, and steadily decreasing wages, conducive to nought but social and moral degradation, and cried out to 'ye Americans, patriots and optimists to awake! Seize the reins of a corrupted government and educate the masses.'

Because he was a convincing talker Jack was appointed one of the debaters for the Christmas week graduation exercises. One may safely assume that the subject of the debate was a goodly distance from socialism, but Jack had been talking only a minute or two when he came to a pause, shifted his weight to the other foot, and began assailing the dressed-up audience of students, their parents and friends with what has been reported by one listener to have been the most truculent socialistic diatribe she ever heard. He told them that the time had come when existing society had to be destroyed, and that he was ready to break it down with any means or force. He talked with such passion that the audience felt he had lost himself and was already clutching at the throats of his enemies in the class struggle. Some were frightened, others thought it a joke, other maintained that it was pitiful, that the boy was not responsible, that he was a supereogist and a latent paranoiac. Members of the Board of Education demanded drastic treatment.

It seems possible that Jack had seized this opportunity to fire his parting shot, for he never returned to Oakland High. It would have taken him two more years to graduate, and since he had just turned twenty he felt that he could not spare the time. Instead he went to a cramming school in Alameda to prepare for the fall entrance examinations to the University. Eliza gave him the money for tuition. He made such swift progress that at the end of five weeks, or at least so Jack reports, the owner returned the money and told him he would have to leave because his school would be discredited if the University found out that two years' work could be covered in the four months that it was going to take him.

His five weeks at the cramming school had been useful not only for what he had learned in facts, but for what he had learned about method. For the next twelve weeks he locked himself in his room at Flora's, where he cracked open book after book with a sledgehammer method of acquiring knowledge. At approximately the same time that Professor Chaney is reported as sitting at his desk in the College of Astronomy in Chicago for nineteen hours a day, studying science and writing nativities, his son Jack is sitting at his desk in Flora Wellman's house in Oakland for nineteen hours a day, studying mathematics, chemistry, history, and English. He gave up the Henry Clay meetings, the socialist meetings, even sacrificed his treasured visits to the home of Edward and Mabel Applegarth. His body and brain began to fag, and his eyes to twitch, but he never faltered.

At the end of the twelve weeks he rode the streetcar to Berkeley, where he spent several days taking the examinations. Confident that he had passed he borrowed a sailboat, stowed a roll of blankets and some cold food into its cabin, and drifted out of the Estuary on the last of an early morning tide. He caught the first of the flood up the Bay, and raced along with a spanking breeze. Carquinez Straits were smoking as he left astern the old landmarks he had first learned with Young Scratch Nelson on the unreefed *Reindeer*. At Benicia he made fast and hurried up among the arks. Here he found his pals from the Fish Patrol. When the word got around that Jack London had returned, the fishermen dropped in to talk over old times and drink his health. Jack, who had not touched a drop of liquor in a year and a half, got roaring drunk.

Late that night his former chief of the Fish Patrol lent him a salmon boat. Jack added charcoal and a fisherman's brazier, a coffee-pot and frying-pan, coffee and meat and a fresh black bass, and cast off his painter. The tide had turned and the fierce ebb, running in the teeth of a fiercer wind, kicked up a stiff sea. Suisun Bay was white with wrath and sea-lump. Jack drove his salmon boat into it and through it. Cresting

seas filled her with a foot of water, but he laughed as he
sloshed about and sang 'Treat My Daughter Kind-i-ly,' 'Come
All You Rambling Gambling Men,' celebrating his admission
to a world where men worked and conquered with their
brains.

After a week of sailing he returned refreshed to enter the
University. James Hopper describes him at this time as a
strange combination of Scandinavian sailor and Greek god,
made altogether boyish by the lack of two front teeth, lost
cheerfully somewhere in a fight. Hopper writes that the word
'sunshine' leapt to his mind the first time he saw Jack on the
campus. He had a curly mop of hair which seemed 'spun of
the sun's gold'; his strong neck in a loose, low, soft shirt was
bronzed with it; his eyes were like a sunlit sea. His clothes
were flappy and careless, the forecastle had left the suspicion
of a roll in his broad shoulders. He was full of irrepressible
enthusiasms and gigantic plans. He has going to take all the
courses in English, nothing less, and most of the courses in
the natural sciences, history, and philosophy. Hopper con-
cludes by saying that Jack's personality shed as much warmth
as the sun itself, that he was intrepid, young and touching,
pure and vibrant.

One of the girls from Oakland High who had been re-
pulsed by his appearance and conduct the year before met
Jack on the campus, and to her surprise found him neat and
clean, happy, well fitted into his surroundings, without the
slouch or gloom or sense of embarrassment that had so
strangled him among the youngsters of the high school. He
spent many hours on the campus with Mabel Applegarth.
Here also were his associates from the Henry Clay Society.
He already possessed a reputation among the students as one
who had done wild and romantic things; he had many friends
and was respected and well liked.

The University of California had a good library and faculty. Jack enjoyed his work heartily. Though he had letters
on economics and political subjects printed in the Oakland
Times, and stories published in such local magazines as *Evenings at Home* and *Amateur Bohemian,* he does not appear to
have submitted any material to *The Occident,* the University
literary publication. He continued to do odd jobs around
Oakland, and when completely broke again went to Johnny
Heinhold, proprietor of the Last Chance Saloon where he
had had his first drink of whiskey when he bought the *Razzle
Dazzle,* and borrowed forty dollars.

Though Jack had known since before he was six that John
London was not his father, he had never had a clue as to

who his real father might be. At this time he somehow came in possession of the Chaney evidence. He never revealed the source of his information, but there were several sources available. John London, realizing that he was nearing the end of his life, might have told Jack so that he could know the truth and understand himself better. He might have heard the talk of old-timers around San Francisco and Oakland, many of whom knew his paternity. His attention might have been drawn to the *Chronicle* article about Flora and Chaney, or he might have been prompted to look up the announcement of his birth and have found that he had been born under the name of Chaney. Lastly, Flora always kept her marriage certificate, which was dated eight months after the *Chronicle* announcement of Jack's birth, and on which she signed herself as Flora Chaney, in a lockbox which did not lock!

Jack confided his discovery to Edward Applegarth while they were walking in the warm sunshine past the old St. Mary's College on Broadway. Applegarth reports that Jack was terribly cut up, and asked permission to use his address when he wrote to Chaney; he did not wish to hurt his mother by any sign that he knew of her troubled background, nor did he want Flora to intercept Chaney's answer. He asked Chaney for information on the three questions that were to torment and torture him to the end of his days: *Who was my father? Was my mother known as a loose woman? Was my mother diseased?*

He received grades of A and B for his first semester, worked during the Christmas vacation, and returned to the University. However, in a few weeks he saw that it was a hopeless struggle. It has long been rumored that he left the University because he submitted a short-story manuscript to an English professor who scrawled across the margin the Greek equivalent for the work 'junk.' The real reason is more prosaic: John London, who had been granted a peddler's license because he was a Civil War veteran, and who was peddling pictures from door to door in Alameda, was in frail health and could not earn a living for himself and Flora. Jack undertook the responsibility. If it had not been for the lack of money there is reason to believe that he would have continued to study at the University, that he would have published articles and stories in *The Occident*, perhaps even have had the patience to fulfill the academic requirements and graduate.

Despite the fact that the family was in desperate need, he took a last gamble before he went out to seek another manual-labor job. He decided that since he eventually was going to be a writer, the best thing he could do was sit down and write. Maybe he would sell something. Maybe he would be able to support his family, earn more than the current dollar a day being paid in the labor market. For five years he had been reading widely, discussing widely, filling and firing his brain, formulating his ideas, seeing unforgettable pictures of nature in beauty and stress and storm, working and adventuring shoulder to shoulder with men from all nations. The time had arrived to give back some of his treasure trove.

Once again he locked himself in his room. He composed steadily for fifteen hours a day, day after day, pouring out ponderous essays, scientific and sociological tracts, short stories, humorous verse, tragic blank verse, and elephantine epics in Spenserian stanzas. In the flush of his first creative fervor he forgot to eat; he said that there never was a creative fervor such as his from which the patient escaped fatal results.

He sent his manuscripts East as soon as he had typed them, using his remaining cash for stamps. When they came back rejected he sold his books and clothing for small sums, borrowed wherever he could, and continued to write. But when the household had used its last dollar, and there was no more food, Jack set aside his pencil and found a job in the laundry of the Belmont Academy, where Frank Norris had been a student. His board and lodging was provided, so that he could turn over the thirty dollars a month wage, after taking out tobacco money, to Flora. His job was to sort, wash, starch, and iron the white shirts, collars, cuffs, and white trousers of the students and professors and their wives.

He sweated his way through long weeks at a task that was never done, working nights under electric lights to keep up with the soiled laundry. The trunk of books he had taken with him so hopefully remained unopened, for when the day's work was done he had his supper in the kitchen of the Academy, and fell into bed. On Sundays all he could do was lie in the shade, read the comics, and sleep after the eighty-hour work week. Occasionally on a Sunday, if he was not too exhausted, he would pedal his bicycle down to Oakland to spend a few hours with Mabel Applegarth. He knew that he was trapped in a blind alley, but he did not know where to turn. Should he quit and take another job? But jobs were all alike; when a man labored for wages that was no time for leisure, for reading and thinking, even for living. He was just another machine into which was poured sufficient food and sleep to do the next day's work. He asked himself how

long he would have to toil thus meaninglessly, and where the
road lay that would lead him to the life he wanted.

Fate presented him with the answer. Gold was discovered
in the Klondike, and when the first great rush started in the
spring of 1896, Jack was in the vanguard. The fact that Flora
and John London had been living on his thirty dollars a
month, that he had given up both the University and his writing to earn it for them, did not detain him. Adventure called.

Once again faithful Eliza came to the rescue. Her husband,
now past sixty, had also caught the Klondike fever. Eliza put
a thousand-dollar mortgage on her home and took five hundred dollars out of her savings to outfit the two men. Jack
and Shepard went across to San Francisco, which was doing
a land-office business in Alaskan outfits, and bought fur-lined
coats, fur caps, high boots, red flannel shirts, blankets, a tent,
stove, runners, thongs, and tools with which to build dog
sleds and boats, and a thousand pounds of grub apiece.

On March 12, 1897, they sailed on the *Umatilla,* the same
ship on which Jack had reached San Francisco at the end of
his tramping days. Once again he was the youngest of a mot-
ley crowd, a husky, handsome, blue-eyed, affable youngster
who could handle himself with the best of them in a discussion, a fight, or a day's work. There was no guile or malice in
him; he liked everybody and everybody liked him. On the
Umatilla Jack became friendly with Fred Thompson, with
Jim Goodman, a miner, and Sloper, a carpenter. These four
men were to remain fast friends during the difficult days to
come.

The *Umatilla,* jammed to the gunwales with venturesome
gold-seekers, took the inside channel and anchored off Skag-
way. Ship-boats took the now excitement-mad miners ashore
to Dyea Beach, where thousands of prospectors stood amidst
their tons of supplies against an Arctic winter, bargaining
frantically with Indians to haul them in. When Jack and Shepard left San Francisco the quoted rate for Indians to portage
over Chilkoot Pass had been six cents a pound. By the time
they reached Dyea Beach so great was the demand for por-
ters that the Indians had raised their rates to thirty and forty
cents a pound, and when a dumbfounded miner hesitated for
a moment, jacked the price to fifty.

If Jack and Shepard had paid this rate they would have
been left without a dollar, and the Northwest Mounted, or
Yellow Legs, who demanded that every prospector carry five
hundred dollars in cash in addition to his thousand pounds of
food, would have turned them back at the Yukon. Many of

the prospectors who could not afford to pay these rates, and who were not strong enough for the back-breaking trail over Chilkoot Pass, sailed back with the *Umatilla* to San Francisco, defeated. Shepard went with them, leaving Jack with Thompson, Goodman, and Sloper.

Though it was only April they had months of hard work ahead if they hoped to cross the Pass, portage the twenty-five miles to Lake Linderman, cross the lake, shoot the rapids, travel the hundreds of miles up the Yukon, and pack into Dawson, close to which flowed the gold-laden Klondike, before winter froze down on them and made further travel impossible. Jack, as the sailor of the crowd, was sent out to buy a small boat, which the men carefully loaded with provisions and pulled up the Dyea River, or Lynn Canal, against the current. The trip was seven miles to the foot of Chilkoot Pass; arriving there the men unpacked the boat, cached the gear, and rode the spring current back to Dyea to fill up again. After many weeks of labor, their bodies straining forward against the ropes, the eight thousand pounds of supplies had been moved to the foot of the Pass.

Chilkoot Pass is reputed to be one of the world's toughest for portage. It is all rocks, and goes very nearly straight up. Jack loaded a hundred and fifty pounds of grub on his back and started the climb; the trail, which is six miles high, was a solid stream of men from top to bottom. Strewn along the sides were older men, weaker and softer men, men from offices who had never lifted anything heavier than a pencil, fallen in exhaustion . . . who would take the next boat back to the States. When the summer sun got too hot Jack peeled off his coat and shirt in the middle of the Pass and startled the Indians by plunging upward in his red flannels. Each trip took a full day, and it required ninety straight days for Jack, Goodman, Thompson, and Sloper to get their eight thousand pounds over the top. More than any book he was to write, Jack derived pleasure from the fact that he started at the bottom of the trail with Indian packers, none of whom was carrying more than he, and often beat them to the top.

On the shores of Lake Linderman another contingent of adventurers was turned back because no boats were available. Jack's party once again cached their supplies and each morning walked eight miles upriver to where Sloper had set up a crude sawmill. They chopped down a number of trees, hung them, and whipsawed the lumber by hand. Sailor Jack was called upon to design two flat-bottomed boats. He named them *Yukon Belle* and *Belle of the Yukon,* and wrote a poem about each the day they were launched.

He cut and stitched canvas sails and sailed the boats across the lake in record time, thus increasing their chances of getting into Dawson before the freeze. Linderman behind them, the party pulled into the headwaters of the Yukon and prepared for the final dash. When they reached White Horse Rapids they found nearly a thousand boats lining the shore, and thousands of men standing by frustrated because every party that had tried to shoot the rapids had drowned. Thompson said, 'Jack, you go look at the rapids, and if they're too dangerous . . .'

Jack tied the two boats ashore. A throng of men, most of whom had never been in a boat before, gathered about to assure him that the rapids were certain suicide. Jack took a look at White Horse, came back, and said, 'Nothing to it. The other boats tried to fight the current to keep off the rocks. We'll go with the current and it'll keep us clear.'

While the crowds of men lined the banks and cheered, Jack nailed his canvas sails over their provisions, stationed Sloper on his knees in the prow with a paddle, put Thompson and Goodman in the center with instructions to give him plenty of speed, and sat himself in the stern to steer. By following the main force of the water they shot the rapids safely, tied up in calm water, and walked back for their second boat.

Instantly Jack was deluged with offers to take other boats through. He charged twenty-five dollars a boat, remained for several days, and earned three thousand dollars for his party. There was another five thousand dollars to be had, but it was already mid-September.

Even so they had delayed too long. At the mouth of the Steward River, seventy-two miles from Dawson, winter fell with a thunderous clap of white snow, and they could go no further. The four men took possession of an abandoned cabin on the bank of the Yukon, cut down spruce trees for firewood, and dug in for a long siege. Between fifty and seventy men were caught at Steward, among them a doctor, a judge, a university professor, an engineer.

There were high hills sloping back from the river, buttressed by an occasional ridge that had been cleft by the stream. All around were forests of spruce and a mantle of snow four feet deep. All men coming over the long trail had to pass Jack's cabin, and the smoke rising white and lazily from the chimney was a temptation, for it spoke of warmth and rest and comfort. To this cabin came Burning Daylight, Louis Savard, Peacock, Keogh, Pruette, Stevens, Malemute Kid, Del Bishop; trappers, Indians, Yellow Legs, *chechaquos*, seasoned sourdoughs, men from all over the world who were to gain immortality in Jack London's gripping tales of Alaska.

Here Jack spent a delightful winter. The company was congenial and varied; there were plenty of books in camp, of which Jack had carried over Chilkoot Pass Darwin's *Origin of Species,* Spencer's *Philosophy of Style,* Marx's *Capital,* and Milton's *Paradise Lost.* One old Alaskan prospector who had been caught in a fierce storm stumbled into camp half dead, threw open the door of Jack's cabin, and found it thick with pipe smoke and men all trying to talk at once, bellowing at each other and waving their arms. The prospector reports that when he heard what the crowd was arguing so fiercely, he thought that in his struggles to escape the storm he had lost his mind. The subject of the argument? Socialism.

One night W. B. Hargrave, who occupied an adjoining cabin, listened in on a heated discussion over a Darwinian theory between Judge Sullivan, Doctor B. F. Harvey, and John Dillon. Jack lay in his bunk also listening, and making notes. When his friends became tangled in a moot point, he called out, 'The passage you fellows are trying to quote runs about as follows . . .' and gave the passage. Hargrave went to another cabin where the *Origin of Species* had been borrowed, brought it back, and said, 'Now, Jack, give that spiel again, I'll hold the copy on you.' Hargrave reports that Jack quoted it word for word.

Hargrave says that the first time he entered Jack's cabin, Jack was sitting on the edge of his bunk rolling a cigarette. Goodman was preparing a meal and Sloper was doing some carpentry work. Jack had challenged some of Goodman's orthodox views, and Goodman was doggedly defending himself against the rapier thrust of Jack's wit. Jack interrupted the conversation to welcome the stranger. Hargrave writes that his hospitality was so cordial, his smile so genial, his fellowship so real that it instantly dispelled all reserve. He was at once invited by Jack to join in the discussion.

Hargrave records that Jack was intrinsically kind, irrationally generous, a prince of good fellows to be with. He had a gentleness that survived the roughest associations. In argument when his opponent had caught himself in the web of his own illogic, Jack threw back his head and gave vent to infectious laughter. Hargrave's parting estimate of Jack is too genuine to be tampered with. 'Many a long night Jack and I, outlasting the vigil of the others, sat before the blazing spruce logs and talked the hours away. A brave figure of a man he was, lounging by the crude fireplace, its light playing on his handsome features. He had the clean, joyous, tender, unembittered heart of youth, yet he displayed none of the insolent egotism of youth. In appearance older than his twenty years; a body lithe and strong; neck bared at the throat; a tangled cluster of brown hair that fell over his brow and which he was wont to brush back impatiently when engaged in animated conversation; a sensitive mouth, but lips nevertheless that could set in serious and masterful lines; a radiant smile, eyes that often carried an introspective expression; the face of an artist and a dreamer, but with strong lines denoting will power and boundless energy. An outdoor man, in short a real man, a man's man. He had a mental craving for truth. He applied one test to religion, to economics, to everything: *What is truth?* He could think great thoughts. One could not meet him without feeling the impact of a superior intellect. He faced life with superb assurance, and faced death serenely imperturbable.'

Fred Thompson bought a sled and a team of dogs and took Jack prospecting up the various creeks that fed into the Yukon. Thompson testifies that Jack was an expert at out-of-doors life, that he could kindle a fire in a storm, make delicious flapjacks and bacon, sling a tent so they could sleep warmly in a temperature of thirty degrees below zero. Jack would have said that all this was apple pie to a Tramp Royal who had spent a year sleeping in the open without a blanket and cooked his food in tin cans over a railroad jungle fire.

Jack and Thompson began prospecting on the Henderson, which emptied into the Yukon a mile below Steward Camp. Where the swift water kept the ice at bay they thrust their shovels into the creekbed and brought them up with shining dust in the bits of gravel clinging to the blades. Breathlessly they staked out their claims, mushed behind their dogs at a swift clip to get back to Steward, and spread the word. Every last man in camp set out on foot or behind his dogs to stake a claim. Thompson told Jack that they were worth a cool quarter of a million. What dreams Jack must have dreamed of bringing his sacks of gold back to Oakland, of supporting Flora and John London in style, repaying Eliza for her many kindnesses, claiming Mabel Applegarth for his wife, and having the leisure to become a writer.

The dreams did not last long; the old sourdoughs who had dashed out to Henderson Creek came in with a loud laugh. Jack's pure gold dust had proved to be mica! Thompson says that Jack did not seem to be too greatly disappointed; going up on the *Umatilla* he had told Thompson that he was not going to Alaska to mine, but to gather material for books.

Still, he could not have been altogether indifferent to that 'cool quarter of a million.'

The best account of Jack to come out of Alaska is given by Emil Jensen, from whom Jack fashioned his Malemute Kid, and whom he later described as a noble man. Jensen writes that Jack gave him the first word of welcome he heard on the cold, inhospitable riverfront. Jack greeted him by saying, 'I can tell that you are a sailor and a Bay man by the way you landed your boat without a jar in spite of the current and the drift ice.'

Jensen writes that the smile on Jack's lips was boyishly friendly and his eyes sparkled as they looked straight into his. He was consistently cheerful, always likable, always a staunch friend. When people disagreed with his socialism Jack would say, 'You are not ripe for it yet, but it will come.'

According to Jensen, the London cabin was the center of attention, for Jack ranked first in versatility and in chaining the interest of his listeners. When men sometimes told tales that seemed a little too tall, and the others withdrew in incredulity, Jack only dug in deeper to extract the last of the details. The little as well as the big things in his daily camp life held for him a stimulus that made his every waking hour worth living. To him there was in all things something new, something worth while, be it a game of whist, an argument, or the sun at noonday glowing cold and brilliant above the hills to the south. Whether silent in wondering awe as on the night he saw the snows aflame beneath a weird sky, or in the throes of excitement while he watched a mighty river at flood tide, he was ever on tiptoe with expectancy.

Jensen tells the amusing anecdote of how Jack loaned him the *Origin of Species*. When Jensen complained that the book was too complex for his simple vocabulary, Jack gave him a copy of Haeckel's *Riddle of the Universe* for lighter reading. This still proving too complex, Jack dug out of his blankets his most valued possession, Milton's *Paradise Lost*. Jensen confessed that he didn't like poetry and couldn't read *Paradise Lost*. Jack set out for a cabin down the Yukon where he had heard it rumored there was a copy of Kipling's *The Seven Seas*, returned to Jensen's cabin with the book, entreating him to read just a few pages so that he might see that poetry was beautiful; and when Jensen read straight through the book, Jack felt he had scored a major triumph.

Jensen's written tribute to Jack also deserves to be given intact. 'Jack's companionship was refreshing, stimulating, helpful. He never stopped to count the cost or dream of profits to come. He stood ever ready, were it a foraging trip

among the camps for reading matter, to give a helpful hand
on a woodsled, or to undertake a two days' hike for a plug of
tobacco when he saw us restless and grumpy for the want of
a smoke. Whether the service was big or little, asked or unasked, he gave not only of himself but of his belongings. His
face was illumined with a smile that never grew cold.'

Jack spent many hours in his bunk reading and making
notes on Alaska, writing down the stories he had heard, the
arguments in which he had engaged, the dialects, philosophies, personalities, and characters of the men who came into
the cabin. As late as 1937 Thompson grumbled that sometimes he couldn't get Jack to split wood because the boy was
too busy extolling the virtues of socialism. A number of old-
time Alaskans have testified that the favorite topic of conversation in Steward Camp that winter of '96 was socialism, for
Jack was by no means alone in believing in its economic philosophy. The miners were not aware of the irony of these
rampant individualists, out gold-hunting to establish private
fortunes, spending their spare hours praising collective socialism. Jack would have answered that there was nothing so
strange in the picture, for these were brave men, pioneers,
the kind that took chances on exploring strange, dangerous,
and far-off lands, and strange, dangerous, and far-off theories.

When spring finally came Jack duplicated the stunt of his
grandfather, Marshall Wellman, who had constructed a raft
and floated it from Put-In Bay to Cleveland on another frontier. Jack and Doctor Harvey dismantled Harvey's cabin, and
Jack lashed the logs together into a raft and floated it down
the river to Dawson, where they sold the logs for six hundred
dollars.

Jack found Dawson to be a carnival tent city with fifty
thousand people and a muddy main street lined on either side
by saloons in which men not only drank but ate, slept,
bought their provisions, arranged business transactions,
danced with the dance-hall girls, and lost their gold dust to
professional gamblers. Food was scarce, ham and eggs sold
for three dollars and a half a portion, laborers were paid an
ounce of gold a day, worth about seventeen-fifty. In the town
were collected some of the world's greatest adventurers and
adventuresses. The prostitutes gathered in such great numbers
that the Mounted Police corralled them across the river in a
space called Louse Town. There was a bridge across the river
a block long, hung on ropes; Jack noted that few of the miners considered the bridge too dangerous to cross.

Thompson says that Jack 'never done a tap of work' in
Dawson. It appears that he did put in a few days finding logs

in the river and towing them by rowboat to the sawmill.
However, there was little reason for him to work when he
could go everywhere without money. He was welcome at the
bars, where the miners bought him drinks for the privilege of
spinning long yarns to him; he was good at drawing people
out, helping them to talk and tell their stories, which he
wanted far more than he did their bad whiskey. The women
liked him because he was good-looking and a good talker;
even though he had no money, he had fun. When there were
no stories to be heard he would sit on the sidewalk and enter-
tain the crowd with tall tales of his own. His nights he spent
in the gambling houses watching and making notes. By listening to the right men, the trappers and sourdoughs who had
been in Alaska before the Klondike strike, he gathered the
first authentic history of the early days of the country. He
knew what kind of material he wanted, and he knew how to
get it, for he was evolving a scientific method of inquiry
which was to enrich his later work.

There being no green foods in Alaska, Jack came down
with the scurvy. His face became covered with sores and his
few remaining teeth weakened in the gums. He was taken
into the Catholic Hospital, where Thompson says he paid a
small sum for Jack's keep. Here he was given treatment until
he was able to travel. In June, Taylor, a Kentuckian, John
Thornson, and Jack left Dawson in a small open boat to
make the nineteen-hundred-mile trip down the Yukon and
along the Bering Sea. Jack did the steering. They traveled in
intense heat at midday and at night tied up and made camp
on shore. They crossed the Yukon Flats with its millions of
mosquitoes, ran the rapids, watched Anglo-Saxons dancing
with Indian girls in native villages.

Despite the fact that the scurvy had Jack almost entirely
crippled from the waist down, and his right leg was so drawn
that he could not straighten it, he went shooting wild fowl at
midnight while his companions slept. He wrote in his notebook every day. After describing the robins singing in the islands, partridges drumming, the discordant cries of gulls and
loons, the flight of plover and wild geese, the beauty of the
night while they drifted downriver, he would note in the margin that the material would go well in *Outing Magazine* or
Youth's Companion.

It took Jack's party nineteen days to cover the nineteen
hundred miles. Without a mishap they sailed along the shore
of the Bering Sea and tied up at St. Michael's. Jack got a job
stoking the furnace on a ship going from St. Michael's to
British Columbia, and from there traveled steerage to Seattle.

From Seattle it was an easy matter for a blowed-in-the-glass tramp to beat his way down to Oakland on the freights.

He arrived home without a penny in his pocket, yet he who had never mined an ounce of gold in Alaska was to make more money out of the gold rush than any sourdough who staked a claim on Bonanza Creek.

4

WHEN Jack reached his home at 962 East Sixteenth Street in Oakland he found that John London had died. Jack was deeply grieved, for he had had from his foster father only kindness and companionship.

Up to this time John London had been the apparent head of the household; he had earned a dollar whenever his advanced years and frail health would permit. But now Jack was the man of the family. To increase his responsibility, Flora had adopted little Johnny Miller, grandson of John London by the younger of the two daughters he had brought to California. Flora became a devoted mother to the five-year-old boy, lavishing on him all the tenderness that had not been forthcoming during Jack's barren childhood.

There was only one thing in the world Jack London wanted to become: a writer. His decision was not reached arbitrarily, because he wanted notoriety or fame or wealth or the sight of his name in print. It had come from within, had been forced upon him by the imperious dictates of his nature and talents. In his notebook he had jotted down character sketches while on The Road, descriptions of the Alaskan countryside, snatches of dialogue and integrations of plot that had poured unbidden through his mind because he had been born with the gifts of perception and sensitivity and a command over words with which to convey emotion. The decision had been strengthened by his learning that his father, Chaney, was an educated man, part of the world of books and writing. In the nineteen-hundred-mile trip down the Yukon, in the ship that carried him from St. Michael's to Seattle, he had planned and organized the stories he would put on paper when he reached home. He had seen sights and witnessed struggles in the Klondike that were hammering at the gates of his brain to be written.

Jack's sense of obligation moved in cycles. When he had been a newsboy and when he had worked in the cannery he had turned over every cent he earned for food and rent and pills for Flora; then he abandoned his steady earnings to become an oyster pirate. For a time he supported his family on the money taken from pirating, then began squandering it on wild drinking bouts. When he returned with his *Sophie Sutherland* wages he bought only a few second-hand garments before turning his pay over to his mother; when he had worked at the jute mill, the electric plant, the laundry, he had kept for himself only seventy-five cents a week. Then after monotonous months of dutiful conduct the springs of responsibility had run down and he had lit out for the adventure trails of The Road and the Klondike. Now, at the age of twenty-two, caught in the focus of a directed impulse to do something constructive with his life, he might for the first time have found some justification for walking out.

Instead he resolutely shoved into the background the stories clamoring for expression. After sixteen months of adventuring the clock of responsibility was rewound; he was not willing to expose his mother and her adopted grandson to privation during the months that it would take to get his stories down on paper and sell them to the magazines. Their needs were immediate; his finding of work would have to be immediate.

Times were hard. The financial depression of 1893 which had forced him into the jute mill at ten cents an hour five years before was still paralyzing the Far West. Muttering to himself that times were always hard in an acquisitive society, Jack tramped the streets and docks for many days, finding even the meanest of manual labor no longer available. Trained in laundry work, he tried for a job in every Oakland laundry. He spent two of his last dollars to advertise in the newspapers. He answered advertisements of elderly invalids in need of companions, hawked sewing machines from house to house as had John London in San Francisco twenty years before. He felt that he was a bargain in the labor market; he weighed a hundred and sixty-five pounds stripped, every pound of which was hardened for toil, but all he could find were the same odd jobs that had sustained him at Oakland High: mowing lawns, trimming hedges, washing windows, beating carpets in back yards. The days were rare in which he managed to earn a whole dollar.

Mabel and Edward Applegarth gave a dinner to welcome him home. They invited a number of his old friends from the Henry Clay Debating Society who wrung his hand, slapped him on the shoulder, and told him how glad they were to have him back in Oakland. Jack was touched by this warm reception, regaled them with tales of the Klondike . . . and got each of them off in a corner to ask if they knew where he might find a job. No one knew.

After his absence of sixteen months and the rough life among the prospectors of Steward Camp and Dawson, Jack found Mabel more delicately beautiful than ever. When the debaters had finally made their adieus and Edward had discreetly withdrawn to his room, Mabel turned the lights low, took him gently by the hand and led him to the piano, where she played and sang the songs she had sung when he first came into the house and she had been both attracted and repelled by his male crudity and strength. She saw the love shining out of his eyes as he leaned opposite her in the bay of the piano enthralled by the music and her fragile scent; and he felt her love for him giving body to the thin sweet voice as she confessed to him in the words of the sentimental ballad that she loved him too. Yet he knew that this was not the moment to speak; he could not take her out of a cultivated home of books and paintings and music until he had something better to offer than second-hand clothing and starvation.

The next morning he saw a notice in an Oakland newspaper that examinations were being held for the mail service. He rushed down to the central post office, took the tests, and passed with a grade of 85.38. If there had been an opening he would soon have been pounding a beat on the Oakland streets with a mail pouch slung over his shoulder.

The odd jobs he was able to find did not fill his days, nor did they provide sufficient money for his family. Reading in a Sunday supplement of the San Francisco *Examiner* that the minimum rate paid by magazines was ten dollars for each thousand words, and having half a dozen exciting articles pulsing on the tips of his fingers, he sat down at the rough wooden table Flora had put in his eight-by-ten bedroom and wrote a thousand-word narrative about his trip in the open boat down the Yukon. That afternoon he mailed it to the editor of the San Francisco *Examiner*. He had no idea that he was beginning a literary career; he was simply trying to earn ten dollars to stave off the landlord until the mail-carrier appointment came through. He decided that his attack upon the literary world would have to be postponed until he could manage to put away a few hundred dollars in savings, or he no longer had other mouths to feed.

Once his writer's brain got a taste of writing he could not

turn himself off. He immediately plunged into a twenty-thousand-word serial for *Youth's Companion,* making the chapter lengths conform to those in serials he had read in that magazine at the library. Before he realized what he was doing he had dashed off seven of the Alaskan stories that were formulated in his mind. He had opened the floodgates but the slightest crack and was being overcome by the torrent.

No appointment came from from the post office. The *Examiner* not only did not send him the ten dollars, but did not even acknowledge receipt of the manuscript. Left without a coin with which to buy food, Jack pawned the bicycle Eliza had given him to ride to Oakland High; when the landlord said pay or get out, he pawned the watch Eliza's husband had given him as a gift, then the mackintosh John London had left him as his sole legacy. When a former waterfront comrade came along with a dress suit wrapped in newspapers, for the possession of which he had no convincing explanation, Jack swapped him some Alaskan souvenirs for it and pawned the dress suit for five dollars, spending the better part of it for stamps and envelopes to send his mounting manuscripts to the magazines. He still had no idea that he was becoming a professional writer; he was simply a man in desperate straits, unable to find work, utilizing his lone talent in a wild effort to earn food money until he was appointed to the civil service.

Winter came on. He was still wearing his light-weight summer suit. The grocer on one corner allowed him credit up to four dollars, and then was adamant; the butcher on the other corner went as high as five dollars before shutting down. Faithful Eliza brought to the London house whatever food she could spare from her own table, and gave Jack enough change to supply him with writing paper and the smoking tobacco without which he could not exist. Jack lost weight, hollows appeared in his cheeks, he became nervous and jumpy, and would no longer have been a bargain in the labor market. Once a week he had an opportunity to eat a hearty meat meal at Mabel's, but with an effort he restrained himself at table so that the girl he loved might not know how hungry he was. Yet his hopes were bright because he remembered that the magazines paid ten dollars per thousand words, and the stories and articles he had sent out ran from four to twenty thousand words, the sale of any one of which would rescue the family. Always in the back of his mind, holding him up as a tentpole holds up a tent, was the hope that maybe he would have several stories accepted. Then he would see his way clear to earn a living from his literary work; he would not be forced by the exigencies of circumstance to become a postman. He did not ask for great rewards or a deal of money; the most he hoped to earn from his work was ten dollars a thousand words, which, even if he sold every line he wrote, could not bring him more than three hundred dollars a month, and more than likely would bring about one hundred and fifty dollars.

He became so immersed in his stories, fighting for that one slim chance of an acceptance, that he found it difficult to stop his writing to mow a lawn or beat a carpet. The family fell into miserable straits; only because Flora was a tough and wiry woman with a twenty-year training in intermittent starvation was she able to stand the privation. Jack became weak and then ill from lack of nourishment. He was so shabby and distrait that he gave up the one evening a week he had been spending with Mabel. At the end of his tether, he was willing to take back the coal-passer's job at thirty dollars a month. As the days passed and he became sicker in body and mind, not only over the starvation but over the uncertainty of his future, his thoughts turned once again to self-destruction, as they had the night he had fallen off the Benicia pier, and when he had grown melancholy on The Road. He says that if he had not been unwilling to desert Flora and little Johnny, the chances were in favor of his suicide. Frank Atherton, Jack's boyhood chum, reports, 'Jack penned farewell letters. There came a friend to say good-bye, who had also decided to end it all.' Jack's arguments in dissuading his friend from suicide were evidently so eloquent that he convinced himself as well.

Then one cheerless morning toward the end of November he received a thin, oblong envelope from the *Overland Monthly,* a literary magazine with a national reputation that had been founded in San Francisco by Bret Harte in 1868. It was an acceptance of one of his Alaskan stories! He had sent them 'To the Man on Trail,' and they were publishing it! Like lightning his mind calculated figures . . . the manuscript was five thousand words . . . they paid ten dollars a thousand . . . the enclosed check was for fifty dollars . . . he was rescued! . . . he would be able to go on writing. He sank down on the edge of his bed and with trembling fingers tore open the envelope just as his trembling imagination was tearing open the bright vistas of the future.

There was no check. There was only a formal note from the editor saying that he found the story 'available,' and would pay five dollars for it upon publication. Five dollars for a manuscript that had taken five days to write! The same old dollar a day he had earned as a laborer in the cannery, the jute mill, the electric plant, the laundry. His eyes glazed, his mind stunned, his body too weak to move, he sat there shivering. He had been a credulous fool. He had been duped. He had believed a Sunday supplement article. The magazines didn't pay the fair wage of a penny a word; they paid a penny for ten words. No man could subsist on that rate of pay, let alone support a family. Even if he wrote great masterpieces, and sold everything that came from his thick, scrawling pencil, there was no hope for him. Only the rich could afford to be writers; he would have to crawl back to the lawnmower and the rug-beater, hang on somehow until the post-office appointment came through.

That very afternoon, by a coincidence that Jack's life could get away with but his fiction never, he received another thin, oblong envelope, this time from a magazine in the East called *The Black Cat,* to which he had sent a story written in that brief, hectic period between the University of California and the Belmont Academy steam laundry. *The Black Cat* was owned and edited by a man by the name of Umbstaetter who had done a great deal to encourage young American writers. Umbstaetter wrote Jack that his story was 'more lengthy than strengthy,' but if Jack would give him permission to cut the four-thousand-word manuscript in half, Umbstaetter would promptly send him a check for forty dollars.

Give permission! It was equivalent to twenty dollars a thousand words, or double the rate he had believed. He hadn't been duped. He hadn't been a fool. He would be able to earn a living for his family by doing the kind of work he loved. He wrote Umbstaetter that he could cut the story in two halves if only he would send the money along. Umbstaetter sent the forty dollars by return mail. And that, says Jack, is precisely how and why he stayed by the writing game.

He went to the pawnbroker and took his bicycle, watch, and mackintosh out of hock. He paid the grocer his four dollars, the butcher his five dollars. He stocked the house with food, paid twelve dollars for two months' rent, bought a second-hand winter suit, some typewriter paper, and a sheaf of pencils, and rented a typewriter. That night he put up a picnic lunch in Flora's kitchen, and the next morning called for Mabel Applegarth. Side by side they rode through Oakland on their bicycles, then climbed to their favorite knoll in the Berkeley hills. It was a clear, beautiful day with hazy sun and wandering whisps of breeze. Filmy purple mists that were fabrics woven of color hid in the recesses of the hills. San Francisco lay like a blur of smoke upon her heights. The intervening bay was a dull sheen of molten metal whereupon sailing craft lay motionless or drifted with the lazy tide. Far Mount Tamalpais, barely seen in the silver haze, bulked by the Golden Gate, beyond which the Pacific was raising on its skyline tumbled cloud masses that swept landward.

Here, lying in the deep grass by the side of the first woman he had ever loved, he told Mabel of his acceptances by the *Overland Monthly* and *The Black Cat.* Remembering how far Jack had come in three short years, Mabel cried out her joy and happiness for him. Jack's arm began to steal behind her and around her, and drew her to him slowly and caressingly. She put a hand on either side of his warm, sunburned neck; his strength seemed to pour into her fragile body.

Mabel Applegarth was the complete antithesis of Jack London. Where he was robust, she was frail. Where he flouted convention, she lived by it. Where he had been exposed to the hardship and cruelty of a man's world, she had been carefully nurtured and protected. Where he broke the rules, she obeyed them. Where he was boisterous, teeming with vitality, she was quiet, retiring. Where he was controlled by no man, she was completely under the dominance of her mother, a selfish, dictatorial woman who controlled her daughter's every move. Jack knew that Mrs. Applegarth had high aspirations for Mabel, that she intended marrying her to a man with wealth in order to recoup the family fortune which Mr. Applegarth had brought over from England and invested in a land colonization scheme that had failed.

Jack had no fear of Mrs. Applegarth. At worst she could be no more difficult to manage than the unreefed *Reindeer,* the wheel of the *Sophie Sutherland* during a storm, the blinds of the Overland Express, or White Horse Rapids.

Munching the thick sandwiches he had put up the night before, the sweethearts agreed that they should be engaged for a year, at the end of which time Jack would have established himself so solidly that they would be able to marry. They would open a little home of their own where they would have shelves of books and paintings on the walls and a piano for Mabel to play and sing to him, and a workroom where he would write gripping short stories and novels, and his wife would correct his manuscripts for occasional errors in grammar; they would make a good living and have intelligent, amusing friends, and raise children and travel and be very, very happy. They sat on through the passing glory of the day, marveling at the wonder of love and at destiny that had flung them so strangely together. The cloud masses on the western horizon received the descending sun and the circle of the sky turned to rose. Holding herself in his arms Mabel softly sang 'Good-Bye, Sweet Day.' When she had finished he kissed her again, and hand in hand, their fates entrusted to each other, they wandered down the hills and rode their bicycles back to Oakland.

Jack had exactly two dollars left out of his forty dollars from *The Black Cat*. This he invested in stamps to send out the manuscripts the Eastern magazines had returned and he had tossed under his table because there was no postage with which to send them out again. Once more he plunged into his writing, mailing the manuscripts as soon as he had finished typing them. But it had been a false dawn. His stories came back with standard rejection slips. The food slowly disappeared from Flora's shelves. The watch, bicycle, mackintosh, and finally the warm winter suit went back into pawn. The magazines might pay a penny a word, or a dollar a word; what good did it do him when he couldn't even sell a sentence?

On the sixteenth of January, 1899, a letter summoned him to work at the post office. The job would be steady, would last all the days of his life. It paid sixty-five dollars a month. He could have plenty to eat, a suit of clothes that was new instead of second-hand, a luxury the twenty-three-year-old boy had not yet attained. He would be able to buy the books and magazines for which he was starved. He would be able to take care of Flora and little Johnny, and if Mabel would be willing to move in with his family for a time, they could be married at once.

Jack and Flora faced the situation squarely. If he continued with his writing they would have to suffer more years of hardship. But if he became a postman what would be the good of his plentiful food and new clothes and books and magazines? He had not been put on earth merely to feed and clothe his body and amuse his mind; he had been put here to create, to contribute great stories to literature. He would be able to endure the privations of the artist because he would be taking a primal ecstasy from his work which would make all other possible pleasures, such as eating and possessing material objects, seem dull and inconsequential. But what would there be to sustain Flora? If she had made a scene, staged a heart attack, cried, or pleaded, Jack might have gone down to the post office and taken the job. But this mother who had borne him out of wedlock, deprived him of love and tenderness, made poverty, bitterness, and chaos the potion of his youth, now firmly told him that he must go on with his stories, that he had it in him to succeed, and that she would stand by no matter how long it took. For if Jack became a successful writer, Flora Wellman, black sheep of the Wellman family of Massillon, would be vindicated.

Now that the decision was irrevocable Jack tackled his job with all the impetuous fire and ardor of his resolute nature. In order to become a writer there were two things he had to acquire: knowledge and the ability to write. He knew that if he thought clearly he would write clearly, for if he were badly educated, if his thoughts were confused and jumbled how could he expect a lucid utterance? And if his thoughts were worthy so would his writing be worthy. He knew that he must have his hand on the inner pulse of life, that the sum of his working knowledge would be the *working philosophy* by which he would measure, weigh, balance, and interpret the world. He felt that he had to educate himself in history, biology, evolution, economics, and a hundred other important branches of learning because they would broaden his thought, lengthen his vistas, drive back the bounds of the field in which he was to work. They would give him a working philosophy which would be like unto no other man's and force him to original thinking, provide him with something new and vital for the jaded ear of the world. He had no intention of writing trivia, of administering chocolate-coated pills to constipated minds.

And so he went direct to the books and laid siege to the citadel of their wisdom. He was no college boy cramming sufficient facts to pass an examination, no casual passerby warming his hands at the great fires of knowledge. He was a passionate wooer and to him every new fact learned, every new theory absorbed, every old concept challenged and new concept gained was a personal victory, a cause for rejoicing. He questioned, selected, rejected, submitting everything he read to a searching analysis. He was not blinded or awed by reputations. Great minds made no impression upon him unless they could present him with great ideas. Conventional thinking meant little to this man who had broken every convention he had met; an image-breaker himself, iconoclastic thinking on the part of others did not frighten or repulse him. He was honest, he was courageous, he could think straight, and he had a profound love for truth, four indispensables for the scholar.

Though he was short on education he had the feeling that he was a natural student. Education seemed to him like a chart-room. He had no fear of unknown books, he knew that he didn't get lost easily, and he had already spent enough time in it to know what coasts he wanted to explore. When he met a book he used no delicate pick covertly to pry open its lock and steal the contents. Jack London about to tackle a new volume upon which he had stumbled in a wilderness trail was like an abysmal brute, a starving wolf poised to spring. He sank his teeth into the throat of the book, shook it fiercely until it was subdued, then lapped up its blood, devoured its flesh, and crunched its bones until every fiber and muscle of that book was part of him, feeding him its strength.

He went back to the father of economics, Adam Smith, and read *The Wealth of Nations*, then worked forward through Malthus's *Theory of Population*, Ricardi's *Theory of Distribution*, Bastiat's *Theory of Economic Harmonies*, the early German theories of value and marginal productivity, John Stuart Mill's *Shares in Distribution* . . . straight down through the historical corollaries until he came to the founders of scientific socialism and was on familiar ground. For his science of politics he went back to Aristotle, followed Gibbon through the rise and fall of the Roman Empire, traced the conflict between Church and State in the Middle Ages, the influences of Luther and Calvin on the Reformation political structure, to the beginning of modern political conceptions in the books of the Englishmen Hobbes, Locke, Hume, Mill; the emergence of the republican form of government to meet the needs of the Industrial Revolution. In metaphysics he read Hegel, Kant, Berkeley, Leibnitz. In anthropology he read Boas and Frazer, in biology he had already read Darwin, Huxley, Wallace, and went back to them with greater understanding. He consumed all the books he could find on sociology: unemployment, business cycles and depressions, the causes and cures of poverty, slum conditions, criminology, charity; burrowed deeper and deeper into trade unionism.

He made careful notes on everything he read, and started a card-catalogue system so that he could lay his hands on his material when he wanted it. But it was not until he struck Herbert Spencer's *First Principles* that he found his long-sought method of correlating the varied trends of thought he had assimilated into a working philosophy. His meeting with the mind of Herbert Spencer was perhaps the greatest single adventure in a life fraught with adventures. One night, after long study-bouts with William James and Francis Bacon, and after writing a sonnet as a nightcap, he crawled into bed with a copy of *First Principles*. Morning found him still reading. He continued reading all the next day, abandoning the bed for the floor when his body tired. He perceived that he had been merely skimming over the surface of things, observing detached phenomena, accumulating fragments, marking superficial generalizations, with everything unrelated in a capricious and disorderly world of whim and chance. Here was the man Spencer organizing all knowledge for him, reducing everything to a unity, presenting to his startled gaze a universe so concrete of realization that it looked like the model of a ship that sailors made and put into glass bottles. There was no caprice; everything was inescapable law. Jack was more thrilled by this discovery than he had been at the discovery of gold on Henderson Creek, for he knew that Spencer's monism could never turn out to be mica.

Herbert Spencer made him drunk with comprehension. All the hidden phenomena were laying their secrets bare. In the meat on his plate that night at dinner he saw the shining sun and traced its energy back through all the transformations to its source a hundred million miles away, traced its energy ahead to the moving muscles in his arms that enabled him to cut the meat, and the brain wherewith he willed the muscles to cut the meat, until with inward gaze he saw the sun shining in his brain, both made of the same substance, both part of each other. Herbert Spencer had shown him that all things were related to all other things from the farthermost stars in the waste of space to the myriads of atoms in the grain of sand under one's foot, and that mankind, man the individual, was just another form of squirming, protoplasmic matter.

Jack's four intellectual grandparents were Darwin, Spencer, Marx, and Nietzsche. His working philosophy, German and English, stemmed directly from these four great minds of the nineteenth century. In 1899 it took intestinal fortitude to read these bitterly attacked and maligned revolutionaries; it also took clarity, intelligence, and penetration to understand them. Jack had the requisite courage and the intelligence; his four masters enriched his life and philosophy. They deepened his healthy skepticism, his love of truth for its own sake, swept away the mental garbage of the Dark Ages, and gave him a ruthless scientific method for the pursuit of knowledge. In his turn, Jack was to dramatize and pass on their teachings.

Frederick Nietzsche had perhaps the greatest emotional effect upon Jack because their experiences were more closely akin. Exposed as he had been to the horrors of spiritualism during his childhood, just as Nietzsche, as a clergyman's son, had been exposed to excesses of piousness, Jack revolted against all manifestations of religion, belief in supernatural powers, in a life after death, and a God-controlled universe. 'I believe that with my death I am just as much obliterated as

the last mosquito you or I smashed.' He believed the entire
Christian religion to be a mass of empty ritual and incredible
fact. He was convinced that religion, any and all religion, was
mankind's greatest enemy because it anesthetized the brain,
doped it with dogma, made men accept blindly instead of
thinking for themselves, kept them from asserting themselves
as masters of the earth upon which they trod, and hence
from bettering their lives. In Nietzsche, Jack found justification for everything he felt about the shams, hypocrisy, and
falsity of religion, stated with such brilliance that he was certain Nietzsche had dug a grave for Christianity.

In Nietzsche too he discovered the theory of the superman
who was bigger and stronger and wiser than all his fellows,
who could conquer all obstacles and rule the slave mass. Jack
found the philosophy of the superman much to his taste, because he conceived of himself as a superman, able to conquer
all obstacles, a giant who would end by ruling (teaching,
leading, directing) the masses. The fact that his philosophy
of the reign of the superman over the slave masses made
Nietzsche detest socialism as a government of the weak and
inefficient, and led him to cry down trade unions as making
the workers dissatisfied with their lot, did not seem to disturb
Jack. He was going to believe in the superman and socialism
at one and the same time, even if they were mutually exclusive. All his life he remained an individualist and a socialist;
he wanted individualism for himself because he was a superman, a blond-beast who could conquer . . . and socialism for
the masses who were weak and needed protection. For a
number of years he was to be successful in riding these two
intellectual horses, each of which was pulling in an opposite
direction.

In addition to becoming learned, Jack had on hand the
more immediate and prosaic problem of earning a living. He
spent long hours in the free reading-room of the library criti-
cally studying the current magazines, comparing the stories to
those that were tumbling off his own typewriter, wondering
what secret trick had enabled them to sell. He was amazed at
the enormous amount of printed stuff that was dead: no
light, no life, no color shot through it. He was puzzled by the
countless short stories written lightly and cleverly but without
vitality or realism. Life was so strange and wonderful, filled
with an immensity of problems, dreams, and heroic toils, yet
these printed fabrications dealt with the sentimental common-
places. He felt the stress and strain of life, its fevers and
sweats and wild insurgences—surely this was the stuff to
write about! He wanted to glorify the leaders of forlorn

hopes, the mad lovers, the giants who fought under stress and strain, amid terror and tragedy, making life crackle with the strength of their endeavors. These magazine writers, typified by Richard Harding Davis (Soldiers of Fortune, Princess Aline), George Barr McCutcheon (Graustark), Stanley Weyman (Gentleman of France, Under The Red Robe), Margaret Deland (John Ward, Preacher), Clara Louise Burnham (Doctor Latimer, Wise Woman), seemed afraid of real life, of its profounder truths and realities. They prettified, evaded, threw a spurious veil of romance over their characters, avoiding anything that cut deep.

The dominant reason for this attitude, he decided after a searching analysis, was fear: fear of shocking or displeasing their editors, fear of alienating their Mid-West public; fear of antagonizing the newspapers, the vested interests, the capitalist-controlled pulpit and educational system; fear of the vigorous, the brutally true; above all fear of the unpleasant. They were stodgy and puny, these fictionizers, with no guts in their bellies or genitals between their legs. They had no originality, no working philosophy, no true knowledge; all they had was a formula for saccharine romance. They were impoverished minds impoverishing literature. He recognized them to be pigmies; only giants dared cross swords with authentic literature. He would make the editors and the public accept him on his own ground.

He turned to the writers whom he judged had truly blazed their own trails: Scott, Dickens, Poe, Kipling, George Eliot, Whitman, Stevenson, Stephen Crane. He burrowed into what he named the triumvirate of geniuses, Shakespeare, Goethe, and Balzac. From Spencer, Darwin, Marx, and Nietzsche he had learned how to think; from his literary parents, Kipling and Stevenson, he learned how to write. He felt that now that he had a working philosophy of scientific determinism with which to focus the characters he drew, and a lucidity of literary expression for the thoughts he uttered, his work would be sane, fresh, and true.

To Jack one of the greatest things in the world was words, beautiful words, musical words, strong and sharp and incisive words. He read the heavy and learned tomes always with a dictionary at hand, wrote down words on sheets of paper and stuck the sheets into the crack between the wood and mirror of his bureau where he could memorize them while he shaved and dressed; he strung lists of them on a clothesline with clothespins so that every time he looked up or crossed the room he could see the new words and their meanings. He carried lists of them in every pocket, read them while he walked to the library or to Mabel's, mumbled them as he sat over his food or prepared for sleep. When the need came in a story for a precise word, and out of the hundreds of lists sprang the one with the exact shade of meaning, he was thrilled to the core of his being.

But how could he get his stories past the stone barricade of editors who protected their genteel publics from the on-slaughts of barbarians from the West? There was no one to help him, to give him a word of advice. He did not know an editor or writer or anyone who had ever attempted to write. He was fighting the battle alone, in the dark, with nothing but his strength, his determination, his convictions, and his feel for narrative to sustain him. He poured his soul into his stories and articles, folded them just so, put the proper amount of stamps inside the long envelope, sealed it, put more stamps on the outside and dropped it into a mailbox. It traveled across the continent and after a lapse of time the postman returned it. He was convinced that there was no human editor at the other end but a cunning arrangement of cogs that changed the manuscript from one envelope to an-other and stuck on the stamps.

Time! Time! was his unending plaint, time to learn, to master his craft before the lack of money for food and rent destroyed him. There weren't enough hours in the day to do all the things he wanted. It was with regret that he tore him-self away from his writing to study, with regret that he tore away from serious study to go to the library and read the magazines, with regret that he left the reading-room to go to Mabel's for the only hour of recreation he permitted himself. Hardest of all was to put aside his books and pencil and close his burning eyes for sleep. In his great passion he limited himself to five hours' sleep a night. He hated the thought of ceasing to live even for so short a time; his sole consolation was that the alarm clock was set for five hours ahead, the jangling bell would jerk him out of unconsciousness, and he would have before him another glorious nineteen hours of work. He was a soul enchanted, a soul inflamed.

At last, in January, 'To the Man on Trail' was published in the *Overland Monthly*. It was Jack's début as a professional writer. The editor had not only failed to send him the five dollars promised on publication, but did not even bother to mail him a copy of the magazine. Jack stood in front of a newsstand on Broadway gazing wistfully, for he did not have ten cents in his pocket with which to buy a copy and see how his story looked in print. He walked uptown to the Applegarth house, borrowed a dime from Edward, walked down town again . . . and bought his copy.

The Oakland newsdealers quickly sold out their supply of the *Overland Monthly*, for Jack's friends in the Henry Clay Society had spread the good word. One of the Oakland newspapers, which had mocked and ridiculed him as the Boy Socialist, now ran a respectful and proud little article about Mr. Jack London, the Boy Author, having a story published in the venerable *Overland Monthly*. Though Jack was in the grip of destitution, still dressed in oddly matched second-hand clothes and living on forced-march rations, he felt a decided change in the attitude of the people about him; if he really were going to succeed as a writer, then they would have to forgive him his eccentricities of dress and manner and thought.

'To the Man on Trail' is not among the best of Jack's Alaskan tales, for the emphasis is more on plot than characterization or nature. Yet from the moment Malemute Kid rises with cup in hand, glances at the greased-paper window where the frost stands three inches thick, and cries: 'A health to the man on trail this night; may his grub hold out, may his dogs keep their legs; may his matches never miss fire,' the reader, gripped and rushed headlong to the end of the story, is aware that a new, youthful, and vigorous voice has arisen in American letters.

The *Overland Monthly* had offered him the princely sum of seven dollars and a half for any additional stories they might buy; in spite of the fact that they had not yet sent him the five dollars for the first story, Jack mailed them 'The White Silence,' which they promptly accepted and published in their February issue. Jack felt the story to be one of his best, and that he ought to get at least fifty dollars for it, but he was prompted to let it go for the dubious seven-fifty for a number of reasons: he hoped that the critics and magazine editors of the East would see the story and be struck by it; he wanted to keep justifying his work to Mabel; and the seven-fifty, if he could collect it, would feed his family roughly for a month.

'To the Man on Trail' had led Oakland to suspect that Jack London might become a successful author. 'The White Silence,' one of our imperishable classics of the frozen country, made them realize that he could write. The story, told with tenderness, depth of feeling, and magnificent imagery, brings one pity and terror and that exultation which can be realized only through experiencing a perfectly conceived art form. Jack had been reading and copying hundreds of poems into his notebooks; he had been writing them every day for facility of expression and because words sang in his brain the same way that musical notes sing in a composer's brain. In 'The White Silence' he proves that he is what we least would have expected from a boy of his background: a true poet. 'Nature has many tricks wherewith she convinces man of his finity—the ceaseless flow of the tides, the fury of the storm, the shock of the earthquake—but the most tremendous, the most stupefying of all is the passive phase of the White Silence. All movement ceases, the sky clears, the heavens are as brass; the slightest whisper seems as sacrilege and man becomes timid, affronted at the sound of his own voice. Sole speck of life journeying across the ghostly wastes of a dead world, he trembles at his audacity, realizes that his is a maggot's life, nothing more. Strange thoughts arise unsummoned, and the mystery of all things strives for utterance.'

Jack believed that dig could move more mountains than faith ever dreamed of. He set himself a quota of fifteen hundred words a day, refusing to stop work until he had set them down in his undisciplined scrawl and had transferred them to the typewriter. He wrote everything in his mind before setting it down on paper, after which nothing could persuade him to make changes other than the substitution of a word or two. With the bicycle, watch, mackintosh, and winter suit in hock again, whole weeks passed in which the family subsisted on beans and potatoes, the diet relieved only when Eliza brought them food from her own table. In desperation Jack began writing triolets and jokes, hoping to earn a dollar from the humorous magazines.

Twice more that spring the Oakland post office summoned him to work, once when there was not a five-cent piece or a slice of bread in the house. He borrowed ferry fare from Eliza, buckled on his fighting armor, and rode across the Bay to the office of the *Overland Monthly* which had ignored his pleading letters and refused to send him the five dollars for 'To the Man on Trail' or the seven-fifty for 'The White Silence.' The moment he entered the office he realized that it was not the prosperous magazine of national importance he had imagined. It was on its last legs financially, being kept alive to support the assistant editor and business manager, Roscoe Eames and Edward Payne, who were to move into Jack's life through this chance meeting and were never to move out again. Eames and Payne were delighted to meet Jack London; they saluted his genius in glowing terms . . . and promised to mail him five dollars the very first thing in the morning. Only the threat of physical violence from the starved author brought forth five dollars in small change from the pockets of the two literary gentlemen.

Sunk in the middle of a crater of debts, Jack's family lived off that five dollars for the month of March. The *Overland Monthly* asked for another story for their April issue; Jack refused to supply it until they remitted for 'The White Silence.' After considerably more dunning they paid, and he sent them 'The Son of the Wolf.' In April he also had published one of his humorous triolets, 'He Chortled with Glee,' in San Francisco's *Town Topics*. Flora and Jack were so harassed by their creditors and landlord that he offered to sell five-thousand-word stories for a dollar, anything to get a few cents in his pocket. Though his confidence was being sustained by the work he was doing, there were periods when he suffered severe nervous attacks; all the uncertainties buried deep in his system would rise to tell him that the odds were too great, that he could never succeed.

May was his first big month. *Town Topics* published a poem, 'If I Were God One Hour,' the *Overland Monthly* ran the fourth of his Alaskan tales, 'The Men of Forty Mile,' a lusty yarn, estimable for its rough Irish fighting and humor, *Orange Judd Farmer* ran 'On Furlough,' and Mr. Umbstaetter of *The Black Cat* finally printed 'A Thousand Deaths.' Jack sat in his cramped, poorly lighted bedroom with the four magazines opened at his contributions, running fingers like a comb through his tousled hair, his gray-blue eyes sparkling with happiness. What did it matter if the house were cold from lack of heat, the larder empty, if his cheeks were sunken and his clothes so shabby that he no longer dared go into the Applegarth home for fear Mabel's mother would see his destitution? He and Flora had a long tradition of starvation; they were sinewy people who could endure on it where softer families would be destroyed. The steel of his character had been tempered by hard usage; he had goaded himself into laughing in the teeth of incredible hardship and dangers as a boy. Should he as a grownup be any the less a Viking? He had set himself the most difficult task that any man could conceive; all the more reason, then, to conquer it, for no adversary less than the most formidable of all adversaries did he deem worthy of his prowess. As a boy he had forced himself to invite and enjoy danger, yet it had not been an unnatural forcing. He was in the true sense of the term a brave man, even if he sometimes did have to romanticize that bravery. Or so he told himself as he sat over his month's literary haul in the humming-wall silence of his bedroom, a man alone with his work.

June saw him published in an Eastern newspaper, the Buffalo *Express* printing 'From Dawson to the Sea,' the account of his nineteen-hundred-mile trip down the Yukon in the open boat. *Home Magazine* ran his 'Through the Rapids on the Way to Klondike,' and the *Overland Monthly* continued its Alaskan series with 'In a Far Country.' However, he had to wait until July to achieve really professional status, for in this month he had stories and articles appearing in five periodicals, a miracle for a twenty-three-year-old who had been writing for only nine months. The *American Journal of Education* published two of his articles on language and the use of verbs, indicating how far he had come in his self-education, while *The Owl, Overland Monthly,* and Tillotson Syndicate released short stories.

Finding this gala month as much a cause for celebration as the sale of his first two stories, Jack took his bicycle out of pawn, called for Mabel, and rode with her into the hills. This time when he laid his triumphs at her feet he noticed that his sweetheart seemed sad. In answer to her direct question he confessed that all five of the sales had netted him only ten dollars in cash, with the possibility of another seven dollars and a half from the *Overland Monthly,* which still owed him for two back stories. Mabel broke down and wept with her head in his lap. The year of their engagement was already half over, and to Mabel's mind Jack's lean earnings from his successful stories only proved that they could never marry or live on his income as a writer. She herself would have been willing to share his poverty, but Mrs. Applegarth had made it forcefully clear that she could not marry Jack until he was making a substantial living.

Jack had brought along a number of his new manuscripts, which he read to her eagerly to prove that it was only a matter of time before the rich Eastern magazines would begin buying. In the face of his booming confidence that his work was true and strong, that it was unlike anything being written in America, Mabel at last garnered the courage to tell him that she did not like it, that the stories were crude, indelicate, bestial in their depiction of raw life, suffering, and death . . . and that the public would never accept them. She loved him more than ever . . . she flung her arms about his neck and kissed him warmly to prove it . . . she would always love him . . . she would marry him right away . . . only wouldn't he be sensible and take a position in the post office . . . or try to get a steady job as a reporter on a newspaper?

Jack was saddened by Mabel's lack of faith in his work, but it did not lessen his love for her. Like the hothouse editors in the East, she had been bred in a genteel and anemic tradition. Well, he'd show them. He'd blast them out of their complacency! He'd teach them what a short story really was!

He returned to his rough wooden table, rolled himself an unending line of bumpy cigarettes, and dug in harder than ever. He wrote blistering articles about the Class War on the same typewriter ribbon with adventure stories for children; gripping tales of death and heroic struggles against fate in the frozen North on the same notepaper with jokes for *Town Topics.* He attacked his books with renewed vigor, making copious notes on war, international trade, graft in government and the courts, the wastes of competitive industry, strikes, boycotts, the woman's suffrage movement, criminology, modern medicine, the progress of engineering and modern science, building file after file of material into his own well-organized reference library. No day passed with less than sixteen hours of study and writing; whenever his physical condition permitted he forced himself to work for nineteen hours, and seven days a week. *Dig can move more mountains than faith ever dreamed of.*

During the months of intense application he had little time for friends or social activity. Mabel and her mother had moved to San José, a small town in the Santa Clara Valley. Now he began to feel that he had cut himself off from people too much; one of the first needs of his nature was for genial and interesting companionship. When the newly formed Ruskin Club, composed of the cream of the Bay area liberals and intellectuals, invited him to join, he accepted with enthusiasm. A few nights later he went unannounced to a meeting of the Socialist Local, where he was given a noisy and heartwarming reception. Urged to speak to the members, Jack walked up to the platform and talked about 'The Question of the Maximum,' in which he tried to show that when capitalism reaches its maximum development it must inevitably become socialized. He had written an article on the subject only a week before. 'The Question of the Maximum,' which was bought by an Eastern magazine but never published, established Jack as a professional economist, for it showed not only a complete grasp of the economic interpretation of history, but indicated the extent of his research in international political economy.

Pleased by the way the Local received his talk, Jack agreed to give several Sunday night lectures in the educational series it was proposing. After his first Sunday talk he was amazed to find the Oakland press writing up his remarks in a serious, friendly fashion. Socialism and Jack London had become respectable together!

In September, October, and November Jack cracked three new magazines—*Conkeys, The Editor,* and *Youth's Companion.* His friends in the Ruskin Club and the Socialist Local considered him a successful writer. Sundays when he wasn't lecturing at the Socialist Local he bicycled the forty miles to San José to visit with Mabel; during the week he spent several evenings at meetings, lectures, and discussions. In the company of Jim Whitaker, a preacher turned novelist, and Strawn-Hamilton, a philosophical anarchist, he rode across the Bay one night to hear Austin Lewis lecture on socialism at the Turk Street Temple. Here he met Anna Strunsky, an ardent socialist whom Jack described as an emotional genius. She was doubtless the most brilliant woman he was to encounter.

Anna Strunsky, a student at Stanford University, was a shy, slender, sensitive girl with dark brown eyes and curly black hair. She came from one of the pioneer families of San Francisco, her parents' home being an outstanding cultural center of the city. Miss Strunsky writes that Jack was pointed out to her as a comrade who spoke on the streets of Oakland and who earned his living writing stories. When she was introduced to him after the lecture, she says that it was as though she were meeting in their youth Lassalle, Marx, or Byron, so instantly did she feel that she was in the presence of a historical character. Objectively she says that she confronted a young man with large blue eyes fringed with dark lashes, and a beautiful mouth which, opening in its ready laugh, revealed an absence of front teeth. The brow, the nose, the contour of the cheeks, the massive throat were Greek. His body gave the impression of grace and athletic strength. He was dressed in gray and was wearing a soft white shirt with collar attached, and black necktie.

Between Jack London and Anna Strunsky there began a tempestuous friendship fraught with terrific arguments on affairs social, economic, and feminine. Jack shocked Miss Strunsky by telling her that although he was a socialist he was going to beat the capitalists at their own game. People thought that socialists were failures, weaklings, and incompetents, but he was going to prove that a socialist could succeed with the best of them, and by so doing he would be serving a propagandistic service to The Cause. Miss Strunsky was repelled by this dream of his, and warned him that real socialists would be incapable of harboring it; to pile up wealth and success—surely anybody who was a beneficiary of the

Old Order must belong to it to some extent in spirit and fact? Jack laughed good-naturedly and replied that the Eastern editors who were starving him now would pay handsomely for stories when they wanted them later; that he was going to extract every last dollar from capitalism he could get.

Aside from family debts and money worries Jack was now enjoying his life. He was earning between ten and fifteen dollars a month; he was being published in a slowly widening circle of magazines; he liked to write, to think, to study, to correlate, to understand. On Sunday nights he lectured to the Socialist Local on such subjects as 'The Expansionist Policy'; he went to dinners given by the Ruskin Club, where he now numbered among his friends young instructors from the University of California, professional men, the new Oakland librarian, who had replaced his old friend and inspirator, Ina Coolbrith. Week-ends he spent as the guest of the Applegarths in San José, reading his new manuscripts to Mabel, weighing her criticisms, stealing a few lover's kisses as they picnicked in the woods or sat on the Applegarth sofa. Completely as he loved Mabel, he never tried to fit her into his tumultuous life in Oakland. It was heresy even to think of her in the smoke and din of a socialist meeting. No, she was the cool goddess who remained above the strife and turmoil of the world; after they were married she would be a gracious hostess to his less rambunctious friends and argufiers, and when he returned from his boisterous meetings, all excited and sweated up, her arms would be a quiet harbor in which he could relax, be quiet, know peace. She had the qualifications for a superman's wife.

At last, a short while before the end of the century, the big break came for Jack London, as he inevitably knew it had to come for all men who had 'faith, dig, and talent.' In the weeks just passed he had written a long story called 'An Odyssey of the North,' which he had had the sheer presumption to send to Boston to the *Atlantic Monthly,* the most blue-blooded, stiff-necked, unapproachable literary magazine in the United States. By all precedent the *Atlantic Monthly* should have sent the manuscript back with a horrified little note. Instead Jack received one of those long, flat envelopes, the arrival of which suffocated him; the editor praised the story, asked him to cut three thousand words out of the opening sections, and offered to pay one hundred and twenty dollars for the publication rights. Once again Jack sank to the edge of his bed, trembling, his eyes glazed, as on that morning the thin envelope arrived from the *Overland Monthly.* A hundred and twenty dollars! Enough to lift the family debts, take his possessions out of pawn, fill the larder, pay the rent for six months in advance! With a terrific leap he sprang off the bed, flung open the door of his bedroom, ran to the kitchen, grabbed Flora, and spun her around with her feet in the air crying: 'Mother, look! look! I did it! The *Atlantic Monthly* is publishing my big story. All the Eastern editors will see it. They'll want to buy, too. We're on our way up!'

Flora Wellman nodded her head and smiled grimly behind her narrow steel-rimmed spectacles as she kissed her only son.

Jack's predictions proved truer than even he had dared hope. The publishing firm of Houghton Mifflin, which was associated with the *Atlantic Monthly* in Boston, and had seen the manuscript of 'An Odyssey of the North' and Jack's other Alaskan tales appearing in the *Overland Monthly*, agreed to bring out a volume of his short stories in the spring. Houghton Mifflin's first reader's report when they were considering publication of the group of short stories is probably the first professional criticism of a collection of Jack's work. 'He uses the current slang of the mining camps a little too freely, in fact he is far from elegant, but his style has freshness, vigor, and strength. He draws a vivid picture of the terrors of cold, darkness, and starvation, the pleasures of human companionship in adverse circumstances, and the sterling qualities which the rough battle with nature brings out. The reader is convinced that the author has lived the life himself.'

No longer would he have to accept seven dollars and a half for a short story, a seven dollars and a half he was having increasing difficulty dunning from the *Overland Monthly*. On December 21, 1899, the contract was signed, and Boston, stronghold of the English stranglehold on American culture, was pledged to sponsor a California-Alaska frontier revolution in literature. With a conservative Boston publishing house backing his radical innovations, his work had a chance for a fair hearing, it would be judged on its merits rather than its departures.

A few nights later Jack sat in his bedroom surrounded by his manuscripts, files, books, and notes for a hundred future stories. In a few hours the twentieth century would be born. He had the feeling that at midnight he too would be born; that he and the new century would be launched together.

A hundred years ago this night humanity had wandered shatter-brained in the miasmic fogs of the Dark Ages, conceiving the world to be preordained, unchangeable; credulously believing that the forms of government, economic structure, morality, religion, and all other aspects of life had been set forever in one unbreakable mold by the Lord God, not the slightest tenet of which might be tampered with or altered. Hegel, rebellious German philosopher, had broken up this rigid concept, which had been forced upon the unthinking mass by king and clergy. Out of the ignorance, the fear, the hypocrisy and sham also had arisen Darwin and Spencer to free mankind from the shackles of religion, and Karl Marx to supply a mechanism with which it might burst its bonds and create a civilization to fit its needs. A hundred years ago this night humanity had been slaves; one hundred years from this night would they be masters? They now had the means and the equipment with which to free themselves; the world could be anything and everything men wanted it to be; all they lacked was the will. He was determined to play his part in providing that collective will.

Quietly, reflectively, he made an estimate of himself, his work, his age, and his future. He had a strong gregarious instinct, he liked to rub against his own kind, yet in society he saw himself as a fish out of water. Because of his background he took to conventionality uneasily, rebelliously. He was used to saying what he thought, nothing more nor less. The hard hand of adversity, laid upon him at the age of ten, had left him sentiment but destroyed sentimentality. It had made him practical so that he was sometimes known as harsh, stern, and uncompromising; it had made him believe that reason was mightier than imagination, that the scientific man was superior to the emotional man. 'Take me this way,' he wrote to Anna Strunsky in the early days of their acquaintanceship, 'a stray guest, a bird of passage splashing with salt-rimmed wings through a brief moment of your life—a rude blundering bird, used to large airs and great spaces, unaccustomed to the amenities of confined existence.'

He had no patience with show or pretense. People had to take him as he was, or leave him alone. He wore a sweater most of the time, and paid calls in a bicycle suit. His friends passed the stage of being shocked, and no matter what he did, said, 'It's only Jack.' He catered to no one, played up to and sought favors from no man, yet he was loved and sought after because, as Anna Strunsky put it, 'To know him was immediately to receive an accelerated enthusiasm about everybody.' His words and laughter and attitudes vitalized those with whom he came in contact; his presence in a group brought that group sharply to life. He had an electric quality that sent a current through people, shocking them into wakefulness so that their bodies and brains came alive when he entered a room.

Perhaps the greatest passion of his life was for exact knowledge. 'Give me the fact, man, the irrefragable fact!' is the motif that runs through all his days and all his work. He believed in the physical basis for life because he had seen the hypocrisy, fraud, and insanity behind the spiritual basis. He wanted scientific knowledge to replace unreasoning faith; only through accurate and penetrating reason could the God of the Dark Ages be taken off the backs of men, could He be dethroned and Mankind set up in His place. An agnostic, he worshipped no god but the human soul. He had learned how vile man could be, but he also had seen the mighty heights to which he could aspire. 'How small man is, and how great he is!'

He demanded virility in a man, first and always. 'A man who can take a blow or insult unmoved, without retaliating —paugh! I care not if he can voice the sublimest sentiments, I sicken.' A man without courage was to him despicable. 'Enemies! There is no necessity. Lick a man when it comes to the pinch, or he licks you, but never hold a grudge. Settle it once and for all, and forgive.' He had an open-handed generosity with his friends; he gave himself to those he loved without reservation, did not abandon them when they hurt him or made mistakes. 'I do not feel that because I condemn the deficiencies of my friends is any reason why I should not love them.'

The backbone of his life was socialism. From his belief in the socialized state he derived strength, determination, and courage. He did not look for the regeneration of mankind in a day, nor did he think that men had to be born again before socialism could attain its ends. He would have liked socialism to filter through gradually, without open revolution or bloodshed, and he was eager to do his part in educating the masses to take over their own industry, natural resources, and government. But if the capitalists made this evolutionary process impossible then he was ready to fight at the barricades for The Cause. What new civilization had ever been born without a baptism of blood?

Organically related to his socialism was his philosophic adherence to a combination of Haeckel's monism, Spencer's materialistic determinism, and Darwin's evolution. 'Nature has no sentiment, no charity, no mercy. We are puppets at the play of great unreasoning forces, yet we may come to know the laws of some of these forces and see our trend in relation to them. We are blind factors in the action of natural selection among the races of men. . . . I assert, with Bacon, that all human understanding arises from the world of sensations. I assert, with Locke that all human ideas are due to the functions of the senses. I assert, with Laplace, that there is no need of a hypothesis of a creator. I assert, with Kant, the mechanical origin of the universe, and that creation is a natural and historical process.'

In his writing he hoped to follow in the footsteps of his master, Kipling. 'Kipling touches the soul of things. There is no end to him, simply no end. He has opened new frontiers of the mind and of literature.' He announced his revolt against 'that poor young American girl who mustn't be shocked or given anything less insipid than mare's milk.' The decade in which he had matured, the last decade of the century, had been its low point, a period of sterility and vacuousness in which the forces of Victorianism had ossified into control. Literature was bounded on all four sides by a Mid-West morality; books and magazines were published for a public that considered Louisa May Alcott and Marie Corelli great writers. Original work was difficult to do, only respectable middle-class or rich people might be written about, virtue always had to be rewarded and vice condemned; American authors were commanded to write like Emerson, to see the pleasant side of life, to eschew the harsh, the grim, the sordid, the real. The American literary leaders were still the pleasantly poetic voices of Holmes, Whittier, Higginson, W. D. Howells, F. Marion Crawford, John Muir, Joel Chandler Harris, Joaquin Miller. American editors, who dwelt in the rarefied and chilly atmosphere of the high places, paid unheard-of prices for Barrie, Stevenson, Hardy, even went so far as to print the daring revelations (editorially castrated, of course) of Frenchmen and Russians, yet demanded of their American authors a repetition of the pseudo-romance formula with only a change in backdrop permitted.

A revolution was being carried on in Russia by Tolstoi and the realists; in France by Maupassant, Flaubert, Zola; in Norway by Ibsen; in Germany by Sudermann and Hauptmann. When he read the stories written by Americans, and compared them to the work of Hardy, Zola, Turgeniev, he no longer wondered why on the Continent America was considered a nation of children and savages. The *Atlantic Monthly*, high priestess of American Letters, had been printing the fiction of Kate Douglas Wiggin and F. Hopkinson Smith. 'It was all perfectly quiet and harmless, for it was thoroughly dead.' Well, 'An Odyssey of the North' would be out in a few days now; neither the *Atlantic Monthly* nor American fiction would be harmless and dead any longer. He determined to do for literature in his own country what Gorky was doing for the art form in Russia, Maupassant in France, and Kipling in England. He would take it out of the Henry James high society salon and place it in the kitchen of the mass of people where it might smell a little occasionally, but at least it would smell of life.

In American literature of the day the three unmentionables were atheism, socialism, and a woman's legs. He would play his part in destroying organized religion, in destroying organized capitalism, and in converting sex from something vile, ugly, and unmentionable into the scientific play of selective forces engaged in the perpetuation of the species. Nor did he intend to become a mere pamphleteer; he was above all a writer, a maker of literature. He would train himself to tell stories so adroitly that propaganda and art would be indissolubly wedded.

In order to accomplish his fourfold purpose he decided that he would have to make himself one of the best educated men of the dawning century. To calculate what kind of start he had in his Herculean task, he looked at the books spread out on his desk and bed, all of which he was in the process of studying and annotating. Yes, he was on the right track: Saint-Amand's *Revolution of 1848;* Brewster's *Studies in Structure and Style;* Jordan's *Footnotes to Evolution;* Tyrell's *Sub-Arctics;* Bohm-Bawerk's *Capital and Interest;* Oscar Wilde's *The Soul of Man under Socialism;* William Morris's *The Socialist Ideal—Art;* William Owen's *Coming Solidarity.*

The clock in his mother's room struck eleven. There was only one hour left to the perishing century. He asked himself what kind of century it had been, what it had left behind for America, the America that had started in 1800 as a group of loosely affiliated agricultural states, had spent its early decades pioneering in the wilderness, its middle decades developing machinery, factories, spanning the continent, its closing decades amassing the greatest wealth the world had ever known . . . and along with its wealth and technological progress had chained the mass to their machines and their poverty.

But the new century, ah! that would be a great time to be alive. The resources, the machines, the scientific skill would be made to serve mankind instead of enslaving it. The human brain would be educated in natural laws, taught to face the irrefragable fact instead of being anesthetized by a religion for the weak and a morality for morons. Literature and life would become synonymous. The true soul of man would emerge in his art and literature and music, niceties which the

triple monster of frontier, religion, and capitalism had strangled in childbed.

What a magnificent America would his sons' sons see one
hundred years from this night as they sat at their desks and
surveyed the century that had just passed! It would be his
fortune to help bring about that new America. He would cast
off the shackles of the dark century now closing; he would
refuse to wear the ugly high stiff collars that dug into men's
flesh, and the ugly high stiff ideas that cut into their brain
and made them miserable. He would turn his back on the antiquated ideology of the nineteenth century and resolutely
face the twentieth, unafraid of what it might bring. He would
be a modern man and a modern American. One hundred
years from this night his sons and his sons' sons would think
back to him with pride.

Flora's clock tolled midnight. The old century was gone.
The new one was beginning. He sprang up from his desk,
donned a turtle-necked sweater, put clasps about his trousers
at the ankles, took out his bicycle, and pedaled the forty
miles through the dark night to San José. What better way to
begin the century than by marrying the girl he loved on its
opening day? If his sons' sons and their sons were to think
back to him with pride one hundred years from this night,
then he had no time to lose!

5

MRS. APPLEGARTH had never wanted Jack for a son-in-law. She had not opposed the engagement too strenuously because she knew the marriage to be predicated on Jack's ability to support a wife by his writing, an eventuality of which she had little fear. When he walked into the cottage on the corner of Elm and Ashbury Streets and showed Mabel and her mother his advance copy of 'An Odyssey of the North' as a good omen of what a happy New Year it was going to be, Mrs. Applegarth changed her mind abruptly. Yes, she would consent to their being married, yes, that very day . . . on one condition. Jack either had to step into the Applegarth house in San José as its provider—Mr. Applegarth was dead, Edward no longer lived at home—or take his mother-in-law with them to Oakland and promise that he would never separate her from her daughter.

Jack, who only a few days before had written to a friend that 'he already had a family to support, and that was hell for a young man,' was less appalled at the prospect of taking on the responsibility of an entire second family than at the unmistakable manner in which Mrs. Applegarth had dug iron claws into her daughter. A scene ensued. Jack insisted that Mrs. Applegarth had no right to stand in the way of her daughter's happiness. Mrs. Applegarth informed Jack that Mabel was a dutiful child, that she was grateful for all her mother had done for her and would not abandon her in her old age—all this in spite of the known fact that Mrs. Applegarth was twice as strong as Mabel, that she had tyrannized the girl into playing nursemaid to her, and even now was demanding of her daughter that she serve her breakfast in bed.

Mabel sat between the two people she loved, pale and distraught, lashed by the mounting quarrel, unable to take sides. She always had been dominated by her mother, and that domination had taken root in the bone. This frail woman who was so weak that she could not lift her voice against her mother, had the astounding strength to sit silently and allow her life to be destroyed, to watch her dreams of love, a husband, and children be shattered.

When Jack reached Oakland that night, thwarted and disconsolate, fresh troubles were added to his burden. Flora informed him that the last of the *Atlantic Monthly* money was spent. In the morning he rode the familiar route to the pawnbroker with John London's mackintosh on the handlebars of his bicycle; when he emerged he had a few dollars in his pocket, but he had to walk home. His journey to the pawnbroker coming on top of Mrs. Applegarth's ultimatum served to show him what an impossible situation he faced. For Mabel to come into his house and share his bed and board would mean but little added expense; their love would enable them to fight their way through hardship. But it would be years before he would earn enough to support his mother-in-law. The idea of bringing her to live with Flora was fantastic; the two women would be at each other's throat inside of twenty-four hours. And even when he was able to maintain two establishments, would he be master in his own home? Wouldn't Mrs. Applegarth run his house just as she would run his wife? Mabel would have to be a daughter to Mrs. Applegarth first, and in her spare time she could be a wife. Such a condition would be intolerable!

His brain churned with frustration at Mrs. Applegarth's domination. At the height of his rage he remembered Mabel, caught between two strong personalities, having her very life squeezed out between them. His anger vanished in the face of his tenderness and concern for her, and he resolved that no matter what the obstacles he would not abandon her to the mercies of her mother; that he would marry her and handle Mrs. Applegarth when the need arose. Quieted, happy in his determination to make everything right, consciousness flooded back, forcing him to realize that every victory he might gain over Mrs. Applegarth in the establishing of a normal marriage would be paid for a hundredfold by Mabel out of her slender fund of health. Again he would decide that he would not allow Mabel to be sacrificed, that as soon as he was earning enough money he would set up a separate establishment and let Mrs. Applegarth rule his household, that nothing he might suffer under her domination would be worse than what he and Mabel were suffering now. Then the torturous cycle started all over and he realized that this surrender too would destroy them, for how could a marriage be a happy one when the wife's body and spirit were in bondage to her mother?

He was undergoing his greatest disappointment. His love for Mabel was a well-rounded love; it would have made a good marriage. He admired and respected her for all the niceties of cultivation he lacked; because of her ethereal quality and the delicacy of her health he would have protected her and exercised care not to hurt her. Mabel in her turn had never loved anyone before Jack, and was never to love anyone after him. She would have made a devoted wife and given him the kind of home he had longed for all the years of his youth. He was intensely unhappy, not only because he was losing his dreams of a wife and home and children, but because the woman he loved was caught in a senseless tragedy he was powerless to right, a tragedy which would not only destroy their relationship, but Mabel as well.

January proved to be a gala month even though his rising sun as yet shed little financial warmth. 'An Odyssey of the North' was released in the *Atlantic Monthly*, which ran only one or two short stories a month; 'Economics in the Klondike' appeared in the *Review of Reviews*, and 'Pluck and Pertinacity' in *Youth's Companion*. 'An Odyssey of the North' tells the story of Naass, headman of Akatan, a modern Ulysses who searches the world over for his wife, Unga, who had been stolen from him on his wedding night by a yellow-haired Viking. As with 'The White Silence,' the reading of this story fills one with tragic ecstasy. It was received in the East with huzzahs of praise, for brave work inspires courage in others. An Oakland newspaper ran an article about the growing literary importance of Oakland, of which Mr. Jack London was the outstanding figure. His friends, remembering the hardships he had endured, were not consumed with jealousy and envy as are most friends when one of their circle rises above the prescribed limit of success; they gave a party for him, and everyone was happy for his sake.

Toward the end of the month he borrowed five dollars from a friend to take his bicycle out of pawn, and pedaled to San José. With the passage of the days he had laid out his arguments with so much clarity and precision he was convinced that Mabel would not be able to resist them, that she would establish her independence. Mabel hardly understood his words; she kept murmuring in a sort of cataleptic trance: 'Mother needs me. She couldn't get along without me. I couldn't desert her.' As late as 1937 Edward Applegarth said sadly, 'Mother was always a selfish woman; Mabel spent her whole life taking care of her.'

He did not altogether give up hope; he loved Mabel as much as ever. But he turned to other women for companionship. He saw a good deal of Anna Stunsky, at whose dinner table there were always several extra places for friends who might drop in . . . and Jack dropped in often. Anna was also writing short stories and sociological essays. They criticized each other's work, argued fiercely about every subject under the sun, admired each other. 'Anna, don't let the world lose you, for insomuch that it does lose you, insomuch have you sinned.' There was a San Francisco newspaper woman by the name of Ernestine whose picture shows her to have had an exquisite profile and a devilish gleam in her eye; she and Jack went on what he called 'far from conventional jaunts.'

Despite the fact that he had had such a brilliant January, he could sell not a line in February. The *Atlantic Monthly* money had paid off debts, bought reputable-looking clothes for Flora and Johnny and himself, and books and subscriptions to the current magazines he needed. Now without a penny in the house, he became hugely disgusted. The economic indignities of his childhood, which he had come to feel no human being should have to endure, taught him to think that pauperism was as objectionable as great wealth. He decided that he would be frankly and consistently brutal about money, that only fools despised it. 'It's money I want, or rather the things money will buy; and I can never possibly have too much. As to living on practically nothing, I propose to do as little of that as I possibly can. It's the feed not the breed that makes the man. More money means more life to me. The habit of getting money will never become one of my vices, but the habit of spending money, ah God! I shall always be its victim. If cash comes with fame, come fame; if cash comes without fame, then come cash.'

So saying, he pawned his books and magazines, the new suit of clothes of which he had been so proud. As always, his first stop after he left the pawnship was the post office where he bought stamps to send his manuscripts on their way again. When *The Editor* magazine offered him five dollars for a seventeen-hundred-word article he was insulted, but he took the money anyway. He went back to his work with double incentive. He had been writing a thousand words a day, six days a week, and made it a rule to make up the next day any amount he fell behind. Now he increased his stint to fifteen hundred words, then to two thousand, but beyond that he refused to go.

'I insist that good work cannot be done at the rate of three or four thousand words a day. Good work is not strung out from the inkwell; it is built like a wall, every brick carefully selected.' The fact that he wanted lots of money, quick money, did not make him careless in his methods or sleazy in his thinking; nor did it change his mind about the type of story he wanted to write. He declared that if the magazines wanted to buy him body and soul they were welcome if they could pay the price, yet all the time he was not writing he spent studying Drummond on evolution, Hudson on psychology, and all the books he could find on anthropology, the inescapable fact that the magazines would not pay ten cents a ton for evolution and anthropology deterring him not at all.

Craving money to release him from his perpetual slavery, he wrote passionate articles on socialism which he knew he couldn't possibly sell, lectured for the Socialist Party in Alameda, San José, and other small towns without pay. He was strangled by the lack of cash, yet his friends of this period report him traveling any distance to get into a group where he could start a heated discussion on anthropology. When he encountered Weismann's radical theory that acquired characteristics cannot be inherited, he was so greatly exercised he dropped all work and made the rounds of his friends, open book in hand, to let them share the great discovery. He who maintained that he would write rot if someone would pay him for it, then proved himself brutally inconsistent by writing about the things he believed in, revolutionary articles and stories whose spiritual brothers were even then reposing on the floor under his desk. He wanted money, but the price the magazine editors demanded for their money was too high for him to pay! 'I am firm. Everybody who has had a chance to know me well has noticed that things come my way even though they take years. No one sways me, save in the little things of the moment. I am not stubborn but I swing to my purpose as steadily as the needle to the pole. Delay, evade, oppose secretly or openly, it's all immaterial, the thing comes my way. Life is strife, and I am prepared for that strife. If I had not been an animal with a logical nature I would have stagnated or perished by the wayside.'

In February, within a very few days of each other, occurred two events, each apparently insignificant when happening, which were to determine the external pattern of his life. He accepted an invitation to luncheon in San Francisco from Mrs. Ninetta Eames, wife of the business manager of the *Overland Monthly*. And Fred Jacobs, a classmate from the University who had enlisted for the Spanish-American War, and had died on board a transport from eating canned meat provided by the ubiquitous war profiteers, was returned to Oakland for burial. Mrs. Eames's luncheon came first; although it took a little longer to exert its influence, that influence was the more lasting.

Mrs. Ninetta Eames was a sweet, mincing, childless woman of forty-seven. Known always as 'poor Netta,' she was a shrewd and clever person whose purpose rarely appeared on the surface, a clinging vine who flexed fingers of steel beneath her softness and sentimentality. Her husband being a pretentious weakling, Mrs. Eames had taken over the affairs of the family, and attained her ends in the only ways open to women of the eighties and nineties who had to control and energize their husbands without the world suspecting.

The purpose of the interview was an article which Mrs. Eames proposed to write about Jack for the *Overland Monthly*. To this luncheon Mrs. Eames also invited her niece, whom she had raised from infancy, Clara Charmian Kittredge, a fairly good replica of her aunt. Clara Charmian Kittredge, vivacious, quick-tongued, with a slender but sensuous figure, was twenty-nine years old and still unmarried; it is not impossible that Mrs. Eames hoped Jack and her niece might become interested in each other. Miss Kittredge, however, sniffed at Jack's shabby clothes and was indignant when Mrs. Eames paid the check; she showed emotion only when Mrs. Eames told Jack that her niece was a typist in an office close by. Miss Kittredge promptly kicked her aunt in the shin for revealing that she had to work for a living.

On the twentieth of February Jack excitedly finished reading proofs on *Son of the Wolf*, his first stories to appear in book form, and mailed them back to the publisher. The following day he attended the funeral of Fred Jacobs, where he met Bessie Maddern, Jacobs's fiancée, a handsome, Junoesque Irish girl whom Jack had known slightly in the Oakland circle. She was well liked and highly regarded by her associates, who were sympathetic over her bereavement. The next morning Jack received a letter from Mabel Applegarth, an old friend of Bessie's, asking him to call upon Bessie and do what he could to lighten her burden. He called at the home of the Madderns that evening.

Bessie Maddern, who was a cousin of Minnie Maddern Fiske, the famous actress, had graduated from Girls' High in San Francisco, attended Normal School for two years, and taught for three years in an Alameda grammar school. At the time of Fred Jacobs's death she was privately coaching in mathematics delinquent grammar-school children, and high-school students who wanted to enter the University. She was a strong woman physically, stolid, phlegmatic, riding her bicycle from house to house in Oakland and Alameda to her various pupils. She was a little older than Jack, had warm, sad eyes, an aquiline nose, a large but well-cut mouth, a strong chin, and black hair with a narrow streak of gray running straight back from her forehead, the result of an accident when she was eighteen. There was a well-poised, quiet assurance about her, and she was entirely forthright in nature.

Miss Maddern was grieving over the loss of Fred Jacobs; Jack was grieving over the hopelessness of his engagement to Mabel Applegarth. They found each other's company pleasant and salutary; they felt comfortable together. Before long Jack found himself spending many evenings with Miss Maddern. She coached him in mathematics and physics, in which he was untutored, while he went back to the beginnings of English literature and reviewed its history for her. On Sundays they took their bicycles across to Marin County, where they wandered through Muir Woods and cooked their dinner of broiled steak, baked sweet potatoes, crab, and coffee over hot coals. On other nights, if Jack had a little money, they would have dinner in one of San Francisco's North Beach Italian restaurants and then go to the opera.

He continued to bicycle the forty miles to San José each week, but his meetings with Mabel left him saddened and disillusioned. It was with relief that he returned to Bessie's cool, undemanding company. She was correcting all his manuscripts by now, polishing down the occasional awkward phrase; she liked his work and believed implicitly that he would become one of the world's great writers, a faith that never wavered.

Jack's rooms on Sixteenth Street had become a meeting-place for the people he knew, for they had begun to clamor for his company. 'I have the fatal faculty of making friends, and lack the blessed trait of being able to get rid of them.' There was nothing he liked better than playing host, but the bicycles began tinkling so frequently outside his house that he often had to do his writing with three or four men sitting on the bed, smoking, talking over old times, arguing whether a belief in materialism necessarily brought about pessimism. Jack could not let his guests go unfed; when a few lonely dollars arrived from the *Overland Monthly* for 'The Impossibility of War,' or from the *National Magazine* for 'A Lesson in Heraldry,' he bought a supply of steaks and chops to keep in the icebox.

Friends from the Ruskin Club dropped in for a smoke and a chat, his comrades from the Socialist Local to ask him to address a meeting, old pals from the Yukon, from the Fish Patrol, the oyster pirates, his brother tramps of The Road. 'That's one of the drawbacks of my present quarters, everybody comes dropping in, and I haven't the heart to turn them away.'

Because his house was becoming too small to hold all his books, his friends, and his work, and because he expected *Son of the Wolf* to earn him royalties, Jack decided to move to larger quarters. He and Flora found a two-story house at 1130 East Fifteenth Street, just a few blocks away, in which there was a large living-room with bay windows, and a good-sized bedroom that could be fitted up to make a workroom and den. Eliza did most of the work of decorating the seven rooms, but Bessie Maddern helped to make Jack's den cozy and colorful. On the night before the family was to move in, Eliza and Miss Maddern were hanging curtains in the den while Jack lay stretched out full length on the rug, his fingers interlaced behind his head, as he had lain so many nights on the prow of the *Sophie Sutherland*. Eliza turned about to pick up a curtain rod and noticed Jack studying Bessie with a curious expression on his face. In a flash she saw a decision settle in his eyes; this sister, who had been more mother than sister, knew at once what that decision was. She was not surprised the next morning when Jack informed her that he was going to marry Bessie Maddern.

Jack had been determined to marry Mabel Applegarth not only because he loved her, but because he was in a marrying mood. He had lived a good deal more than his twenty-three years bespoke; he had a strong feeling for fatherhood, so strong that even as a tramp on The Road he had written in his notebook of his longing for children. 'Divers deep considerations have led me to do this thing; but I shall override just one objection—that of being tied. I am already tied. Though single, I have had to support a household just the same. Should I wish to go to China the household would have to be provided for whether I had a wife or not. As it is, I shall be steadied, and can be able to devote more time to my work. One has only one life, after all, and why not live it? My heart is large, and I shall be a cleaner, wholesomer man because of a restraint being laid upon me in place of being free to drift wheresoever I listed.'

Jack and Bessie were honest with each other. They did not profess to be passionately enamored in the romantic tradition; they knew that Bessie still loved Fred Jacobs and that

Jack still loved Mabel Applegarth. But both had had their hearts set on marriage. They liked and respected and enjoyed each other, felt they could build a good marriage and a solid home, and raise fine children. They agreed that although love was one of the smallest words in the language, it was sufficiently elastic to admit of many definitions. Miss Maddern considered the proposal for a day or two, then accepted.

Unwilling to marry under a name that was not legally his, because of the equivocal position in which it might place his children, Jack told the Madderns the circumstances of his birth. Together he and Bessie went to see an Oakland judge who was a friend of the Maddern family; he assured them that since Jack had been living under the name of London all his life, and had published under it, his right to it was legally established.

On a Sunday, one week after he had made his decision, Jack and Bessie were quietly married. Flora was so outraged by what she considered her son's abandonment of her that she refused to attend the ceremony. The newlyweds rode off on their bicycles for a three-day honeymoon in the country, then returned to Oakland to set up house and dig into work. The Ruskin Club staged a dinner in their honor; the Oakland *Enquirer,* writing up the marriage, said, 'The bride is a beautiful and accomplished young woman,' a compliment which Oakland agreed was well deserved.

During the day Bessie continued her coaching of backward students, earning enough to keep the house going when Jack's income could not. At night she corrected his manuscripts and typed them, read the new books in which he was interested so that she might discuss them with him, copied onto sheets of paper poems he had enjoyed, binding hundreds of them between red cardboard covers, collected and bound magazine articles for him on economic and political subjects, set up a dark room and showed him how to develop his own pictures. On Sundays they took long bicycle rides through the fertile San Leandro Valley, where Jack told Bessie stories of his early days on John London's farm. One week-end they went to Santa Cruz, where they swam in the ocean and frolicked on the beach. If they achieved no ecstasy, they did have fun together, and honest, dependable comradeship. Jack gave every evidence of being pleased with his choice, and pleased with his marriage. Bessie said in 1937, 'I did not love Jack when I married him, but I very soon came to love him.'

The marriage seems to have brought its own good luck, for in May, Jack at last cracked an Eastern short-story magazine,

McClure's, which published action stories for men. There
began a honeymoon period between Jack and the publisher,
S. S. McClure, who gained immortality by paying high prices
for stories from unknown writers on the grounds that 'the
boys have to eat.' McClure bought 'The Grit of Women' and
'The Law of Life,' writing to Jack, 'We are greatly interested
in you and want you to feel that you have the warmest kind
of friends right here in New York. I wish you would look
upon us as your literary sponsors hereafter. If you will send
us everything you write we will use what we can, and what
we cannot we will endeavor to dispose of to the best possible
advantage.'

There was no more heartening message a young writer
could receive. Taking McClure at his word, Jack gathered together a boxful of manuscripts, then dug in to write fresh
ones that had been formulating in his mind. McClure bought
'The Question of the Maximum,' paying him three hundred
dollars in all for the three pieces of work, the largest amount
of money Jack had ever possessed. The material McClure
could not use he sent to other magazines with his recommendation; when the manuscripts became too numerous for him
to handle, he turned them over to a reputable literary agent.
With his sales to McClure, and McClure's sponsorship among
the editors of the New York literary world, the name of Jack
London began to be known.

When *Son of the Wolf* was released in the spring of 1900
it met with instantaneous critical success. The book was like
a time-bomb blowing open the new century. With the exception of an occasional antiquated phrase there was no element
of the now-dead nineteenth century in it. The short stories
spoke vigorously of the new century. The scientific attitudes
toward evolution and the strife among species, the amoral
values of people who lived without fear of being excommuni-
cated by the parson, the bold approach to life's cruelty and
ugliness and grimness as well as the beautiful and the good,
the introduction of whole classes of characters who had never
before been admitted into the polite society of the short
story, the orgiastic action, brute conflict, and violent death
that had been forbidden to the story-teller—all tolled the
death knell of the anemic, the sentimental, the evasive, the
hypocritical, that marked nineteenth-century literature.

Many of the critics of the day picked up the gage for Jack.
The Literary World of Boston said, 'The author's spade goes
down into the root of things'; the *Atlantic Monthly,* 'The
book produces in the reader a deeper faith in the manly
virtues of our race.' Other critics wrote: 'Full of fire and feel-

ing; a natural born story teller; virility and forcefulness throughout; all outward signs of genius; great artist, powerful. . . .' One commented, 'His stories are imbued with the poetry and mystery of the great North. The dominant note is always tragedy (in contrast to the formula of happy endings), as it always is where men battle with the elemental forces of nature. He has brought to the comedy and tragedy of life in the Klondike much of the imaginative power and dramatic force of Kipling. But he has the tenderness of sentiment and a quick appreciation of the finer sentiments of heroism that are seldom seen in Kipling.'

His first published book, and already he was being compared favorably to his beloved master! Elated as he was with the reviews, he found time to be angry with the critics for not realizing Kipling's true greatness, and dashed off a sizzling article on the subject.

The issuance of *Son of the Wolf* marked the beginning of the modern American short story. It had antecedents in Edgar Allan Poe, Bret Harte, Stephen Crane, and Ambrose Bierce, who had all broken with the conventional pattern to write authentic literature, but Jack was the first to bring the story home to the common people, to make it entirely understandable and enjoyable. Up to this time the bulk of short stories had been written for maiden ladies; Jack's stories were for every class of Americans except maiden ladies—and they gobbled them up behind drawn blinds and locked doors. He was also the first to imbue the form with the scientific attitude of the twentieth century, and to give it the force and vitality that Americans had used to conquer the continent and build gigantic industries.

For a long time he had been wanting to try his hand at a novel; since a novel takes from six months to a year to write, during which time there can be no income from the work, the possibility of his getting sufficiently ahead to do a sustained piece of work seemed remote. Now he wrote McClure about his predicament. McClure answered post-haste, 'We will back your novel on your own terms. We will send you a check each month for five months for $100, and if you find that you need $125, why we will do that. I am confident that you can make a strong novel. At any time when you feel in need of any sort of help, please let us know.'

Then, with his career sailing like the *Razzle Dazzle* before the wind, Bessie brought him the news that she was pregnant. Jack was overjoyed and knew at once that it would be a son. Kind as he had been before, he now became gentle as a child, tenderly solicitous of her health and well-being. The knowl-

edge that he was soon to be a father touched off the spark,
and within a few hours of Bessie's revelation he had begun
work on his first novel, *A Daughter of the Snows.*

Though he had figured to a nicety the details of already
being tied down, and having a household to support, Jack
had failed in a typically masculine fashion to realize that no
kitchen has yet been built that is large enough to hold two
women. Flora was raising hell with his wife.

She had been deeply hurt by what she termed her son's desertion at the moment when he was beginning to earn a little
money. Having suffered without complaint during the months
of want, she now felt she was entitled to her reward—instead
of which Jack had brought a strange woman into the house.
She had cooked for him and taken care of him, and now Bessie wanted to do the cooking; she had been the hostess when
his friends came to call, now Bessie was the mistress. Flora
did not like being superseded in Jack's affections; she assumed that she was being shoved into the background. As
she brooded about her troubles the old neurasthenia returned.
She quarreled constantly with Bessie, made things as unpleasant for her as she could. Twenty years after Jack's death,
Bessie commented: 'I should have catered to Flora and pet-
ted her and made her the boss, and we would all have gotten
along fine. But I was young, and wanted to do things for my
husband. So we clashed!'

Oftentimes when Jack was trying to concentrate on the difficult structural problems of his first novel, the angry voices
of the two women would fill the room in which he was working, driving out of his mind *A Daughter of the Snows.* He
would stand it as long as he could, then dash out of the
house, walk at top speed to Eliza's, and implore her to go to
his house and quiet them. When he returned home an hour
or two later Eliza had the situation in hand, and he would go
back to work.

With better facilities for entertaining his friends, Jack
began gathering about him an interesting circle, encouraging
them in their habit of dropping in on Wednesday nights.
Chief among them was tall, athletic, exquisitely sensitive
George Sterling, of whom Jack wrote, 'I have a friend, the
dearest in the world.' Sterling had abandoned the priesthood
of the Catholic Church to become one of those rare poets
who weave beauty, tenderness, and a passion for truth into
his work. An esthete grounded in the classics, he was a split
personality, torn between his love for socialism and the conception of 'art for art's sake,' which had been drilled into him
by Ambrose Bierce, with whose philosophy of defeatism Jack

disagreed violently. Possessing a mind rich in imagery and the music of words, Sterling's loyal comradeship, flaming spirit, and penetrating literary criticism did much to smooth down Jack's rough edges. James Hopper, the husky, powerful football player whom he had known at the University, and who was also trying to write short stories, became an intimate, as did Jim Whitaker, a preacher with seven children who had given up his pulpit to write novels, and Xaviar Martinez, the Spanish-Indian painter. Frederick Bamford, assistant librarian of Oakland and founder of the Ruskin Club, brought his precise goatee and precise bishoplike culture to Jack's board. Anna Strunsky came over from San Francisco, also Strawn-Hamilton, the philosophical anarchist, Austin Lewis, the Social Democrat, and other Bay region radicals. Mrs. Ninetta Eames visited frequently, bringing her literary friends and progress reports of her niece's tour of Europe. Everyone came for supper, after which manuscripts were read, and the new books and plays discussed. Later the men played poker or red dog for small stakes, high excitement, and big laughter. Soon these Wednesday night parties became known as Jack's open house.

Cloudesley Johns, a handsome, lovable young chap, rode up from his post office in a small Southern California town to spend a week. Johns had been the first person to write enthusiastically to Jack when 'To the Man on Trail' was published in the *Overland Monthly;* they had been corresponding ever since. Tramps from The Road, sailors, former waterfront cronies, all liked to show up at Jack's house for a glass of sour Italian wine, a friendly chat. 'Every once in a while some old shipmate turns up . . . just returned from a long voyage . . . big payday coming . . . "Say Jack, old boy, can you lend me a couple of dollars until tomorrow?" ' Jack scaled them down to half, gave them the money, and let them go. He was supremely happy in being able to dispense hospitality; he always liked a crowd of his friends in his house when he had finished the day's work.

Though the hundred and twenty-five dollars from *McClure's* arrived regularly each month, it was no longer sufficient to fill the needs of his family, his rising standard of living, and the influx of friends. He began doubling his working time, devoting the mornings to his serious literature, the afternoons to writing pot-boilers. As a result he sold an article to the Boston *Transcript* on how he had slept on the Common and told the arresting officer tales about Japan to keep out of jail; an article on 'The Husky,' the Alaskan sled dog, which *Harper's Weekly* bought; another on 'Expansion,'

which the San Francisco *Wave* ran as an editorial; two
domestic narratives, 'Their Alcove,' published by *Woman's
Home Companion*, and 'Housekeeping in the Klondike,' by
means of which he crashed *Harper's Bazaar;* a triolet to
Town Topics:

> He came in
>   When I was out
> To borrow some tin
>   Was why he came in,
> And he went without;
>   So I was in
> And he was out.

And Jack was in one dollar!

He worked so steadily at his typewriter and books that
sometimes for days he did not go out the front door except to
pick up the evening paper from the porch. He lost weight,
grew soft, found that he was growing timid in proportion as
he grew soft, that he was becoming afraid to write the things
in which he believed, was asking himself if this manuscript
would sell, or that one would please the public. It had always
been his conviction that a sickly body could not harbor a
healthy brain, so he bought a pair of dumbbells with which
he exercised every morning in front of an open window before sitting down to compose—rarely later than six A.M.—
and after work went hunting behind the Berkeley hills or fishing on the Bay. His body hardened, and with it his nerve and
courage. In a burst of renewed vitality he wrote 'Jan the Un-
repentant' and 'The Man with the Gash.' They were his first
humorous tales of the Klondike, written with the diabolical
sense of humor of the Irishman at a wake who plays tricks
with the corpse.

In spite of its good critical press, *Son of the Wolf* sold but
moderately well. Nor was he getting anything better than
wages from magazines other than *McClure's*, twenty dollars
being a high price for a manuscript. His name was not yet
known to the reading public; he would have to keep writing
for that one smash hit which would put him over. In the
meanwhile he continued to pick up a few dollars wherever he
could; when *The Black Cat* ran a story contest, and he could
think of no major plot with which to win one of the big
prizes, he wrote the ironic 'Semper Idem,' the idea for which
he got out of his evening newspaper, and won a minor prize.
When *Cosmopolitan Magazine* ran a contest on 'Loss by
Lack of Cooperation,' he took a million-to-one shot and
wrote a revolutionary article for them called 'What the Com-

munity Loses by the Competitive System'; he won the first prize of two hundred dollars, which caused him to comment that he was the only man in America making money out of socialism.

After months of interminable wrangling between his wife and mother, Jack rented a small cottage on the street just back of his house and moved Flora and Johnny into it. This excommunication made Flora furious; now she was being put out of her son's home, discarded! Jack achieved little by the maneuver except added expense, for she not only came into his house and caused an even greater amount of confusion, but began rehearsing her grievances with the neighbors, who started unfortunate gossip. Imagining that she was on her own again, Flora began dipping into small business ventures, spending the money Jack gave her no one knew where, running up debts which her son had to cover.

Through the summer and fall Jack continued to work on his novel, lectures for the Socialist Local at mass meetings in San Francisco, attended meetings when other lecturers spoke, joined the Ibsen circle, took fencing and boxing lessons in his back yard, and on Wednesday nights played host to his friends. He was a long way from being a melancholy intellectual—one of the best times he had during the fall was watching California trounce Stanford at football—yet his most consistent adventure of the period was the discovery of great books, to which he gave himself with the whole-hearted abandon of the ragged, uncared-for newsboy, a stack of papers under his arm, who had wandered into the Oakland Library fourteen years before and asked Miss Coolbrith for something good to read. He writes to Anna Strunsky: 'I have been sitting here crying like a baby, for I have just finished reading *Jude the Obscure*. With Jude and Tess to his name, Hardy should die content.' He vowed that he too would die content if he could create one or two books that might stand shoulder to shoulder on the shelves with the books that had so enriched his life.

Between Jack and Anna Strunsky there was developing a curious relationship. That their minds were magnificently mated they had at length come to realize, even though they still were arguing violently over biology, materialism, and socialism. By July Jack's letters to her begin to acquire a tender note. 'For all the petty surface turmoil which marked our coming to know each other, really, deep down, there was no confusion at all. We were attuned somehow, a real unity underlaid everything. The ship, new launched, rushes to the sea, the sliding ways rebel in creaks and groans; but sea and ship hear them not. So with us when we rushed into each other's lives.'

He submitted his serious work to Anna Strunsky, who brought to her criticism a mind finely attuned to spiritual values. In turn he urged her to continue with her own writing. 'Oh Anna, if you will only put your flashing soul with its protean moods on paper! You make me feel as though some new energy has been projected into the world. Anna, read your classics, but don't forget to read that which is of today, the new born literary art. You must get the modern touch; form must be considered, and while art is eternal, form is born of the generations. Oh, Anna, don't disappoint me.'

By the end of 1900 he was writing, 'A white beautiful friendship?—between a man and a woman?—the world cannot imagine such a thing, would deem it as inconceivable as infinity.' Nor had Jack himself conceived it as possible; if he had he might have done his courting in San Francisco instead of Oakland when he was discouraged over Mabel Applegarth. He meant no disloyalty to his wife, yet his mind came to love the mind of Anna Strunsky. He and Bessie had plumbed certain depths together, they had known companionship and created life, and for these things he loved her. But he and Anna had plumbed other depths, depths of the mind and spirit, and for these things he loved Anna.

With Bessie all swollen and big with child, Jack began to torment himself over his feelings for Miss Strunsky, whom he describes as 'a Russian Jewess who happens to be a genius.' Yet no word had been uttered between them about their feelings for each other. 'Ah, believe me, Anna, the things unsaid are the greatest. A happiness to me? Why, you have been a delight, dear, and a glory.' He had married for emotional stability, for a solid, permanent position in society, but '. . . just when freedom seems opening up for me I feel the bands tightening and the rivetting of the gyves. I remember now when I was free, when there was no restraint and I did as the heart willed.'

That he was feeling a genuine emotion for Miss Strunsky there can be no doubt, but mixed in with it are the fears and misgivings, the yearnings for freedom of the young man who is about to become a father, to have further and permanent responsibilities strapped to his back. Yet what would have happened if Mrs. Applegarth had not issued her ultimatum until Jack was writing to Anna, 'A happiness to me? Why you have been a delight, dear, and a glory'?

He continued to write poems for exercise in fluency; to read omnivorously in modern fiction to get well in hand the modern touch; to perform many experiments, not for sale, but to extend his range; to write long criticisms on the technique of story writing; to let no sentence pass in his manuscript in which the words were not smooth and beautiful to his ear. When he thought he was getting too cocky about his work he dug out a batch of old stories and lo! he would be like a lamp. He and Cloudesley Johns, who had had an academic training, exchanged blistering criticisms in the margins of each other's manuscripts. Johns, who was writing a book called *The Philosophy of The Road,* sent it to Jack for correction. Jack's answer contains his literary credo. 'You are handling stirring life, romance, things of human life and death, humor and pathos, but God, man, handle them as they should be. Don't you tell the reader the philosophy of The Road. HAVE YOUR CHARACTERS TELL IT BY THEIR DEEDS, ACTION, TALK. Study Stevenson and Kipling and see how they eliminate themselves and create things that live, and breathe, and grip men, and cause reading lamps to burn overtime. Atmosphere stands always for the elimination of the artist. Get your good strong phrases, fresh and vivid; write intensively, not exhaustively or lengthily; don't narrate—paint! draw! build! CREATE! Better one thousand words that are builded than a whole book of mediocre, spun-out, dashed-off stuff. Damn you! Forget you! And then the world will remember you!'

By the time he reached the home stretch of *A Daughter of the Snows* he knew it was a failure. There was enough good material in it to make two good novels, with sufficient bad material left over to make still a third, bad novel. From *A Daughter of the Snows* emerge his two great weaknesses, implicit here in this beginning, explicit after he had published forty volumes: his conception of the supremacy of the Anglo-Saxon race; and his inability to transcribe to a flesh-and-blood reality on the printed page any woman above the working class.

In Frona Welse Jack tried to create a twentieth-century woman who would be an antithesis of the nineteenth-century woman: strong without being hard, intelligent without being flat-chested, courageous without losing her charm or femininity, able to work and live and fight and think and hold the trail with the best of men. From her character he eliminated everything he detested in womankind: sentimentality, slovenly thinking, coquetry, weakness, fear, ignorance, soft vampirish clinging, hypocrisy. He tried to conceive of a woman who would be a worthy mate for his twentieth-century man; though he was sailing in dangerous, uncharted waters he very nearly makes Frona credible. If he could have gone on from here he might have created in his later work an image that would have served as a model for the new womankind. . . .

Frona appears at her worst when she talks like one of Jack's sociological essays, expounding the chauvinistic fallacy —which Jack had swallowed whole-hog from Kipling—of the supremacy of the white race, of their destiny to rule supreme forever over the red, the black, and the yellow, a gullibility of which he was eagerly guilty because of his own Viking complex. 'The sharp-beaked fighting galleys, and the sea-flung Northmen, great muscled, deep-chested, sprung from the elements, men of sword and sweep . . . the dominant races come down out of the North . . . a great race, half the earth its heritage and all the sea! In three score generations it rules the world!'

Jack permitted his Ango-Saxon myopia to corrupt his thinking about socialism, the one subject above all others in which he wanted to be honest and accurate. When he was writing about the dominant races come down out of the North, he wrote to Cloudesley Johns, 'Socialism is not an ideal system devised for the happiness of all men; it is devised for the happiness of certain kindred races. It is devised so as to give more strength to these certain kindred favored races so that they may survive and inherit the earth to the extinction of the lesser, weaker races.' Thus did Nietzsche speak through Kipling to pervert Karl Marx.

He had bravely turned down the material luxury of a postman's wage for the uncertainties of a writer's career. Now a hundred and fifty dollars a month, an undreamed-of sum less than a year before, was not sufficient to keep him. By the time a check arrived there was a long line of people waiting to cash it. A list of his financial activities between Christmas and New Year's includes a loan to Jim Whitaker; footing the bills for a friend who had had both ankles broken in an accident; paying forty-one dollars of Flora's pressing back debts, giving Mammy Jenny, who was about to lose her home, enough cash to pay the interest on her mortgage, and her delinquent taxes; and, the only unpleasant task in the series, refusing to lend Cloudesley Johns money to leave his desert post office, because he, Jack, had had to go out and borrow money to run his house. And with Bessie expecting to be confined in a week!

Bessie says that she continued her coaching right up to the morning the baby arrived. For a time it looked as though the child might be born on January 12, Jack's twenty-fifth birthday, but Bessie did not go into labor until the morning of the

fifteenth. When she knew that her moment had arrived she
sent for the doctor, who came in such haste he forgot to
bring an anesthetic. Jack was dispatched to buy a bottle of
chloroform. On his way home he rode his bicycle so hard
and fast he fell off, broke the bottle, and cut his hand. Bessie
had delivered of a nine-pound girl, but the afterbirth was
botched and Bessie was ill for a long time. Jack was not able
to hide from his wife his disappointment that it was not a
boy.

Despite the fact that McClure decided against publishing *A
Daughter of the Snows* in his magazine, he continued to send
Jack the monthly check of a hundred and twenty-five dollars.
'Being a married man, and knowing that it costs money to
buy potatoes, I am enclosing . . .' The novel finished, Jack
devoted himself to a series of short stories. With the passing
of the weeks the disappointment at not having a son was al-
layed somewhat; he grew attached to his daughter, Joan, who
favored him strongly in looks. Mammy Jenny moved into the
London house to take care of Joan, just as she had cared for
Joan's father in Bernal Heights, twenty-five years before.

One of the avowed reasons Jack had married Bessie was
because he had believed she would breed strong children; nor
was he mistaken. He had married her on an impulse, to fill
an empty space in both their lives, to plunge them into the
swift stream of living. Bessie was everything she had appeared to be: loyal, devoted, gentle, intelligent, willing to
work with him, share his hardships. He enjoyed being a father, and felt a strong sense of gratitude toward her. Yet sometimes in his fatigue his mind turned against his wife for those
very qualities for which he valued and had selected her. He
was mercurial of nature, he had fire in his veins, he liked to
burn and exult, to live wildly and fiercely, to soar to the
heights in exultation, to drag the depths of despair. In these
spiritual debauches Bessie would not accompany him; she
was emotionally stable, placid, solid, even of temper and
mood. When he was working and accomplishing all the
things he had set out to accomplish he was thankful to her,
but when the work was done there were moments of revolt
when he longed to slip his moorings and beat out to the Bay
on the early morning tide. Then would he sigh for his old
freedom, for the right to move on to another place, another
woman. It was the first time he had not been able to chuck
his obligations and strike out for Adventure Road.

At such times he would write to Anna Strunsky, 'Surely sitting here, gathering data, classifying, arranging, writing stories for boys with moral purposes insidiously inserted, ham-

mering away at a thousand words a day, growing excited over biological objections, thrusting a bit of fun at you and raising a laugh when it should have been a sob, surely this is not all? Were ever two souls, with dumb lips, more incongruously matched?'

They decided to write their spiritual and intellectual feelings into a book. They would call it *The Kempton-Wace Letters,* Jack to be Wace, and Anna to be Kempton, in which Anna would defend the poetic or spiritual wellsprings of love against the attacks of Jack's biological and scientific evolution. Thus would they enjoy the passions and poetries of each other's mind without hurting anyone or violating any codes. Thus would Jack defend his marriage to Bessie, even while escaping it.

While doing double duty at his desk he also had found time to lecture for the Alameda Socialist Party on 'The Tramp,' and at the San Francisco Academy of Science on 'Competitive Waste.' The local press reported his lectures respectfully. When the moment arrived to nominate a candidate for Mayor of Oakland, the first candidate the young Socialist Party had dared put in the field, to whom should the honor go but to their best-known member, Mr. Jack London. In accepting the nomination Jack said, 'It is we, the Socialists, working as a leaven throughout society, who are responsible for the great and growing belief in municipal ownership. It is we, the Socialists, by our propaganda, who have forced the old parties to throw as sops to the popular unrest certain privileges.'

He campaigned in Oakland on the premise that socialism was the hair shirt of capitalism, the irritant which would bring forth from the vested interests certain soothing lotions in the form of better wages, hours, working conditions. He urged the unions and unorganized workers to vote the Socialist ticket so that their display of strength would give them greater bargaining power with their employers.

The workers turned a deaf ear to his economic reasoning. Only the 'intellectual proletariat' stood behind him. To the citizens of Oakland and Alameda he was able to sell but two hundred and forty-five votes in his mild Utopia.

In May there appeared in *Pearson's* magazine 'The Minions of Midas,' as revolutionary a departure in American literature as had been 'An Odyssey of the North' the year before. There was no such pheomenon as a socialist fiction writer in the United States, nor had there ever been one. But Jack had never cast about for the approbation of precedent; he was determined to be a socialist writer in the days when it took as much courage to be a socialist writer as it does nowadays not to be one. In this story he first conceives of a world-wide organization of proletariats so powerful that it cannot be downed by the police, the state militia, or the national government, an organization which is taking over by force the wealth of the world. If 'The Minions of Midas' is not the first proletarian story to have been published in America, it seems to have been the first to appear in a magazine of national importance and distribution. Not that *Pearson's* committed the heresy of buying the story for its socialism; Jack was such a consummate story-teller that *Pearson's* published it for its horror-entertainment value, calculating its socialism to be so far-fetched the readers would think of it as a Jules Verne fantasy.

Jack followed 'The Minions of Midas' with 'The Dream of Debs,' which predicted the San Francisco general strike of 1934, and 'The Iron Heel,' which predicted the rise and current terror of Fascism. After his death the critics were able to agree about few things in his work, but on one point there is little controversy: Jack London is the father of proletarian literature in America. In 1929 the *New Masses* was to say in simple and true words, 'A real proletarian writer must not only write about the working class, he must be read by the working class. A real proletarian writer must not only use his proletarian life as his material; his writing must burn with the spirit of revolt. Jack London was a real proletarian writer—the first and so far the only proletarian writer of genius in America. Workers who read, read Jack London. He is the one author they have all read, he is one literary experience they all have in common. Factory workers, farm hands, seamen, miners, newsboys read him and read him again. He is the most popular writer of the American working class.'

His Wednesday gatherings remained the high spot of his week. His friends now began dropping in about midafternoon; Jack being an inveterate puzzle-worker, they brought pull-aparts, unhookers, mechanical riddles, boards on which marbles or ball bearings had to be rolled into cups and slots. Bessie hunted the magazines assiduously, cutting out the coupons for all advertised puzzles, games, and practical jokes. By suppertime fifteen or twenty people had assembled, and were playing Animals, Statues, Charades, trying to separate interlocking steel rings, drinking water from glasses that had a small hole near the bottom and sprung a stream onto their neckties, or finding a furred mouse in their pocket. The laughter was continuous and uproarious; Jack kept it uproarious because he loved to laugh, and was eager to fill his belly with all the laughter it could hold. He had not had a joyous childhood; he was going to make up for it in simple fun.

Across his big round supper table the arguing was always furious; he knew each man's vulnerabilities, and taunted them with pseudo-serious comments until the battle royal started. A number of young women journalists, musicians, writers had joined the group; after supper there was music, singing, and dancing. Mrs. Ninetta Eames's niece, Clara Charmian Kittredge, was back from Europe. She was an accomplished pianist, and Jack liked to sit on the bench beside her while she played and sang.

After the music, when the crowd was in a quiet mood, Jack brought forth the manuscripts he had written during the week. Seated in a leather chair in the now darkened room, the pages illumined only by the flickering light of the open fire, he read to his friends while they listened attentively. This was followed by an hour or two of solid literary discussion, and then Jack once again started the fun, bringing out the cards and arranging those games in which the most laughter and excitement could be evoked. He laughed lustily at every turn of luck, and at the winning or losing of a pot would become as excited as a child. Men who attended these Wednesday open houses still remember them as the most delightful and stimulating nights of their lives.

There was always a gallon of sour red Italian wine for those who wanted to drink it, but no whiskey. It had been eight or nine years since Jack had done any serious drinking. When going into the Klondike he had carried a quart of Scotch over Chilkoot Pass; six months later he had pulled the cork for the first time, so that the whiskey might be used as an anesthetic, half of it going down the throat of Doctor Harvey, the other half down a man whose leg the doctor was amputating. The patient lived.

Early in the year McClure had suggested that Jack now had published enough stories to put out a second collection of his Alaskan tales. In May *The God of His Fathers* appeared. Though there is no single story in it to equal the brilliance of 'An Odyssey of the North,' the volume has a more consistent level of excellence than his first. Jack carried further his revolution in story-telling, making a rigid elimination of nonessentials, of the gingerbread façade. He stripped the form to fit the action. In these stories he proved that death-appeal in literature is more powerful than sex-appeal. Though some of the critics did not like the second volume as well as the first, most of the press was highly enthusiastic. *The Commercial Advertiser* said, 'The stories ought to be read, and widely read, because they represent one of the most encouraging tendencies in contemporary American fiction'; while *The Nation* reported in July, 1901: 'The stories in *The God of His Fathers* are vivid, concise, dramatic. They are sometimes coarse, generally disagreeable, always cynical and reckless. But if anyone wants to be interested, amused, and thoroughly stirred, he cannot do better than read this volume.' Other papers commented: 'Strongest short-story writer to arise in this country since Poe.' . . . 'A new Kipling come out of the West.' . . . 'Does for Alaska what Bret Harte did for California.' . . . 'We are held spellbound.' . . . 'Power and force . . . true to life . . . first-class raconteur . . . natural-born storyteller . . . realistic, keen observation . . . swift, clean, virile . . . full of healthy optimism . . . gives us new faith in the strength of our race.' The dissenting voices called the stories brutal, vulgar, and unpleasant, written without polish, delicacy, or refinement.

The San Francisco *Examiner* sent a reporter and photographer to the home of Felix Piano, into whose amazing house Jack had moved his family a short time before, to get material for a big spread and pictures of Jack and his study. Felix Piano was an eccentric Italian sculptor who had adorned his house with plaster arabesques, urns, sculptured fawns, angels, devils, dryads, cherubs, centaurs, and lusty nude female torsos reclining under bowers of grapes—all of the rococo ornamentation against which Jack was revolting in literature. Falling upon hard times, Piano had turned over the greater part of the house to Jack rent-free, in return for his board. The inside of the house was large and comfortable even if the outside was incredible.

As result of the article in the *Examiner* Jack found himself definitely famous in the Bay area, although his local fame did him little good financially. Fan letters began to come in. Women in particular seemed stirred by his writing and his pictures, and wrote asking all manner of favors. There was the woman who gave her minister as a character reference, then proposed that Jack be the father of her child so that the child would inherit a magnificent body and brain. Although he heartily approved of the lady's biological thesis, he managed to turn down the proposal.

He was severely in debt: to the stores, to the pawnshop, to his friends. The royalties from *The God of His Fathers* were charged against his advances from McClure, so that no cash was forthcoming. Any check that was due was spent a month before it arrived; though he sold a number of stories and articles to small magazines he could not collect his money. The

business of literature was a wretched one; editors took
months to decide whether they wanted a story, more months
to publish it, and still more months after publication to pay
for it. Jack fumed against this system, crying out that if a
man bought shoes or vegetables he paid cash, so why
shouldn't editors pay cash for stories? This shabby treatment
of a man who needed his wages to buy the necessities of life
for his family made him the more determined eventually to
make editors pay him high prices.

By summer, when he was hopelessly in debt, the San Francisco *Examiner* summoned him to write special articles for
the Sunday supplement, the section for which he had written
his first article, four years before, in an attempt to earn the
requisite ten dollars to feed Flora, Johnny Miller, and himself
until the appointment from the post office came through. He
reported prize fights, wrote a hysterical article about the arrival of the *S.S. Oregon,* which brought down on him the
wrath of the local literati, did articles on 'Girls Fighting
Duels,' the Washoe Indians coming to civilization, and finally
spent ten straight days reporting the German *Schuetzenfest.*
He forced himself to make the articles red-blooded, virile, as
the *Examiner* had promised its readers they would be; as a
result they sound forced and artificial, but the food they
bought for his family was very real indeed.

In August a calamity hit him. After reading a number of
short stories written over a period of months, among which
were 'Moon Face' and 'Nambok, the Unveracious,' and re-
jecting them all, McClure lost faith in him. 'Your work seems
to have taken a turn which makes it impractical for this magazine. Of course I understand that you must follow the lead
of your genius . . . but unless there is a possibility of our
securing the material we can use, do you not think it would
be better for us to drop the salary after September or October?' Six people to support, and his only reliable source of
income cut off!

McClure suggested that if he would turn back to the kind
of story he had written before, the magazine would pay him
high prices. If he obeyed McClure, made a laborious effort to
copy his early material or write according to formula, he
could make good money; if he obeyed the dictates of his
probing mind, which demanded that he continue to explore
new and revolutionary fields of human conduct and artistic
form, he and his dependents would once again face starvation. To this man who claimed that he wanted money passionately, who said that the magazines could buy him body
and soul if they would pay the price, who had vowed to be

'frankly and consistently brutal about money,' only one decision was possible. He threw McClure overboard and went ahead writing the things he felt deeply, that he knew had to be written.

He had two months before McClure was to cut off his hundred-and-twenty-five-dollar salary. If he worked desperately, wrote furiously, surely he could sell something, crack open a new field?

6

~~~~

'FOR ME the New Year begins full of worries, harassments, and disappointments.' He was three thousand dollars in debt, one of his greatest liabilities being that people liked and trusted him and consequently gave him too much credit; he was unable to earn enough to support his growing list of dependents; he was dissatisfied both with the rate of progress he was making in his work and with the speed at which he was becoming known. Yet the greater part of his distress was caused by his recurrent bouts of despondency, the cyclical nature of which had manifested itself early in his youth. 'I dined yesterday on canvasback and terrapin, with champagne and all manner of wonderful drinks I had never tasted before warming my heart and brain, and I remembered the sordid orgies of my youth. [In most vigorous moods he recalled these orgies as romantic adventures.] We were ill-clad, ill-mannered beasts, and the drink was cheap and poor and nauseating. And then I dreamed dreams, and pulled myself up out of the slime to canvasback and terrapin and champagne, and learned that it was solely a difference of degree which art introduced into the fermenting.'

Disillusioned words, sick words, but only momentarily meant, the relapse-mood of the rampant individualist who spends most of his energy conquering the world. Caught in the grip of his dejection he wrote, 'What is this chemical ferment called life all about? Small wonder that small men down the ages have conjured gods in answer. A little god is a snug little possession and explains it all. But how about you and me who have no God? There's damned little satisfaction in being a materialistic monist.'

From a professional viewpoint he had little cause to feel despondent, for on the twenty-seventh of December, George P. Brett, president of the Macmillan Company, one of the most vigorous publishing houses in America, had written to tell him that his stories represented the very best work of the kind that had been done in the country, and expressed a keen desire to publish him in America and England. In reply Jack had sent Brett a group of Alaskan-Indian stories under the title of *Children of the Frost*. Only five days after he had penned his melancholy sentences about this chemical ferment called life, Macmillan accepted *Children of the Frost*, and agreed to his request to advance him two hundred dollars. His weariness disappeared as he wrote to Britt, 'I don't know whether *Children of the Frost* is an advance over previous work, but I do know that there are big books in me, and that when I find myself they will come out.'

In February began Jack's migration to the hills. He found a house in Piedmont on five acres of ground, in a clump of magnificent pines, half the ground in bearing orchard, the other half in golden poppies. There were a large living-room and a dining-room finished in redwood, and in the pines a small cottage for Flora and Johnny Miller. 'We have a most famous porch, broad and long and cool, and our view commands all of San Francisco Bay for a sweep of thirty or forty miles, and all the opposing shores such as Marin County and Mount Tamalpais, to say nothing of the Golden Gate and the Pacific Ocean . . . and all for $35 a month!'

The house was always full of people; rarely were the spare beds unoccupied. Writers on a visit from the East were promptly brought to Jack's house, socialists on lecture tours, actors, musicians, intelligent friends of other friends. Since everyone was welcome and made to feel wanted, Jack's circle grew apace . . . as did his entertainment bills. The *Examiner* continued to give him special assignments such as interviewing Governor Taft when he returned from the Philippines, but Jack groused to Cloudesley Johns: 'Lord, what stacks of hack I'm turning out. I wonder if I'll ever get clear of debt?' When an Oakland grocer wrote him asking for a hundred and thirty-five dollars due, he answered in a fit of temper with a scorching letter in which he upbraided the tradesman for annoying and insulting him, told him to be courteous and wait his turn and he would be paid, that if he attempted to blacklist him or make trouble, he would forfeit his turn among the creditors. The grocer turned the letter over to the newspapers for its advertising value, and the papers played it up with great glee, the picture of a debtor putting a creditor in his place being too delicious to resist. The article was syndicated all over the country, and should have taught Jack not to write tempestuous letters . . . a lesson he was never able to learn.

He was invited to speak before the Women's Press Association of San Francisco, and told them he would lecture on Kipling, who was still thought of by a considerable portion of the American public as a crude and vulgar barbarian. The subject was widely advertised, the combination of Jack London and Rudyard Kipling drawing a large and distinguished audience. When Jack mounted the platform he announced that unfortunately he found he had sent his article on Kipling to an English magazine in the hope of selling it, and since he could not speak without his material, he would give them instead his lecture on 'The Tramp.' The cold waves generated by the rigidly circumspect group of San Francisco women would have frozen anyone less impervious to his audience. However, the women did not remain frigid at the end of the lecture, in which Jack justified the tramp, and blamed his position on society; they attacked him with such vehemence that the chairlady had to bang on the table with her gavel and adjourn the meeting to prevent a free-for-all.—Of course the papers ran the story.

Already known as an odd and colorful character around the Bay, his reputation for eccentricity now became national in scope. A reporter sent to interview him from *The Reader* magazine writes, 'Jack London is one of the most approachable of men, unconventional, responsive, and genuine, with a warmth of hospitality which places the visitor on an immediate footing of a friend. He is boyish, noble, lovable; primitive, free, and unhackneyed.' Jack is reported as saying, 'Any style I have has been acquired by sweat. Light out after it with a club, and if you don't get it you'll get something that looks remarkably like it.' The San Francisco *Chronicle*, which first had begun to publicize him when he was but a month in his mother's womb, gave a full-page spread to the Piedmont Literary Colony, with pictures of Jack and his home in the pines acknowledged to be its center.

In addition to the numerous hack articles he was writing a novel for juveniles called *Cruise of the Dazzler*, a group of adventure stories for *Youth's Companion* under the title of *Tales of the Fish Patrol*, serious Alaskan stories, and *The Kempton-Wace Letters* with Anna Strunsky. *The Kempton-Wace Letters*, a brilliant philosophical analysis of the realist versus the romantic attitudes, continued to be a curious defense by both of their position in their love for each other. Jack, who had married Bessie on what he liked to call the basis of reason, wrote: 'Considered biologically, marriage is an institution necessary for the perpetuation of the species. Romantic love is an artifice, blunderingly and unwittingly introduced by man into the natural order. Without an erotic literature, a history of great loves and lovers, a garland of love songs and ballads, a sheaf of spoken love tales and adventures—without all this man could not possibly love in the way he does.' Anna Strunsky, the poet, insisted that 'the flush of rose-light in the heavens, the touch of a hand, the color and shape of fruit, the tears that come for unnamed sorrows are more significant than all the building and inventing done since the first social compact. You cannot explain the bloom, the charm, the smile of life, that which rains sunshine into our hearts, which tells us we are wise to hope.'

By March they had fifty thousand words written, and Jack was convinced the book would go. In order that their work might be expedited he invited Anna to come and stay in his home. Two years later she was to tell inquiring newspaper reporters: 'I received a letter from Mr. London asking me to come to his house in Piedmont to revise the manuscript. His wife and mother added their requests. During the first days of my stay there Mrs. London was cordial and manifested great interest in our work, but after a stay of five days I became convinced that she had begun to dislike me. [In 1937 Bessie London confided that she had come upon Miss Strunsky sitting on Jack's knee in his study, their heads glued together over the manuscript; no great breach, but upsetting to a woman of Mrs. London's strict sense of the proprieties.]

'She did nothing of any importance to make me feel out of place, but judging from several little occurrences I decided it was best for me to leave. I left very much against Mr. and Mrs. London's will. The farewell between Mrs. London and myself was that of two acquaintances between whom existed a mutual liking. Mr. London and I treated each other as friends, no more. Besides, Mr. London is hardly the man to make love to another woman in his own house. His behavior was most circumspect to me, and always has been. My observation at the time served to convince me that he was blindly in love with his wife.'

That Miss Strunsky, a woman of the highest integrity, was telling the simple truth is confirmed by Jack, who wrote about her, 'It was her intellect that fascinated me, not her womanhood. Primarily she was intellect and genius. I love to seek and delve in human souls, and she was an exhaustless mine to me. Protean, I called her. My term for her of intimacy and endearment was what? a term that was intellectual, that described her mind.'

McClure still owned the rights to *A Daughter of the Snows*. Though he did not like the manuscript well enough to publish it himself, he made every effort to sell it to another house for book publication. At length he was successful, Lippincott's accepting it and paying an advance against royalties of seven hundred and fifty dollars. After McClure deducted what was still owed him, there remained a hundred and sixty-five dollars in cash for Jack. Jack wanted to withdraw the manuscript, but he was powerless to do so; besides, though it was a small sum of money, it enabled him to meet the demands of his more pressing creditors. When galley proof began to arrived for correction he was heart-broken; each batch seemed the worst, until the next batch came, and finally he commented that it was futile to try to doctor a sick thing.

On July 21 he received a telegraphic offer from the American Press to go to South Africa to report the Boer War. He was still three thousand dollars in debt; Bessie was pregnant again, and that would mean more expense; and it was the call of Adventure. He accepted by telegraph within the hour, packed his bag that night, and the following morning kissed Bessie and his daughter good-bye at the Oakland mole—where eight years before, when pursuing Kelly's Industrial Army, he had crawled into an empty freight car. On the train bound for Chicago he encountered a woman whose accidental presence served to accelerate the developments of his own life plot. 'Let me tell you a little affair which will indicate the ease with which I let loose the sexual man. You remember when I started for South Africa. In my car was traveling a woman with a maid and a child. We came together on the jump, at the very start, and had each other clear to Chicago. It was sexual passion, clear and simple. Beyond being a sweet woman, she had no charm for me. There was no glamour of the mind, not even an overwhelming intoxication of the senses. Nothing remained when our three days and nights were over.'

Nothing but the memory of pleasure; for he had always enjoyed women for their entertainment value. He had no horoscope to which he might point and cry, 'Alas! It is my fate,' as had Professor Chaney, even though he had inherited in full measure his father's predatory instincts. 'The flesh, in my cosmos, is a little thing. It is the soul that is everything. I love the flesh as the Greeks loved it, and yet it is a form of love that is almost, if not quite, artistic in nature.' A little later his men friends were to call him, with pride, the Stallion.

Despite the fact that he writes, 'I easily went the limit in those days,' this affair on the train seems to have been the first time he let himself go in the two years of his marriage. Nor was it until he returned from England that his 'little affair which will indicate the ease with which I let loose the sexual man' developed its full psychological consequences.

Once again he arrived in New York in the full heat of summer. This time he did not 'batter the main stem for light pieces' with which to buy glasses of iced milk and imperfect copies of new books to read while lolling in the grass of City Hall Park; instead he went straight to the Macmillan Company, where for the first time he was able to clasp hands with a publisher. George P. Brett was an astute editor, a liberal and honest man with a deep love for literature; he was in addition a staunch friend who was to be Jack's guardian angel through many stormy years, and a lifelong Jack London admirer. Jack had a boat to catch and there was little time for negotiating, but the two men agreed that when Jack returned from South Africa they would enter into a permanent relationship under which Macmillan would publish all the books Jack wrote. Jack told Brett about *The Kempton-Wace Letters*, which he accepted at once for publication.

When he reached England, where he was supposed to interview British generals for their views on the future in the Transvaal before sailing for South Africa, Jack found a cable canceling the engagement. His round-trip transportation had been paid, and a small amount of advance money which he had already spent. Here he was in London, seven thousand miles from home, without resources, and without a job to do.

Always a man of swift adaptability, he decided to go into the East End of London, which his extensive reading in sociology had taught him was one of the worst hell holes for humanity in the western world, and investigate conditions. It did not occur to him that this was a daring and difficult task, that it took almost foolhardy courage for an utter stranger, an American who had been on English soil only forty-eight hours, to attempt to understand, analyze, and then confound a nation with one of its major economic problems. His first volume of short stories had already been released in England, and had received, from a usually conservative press, surprisingly good notices. His publishers were friendly; he could have spent an amusing few weeks among the English literati, enjoyed a vacation. Instead he found a second-hand store on Petticoat Lane, bought a pair of well-worn trousers, a frayed jacket with one remaining button, a pair of brogans which plainly had seen service where coal was shoveled, a thin leather belt, and a very dirty cloth cap, and plunged into the heart of the East End. He rented a room in the most congested district of the slums, then ventured forth to become acquainted. His publishers had been horrified, had told him that it was impossible, that he would be murdered in his sleep. Jack was a son of the people; he laughed at their fears.

He was taken for an American sailor who had been ditched at port. Once again he became Sailor Jack, slipping into the rôle as easily as though he had never left it. He was no outsider, no research man looking down from academic heights; he was one of them, a seafaring man down on his luck. The people of the East End accepted him, trusted him, and talked to him. What he learned about this human shambles he put into a book called *The People of the Abyss,* which is fresh and vigorous and true today, one of the world's classics about the underprivileged.

I took with me certain simple criteria with which to measure. That which made for more life, for physical and spiritual health, was good; that which made for less life, which hurt, dwarfed, and distorted life, was bad.' From the basis of these 'simple criteria' he found that life in the Abyss, where lives one tenth of London's population, was a prolonged, chronic starvation, families of father, mother, and children working long hours and every day, and earning enough to afford only one room in which the entire family had to cook, eat, sleep, and discharge all the duties of intimate living. He found disease, despair, and death the inseparable companions of the People of the Abyss, saw homeless men and women, guilty of no crime but ill health and poverty, pushed about and maltreated as though they were loathsome animals. That some of these people were congenital loafers and wastrels, he soon found out, but just as from his experiences on The Road in America, he discovered that ninety per cent of the East-Enders had been conscientious workingmen until old age, sickness, or business slack had thrown them out of their jobs. Now, unemployed, or at best making sweat-shop products in their rooms, they and their families were left by the City of London to rot away until providential death cleaned them off the streets.

'The London Abyss is a vast shambles; no more dreary spectacle can be found. The color of life is gray and drab, everything is hopeless, unrelieved, and dirty. Bathtubs are a thing totally unknown; any attempts at cleanliness become howling farce. Strange, vagrant odors come drifting along the greasy wind; the Abyss exudes a stupefying atmosphere of torpor which wraps about the people and deadens them. Year by year rural England pours in a flood of vigorous young life that perishes by the third generation. At all times four hundred and fifty thousand human creatures are dying miserably at the bottom of the social pit called London.'

On the coronation day of Edward VII Jack walked up to Trafalgar Square to watch the majestic medieval pageant. For company on his walk he had a carter, a carpenter, and a sailor, old now and out of work. He saw that from the slimy sidewalk they were picking up bits of orange peel, apple skin, and grape stems and eating them; stray crumbs of bread the size of peas, apple cores black and dirty, these things the men took into their mouths and chewed and swallowed. 'It has been urged that the criticism I have passed on things as they are in England is too pessimistic. I must say in extenuation that of optimists I am the most optimistic. I measure manhood less by political aggregations than by individuals. For the English I see a broad and smiling future, but for a great deal of the political machinery, which at present mismanages them, I see nothing less than the scrap heap.'

He rented a room in the home of a London detective which he could use as a place of refuge to bathe, change his clothes, do his reading, and write his book without becoming suspect. In the course of three months he studied hundreds of pamphlets, books, and government reports on poverty in London, interviewed countless men and women, took pictures, trampled miles of streets, lived in workhouses, paupers' homes, stood in bread lines, slept in the streets and parks with his newly made friends, and in addition wrote a complete book—a triumph of energy, organization, and burning passion for his subject.

He arrived in New York in November with the manuscript of *The People of the Abyss* in his suitcase. He hoped that Macmillan would publish it, but he well knew that he could not make money from his sociology. The man who had told Anna Strunsky he was going to extract every last dollar from his writing, who had written to Cloudesley Johns that the magazines could buy him body and soul if they paid the price, here gave the lie to himself. He was a writer first, a socialist second; the man who wanted to earn money ran a very poor third.

A friend who met him at the dock writes, 'He wore a wrinkled sack coat, the pockets of which bulged with papers and letters. His trousers bagged at the knees. He was a minus a vest, and his outing shirt was far from immaculate. A leather belt around his waist took the place of suspenders. On his head he wore a dinky little cap.' George P. Brett, however, had eyes only for Jack's manuscript. He thought *The People of the Abyss* a penetrating job, made some trenchant sociological criticisms, and accepted it at once. Jack told him, 'I want to get away from the Klondike. I have served my apprenticeship at writing in that field, and I feel that I am better fitted now to attempt a larger and more generally interesting field. I have half a dozen books, fiction all, that I want to write. I have done a great deal of thinking and studying in the last two years, since I wrote my first novel, and I am confident that I can today write something worth while.'

Brett was equally confident, and acceded to Jack's plea that Macmillan pay him a hundred and fifty dollars a month for two years. In return they were to publish all the books he wrote during that period. In parting Brett gave him what was perhaps the best single piece of advice he was ever to receive. 'I hope that your work from this time on will show the marks of advancement which I found so strong in your earlier books, but which is not so marked in the last volume or so, these showing signs of haste. There is no real place in the world of literature for anything but the best a man can do.' To which Jack replied, 'My hope, once I am on my feet, is not to write prolifically, but to turn out one book, a good book a year. Even as it is, I am not a prolific writer. I write very slowly. The reason I have turned out so much is that I have worked constantly, day in and day out, without taking a rest. Once I am in a position where I do not have to depend upon each day's work to keep the pot boiling for the next day, where I do not have to dissipate my energy on all kinds of hack, where I can slowly and deliberately ponder and shape the best that is in me, then, at that time, I am confident that I shall do big work.'

On the train headed west Jack spread opposite him on the Pullman seat his three books that had been published in October, just a few weeks before he returned to New York: *A Daughter of the Snows, The Cruise of the Dazzler,* and *Children of the Frost.* He realized that the publication of three books by one man in a single month was not only a record, but also a foolhardy piece of business, the one for which Brett had chided him. He resolved that now that he had 'settled down with one publishing house' he would manage his affairs better. Along with the books, he spread out clippings from the newspapers to see how his work had fared. About *A Daughter of the Snows,* which had been put out by Lippincott, the press made many incisive criticisms, accused him of making Frona Welse unbelievable, and of not handling his construction problems; but for the rest the critics were tolerant, spoke enthusiastically of his strong, graphic style, and predicted that he would do better with his second novel. Jack, who had anticipated a lashing, blew a sigh of relief. *The Cruise of the Dazzler*, which was released by the Century Company, received only the mild reception that he could expect from a novel for juveniles. The most important of his three books, *Children of the Frost*, the Alaskan-Indian stories that were Macmillan's first publication, established him as the dominant figure in the American short story.

Sitting back in his seat pleasedly musing over the past few crowded years as the landscape flashed by unseen, he mingled his memories of his determination to recreate the American short story with the lines of praise the critics had lavished on *Children of the Frost*: '. . . has few superiors as a story-teller . . . a domain which is his by right of conquest . . . marvelous literary development, will last . . . will win fame both wide and permanent.' Though he was happy and proud of himself he realized that he had gained merely the bottom rung of the ladder, that the fight had only begun. Mulling over his ideas and plans, he vowed to do for the American novel what he had already done for the short story. Since Herman Melville there had been no great sea novels in American literature; he would write great sea novels. There were as yet no great proletarian novels in American literature; he would not only write great proletarian novels and make the critics and public like them, but he would also hasten the socialist revolution. He had his work cut out for him; it would take a full twenty years to accomplish everything he had in mind. He determined to fulfill every demand of his program before his time on earth was up.

When Jack reached Piedmont he found that Eliza had been living with Bessie for some six weeks, keeping peace and quiet between Bessie and Flora. His reunion with his family was a joyous one; on November 21, 1902, in writing to Brett a brief survey of his life, Jack said: 'Finding myself anchored with a household, I resolved to have the compensations of a household, so I married and increased the weight of my anchor. But I have never regretted it. I have been well compensated.'

More than ever he found that he had become a busy litera-tor, for not only had he his new work to write, but proofs to read on *The Kempton-Wace Letters*, and corrections and additions to make to the manuscript of *The People of the Abyss*. He so relished being immersed in the welter of books and stories and publications that he went back to his schedule of nineteen hours a day of work, with five hours of sleep.

The only time spent in relaxation was during his Wednesday open house, when his old friends gathered and new friends came into the fold, when he played poker and practical jokes, and initiated his cronies into the intricacies of the English puzzles he had packed into his lone suitcase.

When Bessie came out of her travail she found that she had once again presented her husband with a daughter. Jack's hand was not cut this time; what was cut was the lifeline of hope that he would have a son to whom he could hand down not only his name but his literary tradition. He made himself miserable and ill with frustration; his disappointment made Bessie ill, too.

After wandering about disconsolate for a number of days, a fresh idea shook him out of his lethargy. It was a dog story, which he intended to do in four thousand words, a companion-piece to another dog story he had written the year before. At the end of four days he had written his four thousand words and discovered to his surprise that he had barely begun, that the story was taking on motivation and scope of which he had never dreamed. He decided that he would name it *The Call of the Wild,* and let it grow however it willed, for the story was master now and he the servant writing it; it had taken hold of his imagination and fired him as no other yarn he had ever tackled. For thirty glorious, labor-laden days he wrote with his thick pencil on the rough scratch paper, made his few word corrections, and transferred the material to the typewriter. He neglected everything else—friends, family, debts, the new baby, galley proof arriving in daily batches from Macmillan; living only with his dog Buck, half Saint Bernard and half Scotch shepherd, who had been a country gentleman on a ranch in the Santa Clara Valley until he was kidnapped and shipped into the primitive wilds of the Klondike.

Then at a Wednesday open house Jack made good his neglect of his friends. He settled himself in the comfortable lounging chair by the fire while his guests placed themselves in the window seats and on cushions on the floor. With a grave look in his gray-blue eyes, one hand combing fondly through his hair, he read to them the story of the great dog Buck, who remained faithful to his love of man until the call of the forest and the recollection of wild wolves drew him back to primitive life. There were no card games that night, no wild laughter or practical jokes. Jack read until one in the morning, the silence growing ever deeper about him. When he had finished, his usually loquacious friends could say little, but he saw their thoughts in their shining eyes. His three years of writing Alaskan tales had been at last justified; he had expressed himself in an art form so flawlessly and completely that for these few hours his listeners shared with him the ecstasy he had known in its creation.

The following morning he put the manuscript into an envelope, stamped it, enclosed another stamped envelope to bring it back to him, and sent his story to the *Saturday Evening Post*, the most popular and highest paying magazine in the world. He knew no one on the staff; they had never been hospitable to his work, and he had little expectation of selling them the story. But the 'cunning arrangement of cogs that changed a manuscript from one envelope to another,' against which he had inveighed so strongly four years before when he had been a novice, failed to function. The *Saturday Evening Post* did not use the stamped return envelope with which he had provided them. Instead they sent him a flat, oblong one, in which he found a glowing letter of acceptance, and a check for two thousand dollars.

Two thousand dollars for a month's work! He had always said that serious literature could pay dividends. He had always said he would write his own way, and make the editors like it. Two thousand dollars . . . enough to pay the doctor bills for his second daughter, Bess, the accumulated doctor bills for Flora and for the mother of Johnny Miller, to pay his hundreds of dollars in debts to insurance companies, department stores, grocers, butchers, druggists, clothing, typewriter, and stationery stores, to help all his friends who needed assistance . . . enough to buy those new glass bookcases he wanted, and to order that list of forty books from the East. Not since he had sold 'An Odyssey of the North' had he known such an overflowing measure of exultation. Had he not justified everything he stood for? Had he not, within sixty days of his heroic resolution on the train from New York, begun his revitalization of the American novel? When those friends who had listened to the reading of *The Call of the Wild* thronged back into the house to congratulate him, to wring his hand and slap him on the back, had he not to send down for another gallon of sour Italian wine and get tipsy dreaming more roseate dreams for the future?

Now that things were better for him he engaged a second servant to help Bessie, who was having a difficult time recovering her strength, and entertained more widely. Into his house came many attractive women; after his successful siege of work Jack began to avail himself of them. There perhaps had been an insufficient sexual compulsion in his marriage, but even if that were not so, there was the burden of Bessie having been pregnant for eighteen and recovering from her deliveries for at least another six of the thirty-two months of their marriage. A man of vigorous appetites, accustomed to sexual satisfaction since the days of Mamie on the *Razzle Dazzle,* this had worked a hardship on him; his three days and nights with the woman on the train to Chicago remained strong in his memory. Less than three years after he had written, 'My heart is large, and I shall be a cleaner, wholesomer man because of a restraint being laid upon me in place of being free to drift wheresoever I listed,' he renounced all obligations to abstinence.

'You know my sexual code,' he later wrote, 'you know the circumstances of the period, you know I had no compunction of dallying along the primrose path.' Dally he did, to the fullest extent of his opportunities, yet for him, outside of his marriage, there was no emotion tied up with the sexual act; it was a purely sensory experience, giving pleasure to both parties and hence, since he was a hedonist, a deed of virtue in direct proportion to the harmless pleasure incurred. 'Though I have roved and ranged and looted, I have never looted under false pretense. Never once have I said, "I love you" for the gain it might often have brought me. I have been fair, and fastidiously so, in my dealings with women, demanding no more than I was willing to give. I bought, or took in fair exchange, and I never lied to get the best of a bargain or to get the bargain that was otherwise beyond me.' And, in an effort to justify himself: 'Man can pursue his lusts, without love, simply because he is so made. Mother Nature cries compellingly through him for progeny, and so man obeys her urging, not because he is a wilful sinner, but because he is a creature of law.'

Jack had not mentioned *The Call of the Wild* in the list of books he outlined to Macmillan because he had not known he was going to write it. He sent the manuscript to Brett, who replied on March 5, saying that he did not like the title. 'I like the story very well indeed, although I am afraid it is too true to nature and too good work to be really popular with the sentimentalist public which swallows Seton-Thompson with delight.' Brett then made him an offer of two thousand dollars for immediate publication on an outright sale basis, instead of contracting for it on a royalty basis and postponing publication for a year or two. 'I would like to try an experiment in relation to this book, putting it out in a very attractive typographic form and spending a very large sum of money in endeavoring to give it a wide circulation and thus assist the sale of not only your already published books, but of those still to come. But don't let me overpersuade you in the matter. The decision is entirely in your hands and if you decide not to accept the cash offer we will publish the book in due course under the terms of our agreement.'

He had already spent the two thousand dollars from the *Saturday Evening Post;* the Macmillan hundred and fifty dollars a month was inadequate to support his family of six, two servants, and Mammy Jenny. No book of his had ever earned one thousand dollars in royalties, let alone two thousand dollars, and there was no reason to believe this one would be an exception. Even if the book were to earn two thousand dollars, he would have to wait at least two years for his royalties, and then the money might well have been absorbed by his advance hundred and fifty dollars a month. This was two thousand dollars clear, right now, and money in the hand was money that could be spent . . . particularly for that trim little boat called the *Spray* he had his eye on. He accepted Brett's proposition and sold out all interest in *The Call of the Wild.*

The *Spray* was a sailing sloop with a good-sized cabin in which he could cook and sleep two persons. He bought her not only because he longed once again to live upon the water, but because he had been contemplating a sea novel, and he wanted the feel of a ship under him before he began writing. It was nine years since he had come off the *Sophie Sutherland;* his gear had gone rusty. 'It will be almost literally a narrative of things that happened on a seven months' voyage I once made as a sailor. The oftener I have thought upon the things that happened during that trip, the more remarkable they appear to me.' Brett replied, 'I feel very great hopes for your sea story. So few sea stories are appearing, and none of these good for anything, that a really good sea story at the present time would without question achieve a very remarkable success.'

With Brett's encouraging words ringing his ears, he provisioned the *Spray* with food and blankets and went for a week's sail on the Bay, retracing the trips he had made up the sloughs and straits when he had been a daring oyster pirate and member of the Fish Patrol. At the end of a week, with the sea salt in his nostrils and the feel of sail-ropes in his calloused hands, he returned home, sat down at his desk and wrote *The Sea Wolf,* Chapter One. Whenever the interruptions proved too great, the friends about him too many, he put food on board the *Spray* and pushed off by himself, writing his fifteen hundred words each morning as he sat on the hatch and let the early spring sun warm his body to the pitch that his thoughts about the Sea Wolf were warming his brain. Later in the day he went sailing, shot ducks on the Sacramento River, fished for his supper. On Saturday afternoons and Sundays he sometimes took Bessie and his two daughters, Eliza and her son, and a crowd of his friends for a sail.

It was a busy and exhilarated period. *Wilshire's,* a socialist magazine, published *The People of the Abyss* serially, which put him in the front rank of American socialists; he wrote 'How I Became a Socialist' for *The Comrade,* and a series of critical articles for the *International Socialist Review. Wilshire's* paid him a modest sum for *The People of the Abyss,* but for the socialist newspapers he wrote always without pay. He also composed two new lectures to give to the socialist locals about the Bay, 'The Class Struggle' and 'The Scab,' both of which were published in the socialist press. Fellow socialists began to write to him from all parts of the country; invariably they began their letter, 'Dear Comrade' and ended it 'Yours for the Revolution.' Jack answered every letter himself, beginning 'Dear Comrade' and ending 'Yours for the Revolution.'

With the spread of his name and fame, Jack's home in Piedmont became an intellectual center of the Bay area. No less than a hundred people a week walked through his front door, enjoyed his hospitality. Even with two servants, and Mammy Jenny to care for the children, there was a great deal of work to be done. Bessie was not always in the mood for more and more company and more and more work; for one Wednesday night open house she is reported as purposely preparing less food than would be necessary to feed the horde of people that would be coming in. Nor was she too pleased at the way the women were flocking about her Jack —Jack of the warm, golden smile and booming laugh—flinging themselves at his head. She grew jealous. Jack wanted Bessie to buy beautiful clothes for the many formal affairs to which he was now invited; Bessie declined to buy them. Eliza shopped with her and showed her how stunning she looked in a long velvet gown and a velvet hat with a plume, but she insisted upon wearing blouses, sailor skirts, and sailor hats, even to such affairs as the dinner at the swank Bohemian Club in San Francisco at which Jack was the guest of honor. Jack felt badly about this; he admired Bessie's figure and wanted to show her off to her best advantage. That she was far from well, and had little desire to be out at all, is part of the explanation; the other part is that Fred Jacobs had probably admired her in blouses and sailor skirts.

In spite of these minor frictions, Jack and Bessie got along well together. The one complaint he voiced to her was that he wished she would read more, so they could discuss the new books. Bessie replied that there was nothing she would like better to do, but that she was awakened at six by the baby, and from that moment until ten at night it was an unending round of routine tasks. Jack patted her hand sympathetically, said yes, he knew, and that when the children grew a little older she would have more time for her reading. Though people attest, thirty-five years later, that they appeared an incongruous couple—Bessie seemed middle-aged and matronly, Jack a vivacious young boy—everyone agrees that they lived together harmoniously. Eliza London Shepard, who saw a great deal of them at the time, often staying in their house, attests to this most strongly. Apparently the only criticism Jack made against his wife in his own mind—as reflected by the notes he kept at the time—is that Bessie was literal-minded, that 'she had a narrow band around her forehead.' In all fairness to his wife he also acknowledged that he had always known this, that the emotional stability it gave her was something he sorely needed, and had attracted him to her in the first place. It is at this very time, March, 1903, that Jack wrote to Cloudesley Johns, who at Jack's wedding had said, 'I will withhold my congratulations until your tenth anniversary': 'By the way, I think your long deferred congratulations upon my marriage are about due. I have been married nearly three years, have a couple of kids, and think it's great. So fire away. Or, come and take a look at us, and at the kids, and then congratulate.'

He swung along vigorously on *The Sea Wolf,* the creating of which was bringing him far greater joy than had even *The Call of the Wild.* In his spare hours he wrote such excellent Alaskan tales as 'The One Thousand Dozen,' 'Gold Hunters of the North,' and a dozen others. In additions to the *Spray* he bought a horse and rig to cart his family and friends around the countryside, for warm weather was coming on and he liked to take a crowd into the hills to picnic and play games, swim in the reservoir, and broil steaks over wood fires. Late in April he was thrown from the buggy and had the tip of one of his thumbs cut off. 'It feels as though it had a heart beating at the end of it,' he complained, but the accident did not prevent him from writing his thousand words a day on *The Sea Wolf,* the main character of which was based on Captain Alex McClean, of whose amazing exploits he had heard while he was on the *Sophie Sutherland.* He continued to sail the *Spray* for relaxation and privacy, once having his

sails cut to ribbons in a surprise storm, and finding it difficult
to make the Estuary.

In June *The Kempton-Wace Letters* was published anony-
mously, receiving a good press. 'Unusual . . . thoughtful,
frank . . . sure to have a wide reading . . . has much of the
enquiring spirit of today . . . good meat for the mind . . . a
new departure in novel writing . . . piquant, clever, original
philosophy.' The San Francisco *Argonaut* recognized one of
the authors by the 'evolutionary deductions,' and the news
spread so rapidly that when Macmillan was printing its second edition it asked Jack's permission to acknowledge the authorship. *The Kempton-Wace Letters* sold only moderately
well, having too little action, plot, and swiftness for the general public, but Jack and Anna Strunsky exchanged letters
between Piedmont and New York, where she was now living,
congratulating each other on an important job well done.

Late in June, desiring to take her two children to the
country for the summer, Bessie rented a cabin in a grove of
cabins which had been put up by Mrs. Ninetta Eames as a
summer resort at Glen Ellen, in Sonoma County in the Valley of the Moon. Jack wanted to continue to sail the *Spray*
and concentrate on *The Sea Wolf*, so he remained in Piedmont. One night toward the end of the month when he was
crossing the hills in his buggy with George Sterling and some
other men friends, the buggy ran off the road and plunged
into a ravine. Jack's leg was badly hurt. Charmian Kittredge
came frequently to nurse him. At the beginning of July, as
soon as he was able to walk, Jack left for Glen Ellen to join
his family. Charmian Kittredge also went to Glen Ellen, to
join her aunt.

The *Overland Monthly* having folded up, Roscoe Eames
and Edward Payne were now out of work. Edward Payne
and Mrs. Eames had built a large rambling house called
Wake Robin on the banks of a stream opposite which Payne,
who was a renegade preacher without a pulpit, had put together picnic tables and log seats to hold revival meetings and
philosophical discussions. In order to make money out of the
project, Mrs. Eames had built the cabins and put up tents,
which she rented out to families.

When Jack reached Glen Ellen he found his family com-
fortably entrenched in a cabin with a canvas top, located in a
grove of wine-colored manzanita and madrone. The campers
lived as a communal group; everyone cooked their meals in a
common kitchen by the river bank, and ate on long picnic
tables. Jack spent a few dollars to dam the clear, cool stream
where it flowed along a sandy beach, and the entire camp

collected to swim and sun itself. Here Jack spent his after-noons playing with the youngsters, teaching them to swim. In the mornings he went to a shaded and secluded spot on the bank of the stream where, on the sawed-off trunk of an oak tree, he scrawled his thousand words a day. And one night toward the end of July the entire camp assembled, even the small children, snugly wrapped in blankets, to hear him read the first half of *The Sea Wolf*. He read the manuscript as it rested on the tree trunk on which he had written it, flanked on either side by candles, the campers and neighbors spread out on the ground at his feet. Dawn was beginning to mottle the sky over Sonoma Mountain when he turned the last page. The people alive today who heard Jack London read *The Sea Wolf* by the bank of that stream in Glen Ellen, in late July, 1903, still remember it as one of the most beautiful and mov-ing experiences of their lives.

And then, within a few hours, came the explosion that shattered the existence of the London family. It would per-haps be best to have Bessie tell the story in her own words.

'One day toward the end of July, after lunch, Jack and I stayed down by the stream and talked. He wanted to get away from Oakland for a time, because there were too many interruptions to his work. He said that he had been thinking about buying a ranch on the Southern California Desert, and asked if I would mind going down there to live. I told him, not at all, as long as there would be modern conveniences for the children. [Bessie was mother first, wife second.] Jack promised, and we made plans to leave in the fall.

'At about two o'clock I took my two babies back to the cabin to put them to sleep. Miss Kittredge had been waiting around, and I saw them walk over to a big hammock at the side of Mrs. Eames's house and begin to talk. I thought noth-ing of it. I put the two children to sleep and worked around the cabin straightening up. Miss Kittredge and Jack sat in that hammock for four solid hours and talked.

'At six o'clock Jack walked up to the cabin and said, "Bes-sie, I am leaving you." Not understanding what he was talk-ing about, I asked, "You mean you're going back to Pied-mont?" "No," replied Jack, "I'm leaving you . . . separating. . . ." Stunned, I sank to the edge of a cot and stared at him for a long time before I could stammer, "Why, Daddy, what do you mean . . . you've just been talking about Southern California. . . ." Jack kept repeating doggedly that he was separating from me, and I kept crying, "But I don't understand . . . what has happened to you?" He refused to tell me another word.'

No one, least of all Bessie, knew that Charmian Kittredge had happened to Jack. Of all the women of whom she might have been jealous, it had never entered her mind to be jealous of Miss Kittredge, who was between five and six years older than Jack, not attractive-looking, the subject of a good deal of biting talk and comment among the Piedmont crowd who knew her well. She had been around Jack a good deal, but Bessie was accustomed to that from the house in Piedmont. Jack apparently had not been seeing more of her than of anyone else at the camp. Besides, he had said a number of uncomplimentary things about her to his wife; Bessie knew that he did not care much for her.

In June, 1903, a month before the separation, Miss Kittredge was writing to Jack, 'Oh, you are wonderful—most wonderful of all. I saw your face grow younger under my touch. What is the matter with the world, and where do I belong? I think nowhere, if a man's heart be nowhere.' In the same month Jack writes to her: 'My arms are about you. I kiss you on the lips, the free frank lips I know and love. Had you been coy and fluttering, giving the lie to what you had already appeared to be by manifesting the slightest prudery or false fastidiousness, I really think I should have been utterly disgusted. "Dear man, dear love!" I lie awake repeating those phrases over and over.'

On July 7 Charmian Kittredge writes to Jack: 'I am growing frightened about one thing. I am afraid that you and I will never be able to express what we are to each other. The whole thing is so tremendous and all human modes of expression too inadequate.' A few days later she typewrites from her business office in San Francisco: 'You are a poet and you are beautiful. Believe me, oh my dear, my dear, that I never was SO GLAD, so genuinely, satisfyingly GLAD over anything in my life. To feel that the man who is the greatest of all to me, has not found me wanting.'

In the canvas-covered cabin at Glen Ellen, with his two children sleeping peacefully, Jack spent what was probably the most wretched and confused night of his life. He was above all a gentle, kindly person. Sensitive himself, knowing the nature of pain, he had shrunk from hurting others. It had always been his great joy to help people, to share with them everything he had. Yet he was caught in the grip of such a shattering compulsion that he was walking out on his wife and babies just as he had walked out on Flora and John London when he was younger and emotionally unstable. A tender human being, a socialist who had compassion for all of humanity, who was willing to give the best in him, without hope of reward, to better the lot of the masses, his social and moral consciousness was shoved aside by the conflicting Nietzschean ideal, the strange but constant bedfellow of his socialism, which told him that he was the superman who could wrest from life whatever he wished, that he had no need to concern himself with slave morality, or the feelings of the slave-mass, of which Bessie was an unfortunate member.

In the morning Jack returned to Piedmont, moved his possessions out of the house he had written about so proudly to his friends, and rented a room from the family of Frank Atherton. Within a few days the newpapers had the story of the separation splashed over the front page. Since Jack refused to talk to the reporters, they blamed his separation on *The Kempton-Wace Letters*, for in it Jack had written, 'The emotion of love is not based on reason.' This sentiment was alleged to have hurt Bessie so deeply that it had caused a break-up of their marriage.

7

JACK'S relationship with Charmian Kittredge started on a high plane of avowal and mounted ever higher. On September 1 she writes to him: 'You are my very OWN, and I adore you, just as blindly and madly and passionately and unreasonably as ever girl loved before.' The next day she continues: 'Ah, my love, you ARE such a man. And I love you, every bit of you, as I have never loved, and shall never love again!' Two days later: 'Oh, you are my dear Love my Own Man, my very, actual, true Heart Husband, and I love you so!' In her next letter she says: 'Think of me tenderly and lovingly and madly; think of me as your dear dear friend, your Sweetheart, your Wife. You are all the world to me, and I shall live on the thought of your face, your voice, your mouth, your masterful and tender arms—all the whole, sweet Man —until we meet again. Oh, Jack, Jack! You're so boofull!'

Not to be outstripped in protestation or literary expression, Jack replies, 'You cannot know how much you mean to me. As you say, it is inexpressible. The moments when first I meet you, and see you, and touch you, are unspeakably thrilling moments. When I receive you letters you are with me, in the flesh before me, and I am looking into your golden eyes. Ah, dear heart, my love for woman did begin with you and will end with you.'

For fear of the scandal that would descend upon them when the cause of his separation became known, the lovers met secretly once or twice a week. During the days when they could not be together they released a torrent of letters to each other. From her business office in San Francisco Miss Kittredge wrote daily letters ranging from one thousand to five thousand words; the many hundreds of pages she composed and typed to Jack during the ensuing two years would be the equivalent of half a dozen normal-sized novels. Her letters are artful and coquettish, fluttery and flowery, but beneath the façade of verbiage can be detected the hand of a shrewd and clever woman. Pictured through her letters their love becomes the greatest love of all times. She tells him that she always knew she was intended for some extraordinary destiny. 'Oh, Jack, dear, dear Love, you are my idol, and you cannot know how I love you,' until he comes to believe that he is loved as no man since the beginning of time has ever been loved, and he answers, convinced, 'I doubt if I can ever love you enough, so greatly do you love me.' The way in which he takes her cues, letter by letter, is almost automatic; since he is the literary one of the relationship, can he write any the less gallantly, avowedly, passionately?

'Nay, nay, dear Love,' he writes, 'not in my eyes is this love of ours a small and impotent thing. That I should be willing to live for you or die for you is proof in itself that it means more to me than life or death. That you should be the one woman to me of all women; that my hunger for you should be greater than any hunger for food I have ever felt; that my desire for you should bite harder than any desire I have ever felt for fame and fortune—all, all goes to show how big is this, our love.'

Under the spell of Miss Kittredge's thousands of words beating daily against his eyes, he begins to sound like a fifth-rate Marie Corelli. Mesmerized by her literary style, he replies in her own florid-purple nineteenth-century effusion, a manner against which he had asserted his revolt since the days of his earliest writing; a style of effervescing about love from which he was never to recover, and which was to mar so many of his books. Jack, who in *The Kempton-Wace Letters* had been the antagonist of sentimental and poetic love, the advocate of the theory that love is just a biological urge, suddenly becomes 'God's own mad lover, dying on a kiss.' If Anna Strunsky could have read over his shoulder and seen how completely he had reversed his position, she might have enjoyed an ironic laugh while confronting him with his own line, 'Without an erotic literature man could not possibly love in the way he does.'

Writing from Stockton on November 10, 1903, he reaches the heights of his profusion. 'Know, sweet love, that I never knew how greatly you loved me until there came the free and utter abandonment, the consent of you and your love and of every fibre of you. When you sealed with your dear body all that your soul had told me, then I knew! I knew!—knew that the last of you and all of you were mine. Had you loved me as you do, and yet withheld, you would not have been quite so great a woman to me. My love and worship of you would not have attained the sheer pitch that they have. If you will go over my letters I am sure you will find that I was never utterly *mad* until after you gave greatly. It was *after* you gave greatly that I became your "slave," expressed willingness to die for you, and all the rest of the delicious hyperbole of love. But it is not hyperbole, dear, not the hyperbole of the silly sentimentalist. When I say I am your slave, I say it as a *reasonable* man—which goes to show how really and completely mad I am.'

In 1890, when she was nineteen years old, Charmian Kittredge was, in her own words, 'a rosy-cheeked girl whom many people call pretty, generally in good spirits except when jealous.' By 1903, at thirty-two, she was not considered pretty; she had thin lips, narrow eyes, and drooping lids, but she carried herself with an air of exciting bravado. In many ways she resembled Frona Welse, whom Jack had created to stand as a model for the twentieth-century woman. Forced by the death of her parents to earn her own living in the days when it was not considered genteel for a girl to work, she had made herself into a competent secretary 'earning the small and insufficient salary of thirty dollars a month.' She was well read, unconventional in thought; when Jack first met her, in 1900, she had already begun to collect a library of the more modern and daring novels the Oakland Public Library was banning. She had a genuine love for music, sang pleasingly, and even while working six days a week had had the force and discipline to train herself to become an accomplished pianist.

She had a sexually rich and stimulating voice with a wide tone range, laughed a great deal, even though the point of humor might be obscure, and was an indefatigable talker, being known to speak from four to seven hours without interrupting herself. She could carry on an intelligent and logical discussion, for she had a varied flow of words and phrases. A woman of great physical courage, she was the first to ride astride a horse into the hills when few women were riding at all, and those who dared were riding English side-saddle on the Golden Gate Park bridle paths. She had a deep love of horses. Ambitious, both socially and intellectually, she worked hard to advance herself, and saved her money with which to take a trip through Europe, did a little painting on China dishes, tried hard to make progress each year over the last.

However, as reflected by her frothy language and frilly lace caps, by her fluttering manner, in anything relating to love and sex she was a perfect blooming of the nineteenth-century woman, the exact opposite of Frona Welse. Many facets of her complex nature are revealed in her diary: her saccharine, sentimentalist approach to romance; every man she meets, no matter how casually, instantly becomes in her mind the source of a great romance. Every man looks at her either admiringly or passionately, and cannot tear his eyes from her. She has little use for her own sex; every woman is jealous of her and she is jealous of every woman. When there were men about she dramatized herself with verve, with gusto, making a conscious bid for the focus of attention. People who knew her disclose that she was no respecter of private property as far as men were concerned. Because of her preoccupation with the snaring of a husband, young women who were keeping company or were married were suspicious and afraid of her.

There is a continuous string of men who come into her life and are soon gone. One is hard-pressed to understand why so attractive a young woman was not able to achieve marriage. Miss Kittredge, too, is stumped. Auntie, who demands immediately if each new man's intention is marriage, is getting nervous as the years pass by and all the other girls marry but her niece somehow always misses out.

Miss Kittredge had been a frequent visitor at the London house in Piedmont on her return from Europe, and in his vagrant mood Jack went on the make. 'I confess what you already know, what you knew from the very first moment. When I first broke silence it was with the intention of making you my mistress. You were so frank, so honest, and not least so unafraid. Had you been less so, in one touch, one pressure, one action, one speech, I think I should have attempted to beat down your will to mine. . . . I remember when we rode side by side on a back seat, and I suggested "Haywards" and you looked me in the eyes, smiling, not mocking, with no offended fastidiousness in your face, no shock, no fear, no surprise, nothing but good nature and sweet frankness—when you looked me thus in the eyes and said simply, "Not tonight." '

Two months after his separation from Bessie, Jack writes, 'Sometimes I wonder why I love you, and I am compelled to confess that it is not for your beautiful body or mind that I love you, but for the flash of spirit that runs through all of you, that makes you carry your clothes, that makes you game, that makes you sensitive; that makes you proud, proud in yourself, proud of your body, and that makes your body in itself and apart from you, proud.'

There can be little doubt but that he had become entangled with Miss Kittredge during the month of June, when he was alone in the house in Piedmont, and that his suggestion to Bessie that they move to Southern California, leaving behind the San Francisco Bay he loved so dearly, was an attempt to escape from the situation in which he found himself. It apparently took Miss Kittredge four hours of solid talk to change his mind.

'If either of his two daughters had been a son,' observed one of Jack's closest friends, 'no force on earth could have torn him away from his family.'

Charmian Kittredge was genuinely convinced that Jack was mismated; she believed she could be the kind of wife he needed, one who would roam and adventure and dare with him, and not be tied down to a home and routine. Abetted by her Aunt Netta, who harbored the lovers from the very beginning, she appears to have been the motivating force behind the break-up of the London family, yet the fact that Jack was vulnerable is evidenced by the completeness with which he gave his mind's love to Anna Strunsky, and his body's love to the woman on the train to Chicago. It is likely that if not for the advent of Miss Kittredge with her particular background, Jack would have remained married to Bessie, using his home for headquarters while he traveled and adventured by himself. There is always the possibility, however, that if Miss Kittredge had not been successful in capturing him, the next woman, or the tenth from the next, might have. . . . As Jack had written so often in his stories, this was a world of dog eat dog, with the wolves devouring those who fell behind; if Bessie were too weak to hold her husband, that was no concern of Miss Kittredge; she had the right to fight for what she wanted and to take all she could get. Where Jack would be hurting three of the people he loved most, two of whom he had caused to be brought into the world, she would be hurting no one she loved.

In order to allay suspicion, Miss Kittredge went frequently to Bessie's house and accepted Bessie's confidences about her marital difficulties. On September 12, 1903, she writes to Jack, 'Last night I went to see Bessie. She was lovely to me —so lovely it made me sick. She begged me to come and stay all night with her, any time. She was so sweet and hospitable that it seemed as if all the trouble and tearing apart might be a dream. Sometimes I have to fight off a feeling of actual WICKEDNESS, when I think of it all, but my reason enters and helps me out; but oh!!!' Five days later she continues: 'I have about given up thinking Bessie really suspects me, though I would not be surprised at ANYTHING she did! She is deep, and I do not understand deceitful people.' Miss Kittredge played her part so adroitly that on October 2 Jack was able to write to her, 'All goes well with Bessie, so far as you and I are concerned. She told me last night she wouldn't know what she would do if it weren't for you. In fact you were exalted above all people.'

Though Bessie was stricken, she was too proud to fight, to cause scenes. Completely in the dark as to her husband's motives, she sat quietly and wondered why the man who had insisted that she marry him, who had insisted that she bear him children, who had accepted her financial help during the first year of their marriage and her assistance on manuscripts, notes, and the assembling of material, who had lived with her in peaceful comradeship for three years, should suddenly, without warning, discard her.

In her troubles she found one friend: Flora London. For three years Bessie and Flora had quarreled, driving Jack to distraction, but Flora had learned the meaning of motherhood through her love for little Johnny Miller; she now turned against her son for abandoning his family. Bitter at what he termed his mother's treachery, Jack's mind fell into chaos. He developed a persecution mania, charging that everyone was against him, that the world was conspiring to keep him from his 'love-woman.' On September 22 from the *Spray* he writes to Miss Kittredge, 'By every human right I should not have ridden off into the dark. You were mine, mine, and the world had no right to drive me away. And yet I was driven, ignobly driven, from the woman I love dearer than life.'

His thoughts became so confused that in spite of the magnificent critical reception of *The Call of the Wild,* which the press agreed was a 'classic enriching American literature,' he could not do a stroke of work. He decided that the only way he would ever finish *The Sea Wolf* was to escape the churning currents about him by slipping his cables. He had the *Spray* overhauled, then sent transportation money to Cloudesley Johns, who lived in Southern California, and knew little of his troubles. The two men headed for the mouth of the Sacramento River; in the mornings they worked at their books, in the afternoons they swam, shot ducks, fished. After his woman-complicated world—though he himself had made the complications—he found the companionship of a man salutary. 'The more I see of Cloudesley, the more I like him. He is honest and loyal, young and fresh, understands the discipline of a boat, and is a good cook, to say nothing of being a good-natured and genial companion.'

Man fashion, he shoved his troubles out of his mind and wrote his thousand words on *The Sea Wolf* every morning. The only trouble he could not successfully ignore was that by Semptember 14 he was again without funds. He wrote to Miss Kittredge, 'Bessie makes out to you that I am almost destitute. I feel pretty close to it, when all I have between me and pauperism is a bare $100, and an unexpected doctor bill comes in for $115.' He put aside the *The Sea Wolf* to write a story for *Youth's Companion*, plotting a whole month of hack work in order that he might get a little ahead.

Every few days he called in at a small town, Stockton, Antioch, Vallejo, for his mail. One day he received a letter from Bessie telling him that Joan was down with typhoid. He raced back to his daughter and was at her beside constantly, in anguish lest the child die. When the doctor reported that she was sinking, Jack felt it was retribution being visited upon him. He vowed that if only the child would get well he would give up his great love and return to his home. The newspapers reported that the Londons had been reconciled at the bedside of their daughter. However, when Joan began to recover, Jack was like a shipwrecked man who fell on his knees on the raft and prayed, 'Dear God, if you will only send me a ship I promise to be good for the rest of my life . . . never mind, God, I see a sail.' When Joan was up and about again, he went back to the *Spray*.

Though the present might be muddled he had done good work in the past and that good work brought its reward. *The Call of the Wild* caught the popular favor, and because of its universal theme was selling to all classes and ages of people. By November it was number three on the best-seller lists, topped only by *The Bar Sinister* and *The Little Shepherd of Kingdom Come*, and leading such favorites as *Mrs. Wiggs of the Cabbage Patch*, *Rebecca of Sunnybrook Farm*, and *Pigs in Clover*. In November *The People of the Abyss* was released to very nearly solid praise, the critics claiming that as a sociological document the book stood unequalled, that if he had never written anything beside *The People of the Abyss*, Jack London would deserve to be famous, and that it would make a smugly complacent civilization sit up and wonder if it had been making the best use of its opportunities. The English press, which might have been expected to consider him an unqualified intruder, accused him of exaggeration and of tackling his subject with an axe, but also admitted that no one had succeeded as he had in getting close to the heart of the London slums.

Jack had sent Brett the first half of *The Sea Wolf*. Brett was so excited by the tale that he sent it to the editor of *Century* magazine with a glowing recommendation. When he heard what Brett had done Jack shook his head in perplexity, for he knew the *Century* to be a staid and conservative family organ. It was unthinkable that it should run the vigorous and bitterly real *Sea Wolf*. The editor of *Century* was thrilled with the manuscript, agreeing that if he were given the right to blue-pencil the latter half, on which Jack was still working, if the man and woman when left alone on the island would do nothing to offend the subscribers, he would pay four thousand dollars for the serial rights.

Four thousand dollars! For the magazine rights alone! As much money as he had received for the total rights to *The Call of the Wild*. He spread full canvas and sailed at top speed down the Bay and through the Estuary to his dock. Immediately on landing he telegraphed the editor of *Century* that he could blue-pencil to his heart's content, that he 'was absolutely confident the American prude would not be shocked by the second half of the book.' The deal was closed and Jack dug in with renewed vitality and concentration, completing the book in thirty feverish days of writing. The *Century* magazine was already blazoning his name to the four winds in advertisements astounding in size and vigor as they told the whole world that Mr. Jack London, author of the popular *The Call of the Wild*, would have his new book, *The Sea Wolf*, published in the pages of *Century*.

Within a few months he was to be the possessor of four thousand dollars in cash. In the meanwhile, just one week before Christmas, he found himself practically penniless. He had exactly $20.02. In the bank, and no Christmas presents bought. 'I wonder if on the strength of the sale of *The Call of the Wild* Brett is going to give me an honorarium for a Christmas present? It would come in handy.' *The Call of the Wild* was having what the publishers term a runaway sale, but Brett did not send him the honorarium. This does not appear to have been stinginess on his part, for he was liberal with his star author over a period of exacting years. Brett felt that Jack had made a bargain and that if he sent him an honorarium he would be breaking the agreement and setting a precedent. If Jack had kept his rights to *The Call of the Wild* the royalties during the next few years would have earned him close to a hundred thousand dollars—assuming that Brett would have invested as much money in promotion under the changed conditions. Jack never regretted his bargain; Brett had spent a fortune in advertising his name, and he knew the worth of advertising to his future career.

By New Year's Day of 1904 it appeared certain that Russia and Japan would go to war. Jack did not want this to happen; as a socialist he was against all war because he knew that in war the working people of the world were shot down to further or protect the moneyed interests. However, if war did begin he wanted to be on the spot to see it. He had studied military tactics and equipment for destruction, was interested to observe what modern warfare could do to destroy civilization. He also had a lot of theories about the Yellow Peril to investigate. In addition he felt that if he made his reputation as a war correspondent he would always be able to earn money. It was Adventure Road once again, offering an escape from his marital and love complications.

Magazines and newspapers began sending their correspondents to Japan. Jack received offers from five syndicates, and accepted the one that bid the most money, the Hearst chain. In the first week of January he went to the offices of the *Examiner* and had his picture taken on the roof of the building. Wearing a workingman's dark suit and high shoes and needing a haircut, he looked as though he had just come off a shift at the Belmont Steam Laundry. The pictures reveal the stress and anxiety of the six months since he had separated from Bessie in their cabin at Glen Ellen; the look of boyishness has been dissipated, he appears troubled and harassed.

He ordered Macmillan to send his monthly check to Bessie, asked Eliza to give Miss Kittredge anything she might need, the first intimation Eliza had had of what was going on, then commissioned George Sterling to edit *The Sea Wolf* before Macmillan sent it to press. On the seventh of January, 1904, five days before his twenty-eighth birthday, he crossed on the ferry to the Embarcadero and sailed on the *S.S. Siberia* for Yokohama.

On board the *Siberia* was a jolly group of newspapermen, which promptly named itself the Vultures. On the first day out from Honolulu, while playing jumping games on deck, Jack landed on a round stick and sprained his left ankle. His right ankle being weak from a spill off an express train when a Tramp Royal, this accident crippled him. 'For sixty-five sweaty hours I lay on my back. Yesterday I was carried on deck on the back of an English correspondent.' He had little time to brood over his ill fate, for the Vultures thronged his cabin, regaling him with yarns of other wars and other assignments.

When he docked at Yokohama he had a drink at each of the bars where as a boy of seventeen he had drunk shoulder to shoulder with Big Victor and Axel when they had been the Three Sports of the *Sophie Sutherland*. Then he took the train for Tokio, where he found correspondents assembled from all over the world, awaiting permission from the Japanese Government to go into the field. Because war had not been formally declared the Japanese officials were evading the requests, providing the correspondents instead with sightseeing trips, sumptuous banquets, diverting entertainment.

Jack had not come to Japan to attend banquets. After two days of encountering exquisitely polite evasions he did a little sagacious interviewing and learned what the other correspondents did not yet suspect, that the Japanese Government had no intention of allowing the newspapermen anywhere near the firing line. He realized that if he wanted to report the war he would simply have to go out and find it. Without breathing a word to any of the Vultures he slipped out of Tokio on a train for Kobe and Nagasaki, where he hoped to catch a boat for Chemulpo in Korea, where the Japanese forces were being rushed to the front.

After a few days of hunting up and down the coast he found a vessel going to Chemulpo on February 1. He bought his ticket, thinking of how he would be with the Army in Korea while the other correspondents were still being fed sumptuous dinners in Tokio. To fill his spare hours he went into the streets to take photographs of coolies loading coal and bales of cotton. Within a few moments he saw the inside of the first of a string of Korean jails and Japanese military prisons that must have made him long for the comparative security of the hall man's job at the Erie County Penitentiary: for the Japanese officials had arrested him as a Russian spy! He was put through eight hours of grilling, moved the next day to a larger jail for more questioning, and finally released . . . too late to catch his boat.

Learning that soldiers were being called from their homes in the middle of the night, he frantically searched the coastline for another ship bound for Chemulpo. Finally on the eighth of February he secured passage on the *Kieogo Maru*, but the Government confiscated the vessel just before it was to sail. Outraged at the thought that he might not be at the front to report the first battle, he made a wild dash in a steam launch for a small steamer going to Fusan, a port en route to Chemulpo, catching it amid such confusion that one of his trunks was lost overboard. It was a native ship, with not a bite of white man's food aboard; in spite of the fact that it was alternately snowing and sleeting, he had to sleep on the open deck, reminding him of the nights he had lain shivering in the railroad jungles without a blanket.

At Fusan he made connections with a second boat, but when they reached Mokpo the Government seized the vessel and unceremoniously dumped passengers and baggage ashore. The speed with which the Japanese were shipping soldiers to Korea convinced him that war was about to be declared, yet here he was, several hundred miles from Chemulpo, and no ship to be had. He was being paid to write up the war, and by God! he was going to write it. But how was he going to get to it? The voice of Marshall Wellman, his maternal grandfather who had built a raft at Put-In Bay and floated it back to Cleveland, told him in clear and unmistakable terms. Charter an open native junk and sail it across the Yellow Sea, then along the Korean coast until he reached Chemulpo!

The thermometer read fourteen degrees below zero, but he had endured sixty below in the Klondike; the wind was howling over the Yellow Sea, but not any worse than it had howled over Lake Linderman; it was a magnificently courageous, foolhardy thing for him to try, but no more foolhardy or courageous than for the twelve-year-old lad to have sailed a leaky catboat across treacherous San Francisco Bay in a lashing southwester. That his journey would be as difficult and dangerous as that made by the Vikings who crossed the Atlantic in an open boat only made it the more appealing. He purchased what he considered a seaworthy junk, engaged three intrepid Koreans to help him man it, and set sail for Chemulpo.

'The wildest and most gorgeous thing ever! If you could see me just now, a captain of a junk with a crew of three Koreans who speak no English. Made Kun San at nightfall, after having carried away a mast and smashed the rudder. We arrived in the driving rain, with the wind cutting like a knife. You should have seen me being made comfortable—five Japanese maidens helping me undress, take a bath, and get into bed, passing remarks about my beautiful white skin.'

For the next six days and nights he was out in freezing weather, the tiny boat tossed by a fierce gale, in danger every moment of going under. There was no heat except from a charcoal burner, the fumes of which poisoned him even worse than the cold native food upon which he had to subsist. Both ankles being weak, he sailed the junk in a crippled state. His condition when he reached Chemulpo is described by an English photographer who had arrived there on the last boat to clear.

'When London arrived at Chemulpo I did not recognize him. He was a physical wreck. His ears were frozen, his fingers were frozen, his feet were frozen. He said he didn't mind his condition so long as he got to the front. I want to say that Jack London is one of the grittiest men it has every been my good forture to meet. He is just as heroic as any of the characters in his novels.'

Jack bought several horses, learned to ride, engaged servants and a *mapu*, or horse-boy, and started north across Korea in the direction of the Russian troops. The roads were covered with mud and ice, and by nightfall each day they had to beat the Japanese soldiers to the next village in order to find a place to sleep.

After several weeks of forced march during which he endured incredible hardship, he finally got to Ping Yang, the farthest point north to be reached by any war correspondent. Here he was held in jail for a week on a complaint lodged with the Japanese Government by the correspondents who were still being entertained in Tokio, and whose papers were sending sizzling cables demanding to know why Jack London could send dispatches out of Korea when they couldn't. Ordered back to Seoul, two hundred miles behind the front, he was thrown into a military prison on orders from Tokio because he had no permit to accompany the Army.

The Japanese Government then decided to make a friendly gesture to the other nations. 'Fourteen of us correspondents, who had refused to remain pickled in Tokio, were allowed to travel with the Army, but it was like a party of Cook's tourists with the supervising officers as guides. We saw what we were permitted to see, and the chief duty of the officers looking after us was to keep us from seeing anything. We did see part of the battle of the Yalu from the walls of Wiju, but when one Japanese company was annihilated, we were ordered back to camp.'

With the arrival of spring weather the correspondents were permitted to cross the Yalu River; in a grove beside a temple the Army built each of them a magnificent little camp. Jack swam, played bridge and other games, but his movements were limited to a radius of a mile and a half . . . while the Japanese were out bombarding the Russian entrenchments.

It was difficult to work when held captive forty miles behind the line of action, yet he did his best. He made a careful estimate of the Japanese Army: 'The Japanese soldiery and equipment command universal admiration.' He wrote analyses of the military tactics and maneuvers of both armies. He took photographs, utilizing the training Bessie had given him with a camera, of the Army on the march, digging trenches, making camp, caring for its wounded, the first war pictures to reach America. Though he sent out nineteen dispatches and hundreds of photographs, he had to wait until he got back to San Francisco to learn if the *Examiner* had received them. 'I am disgusted!" he cried. 'I'll never go to a war between Orientals again. The vexation and delay are too great. Never were correspondents treated in any war as they have been in this.' By June he was ready to go home, for he knew that he was wasting his time. 'I am profoundly irritated by the futility of my position in this Army and sheer inability to do any decent work. The only compensation for these months of irritation is a better comprehension of Asiatic geography and character.'

A threat of court martial gave impetus to his desire to leave. One day his *mapu,* reporting to Army headquarters for feed for his master's horses, was prevented from getting his full share by a Korean whom Jack had long suspected of robbing him. When Jack accused the Korean of this, the man made a threatening gesture with his knife. Jack knocked him down with a blow of his fist. He was promptly commanded to report to General Fuji, who threatened drastic punishment. When news reached Richard Harding Davis, splendidly marooned in Tokio, that Jack London was in danger of being executed, he burned the cables to President Roosevelt, who in turn sent angry protestations to Japan. General Fuji was ordered to release him. Jack packed his kit and made his way back to Tokio, where he found the correspondents he had left behind four months before, still awaiting official permission to join the Army. Davis rode with him to Yokohama to see him off, swearing that as soon as he heard a shot fired he was returning home, but after having waited all these months he couldn't leave without hearing that one shot!

'Only in another war, with a white man's army,' mourned Jack, 'may I hope to redeem myself.' He need not have felt badly; he had gotten out more dispatches than any other correspondent, had given his paper several scoops, especially with the war photographs, and they were well enough pleased with his work. Not the least important aspect of his Oriental junket was that the newspaper chain had given his stories flaming headlines. What with the success of *The Call of the Wild,* and the spectacular advertising *Century* had given *The Sea Wolf,* by the time he reached San Francisco the name of Jack London was becoming more widely known than that of any other American writer.

He confidently expected that when his ship tied up at the

Embarcadero he would be greeted by Miss Kittredge's out-stretched arms; instead he was greeted by the outstretched hand of a process server with a copy of Bessie's divorce complaint. Bessie had put an attachment on the earnings still due him as war correspondent for the *Examiner*. He flinched under the blow, but what stunned and made him heartsick as he read further in the complaint was that Bessie had named Anna Strunsky as the cause of her marital troubles!

Jack had been eager for Bessie to begin her divorce proceedings, but to involve Anna in a scandal, Anna whom he had not seen for two years . . . ! When he was able to blink the mist out of his eyes he saw to his relief that Bessie had not accused Anna of wrongdoing; she had merely charged that their collaboration over *The Kempton-Wace Letters* had caused her husband to become cold and indifferent to her.

There was no sign of Miss Kittredge anywhere on the dock. When Eliza, who had come down to greet him, handed him his mail, he found a letter from Newton, Iowa, where she was staying with an aunt. He read, 'I fear you will be disappointed that I am not in California. The terror of all my dear ones, the scandal, makes me sicker every time I think of the possible happenings during the next few months. I am not writing coldly, dear; indeed there never was a moment since we loved each other that I was madder for you than right now, but I am forced for the sake of others, as well as my own, to be level-headed.'

Jack was hurt, angry, disgusted. When he went up to Piedmont to greet Bessie and to hold his two daughters in his arms, the thought came to him, 'If I was brave enough to sail the Yellow Sea in a sub-zero gale, in an open junk, then why am I not brave enough to stand by my wife and obligations even though I have fallen in love with another woman?'

The next morning the news flashed across the continent that Jack London's wife was divorcing him, and named Anna Strunsky. The San Francisco papers announced it in bold streamers; from that moment forward Jack found that he would live the smallest and most intimate details of his life on the front page of the newspapers. Cornered by reporters he cried, 'The only feature of the case that stirs me up is that Miss Strunsky's name should be mentioned for she is an extremely sensitive person.' Miss Strunsky told the newspapermen: 'I am astonished. I have seen Mr. London only twice in the past two years, for I have been in New York and Europe. My visit to the London house occurred two years ago, and at that time there was not a breath of rumor to the effect that their married life was not a happy one.' Asked in 1937 why she had named Miss Strunsky, Bessie said that she regretted her mistake. 'I knew that Jack would never have left me except for another woman, and I couldn't think who it might be, except Anna Strunsky.'

It took Jack but a short time to convince Bessie that Anna Strunsky had nothing to do with their separation; once convinced, she withdrew Anna's name from the case. He then pointed out that if she stuck to her lawyer's advice to keep an attachment on his earnings, the lawyers would get most of the money and there would be little left for the children. Quite gray now, saddened, bitterly wounded, Bessie asked if he would build her a house in Piedmont so that she would always have a secure roof over her children's head. When he agreed, she withdrew the attachment, amended the suit to simple desertion. Jack wrote to Miss Kittredge, 'It has taken all the resolution I could summon to prevent my going back, for the children's sake. I have been sadly shaken during the last forty-eight hours—so shaken that it almost seemed easier to sacrifice myself for the little ones.'

Instead he told Bessie that Charmian Kittredge was the other woman. Bessie received the news in stony silence, her only comment being that she never cared to see Miss Kittredge again.

In July he went up to Glen Ellen, rented a cottage from Ninetta Eames, and waited for Miss Kittredge to come back to him. When she wrote that she needed money for transportation he sent her a check for eighty dollars. Still she kept writing that she was afraid to come home for fear of the scandal. At length Jack burst out: 'Am hugely disgusted. Somebody is not playing fair. I talked it over with Netta and Edward and both were satisfied that there was nothing to apprehend from Bessie. I wrote a check, which Edward cashed and mailed to you . . .' after which follows ten tumultuous pages of how 'hugely disgusted' he was with Ninetta Eames and Edward Payne, the first of a long series of disgusts that were to extract their toll on his psyche.

The only pleasure he derived from the hot summer weeks was taking the *Spray* for long sails. The boys along the banks of the creeks recognized him and cried out, 'Hello, Jack, how's every little thing in Korea?' When Manyoungi, the loyal and devoted Korean boy who had served him so well, and to whom he had given transportation money, arrived, Jack rented a roomy flat on the corner of Sixteenth Street and Broadway, where he installed Flora as his chaperon. Happy to have her son to herself once again, Flora forgot about her quarrels with Jack when he had left Bessie, and settled down to become a charming hostess, with Manyoungi keeping the house clean and cooking for 'Master.'

Jack entered one of the most unhappy and unproductive periods of his life. He was unhappy about losing his two children; he was unhappy about hurting Bessie and Anna; he was unhappy about Charmian not standing by; he was unhappy about having squandered his time and health in Korea and producing no good work; he was unhappy because his thoughts were dry and brittle, because no big ideas came to him, no internal force to conceive and execute big projects. At the bottom of his despair he wrote to Anna Strunsky, 'I wander through life delivering hurts to all that know me. And I am changed. Though I was a materialist when first I met you. I had the saving grace of enthusiasm. That enthusiasm is the thing that is spoiled.'

The Faith of Men, his fourth collection of short stories, which had been released by Macmillan in April, was selling so well that it had to be reprinted in June, and now again in August, but even this did not hearten him. He agreed with the critic of The Nation who regretted that a man with his powers should spend all his time in the frozen North. Both his body and mind went soggy and stale. He came down with the grippe; when he recovered he developed a nervous skin itch that put him through torture. He could not exercise, his weight fell off, he became thin, soft, jumpy. Because of his physical affliction and the low state of his mind he lived as a recluse.

In August he paid sixteen hundred dollars for a lot in Piedmont, called in an architect, let Bessie say what kind of house she wanted, and watched the work begin. When he had returned from Korea he had four thousand dollars in the bank from the Century and the Examiner; every dollar of it, plus a good-sized mortgage, went into the building of the house, leaving him once again without funds. Determined not to let his melancholia disrupt his discipline, he plunged into work. He read the dozens of books he had missed while in Korea; wrote articles, such as 'The Yellow Peril,' for magazines and newspapers; began a short prize-fight novel called The Game; lectured to every socialist organization in the vicinity; spoke free of charge to clubs and churches in order to make converts to socialism and thus hasten the revolution. He began work on his first play, The Scorn of Women, based on one of his Alaskan tales, gave readings on The People of the Abyss and The Class Struggle. His skin ailment receding, he again entertained his friends on Wednesday nights, went on swimming parties at the Piedmont Baths and on picnics in the hills. He worked hard and played hard because he did not want to have time to realize how wretched he felt. Yet he did not fool himself about the quality of the work he was doing. 'Still plugging away at *The Game*. Believe it is a failure, but the work is good for me. *The Scorn of Women* is not a big effort, I wouldn't dare a big effort.'

His one sustaining force was Brett of Macmillan. On the strength of the advance sale of *The Sea Wolf*, which reached twenty thousand by the beginning of October, Brett increased the monthly allowance to two hundred and fifty dollars. He assured Jack that it was a truly great book, and finally, at the beginning of November, communicated the magnificent news that *The Sea Wolf*, Jack's tenth publication in less than four years, had sold forty thousand copies to the bookstores before its release. In December he sent Jack a check for three thousand dollars, which Jack had figured he would need to get him out from under his load of insurance, mortgage, and personal debts.

The Sea Wolf shot onto the market like a thunderbolt, became the rage overnight, was on everybody's lips to be praised or cursed. Many readers were insulted and offended by its attitudes; others valiantly took up the cudgels in its defense. Part of the press called it cruel, brutal, and revolting, but the greater part agreed that it was 'rare and original genius . . . raises the quality of modern imaginative literature.' It marked another milestone in American literature, not only because of its realism and vigor, the wealth of characters and situations unknown to American literature, but also because it heightened the intellectual tone of the modern novel. Where before had Americans encountered such dread suspense, such authentic death-appeal as found in the conflict of the spiritual versus the materialistic as took place on board the *Ghost* between Wolf Larsen and Peter Van Weyden? Where before had they been presented with mature philosophy, had they found it made exciting, something to fight about? Jack had taken the scholar's revolution of the nineteenth century, dramatized it, popularized it, made it thrilling and intelligible to the great mass of people who had never even heard of evolution, biology, or scientific materialism. Darwin, Spencer, Nietzsche stalk through the book, its unseen protagonists. In dramatizing the teachings of his beloved masters he made the battles of the mind as exciting as the Irish bricklayers' free-for-all in Weasel Park in his later novel, *The Valley of the Moon*, no mean accomplishment.

Toward the end of the book Jack introduces its only

woman character and thereby marred what was, and is still, a nearly perfect example of the novelist's art. When the literary critics declared that the woman was unbelievable, Jack cried, 'I was in love with a woman, and I wrote her into my book, and the critics tell me that the woman I love is unbelievable.' He had not only written Miss Kittredge into the book but also the poetic-hysteric manner of writing about her which he had absorbed while answering her letters. In everything pertaining to the woman and the love between her and Peter Van Weyden, *The Sea Wolf* shows the worst of the rococo nineteenth century; on all other counts it is a forerunner of the best in twentieth-century literature.

A few weeks after its release it ran fourth to such raspberry-syruped sawdust as *The Masqueraders* by K. C. Thurston, *Prodigal Son* by Hall Caine, *Whosoever Shall Offend* by F. Marion Crawford, and *Beverly of Graustark* by George Barr McCutcheon. Three weeks later it was leading the best-seller lists, far out in front, and the twentieth century at last had thrown off the shackles of its predecessor. *The Sea Wolf* is as thrilling today, as profound a reading experience, as it was in November, 1904. It dates very little. Many critics consider it London's most powerful work; readers who pick it up again are enthralled by it.

Miss Kittredge returned from Iowa; they had several rapturous though fugitive engagements in Oakland and San Francisco, then she left for Glen Ellen to live with Ninetta Eames. There followed an occasional impassioned meeting, Jack penned a few rhapsodic messages, but for the most part his letters became newsy and casual. He is no longer God's own mad lover dying on a kiss. Once again his fancy roamed. Miss Kittredge tells of the development. 'I know that your thoughts and interests for the past few weeks have been taken up by another woman. You're only a boy, after all, dear Man, and transparent enough. But the shock you gave me the night of your "Scab" lecture in the city, made me very thoughtful. I saw you watch for her in the audience when you were through speaking; I saw you wave to her; I saw her backing and filling and fluttering after her manner. I saw you come together in the light of your cigarette, and I knew that you had been together the evening before. It isn't the mere fact of your unfaithfulness—you haven't that kind of integrity, very few men have, and I have faced the probability of your infidelity for a long time, and accepted it in a way. You have been very happy of late, and I knew I was not responsible for your light-heartedness. Somebody was, of course, and so . . .'

The year 1904 was one of headlines for Jack; everything he did excited the press. He began the year peacefully enough with a trip to Los Angeles, where he had been invited to address the local socialists. Julian Hawthorne wrote of him in the Los Angeles *Examiner:* 'It is pleasant to look upon Mr. London. He is as simple and straightforward as a grizzly bear. Upon his big, hearty, healthy nature is based a brain of unusual clearness and insight. His heart is warm, his sympathies wide, his opinions are his own—independent, courageously expounded.' He had no sooner returned to Oakland than he was invited by the liberal-minded president of the University of California to address the student body, an honor for a man who had been forced to leave the University only seven years before to work in a steam laundry. Jack harangued the young people with one of the most fiery speeches he had ever made, telling them that the greatest revolution the world had known was in the making before their very eyes, that if they did not wake up it would descend upon them in their sleep. After the lecture, when he complained to a professor of English that the students were given literary pap to feed upon, the professor replied, 'I wouldn't say that, Mr. London. A chapter of *The Call of the Wild* is included in our new reference book.' The circle of faculty members laughed, Jack flushed, murmured something about being canonized, and subsided. The following day the president of the University was attacked for permitting Jack London to preach revolution. He replied calmly, 'It is the man we invite, not the subject. London has earned his right to appear before us.'

It was at Stockton, where Jack accepted his first invitation to speak to a club of businessmen, that he got into his initial embroilment of the year by an act comparable in its foolhardiness and courage with crossing the Yellow Sea in a howling gale, or descending into the slums of London to write *The People of the Abyss*. The report of the Stockton paper, though a little biased, is a vivid one: 'He lectured the club of businessmen as though they were unruly schoolchildren; he demanded to know what each of them knew about the subject of socialism; he informed them that they had read little and seen less; he pounded the table and puffed out volumes of cigarette smoke—all of which so alarmed and befogged his auditors that they subsided into embarrassed silence.'

They did not remain silent long; at the close of his talk Jack horrified the businessmen of Stockton by telling them that the socialists in Russia who had participated in the 1905 uprising and killed several of the Czarist officials were his brothers! The audience jumped to its feet, storming at him. The next morning headlines screeched across the country: 'JACK LONDON CALLS RUSSIAN ASSASSINS HIS BROTHERS.' A furor arouse, retractions were demanded, editorials flamed out against him, one of the papers cried, 'He is a fire-brand and red-flag anarchist, and should be arrested and prosecuted for treason.' Jack stood his ground. The Russian revolutionists were his brothers, and no one could make him repudiate them.

Society had persistently tried to lionize him as California's one literary genius, saying, 'Socialism is his hobby. A little extreme, but he's so young and original. His socialistic theories are only a fad, he'll get over them.' Now the gates were locked against him as tightly as though he were still a tramp on The Road. No longer was he invited to what he called pink teas, or to formal dinners where he wore his soft white shirt and flowing tie in a sea of starched linen; for society at last concluded that he had been serious when he had so charmingly told them over their dinner tables that as a class they were a parasitic fungus growth.

The scandal had no sooner died down than Jack gave another lecture in which he mentioned that William Lloyd Garrison had said, 'To hell with the Constitution!' when he was condemning slavery in 1856, and that General Sherman Bell had said it more lately in putting down strikers. The next morning he was once again the man of the hour, with hundreds of newspapers from California to New York shouting: 'JACK LONDON SAYS TO HELL WITH THE CONSTITUTION.' He did his best to explain that he was not the author of the phrase, but newspapers are rarely interested in the aftermath of a flash story.

If the freedom of the press allowed bigots to tear a man to shreds, it also permitted wiser men to speak their piece. In the San Francisco *Bulletin*, by no means a radical paper, he read, 'The hot sincerity and hatred of wrong that burns in the revolutionary heart of young Jack London is the same spirit that characterized the tea-overboard party in Boston Harbor. It is the spirit that will ultimately reserve for the Republic all that is best, for it is the opposite of the dull spirit of slavish respect for the Established, which slavishness is composed of abasement of mind, and selfishness of character.'

A few days later he was invited to speak by the debating society of his own Oakland High School. When the principal learned about it he refused them the use of the school building. Once again the papers played up the story, and every man and woman in the state discussed the merits of the case.

The San Francisco *Post* remarked caustically, 'Socialism may be all that is urged against it, but the best way to propagate its doctrines is to forbid their propagation.'

Jack was delighted at the nation-wide publicity that socialism was earning through his efforts. Besides, the free advertising, which would have cost him thousand of dollars if he had had to buy it, was booming his work. *The Call of the Wild, The Sea Wolf, The People of the Abyss* were being widely bought, and even more widely read and discussed. People might disagree with his ideas for an economic democracy; they might quarrel with the manner in which he was revolutionizing American literature; but it was no longer possible to gainsay the fact that he was the leading young writer in America. And his enemies had helped him arrive!

In the midst of the furor over his socialism, Macmillan released his *War of the Classes*. The book aroused so much interest that it had to be reprinted in June, October, and November, an astounding accomplishment for a collection of revolutionary essays in a country which denied vehemently that there was such a thing as a war between the classes, where socialism was ridiculed and despised, accused of being a hydra-headed monster that devoured its young. His was a voice crying in the wilderness, but more and more people were coming to hear that voice, particularly the generation just growing up, just throwing off the shackles of a restricted pioneer mentality, and beginning to count the human costs of large-scale industrialism. Jack London was a great name to this generation; it went to his books with burning faith. All over America one still meets people who relate with pride that Jack London turned them into socialists; the fact that their socialism did not always stick is perhaps not Jack's fault.

In March he once again agreed to run for Mayor of Oakland on the Socialist ticket, receiving 981 votes, exactly four times as many as he had received in 1901. In April he and Manyoungi went to Glen Ellen, where he paid Ninetta Eames six dollars a week for a cabin at Wake Robin. Mrs. Eames gave out the report that 'Jack had come home to Mother because of troubles in Oakland.' The trusting farmers of the neighborhood suspected nothing.

Spring in Sonoma County was beautiful. He regained his good spirits and full working force; the melancholia of the winter was forgotten. Having sold a story to *The Black Cat*, he spent two hundred and fifty dollars of the three-hundred-dollar check for a saddle-horse which the indefatigable Miss Kittredge rode all the way from Berkeley to Glen Ellen, a distance of thirty miles. They rode horseback among the groves of redwood and pine on Sonoma Mountain, over the trails through the wine-colored manzanita and madrone. The air was clear, fragrant, and intoxicating, and when the full moon rose the valley was filled with a luminous white mist. 'Now I know why the Indians named this place the Valley of the Moon,' commented Jack.

His creative force in full flower again, he wrote *White Fang*, a sequel to *The Call of the Wild*, the story of how White Fang, instead of going from civilization back to the call of the primitive, comes out of the wilds to live with mankind. Although the book does not rise to the heights of *The Call of the Wild*, it is a beautiful and moving dog story, carrying with it the thrill of first-rate literature. Each week he did a full-page book criticism for the Hearst chain, outlining the existing struggle between labor unions and employers when he reviewed *The Walking Delegate*, giving the sweatshop system a blasting when he praised *The Long Day*, which told of the privations of a factory girl in New York. The Intercollegiate Socialist Society was organized in the East by Upton Sinclair and J. G. Phelps-Stokes, and Jack was elected president at the first meeting of the executive committee. When Macmillan published his first story, *The Game*, and the critics condemned it as trivial and unbelievable, he sent them news clippings to prove that a fighter could smash in the back of his skull when falling to the mat from a hard blow.

The heat of summer coming on, he again spent a few dollars to have the creek dammed. Here his neighbors collected to swim. He worked in the mornings, swam in the afternoons, and enjoyed himself . . . except that he missed his two children. Then one hot afternoon, when he was riding across the mountains inhaling the sage scents that beat upward from the slope, he stumbled onto the Hill Ranch, one hundred and thirty acres of majestic land leading up from the floor of the valley to Sonoma Mountain. 'There are great redwoods on it, some of them ten thousand years old. There are hundreds of firs, tan-bark and live-oaks, madrone and manzanita galore. There are deep canyons, streams of water, springs. It is one hundred and thirty acres of the most beautiful, primitive lands to be found anywhere in America.'

He went wild about the place and decided at once that he must own it, a sentiment in which Miss Kittredge heartily encouraged him; only by getting him away from the city and from contact with other women would she avoid the danger of losing him, as she had almost lost him a few months before. Jack rode into the small village of Glen Ellen where he learned that the land was for sale and that the price had been set at seven thousand dollars. That afternoon at five he was at the home of the Hills, excited as a schoolboy, ready to buy. 'I hear you set the price of the land for Chauvet at seven thousand dollars,' he said to Mr. Hill. 'Yes,' replied Hill, 'that was the price I set him ten years ago.' 'I'll buy it!' cried Jack. 'Not so fast,' said Hill, 'you'd better go home and think it over for a few days.'

After Jack left, Mr. Hill told his wife that he had asked seven thousand dollars of Chauvet because Chauvet had wanted to utilize the water rights, but since Jack expected to farm the piece, five thousand dollars was all he could ask. The next day Jack dashed in more excited than ever; he had been unable to sleep for the planning of his beautiful ranch. 'Now I want to talk to you about the price . . .' began Hill. Jack leapt out of his chair, his face reddened, and he shouted in a burst of anger, 'You can't do that to me! I won't stand for it! You can't rise the price! Everybody around here is trying to do me. Seven thousand is the price you agreed to and that's the price I'm going to pay!' Unable to break into the torrent, Hill waited until he had subsided, then said quietly, 'All right, Mr. London, take it at your price.'

Years later, when Jack and the Hills had become close friends, Mr. Hill told him how he had done himself out of two thousand dollars. Jack laughed heartily, said that it ought to teach him to control his temper.

That night he and Miss Kittredge laid their plans. There was a ramshackle barn on the Hill Ranch that could be remodeled to house their horses and hired man. While Jack was away that fall on a lecture tour of the country, the hired man could clear a number of the acres, plant hay and corn, build pigsties and chicken houses, and get the ranch in working order against the day when Bessie's divorce would be granted and they could marry.

Jack wrote to Brett for the seven thousand dollars with which to buy the Hill Ranch. Brett replied, 'I am doubtful as to the advisability of any man who has a part to play in the world tying himself down to the purchase of real estate in any part of the country, no matter how beautiful and productive.' Jack wrote back, 'I was careful to buy a piece out of which no profit could be made. I'll never be bothered with a profit or loss account, but in twenty years it will be worth one hundred and twenty thousand dollars. I am anchoring good and solid, and anchoring for keeps.' Resignedly, Brett sent him the seven thousand dollars against the *Sea Wolf* royalties, and Jack exultantly became owner of the Hill Ranch.

He then hired a farm hand, bought several horses, a colt, a cow, a calf, a plow, a barrow, a wagon, a buggy, harnesses, chickens, turkeys, and pigs.

When he finally came out of the wild buying spree he found that he did not have a dollar left, and that no money would be due from Macmillan for a long time. 'All this buying was unexpected, and has left me flat broke. Also I am expecting to receive, and dreading to receive, a notice from Bessie that she wants several hundred dollars with which to buy a horse and surrey. I've taken all the money I could get from Macmillan to pay for the land, and haven't enough left to build a barn with, much less a house. Am writing some short stories in order to get hold of some immediate cash.'

By October 4 he had overdrawn so heavily from Macmillan that they asked him to pay interest on the new advances. His bank book showed $207.83 to his credit, while among the immediately necessary outlays were $75 to Bessie, $55 to his mother, $57.60 for ranch tools, $24 for rent at Glen Ellen, $50 for store bills. 'I must pay my way and Manyoungi's way to Chicago; Charmian follows in twenty-four hours, and there are her expenses. My mother wants me to increase her monthly allowance. So does Bessie. I have just paid hospital bills of over $100 for Johnny Miller's mother. I have promised $30 to pay for printing of the appeal of Joe King, a poor devil who had a fifty-year sentence hanging over him and who is being railroaded. There is a bill for over $45 for the hay press, and in November I must meet between $700 and $800 in insurance. So you see I am not only sailing close into the wind but that I am dead into it and my sails flapping.'

During his lifetime, in the course of which he earned well over a million dollars from his writing, he was almost never the owner of his money when it reached him. He always spent first, then split his head trying to figure where the necessary money was to come from. As Emil Jensen had said in the Klondike, he was never one to count the cost. It apparently never occurred to him that if he didn't spend his money until he had earned it he would not only keep out of debt, but out of trouble as well. 'The habit of spending money, ah God! I shall always be its victim!'

In October he started on his lecture tour attended by Manyoungi. Miss Kittredge returned to her aunt in Newton, Iowa, so that she could be closer to him. The tour, which included most of the large cities of the Mid-West and the East, was carried out in a blaze of publicity, for he was rapidly becoming one of the most romantic figures of the period. In addition to being the voice of socialism, the voice of scientific evolution, the voice of a new and robust realism in American literature, he also represented the youth and courage of the world. The women's clubs liked his virile figure, his smoke-puffing masculinity, his passionate sincerity on questions of social reform, his golden smile and infectious laughter. He made several hundred dollars a day, found amusing and intelligent company in each town, and was treated with friendliness by the newspapers. 'Jack London is a personality of unusual magnetic attraction. If it had been possible to spoil him he would have been spoiled by the regiment of adorers who beset him. He has been subjected to the same experiences as the matinée idol. However, he is without personal vanity.'

Then, on Saturday, November 18, he received a telegram in Chicago that Bessie's final divorce decree had been granted. He wired Miss Kittredge to come on at once from Newton to be married. She reached Chicago Sunday afternoon at five, but Jack had no marriage license. The bureau of course was closed, so he engaged a carriage and drove at top speed through the Chicago streets to enlist the aid of influential friends. The first two visits proving fruitless, a third friend was taken from his dinner table because he knew a city official. After another long drive they reached the home of the official, who said that he would be glad to do anything to help Jack London, but what was his blistering hurry, anyway? Why couldn't he wait until morning when the license bureau would be open and he could do everything in apple-pie order? Jack refused to wait, brought all his considerable force of argument to bear, ended by persuading the official to get into the carriage and drive with them to the south side of town, where the marriage-license clerk was routed out of bed. The clerk was dumbfounded, but under Jack's determined will he dressed and accompanied the party to the City Hall, opened his office, and made out the license. After several vain attempts they located a justice of the peace, Mr. Grant, who married Jack to Charmian Kittredge in the library of his home.

The following morning, November 20, 1905, the press of the nation was shocked by what they termed the 'indecent haste' of his marriage. Up to this time people had assumed that his separation from Bessie was caused by internal differences which made it mutually desirable. By his terrific sweat to remarry Jack showed that he had broken up his home for another woman . . . and that put an unpleasant face on affairs. Friendly as the press had been up to Saturday, on Monday it turned against him, not only its anger and indignation, but its ridicule as well. On Tuesday morning the nation was informed 'JACK LONDON'S MARRIAGE INVALID,' for the new divorce laws of Illinois, which were still in confusion, declared that no marriage could be valid unless it took place a year after the granting of the final decree. Cornered by reporters, Jack, once again feeling that he was being persecuted, cried out in impetuous ardor, 'If necessary I'll get married in every state in the Union, as fast as I can get from one to the other!' Many witty stories were written about the much-marrying Mr. London.

Had he waited until he returned to California, had he waited a few circumspect months he could have avoided the entire scandal. His marriage would have passed with brief notice. Instead he laid himself open to attack from every quarter. Sermons against him were preached from pulpits; the towns of Pittsburg and Derby banned his books from the public library, suggesting that other cities follow their lead; syndicated dispatches were released urging the women's clubs to cancel his lectures; many papers commented that it was strange that persons who were unable to regulate their own domestic affairs set themselves up as teachers of humanity at large. Articles were written questioning the mystery and haste of his second marriage. Miss Kittredge was attacked for breaking up his marriage to Bessie.

Because of the conduct of their leader, the socialists of America took severe punishment. The capitalist press utilized the weapons at hand: 'There's socialism for you! Deserts its wife and babies . . . sanctions immorality . . . would bring about chaos . . . socialism is anarchism, would destroy our civilization . . .' It was bootless for his comrades to protest, 'You cannot blame London's erratic conduct on socialism! Socialism disapproves of this sort of thing as vigorously as does capitalism!' Their leader had violated certain codes, and their Cause consequently had to suffer. Accused by his comrades of retarding the socialist revolution in America by at least five years, he smilingly replied, 'On the contrary, I believe I still have accelerated the revolution by at least five minutes.'

Just what motivated his theatrical rush to have that belated ceremony performed, to flaunt a new marriage in the face of the public? Part of it was a romantic gesture for Miss Kittredge. Part of it was rash, impetuous thoughtlessness, the act of a man who doesn't stop to question what the world will think. Part of it was sheer bravado, the act of a thick-skinned Irishman who doesn't care what it thinks. Lastly, the immediate taking of another wife was an appeasement to his con-

science for the wrong he had done Bessie, and hence all
wives.

The attacks against him in press and pulpit continued for
several weeks. The seriousness of his work was injured in the
minds of many readers, but in return the blazing publicity extended his public. It remained for the fashionable Averill
Women's Club to administer the crowning blow, and close
the discussion. At an open meeting the ladies passed a resolution approving free textbooks for public schools, and resolu-
tions denouncing college football and Jack London.

8

IN JANUARY of 1906 the lecture tour finally brought Jack to New York, where he was met by Doctor Alexander Irvine, handsome Irish idealist, minister of Pilgrim's Church in New Haven and head of the New Haven Socialist Local. Doctor Irvine had come to New York to persuade him to lecture at Yale University. Jack heartily concurred that the opportunity of launching a bolt of socialism at three thousand Yale students was too good to pass up. Doctor Irvine took the next train back to New Haven, where he then proposed to the Yale Debating Club that they sponsor the lecture. The members nervously agreed to present Jack London the following evening—on condition that he was not to say anything radical.

Elated, Doctor Irvine went that night to a socialist painter by the name of Delfant, who made ten posters on which were drawn a likeness of handsome Jack in his turtle-necked sweater, and under it a mass of red flames with the title of the lecture, 'REVOLUTION.' Just before dawn Delfant and Doctor Irvine went about the campus tacking up the posters on trees. Yale was aghast when it awakened and saw the glaring announcements. A faculty member immediately summoned the chairman of the Debating Club and informed him that the meeting would have to be canceled, that if it were not, he would have permission to use Woolsey Hall revoked. There would be no revolution preached at Yale University! The club was about to obey when Doctor Irvine urged its members to go to the younger professors and see if they couldn't raise support against the reactionaries. The first professor to whom the chairman presented his problem was William Lyon Phelps, who asked, 'Is Yale a monastery?'

The rebuke was so adroitly yet gently put that it silenced the opposition. At eight o'clock that evening three thousand students and three hundred faculty members, nearly the entire university, jammed Woolsey Hall. Jack was given a warm reception as he walked onto the stage, and was listened to attentively as he told of seven million men in all countries of the world who 'are fighting with all their might for the conquest of the wealth of the world, and for the complete overthrow of existing society. They call themselves comrades, these men, as they stand shoulder to shoulder under the banner of revolt. Here is tremendous human force, here is power; the revolutionists are swayed by a great passion, they have much reverence for humanity but little reverence for the rule of the dead.' After an hour of dissecting the capitalist system with an economic scalpel he concluded with the challenge, 'The capitalist class has failed in its management, and its management is to be taken away from it. Seven million men of the working class say that they are going to get the rest of the working class to join with them, and take that management away. The revolution is here, now. Stop it who can!'

In spite of the fact that he 'shocked them out of their socks,' as Doctor Irvine put it, and that not twenty students in the audience agreed with a word he uttered, he received an ovation when he finished. Yale University sportingly refused to take any rent for the Hall, and the entire gate, at twenty-five cents a head, went into the treasury of the New Haven Socialist Local, a windfall.

After the lecture Jack, Doctor Irvine, and a hand-picked group of a dozen of the best debaters at the University went to Old Mory's for beer and solid talk. It was Jack against the field; from all reports of the rough-and-tumble discussion, in which he tried to prove that private property is based on either seizure or theft, Jack held his own even if he did not make any converts. When he and Doctor Irvine reached the latter's home at four o'clock in the morning they found a group of workingmen waiting to thank him for his lecture. At eight o'clock the next morning the doorbell was rung by a gangling, red-headed reporter from the Yale *News* who wanted a personal interview with Jack London because it would help his chances on the paper. The reporter's name was Sinclair Lewis.

By January 19 he was back again in New York after two weeks of lecturing to speak on 'The Coming Crisis' for the first open meeting of the Intercollegiate Socialist Society, of which he had been named president. Reports of how many people crowded into the Grand Central Palace vary from four to ten thousand, but every socialist on the Atlantic coast who could scrape up the fare to New York was present. In spite of the title of the organization, there were probably not a hundred college students scattered among the thousands of working people. On his way north from a lecture in Florida, Jack's train was late. Upton Sinclair, who was just having published a book about the Chicago stockyards titled *The Jungle,* and who was the organizing force and brains behind the Intercollegiate Socialist Society, kept the crowd interested by telling them that they could help bring economic democracy to America. At ten o'clock, when Jack appeared in a black cheviot suit, with a white flannel shirt and white tie, and well-worn patent leather pumps, his hair flying, the crowd thronged to its feet to give him the greatest reception of his life: Eugene V. Debs was their giant, but Jack London was their fighting young leader and prophet. Upton Sinclair says that the audience cheered and waved tiny red flags for fully five minutes before Jack had a chance to make himself heard. When he predicted the downfall of capitalist society by the year 2000, the crowd went delirious with delight even though not a soul among them would be present to witness that great Judgment Day.

He remained in New York for a week. New York always had a strange effect upon him; it excited him physically and depressed him nervously. He told Doctor Irvine that every time he found himself entering the city he wanted to cut his throat. The day following his lecture for the Intercollegiate Socialist Society he met Upton Sinclair at luncheon to discuss plans for the Society. Sinclair, who was an ardent prohibitionist, reports that Jack had been drinking before he arrived, that his eyes were excitedly bleary, that he continued to drink straight through the luncheon. Before reaching New York Jack had written a glowing review of *The Jungle* which now sent that muckraking classic and its author on their way to fame.

On February 3, when lecturing in St. Paul, he fell ill and his mouth became covered with cold sores. He canceled the balance of his lectures to return to Glen Ellen, where he rented part of Wake Robin from Ninetta Eames and Edward Payne, the joint owners. It was here he hatched his plans for an adventure which was to make all other adventures of his thrill-packed life seem pale by comparison.

The summer before, while sunning himself on the beach at the swimming hole at Glen Ellen, he had read to the group of vacationers from Captain Joshua Slocum's book *Sailing Alone Around the World.* Captain Slocum's boat had been thirty-seven feet long; Jack mentioned jokingly that he would

not be afraid to sail around the world in a small boat, say
forty feet long. Now, back at Wake Robin, having had his fill
of crowds and cities and adulation, sensitive to the fact that
he was being attacked from many corners and for many reasons, that the people of Glen Ellen were hostile because of
the haste and circumstances of his second marriage, he once
again began talking about the voyage around the world. He
had long planned just such an expedition to the South Seas; it
was one of the great dreams of his life, kindled by the romantic tales of Stevenson and Melville. Charmian, whose forte
was adventure, encouraged him, as did Ninetta Eames and
Edward Payne, who hoped Roscoe Eames would become
captain of the ship.

'I had a house to build on the ranch, also an orchard, a
vineyard, several hedges to plant, and a number of other
things to do. We thought we would start in four or five years.
Then the lure of adventure began to grip us. Why not start at
once? Let the orchard, vineyard and hedges be growing while
we were away. After all, I'd never be any younger.' Always
impetuous, swift of decision, heedless of cost, he resolved
that he too was going to circle the globe in a small boat.

Ten days after his return to Wake Robin he wrote to half a
dozen of the leading Eastern magazine editors in an attempt
to get them to underwrite his adventure with hard cash. 'The
boat is to be forty-five feet long. It would have been a bit
shorter had I not found it impossible to squeeze in a bathroom otherwise. I sail in October. Hawaii is the first port of
call; from there we shall wander through the South Seas,
Samoa, New Zealand, Australia, New Guinea, and up
through the Philippines to Japan. Then Korea and China,
and on down to India, the Red Sea, Mediterranean, Black
Sea and Baltic, across the Atlantic to New York, and then
around the Horn to San Francisco. I shall certainly put in a
winter at St. Petersburg, and the chances are that I shall go
up the Danube from the Black Sea to Vienna. I'll go up the
Nile and the Seine; there is no reason at all why I shouldn't
come up to Paris and moor alongside the Latin Quarter, with
the bow line out to Notre Dame, and a stern line fast to the
Morgue. I shall not be in a rush; I calculate that seven years
at least will be taken up by the trip.'

Although there were several seaworthy boats on San Francisco Bay that could be bought for a reasonable price, Jack
discarded this idea; he would sail no man's boat but his own.
There were expert ship architects in San Francisco, but he
would sail in no vessel but one that had been fashioned in his
own mind. There were competent shipbuilders with yards on

the Bay, but he would be master of no boat but the one he had built himself.

He decided to design a boat that would be a departure in sailing vessels, even as everything in his life design had to be a departure. He hit upon the idea for a 'ketch,' a compromise between a yawl and a schooner which would retain the virtues of both, but he frankly admitted that he had never seen a ketch, let alone sailed one, that the whole thing was a theory in his mind. He sunk himself in the details of boat-building, pondering such problems as whether a two-, three-, or four-cycle engine would be best; whether he should use a make-and-break or jump spark for ignition; what was the best kind of windlass; whether the rigging should be set up with lanyards or turn buckles. Always a swift and penetrating student, in a few weeks he taught himself a great deal about modern shipbuilding.

Roscoe Eames in his palmier days had sailed small boats around San Francisco Bay. On the basis of this experience Jack hired him at sixty dollars a month to take the plans down to San Francisco and supervise the building of the *Snark,* an arrangement which pleased everyone concerned and gave to the aging and cantankerous Roscoe the first wage he had earned in years. Jack decided to call his boat the *Snark* after an imaginary animal in *The Hunting of the Snark. Cosmopolitan* had suggested that he name it after their magazine; Jack agreed that if they would pay the cost of building the boat he would not only name it *Cosmopolitan Magazine,* but would also take subscriptions along the way. He calculated the *Snark* would cost seven thousand dollars to build and, so calculating, said to Roscoe, 'Spare no money. Let everything on the *Snark* be of the best. Never mind decoration; pine board is good enough for me. Put the money into construction. Let the *Snark* be as staunch and strong as any boat afloat. Never mind what it costs to make her staunch and strong; I'll go on writing and earning the money to pay for it.'

Having dispatched Roscoe with the boat plans and an open check book, Jack cast about for his next serious project. It was four months since he had done any creative work. Among the many books he had ordered from England by catalogue was Stanley Waterloo's *Story of Ab,* one of the first attempts to re-create in literature the life of man when he was still more animal than human. Waterloo had put in ten years of study and work on his book; the result was erudite but unexciting. Jack saw his opportunity: here was a mechanism with which he could bring to life Darwin's theory of evolution! That afternoon he formulated his outline, leaning heavily on Waterloo's book, and the next morning he began to write *Before Adam,* illustrative of his talent for conceiving titles. By using the simple device of a modern boy who dreams at night that he is growing up as a primitive child, he contrasts the two periods with telling effect. The writing is so warm and honest that the reader believes this is how man really lived after having taken his historic step forward from the ape. 'It is going to be the most primitive story ever written!' exulted Jack.

Conceived in the dark days when organized religion was fighting the theory of evolution as a diabolical concoction of sacrilegious souls, before the methods of scientific investigation had made much headway against the stone wall of ritualistic dogma, *Before Adam* was a brave attempt to popularize Darwin and Wallace, to bring the meaning of their work to the masses so they might better understand their antecedents. He was a superb story-teller, and this book about primitive people is as absorbing as any of his Alaskan tales. Though *Before Adam* misses being first-rate literature because of the tumultuous haste in which it was poured out, it makes delightful and illuminating reading, particularly for young people just beginning to sharpen the teeth of their mind.

Roscoe bought supplies, hired workmen, rented space in a shipbuilding dock, then informed Jack that the keel of the *Snark* would be laid on the morning of April 18, 1906. On the eve of the eighteenth Jack talked for hours about his trip, recalling that 'when I was a small boy I read a book of Melville's called *Typee,* and many long hours I dreamed over its pages. I resolved then and there, mightily, come what would, when I had gained strength and years I too would voyage to Typee.' In the very early morning, awakened by the floor shaking under his bed, he assumed that he had been dreaming of the valley of Typee and had tossed in his sleep in excitement. When dawn finally came he saddled Washoe Ban, rode to the top of Sonoma Mountain, and saw San Francisco in flames. He returned at top speed to Wake Robin, caught a train to Oakland, and then a ferry across to San Francisco, where he took photographs and dashed off a telegraphic story for *Collier's.*

Among the many major tragedies brought on by the San Francisco earthquake and fire, there was the minor tragedy that the keel of the *Snark* could not be laid. Supplies that had been paid for were burned; there were no workmen to be had; the ironworks had been razed, equipment ordered from

New York could not be brought into the city. There could be no lick of work done on the *Snark* for many weeks. Jack left Roscoe behind to get construction under way again just as soon as possible, and returned to Glen Ellen to write some of his finest Klondike stories, among them 'Love of Life,' 'The White Man's Way,' 'The Story of Keesh,' 'The Unexpected,' 'Negore,' 'The Coward'; he had begun to suspect that the *Snark* might cost a little more than his original estimate of seven thousand dollars to build.

In June the keel of the *Snark* was at last laid. Jack also conceived the motif for the novel based on the economic life of the people, for which he had long been casting about in his mind. 'I am deep in the beginning of a socialistic novel! Am going to call it *The Iron Heel*. How is that for a title? The poor futile little capitalist! Gee, when the proletariat cleans house some day!' Again his vigorous imagination, which just two months before had invented a device to plunge a story backward in time some tens of thousands of years, now created a device to project *The Iron Heel* forward by seven hundred years: the finding of the manuscript of Ernest Everhard where it had been hidden just after the Second Revolt of the People had been bathed in blood by the Oligarch. Anatole France, who called Jack the American Karl Marx, wrote in an introduction to *The Iron Heel*, 'Jack London has that particular genius which perceives what is hidden from the common herd, and possesses a special knowledge enabling him to anticipate the future.'

A special knowledge inherited straight from Professor Chaney, one of whose greatest delights was predicting the future, nearly always accurately. In *The Iron Heel* Jack once again proved that ideas can be more exciting than action, and that they control the world; just as in *The Sea Wolf* and *Before Adam* he had paid his debt to his masters, Spencer, Darwin, and Huxley, he now paid his debt to his master, Karl Marx, popularizing his teachings, dramatizing socialism and the revolution, making it intelligible to the masses. Karl Marx would have been pleased with *The Iron Heel*.

In writing his book Jack went to the extensive files and catalogues he had studiously compiled over a period of years, drawing from them sufficient factual material to make it one of the most scathing indictments against capitalism ever conceived. Economics was not only considered dry and dull and boring by Americans, but any discussion of principles underlying private property and distribution of wealth was as tabu as discussions of evolution. Industrialists and bankers ruled by what had been known before the republican revolution as the Divine Right of Kings; workmen were told to be grateful for the labor and bread provided them through the wisdom and goodness of their employers. The Church, as exemplified by Jack's contact with it in Chicago while on his lecture tour, when the only two allegedly liberal ministers in the city refused to speak at the funeral of former Governor John P. Altgeld because he had pardoned the men railroaded in the Haymarket Riot, was a pot-bellied handmaiden of industry, as was the so-called higher education in the colleges, which taught only what its paymasters permitted.

All this he documented and wrote into one of the most terrifying and beautiful books ever written; if *The Iron Heel* is not his greatest contribution to the realm of literature, it is certainly his greatest contribution to the economic revolution. In it he not only predicted the coming of the now current Fascism, but detailed the methods by means of which it would murder all opposition and wipe out existing culture. *The Iron Heel* reads as though it were written yesterday . . . or ten years from today. In all contemporary literature there is no chapter more exciting than the one in which Ernest Everhard faces the Philomath Club (note the resemblance of the club name to the one Chaney invented, the Philomatheans), whose members formed the wealthiest Oligarch on the Pacific coast. Nor was there ever a more prophetic paragraph than the one in which the leader of the Oligarchs answers Everhard, who has just laid bare the waste and rapine of the profit system, and predicted the taking over of industry by the working people. 'When you reach out your vaunted strong hands for our palaces and purple ease, we will show you what strength is. In the roar of shell and shrapnel and the whine of machine-guns will our answer be couched. We will grind your revolutionists down under our heel, and we shall walk upon your faces. The world is ours, we are its lords, and ours it shall remain. As for labor, it has been in the dirt since history began, and in the dirt it shall remain so long as I and mine have the power.'

In the extensive bibliography on communism, Bukharin lists only one book by an American author, *The Iron Heel*.

Compared in scope as an adventure of the mind to his seven-year plan of sailing a forty-five-foot boat around the world, *The Iron Heel* makes the contemplated *Snark* voyage seem like a ferry ride across San Francisco Bay. He wrote the book in full consciousness that it would make him bitter and powerful enemies; he wrote it in full knowledge that it would injure his career, that it might hurt his past books and kill any new ones he might write. He wrote it in full awareness that Macmillan's might be forced to refuse to publish it, that no magazine would dare serialize it, that there was no way to make enough money from it to pay for the food he consumed during the months of writing it.

All of which was even more courageous in view of what was happening to his bank account over the building of the *Snark*. Fulfilling his own command, 'Never mind what it costs to make her staunch and strong,' he ordered the most expensive Puget Sound planking for the deck so that there would be no butts to allow leakage; built four watertight compartments so that no matter how large a leak the *Snark* might spring, only one compartment could fill with water; sent to New York for a costly seventy-horse-power engine; bought a magnificent windlass and had castings specially made so that the engine could transmit power to the windlass to haul up the anchor. He built a dream of a bathroom, with schemes, devices, pumps, levers, and sea valves. He bought a rowboat, and then a small launch with a motor in it. He had a bow built on the *Snark* that cost a small fortune, but over which no sea could break, the most beautiful bow he had ever seen on a boat. Reporters sent to interview him wrote that he became 'all boy' when the subject of the cruise was mentioned, that it was a new toy and he was going to have a lot of fun playing with it.

By midsummer he found that he already had ten thousand dollars in the *Snark*, and that she was not half finished. The ten thousand dollars had taken from him every dollar he could command; royalties and advances from Macmillan and his English publishers, the four hundred dollars he got from McClure who had bought *Love of Life*, the money he had received from other stories he had written after completing *Before Adam*. In addition to building his boat, he supported Flora, Johnny Miller, and Mammy Jenny in the house he had bought for Flora; Bessie and his two daughters in the house he had built for Bessie; Charmian, Roscoe Eames, and in part, Ninetta Eames and Edward Payne in Wake Robin; and had a foreman and hired men on the Hill Ranch who were planting and clearing, buying equipment and materials.

The editors to whom he had sent his excited letters in February were turning a cool cheek to his plea for advances against articles about the voyage. The acquiring of enough money to support his list of fourteen relatives, dependents, and workmen, and in addition to pay wages to the workmen on the *Snark*, became known as London's monthly miracle. Common sense told him to abandon the *Snark*, for the present at least, as he could not foot the bills. Or, if he wanted to

continue pouring money into the *Snark,* to give up writing on
The Iron Heel. He was a poor one for compromise. He continued his impassioned thousand words a morning on *The
Iron Heel,* and in the afternoons, Sundays, and holidays
turned out stories, articles, essays, anything to earn the hundreds and hundreds the *Snark* was consuming. In addition to
buying a series of articles about the days when he had been a
tramp on The Road, *Cosmopolitan* at last sent him a thousand dollars against an article he was to write about the
Snark before he sailed; apparently *Cosmopolitan* entertained
serious doubts about the forty-five-foot boat ever reaching another port.

By October 1, the date on which he had planned to cast
off, he had fifteen thousand dollars in the *Snark,* and it was
only half finished. He had poured into it the two thousand
dollars from *Everybody's* magazine for the serialization of
Before Adam, the two thousand dollars from *Cosmopolitan,*
the two thousand dollars from the *Woman's Home Companion* which it had agreed to advance him against articles on
the domestic life of the aborigines, and at least another two
thousand dollars earned by the batch of Alaskan tales, but he
found that if he wanted to continue work on the boat he
would have to borrow against the house he had bought for
Flora. And at last he perceived that Roscoe Eames was a
tragic error. Eames was quarrelsome and could get little work
out of his men; he was inefficient, the workmen were dupli-
cating their efforts; he was so garrulous and chaotic-minded
that he was paying three prices for gear, buying materials for
which he had no use, giving checks for equipment no one
bothered to deliver. Uncompromising in his demands upon
himself that he master any field of knowledge or endeavor
before he wrote about it, Jack had not thought to make such
demands of the people he employed, accepting them on their
self-evaluation.

To complicate matters further, *Cosmopolitan,* which had
had to be bludgeoned for a thousand-dollar advance, ran
full-page advertisements that they were sending Jack London
around the world in the *Snark* to write stories for them. 'Everywhere prices have been raised, and stuck into me, and
broken off, all upon the understanding that I wasn't spending
my own money, but the money of a rich magazine.'

In addition to this false advertising, which hurt Jack doubly because it put his voyage in a different light, making him
look like an employee rather than an adventurer, *Cosmopolitan* also mutilated his first article about the *Snark.* Jack was
never in better form than when he was writing angry letters

to people whom he felt had taken advantage of him. 'You're treating me scurvily. This is the first squabble I've ever had with a magazine. I hope it will be my last, but I'll make it hum while it lasts. Either we're going to work together, or we're not. Frankly I'd like to call the whole thing off. If you can't find a fair and square basis for treating me, then on your head be it. I'll neither give nor take quarter. You want to know when my next article will be sent to you. There are a few things I want to know first or else you will never know when that second article will be sent to you. You'll think the Day of Judgment will be a whole lot quicker in coming than that second article. I weave my stuff; you can't cut out parts of it and leave mutilated parts behind. Who in the dickens are you, anyway, to think that you can better my work? Do you think that I'll write my heart, my skilled professional heart into my work to have you fellows slaughtering it to suit your journalistic tastes? I refuse flatly and definitely to collaborate with anyone in your office!'

What vexed him more than the wasteful expense were the prolonged delays. The *Snark* was promised for November 1, then November 15, then December 1. In desperation he moved to Oakland, sent Roscoe home to study navigation, and undertook supervising the completion of the boat himself. He hired fourteen men, paid them earthquake wages, and a dollar a day bonus for working fast. In order to do this he had to mortgage the Hill Ranch. By December 15 in spite of the tremendous outlay of cash, he saw that the *Snark* was as far from completion as it had been on October 1; once again he had to postpone his announced sailing date.

The newspapers began to publish satiric rhymes about the procrastinating Mr. London; the *Woman's Home Companion*, upset because *Cosmopolitan* beat them to publication with an article about the *Snark*, protested against his not sailing and demanded an article on the aborigines while he was still in San Francisco; his friends bet with him against his sailing date.

His foreman at the Hill Ranch collected his first bet on New Year's Day, 1907, and this amount was added to the twenty thousand dollars invested in the *Snark*. 'After that the bets came fast and furious. My friends surrounded me like a gang of harpies, making bets against every sailing date I set. I was rash, and I was stubborn, and continued to bet, and paid them all.'

So well had the voyage of the *Snark* been publicized by the newspapers and magazines that he received thousand of letters from all over the country, the writers pleading to be

taken along. Ninety per cent were willing to work in any capacity, and ninety-nine per cent were willing to work without
pay. 'Physicians, surgeons and dentists in large numbers
offered to come along without pay; there were reporters, va-
lets, chefs, illustrators, secretaries, civil engineers, machinists,
electricians, retired sea captains, schoolteachers, university
students, ranchers, housewives, sailors, riggers.' Only one of
them was Jack unable to resist, a seven-page letter from a
young lad in Topeka, Kansas, by the name of Martin Johnson. Jack wired him, 'CAN YOU COOK?' and Martin Johnson
telegraphed back 'JUST TRY ME,' then rushed out to get a job
in the kitchen of a Greek restaurant in Topeka. By January
the future African explorer was in Oakland, ready to sail on
the *Snark*, but the *Snark* was not ready for him. Because
Jack insisted upon paying a fair wage to everybody who
worked for him, Martin Johnson's wage was added to the
roster.

Despite the fact that he now knew Roscoe to be incompetent, Jack did not fire him and engage one of the many available accredited sea captains to command his ship, any one of
whom he could have had for the same one hundred dollars a
month he was to pay Roscoe after they sailed. Nor did he
accept the offer of any of the able-bodied seamen who
begged to come along, with or without pay. Instead he hired
for his lone engineer and sailor a Stanford University student
by the name of Herbert Stoltz, who was a husky and willing
young man. That was to be his crew: Jack, Charmian,
Roscoe Eames, Martin Johnson, Herbert Stoltz, and a Japanese cabin boy, not one of whom, aside from Jack, knew
how to reef a sail or haul up an anchor.

Having completed *The Iron Heel* he read the first two
chapters to the Ruskin Club. An Oakland newspaper commented that he always tried out his socialistic ideas on Oakland because he knew that if they went there, they would go
anywhere. He then sent the manuscript to Brett, who predicted that the newspapers would ignore it, or come down on
the head of the author and publisher, but claimed that it was
good work and agreed to publish it regardless of the consequences, a brave decision. His only request was that Jack de-
lete a footnote which Brett was sure would land them both in
jail for contempt of court. Jack replied, 'If they find me
guilty of contempt I'd be only too glad to do six months in
jail, during which time I could write a couple of books and
do no end of reading.'

He had good reason to yearn for the comparative peace
and quiet of a jail, for the *Snark* had landed him in a verita-

ble bedlam. In February, one year after he had written his enthusiastic letters to the editors, the *Snark* had been so long in the building that she was breaking down faster than she could be repaired. The boat became a farce, London's folly. The newspapers laughed openly. Nobody took her seriously, least of all the men who were working on her. 'Old sea dogs and master sailors by the score have made pilgrimages to the *Snark* and gone away shaking their heads and voicing misgivings of many sorts.' Sailors said the *Snark* was badly planned and badly rigged, and would founder at sea. Bets were laid against the *Snark* ever reaching Hawaii. Manyoungi, the Korean boy who had served 'Master' faithfully for three years, was so sure he would never reach Hawaii that he forced Jack to fire him by demanding, 'Does God wish his coffee now?' Day and night the boat was surrounded by a crowd of curious jeering spectators.

Realizing that 'the stage was set against him,' that he could never complete the boat in San Francisco, Jack decided to sail her to Honolulu as she was and finish her there. His decision was no sooner made than the *Snark* sprang a leak that took days to repair. When he finally was able to start her for the boatways, she was caught between two barges and severely crushed. The workmen moved her to the ways and started her for the water, but the ways parted and the *Snark* dropped stern-first into the mud. Twice a day for a week, at high tide, two steam tugs pulled and hauled at the *Snark*, trying to get her out of the mud. When Jack tried to help by using the windlass, the specially made castings shattered, the gears ground, and the windlass was put permanently out of commission. In despair he turned on the seventy-horse-power motor, but it shattered the cast-iron bedplate that had come all the way from New York, reared up in the air, smashed all connections and fastenings, and fell useless on its side.

By now Jack had twenty-five thousand dollars in the sunken boat. His closest friends advised him that he was whipped, that he had better leave the *Snark* where she was and abandon the voyage. They assured him that to sail in her, if he could ever get her to sail, was courting suicide. Jack cried, 'I can't quit!' Day after day he spent in a rage against the incompetent workmen, the defective materials that had been sent him, the merchants dunning him with bills, the newspapers that were openly ridiculing him. If he admitted defeat now he would be the laughing-stock of the country; he would never be able to live down the shame and disgrace! He was a man of his word. He'd sail that boat to Hawaii if it was the last thing he did. Better to die a hero's

death in the deep Pacific then be jeered at by the workingmen and merchants who had mulcted him, the newspapers
that had satirized him, the crowds of onlookers who had
laughed and called him crazy, that had raised the odds
against his ever reaching Honolulu to twenty to one, with no
takers!

'By main strength and sweat we dragged the *Snark* off the
wrecked ways and laid her alongside the Oakland City Wharf.
The drays brought the outfit from home, books, blankets, and
personal luggage. Along with this, everything else came on
board in a torrent of confusion—wood and coal, water and
water tanks, vegetables, provisions, oil, the lifeboat and
launch, all our friends and those who claimed to be their
friends, to say nothing of some of the friends of the friends
of the crew. Also there were reporters and photographers,
and strangers, and cranks, and finally, over everything, clouds
of coal dust from the wharf.'

But at last the long, heart-breaking travail was over; they
were to sail on Saturday, April 20, 1907. On Saturday morning Jack went on board with a check book, fountain pen, and
blotter, and nearly two thousand dollars in cash, all he had
been able to collect in advances from Macmillan and the
magazines and waited for the balances due the hundred and
fifteen firms whom he felt had delayed him so long. Instead
of the merchants coming on board for their pay, a United
States marshal arrived and tacked a notice on the *Snark*'s
mast that she was libeled for debt by a man by the name of
Sellers to whom he owed $232. The *Snark* was a prisoner
and could not move; Jack thrashed about the town trying
madly to find his creditors, the sheriff, the mayor, anything to
get clear. Everyone was away for the week-end.

On Monday morning he sat once again on the *Snark* pouring out greenbacks, gold, and checks to his creditors, so
blinded with anger and frustration that he could not even
itemize the bills, make sure he owed the money, or that he
hadn't paid the bills before. When he added it all up he
found that the *Snark*, whose seventy-horse-power engine was
lashed down for ballast, whose power transmission was a
wreck, whose lifeboat leaked and motor launch wouldn't run,
whose one coat of paint had already worn off, had cost him
thirty thousand dollars.

Robbed, ridiculed, cried over, given up for a hopelessly romantic idiot, Jack hoisted Jimmy Hopper's California football sweater to the top of the mast, and raised his anchor by
hand. Then, with a navigator who couldn't navigate, an engineer who couldn't engineer, and a cook who couldn't cook,

the *Snark* limped down the Estuary, crossed the Bay, and sailed out the Golden Gate Strait into the Pacific.

Though his lack of practicality started his troubles, those troubles were usually compounded by the cupidity of the people around him. When he came to inspect the forward beams, which had cost him seven dollars and a half each because they were supposed to be oak, he found that they were pine, worth two-fifty each. The special planking brought from Puget Sound spread, and the deck leaked so badly it flooded the bunkrooms, ruined the tools in the engine room and the provisions in the galley. The sides of the *Snark* leaked, the bottom leaked, and then the expensive watertight compartments began leaking into each other, including the one in which the gasoline was stored. The ironwork broke off in his hand, particularly the portion used in the rigging. Every gadget in the dream bathroom went out of order within twenty hours. When he came to inspect the provisions he found that the oranges had been frozen before being put on board, that the apples and cabbages, having been put on for one of the earlier announced sailings, were spoiled and had to be thrown overboard, that kerosene had spilled on the carrots, the beets were woody, the kindling wouldn't burn, and the coal had spilled out of the rotting potato sacks and was being washed through the scuppers.

Not until they were several days at sea did Jack discover that Roscoe Eames had failed to learn anything about navigating during the months when he was being paid to do so, that Roscoe couldn't take an accurate bearing, and that the *Snark,* leaking like the proverbial sieve, was lost somewhere in the Pacific! He dug out the navigation books and studied them, then drew his charts and took a shot at the sun. 'Navigating by observation of the sun, moon, and stars, thanks to the astronomers and mathematicians, is child's play. One whole afternoon I sat in the cockpit, steering with one hand, studying logarithms with the other. Two afternoons, two hours each, I studied the general theory of navigation and the particular process of taking a meridian altitude. Then I took the sextant, worked out the index error, and shot the sun. Proud? I was a worker of miracles. I had listened to the voices of the stars and they had told me my place upon the highway of the sea.'

They ran into heavy weather that sent Martin Johnson and Tochigi, the cabin boy, into their bunks with acute cases of seasickness; in addition to his other duties Jack stood knee-deep in water in the galley trying futilely to manage a hot meal. Charmian not only took her regular trick at the wheel, but two four-hour tricks in a row, holding the course in rough and black seas while the five men slept securely below deck. Roscoe, who had put aboard hundreds of dollars worth of specially canned health foods, at Jack's expense, sat in his cabin eating the health foods. When Jack asked him why he didn't scrub down the decks and make some attempt to keep the boat clean, Roscoe replied that he couldn't work because he was constipated.

In the midst of the dirt, danger, and confusion, with his world almost literally sinking beneath him, Jack sat down on the forward hatch and began writing *Martin Eden,* perhaps the finest novel he ever wrote, and one of the greatest of all American novels. The original ink-scrawled manuscript shows few changes, indicating the tremendous powers of organization he had developed, and the concentration with which he pitched into his work. After a week the sun came out, Martin Johnson and Tochigi climbed weakly from their bunks, and Herbert Stoltz, without a captain to command him, did his best to keep the *Snark* before the wind. Jack wrote his thousand words a morning, pushing forward into the autobiographical story in which he tells of his own struggles to overcome his lack of book-learning, to turn himself from a rough sailor into a cultivated man and a successful author in the short period of three years. The main characters are himself, Mabel Applegarth and her family, and George Sterling as the poet Brissenden. Ruth Morse, the name Jack gave his heroine, is convincing because she is taken from a life model, the only woman above the working class he ever made believable. Warm, crude, vital, *Martin Eden* is strikingly prophetic; the poet Brissenden warns Martin Eden that he must tie himself to socialism or when success comes he will have nothing to hold him to life. Martin renounces his socialism, and then, sated with success, drowns himself.

When the book was published, two years later, the San José Women's Club invited a book-reviewer by the name of Mira MacClay to review *Martin Eden* for them. In the course of her review Mrs. MacClay lashed the heroine for being a coward and a weakling, for ruining Martin Eden's life as well as her own. She had no way of knowing that the pale, ethereal, spinsterish-looking woman in the front row, gazing up at her with death in her eyes, was Mabel Applegarth.

After twenty-seven days of sailing, during which the magnificent prow of the *Snark*, into which Jack had poured so much love and money, proved not only useless but dangerous because she would not heave to in rough weather, land was sighted. Jack was chagrined over his navigation; according to his charts the nearest land should have been a hundred miles distant. It soon proved to be the summit of Haleakala, towering ten thousand feet above the sea, and fully a hundred miles away. Always prouder of his physical than his intellectual accomplishments, he was more elated that he had been since he held firm the wheel of the *Sophie Sutherland* in the typhoon off the coast of Japan.

Early the following day they drifted around Diamond Head and into full view of Honolulu. A launch of the Hawaiian Yacht Club came out to meet the *Snark,* bringing with it newspapers with cable dispatches from the States that the *Snark* had foundered. The commodore of the club bade them welcome to Hawaii, led the way to Pearl Harbor, and took them home for a hot bath and *poi* cocktails; a friend by the name of Tom Hobron placed a cottage on the Island of Hilo at their disposal. Each morning Jack was awakened by mynah birds. He walked the few steps to an emerald-colored lagoon for a swim, sat down to breakfast at a table under the trees that Tochigi had strewn with red hibiscus and glassy coral peppers, and after breakfast worked in a blue kimono at an improvised desk set up on the lawn. He wrote the details of his difficulties in getting the *Snark* built and launched into 'The Inconceivable and Monstrous'; told of the thousands of letters he had received from people who had wanted to join his adventure in *Adventure,* and the story of how the *Snark* was lost because Roscoe Eames couldn't navigate, and how he had taught himself to navigate in 'Finding One's Way About.' He was in desperate need of funds, the articles were amusing, and they sold to the magazines. He wrote one short story, 'To Build a Fire,' an Alaskan tragedy.

For the first twelve days the *Snark* was in Pearl Harbor he did not go aboard. On the thirteenth when he rowed out to the boat he found that the decks had not been hosed down even once, that along with the exposed gear, they were rotting under the tropical sun. He promptly fired Roscoe Eames and Herbert Stoltz and sent them back to California. The newspapers told the American public that there had been quarreling and dissension on the *Snark.* Because Jack did not want to hurt Ninetta Eames by exposing Roscoe, he made no attempt to defend himself. He then sent transportation money to Eugene Fenelon, a friend of George Sterling, to join the *Snark* as its engineer. Fenelon, who, as the newspapers com-

mented, 'gained his knowledge of the sea while traveling as
strong man of the circus, and while studying for the priesthood,' arrived, spent several months attempting to put the
Snark in shape, and returned to Carmel leaving the equipment in worse condition than ever.

Not only was Hawaii 'a great land, but the people were
sweet people.' The editors of the Star and the Pacific Commercial Traveler gave a dinner in their honor, they were invited to a reception for Prince Kalamanaole and Her Majesty, Liliuokalani; everywhere they were entertained and
shown the majesty of the islands. Every day held a new and
dramatic adventure: he fished by torchlight with Prince Kalamanaole, went to native luaus, or moaning feasts, swam in
the bright, warm moonlight, lived on the Haleakala Ranch on
the Island of Maui. The manager, Louis von Tempsky, took
him to watch cattle drives, colt-breakings, and brandings, and
on the ride of incredible beauty and danger eight thousand
feet up the sides of mountains, and across shaky hempen
bridges which spanned great gorges, to Haleakala crater,
from the crest of which he saw all of the islands and the sea
beneath them. Out of this adventure came the article, 'The
House of the Sun.'

He spent a week on the leper island of Molokai, where he
and Charmian lived and mingled with the lepers on terms of
physical equality, sitting side by side with them at their shooting club and standing in the rifle boxes, shooting with rifles
still warm from their hands, or attending the horse races they
staged. The lepers pleaded with him to write an article which
would tell the truth about the maligned Island of Molokai so
that the world might know that they lived well and happily,
and in 'The Lepers of Molokai,' written as soon as he returned to his bungalow in Hilo, Jack fulfilled his promise
with a tender and tragically beautiful description of his stay
there. Alexander Hume Ford, authority on surf-riding, taught
him to ride the breakers; although he received a sunburn that
kept his sensitive skin blistered for two weeks, he wrote an
article called 'A Royal Sport' which did much to popularize
surf-riding among Americans. He loved the easy, beauty-
drenched life of the islands, and worked well on Martin
Eden, in addition to his other writings.

When the series of tramp articles appearing in the Cosmopolitan were ready to be issued in book form, Brett wrote to
Jack asking if he would still be willing to publish The Road if
he, Brett, could prove that the book would hurt him with his
public. Jack replied, 'In The Road, as in all my work, I have

been true. As my character has developed through my work there have been flurries of antagonism, attacks, and condemnations. But I pulled through them all. I have always insisted that the cardinal literary virtue is sincerity. If I am wrong in that belief, if the world downs me on it, I'll say, "Good-bye, proud world," retire to the ranch, and plant potatoes and raise chickens to keep my stomach full. It was my refusal to take cautious advice that made me.'

There was one piece of cautious advice that he did take, one that probably saved his life: in mid-October he set sail from Hilo for the Marquesas with a registered sea captain and a Dutch sailor on board. Captain Warren had been paroled from the Oregon penitentiary on a charge of murder; Hermann had once captained his father's fishing ketch off the coast of Holland. If he had had the caution to hire experienced seamen while building the *Snark,* or before sailing her to Hawaii, he could have saved himself twenty thousand dollars and endless aggravation. The only one from his original crew to prove himself a worthy adventurer was six-foot, handsome Martin Johnson, who was promoted from cook to mechanic, and thereafter was an asset to the *Snark.* During the two years of its adventuring, Charmian too proved her worth to Jack. She was dead game, a woman of inexhaustible courage, cheerful in the face of hardship, as staunch as a man companion when bucking danger. Whether it was spending the week among the lepers of Molokai, recruiting among the head-hunters of the Solomon Islands, riding a horse over hempen bridges and across tropical canyons, traversing a portion of the Pacific that no sailboat had ever attempted, she had spunk and resourcefulness. She was calm in troubled times, a joyous companion in good times. If Jack had wanted someone to roam side by side with him, in Charmian he found that woman.

Several days out of Hilo Jack opened his book of sailing directions for the South Pacific Ocean, and read that not only had no sailing-boat in recorded history made the cross from Hawaii to the Marquesas, but that, owing to the equatorial currents and the position of the southeast trade winds, it was considered impossible to fetch the Marquesas. 'The impossible did not deter the *Snark,*' commented Jack, and continued merrily on his way, fetching the Marquesas by a stunning feat of navigation and sailing, escaping death only because the larger fates said that the man called Jack London had a number of books in him that had to be written before he could be killed off.

They found themselves wedged between the trade winds and the doldrums, with the *Snark* standing motionless for days. They were buffeted by storms of wind, rain, and sea, by squalls that time and again seemed as though they would snap the tiny, leaking *Snark* like a matchstick. In sixty days they sighted no sail or steamer's smoke; they lost half their water overboard and were saved from perishing of thirst by a providential rain. To Jack, death-appeal was the greatest of all thrills; he was living as ecstatically as a young boy. He navigated the *Snark* through uncharted waters, fished for dolphins and sharks and sea turtles, stretched out on the hatch with the sea-salt in his nostrils and the roll of the ocean caressing his body, wrote his thousand words every day on *Martin Eden,* and exciting articles such as 'A Pacific Traverse.' On warm days he sat on deck and read to Charmian, Captain Warren, Martin Johnson, Hermann, Nakata, the jovial Japanese cabin boy who had replaced Tochigi, and Wada, the cook, from Stevenson's books on the Marquesas and Tahiti, from Conrad's *Typhoon* and *Youth* and Melville's *White Jacket, Typee, Moby Dick.* The troubled background of the *Snark* was forgotten as he fulfilled his promise to the romantic boy of thirteen who had read every travel book Miss Coolbrith could find for him in the Oakland Public Library.

Two months of sailing brought him to Nuka-hiva, in the Marquesas. 'The trade blew out of the northwest, while we steered a steady course for the southwest. Ten days of this and on the morning of December 6, at five o'clock, we sighted land just where it ought to have been, dead ahead. We passed to leeward of Uahuka, skirted the southern edge of Nuka-hiva, and that night, in driving squalls and inky blackness, fought our way in to an anchorage in the narrow bay of Taiohae. The anchor rumbled down to the blatting of wild goats on the cliffs, and the air we breathed was heavy with the perfume of flowers.'

In Nuka-hiva it was a source of pleasure and gratification to him to rent the clubhouse in which Robert Louis Stevenson had spent frequent afternoons when he lived in the Marquesas. On the second day, as soon as they were able to ride, the entire crew set out for Melville's magnificent valley of Hapaa, which Melville had pictured in *Typee* as peopled by a strong and warlike tribe living in the midst of a tropical and fertile garden. Alas for the disillusionments of youth's dreams: by the time Jack rode through the valley of Hapaa it had become an untenanted, howling, tropical wilderness, with the few Marquesans who had escaped the ravages of the diseases brought in by the 'inevitable white man' dying in their wretched huts of galloping consumption. He wrote a heart-broken article about the extinction of this glorious race, which he named, in deference to Melville, 'Typee.'

'All the strength and beauty has departed, and the valley of Typee is the abode of some dozen wretched creatures af-flicted by leprosy, elephantiasis and tuberculosis. Life has rot-ted away in this wonderful garden spot.'

After twelve colorful days in the Marquesas, during which he hunted wild goats, and witnessed native festivals, dances, and feasts, he hoisted anchor and sailed through the Paumo-tan Islands for Tahiti, where he was to pick up his mail. Here he learned that the *Snark* had once again been given up for lost, that the San Francisco sailors were recalling their proph-ecies that she was badly planned and badly rigged. Many of the papers ran stories of genuine regret over the loss of so able a young writer; others accused him of staying lost merely to get publicity, and one editorial even charged him with employing a very clever press agent who had secured for him free advertising worth more than the cost of the boat.

Though he had been gone only eight months, an examina-tion of the many boxes of accumulated mail showed him that when the master is away his affairs soon fall into chaos. The Oakland bank, convinced that he was on the bottom of the South Pacific, had foreclosed the mortgage on Flora's house. A number of checks he had issued in Hilo, totaling eight hundred dollars, had been returned by another Oakland bank marked 'Not sufficient funds,' causing an uproar in the press.

When Jack left Glen Ellen he had given Ninetta Eames his power of attorney and made her his agent and business man-ager. She had set her own salary at ten dollars a month, which she now raised to twenty dollars a month, in addition to the forty dollars a month she was charging as rent for the rooms at Wake Robin he was not occupying. Poring over the bills, Jack learned that she had spent a thousand dollars to build an annex to the barn on the Hill Ranch so that the fore-man might live there with his wife; fourteen hundred dollars in the month of December to take care of Flora, Johnny Miller, Mammy Jenny, Bessie, and the two girls, to pay wages, buy supplies and equipment for the ranch, to pay in-surance, and keep up Wake Robin. Another bill totaling a thousand dollars was a three-page list of equipment for the *Snark,* including everything from a thousand gallons of gaso-line to a hundred boxes of Jack's special Egyptian cigarettes and a dozen boxes of candy. All of these myriad expenses in addition to the thousand dollars a month it was costing him to man and run the *Snark!* Despite the fact that in December Macmillan had paid him fifty-five hundred dollars in royalties; Reynolds, his occasional agent in New York, had sold 'To Build a Fire' to *Century* for three hundred and fifty dollars; Ninetta Eames had sold 'The Lepers of Molokai' to *Woman's Home Companion,* 'Finding One's Way About' and 'The Inconceivable and Monstrous' to *Harper's Weekly;* that money had come in from English magazines and English publishers, from his Scandinavian, German, French, and Italian publishers, he learned that in the first week of the year 1908 he had exactly sixty-six dollars in the world, and no immediate promise of anything more.

When he had arrived in Honolulu on May 28 of the previous year, almost the first thing he had said was, 'I am bankrupt and shall probably have to stay here until I raise some money.' He had then written a number of articles about the voyage and stories about Hawaii which had brought from three hundred to five hundred dollars apiece. It was only four and a half years since the success of *The Call of the Wild;* he had earned enough to spend forty thousand dollars on the *Snark,* eleven thousand on the Hill Ranch, ten thousand on Bessie's home, eight thousand on Flora's home, and about thirty-five thousand more to support his ever-growing entourage. It was now costing him three thousand dollars a month to navigate, yet here he was stranded in Tahiti with sixty-six dollars in the world!

The *S.S. Mariposa* was scheduled to sail from Tahiti for San Francisco. Jack decided to leave with her, to go home and try to straighten out his affairs. How he got together the money to buy the tickets for himself and Charmian remains a mystery. He left the *Snark* in the hands of Captain Warren and the crew, and returned to California. His horde of anxious relatives, who had hoped to receive mail on the *Mariposa* to assure them that he was safe, were stunned when they learned he was in San Francisco. The newspapers broke out the boldest headlines yet to herald his arrival. One reporter stated, 'The smile that won't come off doesn't half express the London smile. This is hearty and soulful, of wide expanse, and good to look upon.' Many accused him of abandoning his voyage. When he told everyone that he was returning with the *Mariposa* when it sailed a week later, those of his friends who did not laugh at him in disbelief tried to persuade him against it, urging that since he had demonstrated he could do it, he should let well enough alone and remain home. They evidently did not believe his statement to the reporters that the days spent on board the *Snark* were among the happiest of his life.

He immediately wired Macmillan for an advance against the almost completed *Martin Eden,* with which he lifted the mortgage on Flora's house and paid the ever-mounting bank interest on the Hill Ranch. He arranged with *Harper's Weekly* to publish a series of the *Snark* articles, using the money to pay his most pressing debts and to give Flora her fifty-two-dollar check for February, Bessie her seventy-five-dollar check, Mammy Jenny her fifteen dollar . . . By glancing at the back files of the *Woman's Home Companion* he learned why he had been charged double prices in Hawaii and Papeete: the *Companion,* to whom he had transferred his contract because *Cosmopolitan* had broadcast the news that they were sending him around the world, had found that identical piece of false advertising too juicy to resist.

The year 1907 had seen four of his books published, one better than the record he had set in 1902. He was but thirty-one years old and he had published twenty books, for he was as profligate with the great riches of his mind as he was with the riches they earned for him.

Before Adam, his dramatization of evolution and primitive life, is still read with delight by Americans. *The Road,* though it received scant attention when released, is now recognized as one of our few genuine source books on tramp life. *Love of Life* includes some of his most finely wrought Alaskan tales. Written for the cash he needed to pour into the *Snark,* the excellence of these tales indicates that some men who write for literature, with nary a tarnishing thought of money in mind, can create trash, while others who write for money can create literature. A man's gifts, and not what he plans to do with the rewards of those gifts, are the determining factors. Jack had a love of truth, an ability to think straight, a vigorous education, deep understanding of people, and the courage to say what he felt and thought. Coupled with this richness and integrity of mind was a native story-teller's gift whipped into shape by hard and intelligent work. The fact that he needed money had not caused him to give short measure or sabotage his craft; his career was founded on the belief that good work deserved good money.

Brett's prediction about *The Iron Heel* proved accurate; the majority of newspapers did not mention its publication; the few that did declared that 'the hand of the law should descend heavily upon him.' Ignored, unfavorably reviewed, the book received no recognition and no sale except among the handful of Marxian socialists in America. Ten years later it was to emerge as one of the world's great classics of revolution, and to make of Jack London a veritable God to the Russian people. Bitter as was the capitalist press against *The Iron Heel,* the socialist press, which the year before had berated him for walking out on a luxurious yacht when there was so much work to be done at home, was even more bitter. He was accused of betraying the Cause, of antagonizing the public by preaching bloodshed, of alienating the party membership, which was peaceful and wanted socialism to filter through gradually by means of education, legislation, and the ballot, and not by death at the barricades. Though the capitalist and socialist presses united in calling him a menace, by April, three months later, the socialists had forgiven him sufficiently to suggest that he run for the presidency of the United States on the Socialist ticket.

He fulfilled his promise and returned with Charmian on the *Mariposa* to continue his seven-year voyage around the world. On April 9 he sailed in the *Snark* from Tahiti to Bora Bora, gem of Polynesia. In Bora Bora he joined the native stone fishers; in Raiatea he lived with the aborigines amid a wealth of food and gifts showered upon him in a profusion unknown to more civilized countries; in Pago Pago he was entertained by a native king. Sailing onward to Suva in the Fiji Islands the *Snark* was buffeted by storms and lost for days because the chronometer went out of order. They reached Suva, capital of the Fijis, in June. Here Captain Warren, who had grown melancholy during the month of May and twice gone berserk, went ashore, leaving the *Snark* badly in need of repairs, and did not return. Jack had his possessions sent after him, and from that time forward captained his vessel himself without mishap. He cruised through the Solomon Islands, lived on the copra plantations in the bush 'as near the rawest edge of screaming savagery as any place to be found on this earth.' At Malaita, where many white men lost their heads to the savages, he joined friends on the *Minota* and went recruiting with them among the bushmen for slave labor for the plantations. He was attacked from ambush by cannibals, by natives on board the boat who wanted to loot and scuttle her and *kai-kai* the white crew. When it looked as though the ship would pile up on the reef he was shot at by Sniders, by poisoned arrows, was attacked by tribes of screaming black natives. 'When the *Minota* first struck there was not a canoe in sight; but like vultures circling down out of the blue, canoes began to arrive from every quarter. The boat's crew, with rifles at the ready, kept them lined up a hundred feet away with a promise of death if they ventured nearer. There they clung, black and ominous, holding their canoes with their paddles on the perilous edge of the breaking surf.' Here indeed was adventure worthy of the boy who had sailed the *Razzle Dazzle* without reefing, who had four times stopped the Overland Express, who had shot White Horse Rapids, and sailed a native junk across the Yellow Sea. 'I'm having the time of my life!' he cried.

He made copious notes, took photographs, at each island collected native canoes, paddles, shells, wood carvings, spears, calabashes, bowls, mats, tapa cloth, jewels, coral, and aboriginal ornaments that formed a complete South Seas museum when he took them back to Glen Ellen. And everywhere he went, Fiji, the Marquesas, Samoa, wherever he could gather together ten white men, he gave his lecture on revolution!

Living as he did in the midst of leprosy, elephantiasis, malaria, ringworm, gari-gari (a horrible skin itch), Solomon sores, or yaws, skin ulcers, and a hundred other jungle diseases, the *Snark* was converted into a hospital ship. Every time a member of the crew bruised himself on board or cut his leg while beaching the boat or treading through the jungle, a yaw developed which spread over his body, the individual ulcers becoming big as silver dollars. In the Solomons the entire crew contracted malaria, sometimes as many as five of them being down with it, leaving the sixth to sail the *Snark* through fair weather or foul. Jack had so many bouts of malaria that for months he was as much on his back as he was on his feet, doped with forty grains of quinine. On the way to Fiji he scratched some mosquito bites and his body became covered with yaws. Even these hardships he enjoyed because they seemed to him the romantic hardships of the explorer, the intrepid and inevitable white man who conquered the world. He liked to call himself an Amateur M.D.; he pulled teeth, treated Charmian's and Martin Johnson's open yaws with corrosive sublimate, slammed quinine down the throat of Wada, who had contracted blackwater fever and with Oriental fatalism had given over to dying.

Except when down with malaria, he kept rigidly to his routine of composing a thousand words every morning. Charmian, equally faithful to her duties, typed his manuscripts and took dictation for the replies to his voluminous

correspondence. His one novel to come out of the South
Seas, *Adventure,* which took him many months of painstak-
ing labor, was laid on a copra plantation he had visited on
the Solomon Islands. When the critics complained about his
'screaming savagery,' Jack defended himself on the ground
that he had portrayed only what he had seen with his own
eyes. Veracity of reporting, however, does not make convincing literature; *Adventure* is adequate escapist entertainment,
but no better than could have been done by a dozen of his
contemporaries. It was serialized by *Popular Magazine,*
whose readers had a low literacy quotient, and when published in book form died a quick death.

His articles about the voyage, later collected in *The Cruise
of the Snark,* are colorful and dashing journalism, told in the
warm, infectious, friendly style of narrative which so precisely reflects his character; but he would have been the last
to imagine they had any solid literary value. On board the
Snark, and in the years to come, he was to write thirty short
stories laid in the South Seas; while some of them, such as
'The House of Mapuhi,' 'The Heathen,' 'Koolau,' 'The
Leper,' 'Chun ah Chun,' 'Yah! Yah! Yah!' are good yarns,
the reader sits apart in wonderment, as though watching
some aboriginal sideshow. The stories of the 'inevitable white
man' who tames the blacks and farms the world are exciting
and exotic, but they have little of the universal in them. The
reader is rarely able to identify himself with the main character, to live and fight and die with him, as he does with Jack's
Alaskan heroes, with his native American protagonists. His
South Seas adventures could be important to no one but himself. His socialist comrades had criticized him for going away
when there was so much work to be done at home. They
were right in a profounder sense: Jack's simplest writings
about his own people and customs and conflicts create literature, stay with us to enliven our memories and broaden our
concepts, and our love of the printed page.

The voyage of the *Snark* repaid him many times over in
adventure; if as an investment in literary materials it was not
to prove profitable, Jack would not have been concerned over
this aspect of the bargain. He loved to cry, 'I have always
stood for the exalting of the life that is in me over art, or any
other extraneous thing.'

In addition to maintaining rigid discipline in his work, he
strove valiantly to keep his business affairs in order. Wanting
some guest houses built near Wake Robin to accommodate his
friends when he returned, he wrote Mrs. Eames a nine-page

letter of instructions containing a mass of technical information about building. While thousands of miles away in the Solomon Islands he detailed which way each door should swing, where the washbowl should stand in relation to the toilet. He wrote beautifully clear, logical comprehensive letters to his business associates, but the more instructions he wrote the greater confusion his affairs fell into; he had not yet come to realize that any man who earns between twenty thousand and thirty thousand dollars a year is running a big business and has to remain close to the factory. His agent in New York would sell a short story to an English magazine while Ninetta Eames was in the process of selling the same story to an American magazine; after Jack had spent the money the American magazine had paid, it would irately demand a refund because it had been cheated out of the English copyright. His American and English book publishers were quarreling over who owned the distribution rights in the Colonies, which resulted in publications being held up; editors who would have bought stories and articles if certain details could have been adjusted, returned the manuscripts because it took too many months to negotiate through the Solomon Islands. His value in the market had gone up, he had been receiving five hundred and six hundred dollars for a manuscript from such magazines as *Cosmopolitan* and *Collier's;* when the editors stopped buying, Ninetta Eames began hawking stories and articles as though they were fish, demanding, 'How much will you give for this Jack London story?' and taking any price offered. The editors soon began to sense that the London material was being sent out under panic conditions; they refrained from buying altogether, the market became glutted with his manuscripts, his income halted abruptly.

The hundreds upon hundreds of frantic typewritten pages Ninetta Eames sent to Jack during this period constitute an amazing document. In sentiment as well as language they bear a family resemblance to the hundreds of typewritten pages sent to Jack by Mrs. Eames's niece five years before. Fluttery, flowery, bathed in saccharine protestations of undying love and sacrifice and devotion, the steely fingers are visible beneath every line. Ninetta Eames built an annex to her Wake Robin home; when Jack returned to Glen Ellen she charged him rent to occupy the rooms his money had built. For a second time she raised her own salary, this time to thirty dollars a month, back-dating the raise, and demanding to know of Jack if he were not willing to pay her a living wage. Anguished by this attack, Jack protested, 'One of the things I have prided myself on since I have had a dollar to spend has been that everybody who ever did anything for me has always been well paid.' After months of crying about her poverty, her hardships, her inability to repay Jack the loan he had made her at Wake Robin before he left on the *Snark,* he finally wrote, 'My money on deposit at the Bank of Oakland is earning me no interest; help yourself to it for whatever you need.' An examination of the check books today reveals that Ninetta Eames took him at his word: there are hundreds of checks to sanitariums, doctors, drugstores; there are checks for clothing, furniture, repairs to Wake Robin, and for grocery bills that would have fed a large-sized institution.

If all of this was without Jack's knowledge, it was at least with his overt permission. What he did not know was that he was getting about twenty-five cents' worth for every dollar being spent on the Hill Ranch. He was paying to have a solid stone wall built in the new barn he had ordered, but a few years later when an earthquake hit Glen Ellen, the walls cracked and he discovered that they were not only hollow but that the workmen had thrown into them the tin cans and refuse from their lunches. There was the matter of the bathroom equipment bought for the foreman's house, for which he paid full price, but which proved to be second-hand when it was deposited at Glen Ellen railway station. However the worst blow to Jack was that Mrs. Eames stopped sending him his monthly accounts. In an agonized letter written to her from Penduffryn, in which he tries to set her straight on a score of business complications, he complains that although he received mail from her every month of the year 1908, she had sent him accounts for only February and May.

Then, in the midst of the chaos, Ninetta Eames concluded an astute business deal and Jack forgave her everything. She sold the serial rights of *Martin Eden* to the *Pacific Monthly,* for the princely sum of seven thousand dollars, which covered his debts and put him a few thousand dollars ahead.

Adjoining the Hill Ranch in Sonoma Valley was the Kohler vineyard property of eight hundred acres and the Lamotte Ranch of one hundred and ten acres. For many months Ninetta Eames kept reminding Jack that the Kohler property was for sale for thirty thousand dollars and a great bargain, and repeatedly informed him that the Lamotte Ranch could be bought for ten thousand dollars. There was no reason for him to buy either of these ranches; he already owned a hundred and thirty acres of magnificent land on which he had not yet passed a single night; there remained another five years in which he intended to sail around the world; and the seven thousand dollars he had just received from *Martin Eden* had saved him from imminent bankruptcy. But he remembered the rolling hills and redwoods of the Lamotte Ranch, the happy hours he had spent riding down its canyons and across the trails through the vineyards and madrone. By return mail he ordered Mrs. Eames to buy the Lamotte Ranch for him. She paid about three thousand dollars down, and mortgaged the balance. Sailing a ketch among the Solomon Islands, headed for Japan, India, and the Suez Canal, uncertain whether he could sell tomorrow's story or meet next month's bills, Jack was now owner of two hundred and forty acres of the most beautiful foothill country in California. . . .

By September 18, 1908, the fun of playing the Amateur M.D. was gone; his hands began to swell with dropsy; only by the most painful effort could he close them. Then the skin began to peel off, first one layer, then two, then five and six layers. He was in constant agony. No one could diagnose the strange disease he had contracted. A nervous affliction seized his whole body; at frequent intervals he became helpless, unable to stagger about the deck for fear of being forced to clutch something with his hands. The nervous disturbance began to affect his mind; his persecution mania returned, there was a conspiracy against him, people were trying to prevent him from completing his voyage around the world.

Danger nor hardship had been able to deter him, expense and ridicule had only whetted his determination. But illness at last conquered him. Helpless with pain, he arranged for a retired captain to watch over the *Snark*, then engaged passage for himself, Charmian, Martin Johnson, and Nakata on the *S.S. Nakomba* for Sydney.

The night before he was to sail he went alone aboard the *Snark*. A full moon lighted the deck of the ship that had grown under his own brain and his own hand. He loved every part of her, even her weaknesses and faults, for they too had been of his making. She was worth every dollar he had poured into her, every ounce of energy he had expended in her behalf, all the abuse and ridicule he had borne in her creation. At times she had been errant and self-willed, at others weak and incompetent, but she had served him well, she had been faithful to him, had carried him safely over the thousands of miles of ocean at his bidding, had brought him great happiness and heroic adventures, had provided his mind with rich and exotic scenes upon which his memory might feed in leaner, duller days. Together they had faced death unflinching, had battled stormy seas, been lashed by wind and rain, lay quiescent in the doldrums; been warmed and made joyous by the strong clean sun and the salt sea air. The *Snark* had been a good friend to him, and in separating he ran a pain-racked hand fondly across her railings and riggings and gear, shedding an honest, sentimental tear, as he felt all true friends should at parting.

After twelve wretched days at sea he entered a hospital in Sydney, and stayed five weeks there on a white cot. His malady baffled the Australian specialists, appeared to be unknown in the history of medicine. 'I am as helpless as a child. On occasion my hands are twice their natural size, with seven dead and dying skins peeling off at one time. My toenails, in twenty-four hours, grow as thick as they are long.'

Finding that they could do him no good in the hospital, Jack spent the next five months in Sydney hotels and apartments, hoping for a cure that would enable him to return to the *Snark*. He was unable to write, and in such pain that he was hardly able to read. The only job he turned in was a report of the Burns-Johnson fight in Australia. What a newspaper reporter had described only a year before as 'the smile that won't come off' was now completely gone. He was a sick, discouraged, and confused young man.

By the beginning of March, 1909, he realized that if he did not go home to California he would leave his bones in the tropics just as surely as he would have if the bushmen of the New Hebrides had cut off his head and *'kai-kai'd* along him.' He sent Martin Johnson with a navigator to the Solomon Islands to bring the *Snark* down to Sydney. 'I left the *Snark* in charge of a drunken master, and when she was brought back to Sydney she had damned little left upon her. I am still wondering what became of my automatic rifles, of my ship's stores, of my naturalist's shotguns, of my two cameras, of my three thousand French francs.' He took his personal possessions off the *Snark*, then offered her up at auction. She fetched three thousand dollars, and was put into recruiting slave labor among the Solomon Islands, an ironic end for a ship built by one of the world's leading socialists.

Arriving in San Francisco on July 23, 1909, after more than two years of wandering, he told newspapermen at the dock, 'I am unutterably weary, and I have come home for a good rest.' He was under a staggering load of debt, his health was badly undermined, the newspapers of the country were either hostile or disinterested, the magazine editors had seen so little real material from him in the past year that they suspected he was through; even the public was tiring of his recent work, in which he was fulfilling too well the accusation that Jack London began a story with three characters and ended by killing four of them. By poor navigating he had piled his craft on a tropical coral reef, where it was slowly breaking up under heavy seas.

9

JACK'S health had improved on the voyage from Sydney which he made in leisurely stages by way of South America and Panama; once home, the temperate California climate soon brought him back to normal. When he stumbled on a book called *Effects of Tropical Light upon White Men,* and learned that his baffling affliction had been nothing more sinister than the ultraviolet rays of the tropical sun tearing at his skin, his psychological recovery was completed. By August he was swimming in the creek he once again dammed, riding Washoe Ban across the Hill and Lamotte Ranches, inhaling the hot curative scents of sage and pine and baking native earth.

Construction never having been begun on the guest houses about which he had written Mrs. Eames from the Solomon Islands, he once again moved into Wake Robin, occupying the annex that had been built during his absence. Not a man to harbor past injuries, he gave Ninetta Eames an honorable discharge, bought the seventeen-acre Fish Ranch so that she would have a meadow to pasture her cow, and when she divorced Roscoe Eames and married Edward Payne, gave her a five-hundred-dollar gift in addition to her wedding outfit.

With the intelligent Nakata to cook and care for him, and Charmian guarding his privacy, he set to work in deadly earnest to straighten his affairs. His first move was to recall every manuscript from the market, and to inform the editors that he was home to stay, that he had magnificent new material, that there would be no more confusion in the marketing of his wares. For a period of three months not a line appeared in a magazine under the by-line of Jack London, the first time he had been missing from the reading world of America since the appearance of 'An Odyssey of the North' at the opening of the century. These months he devoted to heroic labor, nineteen hours of concentrated work a day, seven days a week, the identical schedule he had imposed upon himself in his novitiate: for he knew it to be more difficult for a man to climb to favor a second time than a first. Editors and critics were saying he was through, that he had shot his bolt, that the public was tired of him; he knew that he had barely scratched the surface of the fine and moving stories he had to tell.

When *Martin Eden* was released, though it deserved the finest reception of all his books, the novel was so neglected or abused by the unfriendly press that Brett could find no laudatory lines from the reviews to quote in his advertisements. Jack complained that the critics had not understood him, that the reviewers were accusing him of abandoning his socialism and making individualism sound alluring, whereas he had written the book as an indictment of the Nietzschean superman philosophy. On the fly leaf of the copy he sent to Upton Sinclair, he wrote, 'One of my motifs in *Martin Eden* was an attack on individualism. I must have bungled, for not a single reviewer has discovered it.' He had not bungled; he had merely written such a gripping human life story that his conflicting philosophies had fallen by the wayside. If he could have known that *Martin Eden* was going to inspire an entire generation of American authors, if he could have known that thirty years later *Martin Eden* would be considered by thousands of fiction lovers as the greatest of American novels, he would not have been so heart-broken over the treatment afforded what he always called his best book.

The deeper he was in debt the better he worked; the greater the odds against him, the more passionately he attacked his adversaries. He began work on the boldly conceived *Burning Daylight,* a novel of the Klondike and San Francisco; he wrote four of his best South Sea tales; he wrote 'Samuel' and 'The Sea Farmer,' two stirring dialect yarns laid on the coast of Ireland. Anger had always been one of his most potent motivations; he burned at white heat, for he was madder'n hell at having almost destroyed himself, at the critics for saying he was washed up. The sheer ecstasy of creative writing having palled after the publication of twenty volumes, pressure helped him to turn out his daily stint. For the following seven years that pressure remained so heavy and constant one comes to suspect he knew he had to keep himself in debt in order to get his work done. 'I am swinging along a thousand words a day on a novel, and I wouldn't break it off for anything short of the trumpets of doom.'

By November he had worked so faithfully and so well that

he sold the best of his prize-fight stories, 'A Piece of Steak,' to the *Saturday Evening Post* for seven hundred and fifty dollars, and received a contract to supply them with twelve stories the following year. When *Burning Daylight* was completed he sold the serial rights to the New York *Herald* for eight thousand dollars. Having acquired the privilege of selling the reprint rights to as many newspapers as would purchase them, the *Herald* wrote glowing, promotional articles about Jack London and *Burning Daylight* which were reproduced in the hundreds of newspapers buying the serialization. This favorable publicity offset the abuse and ridicule he had been enduring.

Burning Daylight ranks with *Call of the Wild, The Sea Wolf, Iron Heel, Martin Eden, John Barleycorn, Valley of the Moon,* and *Star Rover* as important American novels. The first third, in which Jack portrays the history of Alaska before the Klondike gold strike, and Burning Daylight's dash with the mail from Circle City to Dyea, is the most stirring writing to come out of the frozen North; in the last third the descriptions of the beauties of the countryside at Glen Ellen reveal him to be a faithful lover of nature to whom nature in turn reveals her beauties and subtleties; but the real accomplishment of *Burning Daylight*, which purports to be an action and adventure story, is the manner in which he wove his socialism into the middle third, making it such an integral part of the action and suspense that the reader unsuspectingly drinks it in as a necessary development of the tale. Burning Daylight, a Nietzschean blond-beast buccaneer, while raiding the business pirates of San Francisco, muses, 'Work, legitimate work, was the source of all wealth. Whether it was a sack of potatoes, a grand piano or a seven passenger touring car, it came into being only by a performance of work. Where the bunco came in was in the distribution of these things after labor had created them. By hundreds of thousands men sat up and schemed how they could get between the workers and the things the workers produced. These schemers were business men. The size of the whack they took was determined by no rule of equity, but by their own strength and swinishness. It was always a case of "all the traffic could bear." '

Rank heresy to unawakened America of 1910, this was authentic proletarian writing; because the sentiments were not superimposed upon the story, because they appear to be a necessary part of Daylight's observations and conclusions about the local scene, they become at one and the same time proletarian writing and art. When *The Iron Heel* had been published Jack had been accused of destroying a good novelist to become a mediocre propagandist; he had replied that he could weld propaganda and art so that the reader could never see where they had been joined. In *Burning Daylight* he was successful at this most difficult of all writing tasks. With millions of people thrilling to the exploits of Burning Daylight, he was reinstated in favor with both the bourgeois and socialist publics.

Confirmed in his knowledge that he had lost none of his powers, and desirous of firing a twenty-one-gun salute in honor of Charmian's announced pregnancy, Jack began the fulfilment of another of his great life dreams. He started work on the house in which he planned to live for the rest of his life, choosing for its site a magnificent spot in a canyon of the Hill Ranch, surrounded by redwoods, vineyards, prune orchards, and forests of manzanita. Here he would have room for his library of four thousand volumes, for the stacks of broad white cardboard boxes in which he arranged his government reports, socialist pamphlets, newspaper clippings, national dialects, names and customs, the poems he still bound together between red covers. Here he would have room for his steel files, crammed with business and personal correspondence, for his thirty-high rows of narrow black boxes in which he treasured his souvenirs from The Road and Alaska, from his trips to Korea and the South Seas; in which he kept his hundreds of jokes, puzzles, games, pull-a-parts, water pistols, coins with both sides the same, decks of strange cards. Here he would be able to make his guests comfortable, provide them with such modern conveniences as electricity and running water in their rooms; build a huge playroom in the cool basement for men only, in which they could hatch political schemes, tell stories, play billiards and poker, bowl, concoct any amount of noisy nonsense. Here he would have a beautiful music room in which Charmian and his many musician friends could play, a huge dining-room where he could seat fifty people for good food and good talk, a redwood-lined bedroom for himself in which there would be space for an ingeniously devised night table to hold the accouterments Nakata deposited for Master at bedtime, and on which he wouldn't be so crowded he would forever be spilling his iced drink on his books. Here he would at last have an adequate workroom with provision for a dictaphone and space set aside for a professional secretary.

He maintained that he was building his 'historic home.' The Indians of Alaska had called the conquering white man 'Wolf'; that one word had come to dominate much of Jack's

thinking, for he always thought of himself as the conquering
Wolf. He used it in such titles as *Son of the Wolf* and *The
Sea Wolf*, signed himself as Wolf in his letters to George
Sterling, and now he was building the Wolf House of the
great white chief. He hoped with all his considerable might
that Charmian would give him a son so that he could start a
London dynasty that would live forever in the Wolf House.

He determined that it must be the most beautiful and orgi-
nal home in America; to achieve that end he was willing to
spend any amount of money. The house must be constructed
of the huge red stones the Valley of the Moon grew more
plentifully than any other crop; the ten-thousand-year-old
redwoods must be cut down for timber. He called in San
Francisco architects and spent many happy hours mulling
over blueprints, arranging the rooms, designing the exterior
to fit indigenously into the hills. In Santa Rosa he found an
Italian master stonemason by the name of Forni, whom he
ordered to build a house that would stand through the centuries. Every inch of rock had to be washed with water and
scrubbed with a steel-wire brush; more cement had to be
used, and less lime, so that the walls would stand forever; one
workman had to spend all his time keeping the walls wet so
the cement wouldn't harden too fast and turn to powder;
there had to be two floors between each stage, and sometimes
three; the inside walls had to be of solid timber, the outside
logs bolted into the inside studs for double security; copper
had to be used for the roof gullies and copper for all lead-in
pipes.

As a rampant individualist he was going to build himself
the greatest castle in the United States. As a socialist he was
going to give workingmen good jobs, and devote more than
half of the twenty-three rooms to guests. In order to expedite
construction he had Forni put thirty men to work.

In the spring of 1910 he made one of his wisest moves: he
invited Eliza London Shepard to live with him permanently
and take care of his ranches. Mrs. Shepard was now forty-
three years old, separated from her seventy-one-year-old husband; she had suffered hardship and spiritual adversity since
leaving John London's ranch in Livermore, and had developed into a sympathetic woman. She was still plain of face
and manner, honest, capable, hard-headed, having trained
herself to become a lawyer so that she might help her husband in his patent office. Without froth, frill, or pretense, she
was loved by everyone who came in contact with her. She
had been faithful to Jack through the years, loving him as
devotedly as she did her own son, Irving.

Jack's first move, now that he had Eliza to manage for him, was to complicate her task by buying the Kohler vineyards about which Ninetta Eames had so often written him when he was away on the *Snark,* eight hundred acres of land joining the Hill, Lamotte, and Fish Ranches. The Kohler vineyards cost him thirty thousand dollars, very little of which he had in his possession, for the Wolf House had already been started and was also scheduled to cost thirty thousand dollars. What prompted him to buy that additional eight hundred acres when he had no money with which to pay for them, when he already had so much beautiful land to live upon, cultivate, and enjoy? Thirty thousand seemed a cheap price for so much fine land, it would connect his other two ranches, make him monarch of all he surveyed. . . . But he always insisted that there was no explaining the why of 'I Like.' 'When philosophy has maundered ponderously for a month telling the individual what he must do, the individual says in an instant, "I like" and philosophy goes glimmering. It is "I like" that makes the drunkard drink and the martyr wear a hair shirt; that makes one man pursue fame, another gold, another love, another God.' He liked the Kohler vineyards, and so he bought them.

By June of 1910 he was once again sending frantic letters East for money. 'I have a pressing need of money on account of a ten-thousand-dollar payment I have to make in buying some land. By throwing myself on others' mercy I had the time extended to June 26, but if I do not pay then I stand to lose not only the land but the advance payment.'

Charmian left for Oakland to prepare for the coming of her baby. Jack set a corps of men to work clearing a new riding path which would join his ranches and circle the site of the Wolf House, a surprise for her against the day he would bring her back to the ranch with her son: for he was positive this time it would be a son. He dreamed away pleasant hours thinking of the great moment when he would be able to put his boy on a pony and have the lad ride by his side through the eleven hundred acres which would one day be his domain.

On June 19, Charmian gave birth to a daughter. The baby lived for only three days. Eliza took care of the burial. Grieving, inconsolable, Jack wandered into a saloon near his old waterfront haunts at Seventh and Webster Streets, a bunch of newspapers under his arm. Muldowney, the proprietor, accusing him of wanting to paste circulars on the walls started a fight in which four of his hangers-on joined. Jack was severely beaten before he managed to escape. He had Muldow-

ney arrested, but the judge dismissed the case, implying it had
been a drunken brawl in which the court had no concern. Police court reporters sprayed the story of the 'drunken brawl'
over the nation's papers, heaping double invective upon him
for getting drunk with his wife in the hospital, and his baby
just dead. When well-wishers wrote him that the judge had
not vindicated him because he owned the premises upon
which the saloon was located, Jack sent a raging letter to the
judge, copies of which he mailed to the press syndicates, in
which he reviewed the case and ended with, 'Someday, somewhere, somehow, I am going to get you, and I shall get you
to the full hilt of the law.' He then inserted an advertisement
in those Bay papers that would carry it, asking for information concerning any political, judicial, or social corruptiveness
of the judge who owned the land occupied by Muldowney's
tenderloin resort. The false charges of drunken brawling had
been wretched business, but when his letter to the judge was
reproduced all over America, people shook their heads in
amused despair. The only revenge he was to enjoy was in the
form of the writer's perennial revenge: he wrote a story
about the affair called 'The Benefit of the Doubt,' in which he
thrashed the judge . . . and then sold it to the *Post* for seven
hundred and fifty dollars.

Several days later, with a swollen and purple eye, he departed for Reno, where he spent ten days writing up the
training camps and the Johnson-Jeffries fight for the New
York *Herald*. He enjoyed prize fights; the ten days at the
training camps with the other correspondents, most of whom
were friends from other campaigns, provided him with an escape from the bitterness of having lost his child. He now had
the prescience that he would die without ever having bred a
son, a conviction that made him feel dry and barren despite
the twenty-four books he had begot.

Back in Oakland he spent the money he had just earned to
buy the *Roamer*, the fourth of his sailboats in which to cruise
about the Bay. As soon as Charmian had recovered they went
together for a vacation on the water, working, sailing, fishing
for their supper. When he returned to Glen Ellen, his neighbors, thinking to hear romantic tales of the South Seas, invited him to lecture in the local Chauvet Hall. Since he declined to speak from the stage, the chairman went to the grocery next door and brought back a soap box for him to stand
upon so that the audience might see him. The farmers of
Glen Ellen heard not one word about his adventures in Tahiti, Fiji, or Samoa; instead he spent the hour trying to prove
Eugene V. Debs's theory that 'So far as the class struggle is

concerned there is no good capitalist and no bad working-man. Every capitalist is your enemy and every workingman is your friend.'

The passage of the summer months healed the wounds of the loss of the baby, and the Oakland trouble. His greatest pleasure was to call his favorite dog, Brown Wolf, and ride Washoe Ban across the fields to the Wolf House to note its daily progress and talk with Forni and the workmen; to observe with gratification that the workmen were coming to love the house as much as he loved it, to feel that it was a great work of art they were helping him create. The workmen lived in tents on the ranch, and after work they would climb to the highest knoll with a jug of wine and an accordion and sing sentimental Italian songs to the warm, close stars. Often of a clear evening Jack came to sing with them, to drink a glass of their sour red wine and discuss the building problems that had arisen during the day. Forni says, 'Jack was the best human man I ever met. He was kind to everybody, never saw him come on job without smile. Was very good Democrat—very noble gentleman, a man for family love and for the workingman. Never heard a word from him in four years that we was working bad or too slow.' When the workmen were ready for sleep he would shake hands with each of them, wish them a good night, and then walk with Brown Wolf through the prune orchard with the smell of the plums and the leaves and the rich, exuding earth in his nostrils.

He was completely devoted to Charmian. With Nakata they took a driving trip behind four spirited horses through the wilds of Northern California, Oregon, and Washington. She was still game for any adventure, rode and swam and sailed with him, played the piano and sang for him, typed his manuscripts and took dictation on his mail. He also maintained friendly relations with Bessie, going to the house in Piedmont several times a month to visit the children, play with them, take them to the theater or the circus. Bessie told newspaper reporters, 'Mr. London is doing all he possibly can for his two daughters. He loves them devoutly. He comes here often to see them when he is in Oakland, and they consume hours playing and talking together. They love their father and there is no reason why they should not. There is no bitterness in my heart toward him. In doing for the children as he is, he is doing for me far more than he can realize.' There was always a touch of the tragically noble in Bessie Maddern's character.

Flora, with the encroachment of old age, was growing

more erratic than she ever had been in the early days with John London. Despite the fact that Jack had bought her the house in which she lived, that he had put Mammy Jenny into it to look after her, and sent her a fifty-five-dollar check every month of his life, she went about to her neighbors in Oakland telling them that Jack London wasn't supporting her, that she needed money to live on, and wouldn't they buy the home-made bread she was about to go into the business of baking? Profoundly distressed by such callous treatment of an aging mother by a wealthy and famous son, the neighbors signified their willingness to buy a loaf of home-made bread daily. Flora then bought a stove and began baking. The story was quickly spread by word of mouth, and Oakland was horrified. At his wit's end to know how to control his mother, Jack wrote her the most patiently tender but pathetic letter he ever penned. 'Dear Mama: I just want to give you the figures and reasoning in your bread-making. In your most prosperous month you have cleared $7.50. You paid $26 for the stove. If, for three months, you devoted your total profits of $7.50 to paying for the stove, you will have worked those three months with no profit to yourself, and at the same time, since you say you are no longer able to do your share of the housework, you will have to hire somebody else to do your share of the work, and that will cost you at least the $7.50 profit you are making on the bread. . . .' He knew his mother too well to appeal to her on the grounds that she was hurting his name in Oakland; only by appealing to what she liked to think was her business sense could he dissuade her.

The letter worked; Flora gave up bread-making. Needing some business on which she could expend her manifold energies, she next started to open a newsstand on Broadway. He spiked that activity just in time. Soon collectors began arriving at the ranch with bills for articles Flora had bought, and for which she had no earthly use, chief among which was an item of six hundred dollars for diamonds. Jack was always gentle with her, as each new book appeared he sent it to her with a loving inscription, never did he let on that she was hurting him with her eccentricities, but he was forever afraid of the new scheme she would hatch behind those tight, peering eyes and narrow, steel-rimmed spectacles. In time he was to begin brooding over the horrible possibility that his mother had never been altogether sane. Yet so strange is the sum total of human attributes that Johnny Miller remembers Flora as the finest woman he ever knew, a gentle, loving, and altogether rational mother and friend to him; while people who took piano lessons from her at this time remember her as a sweet and kindly old lady.

The *Post* was now paying him seven hundred and fifty dollars for all the stories he could supply, *Collier's* offered one thousand dollars, the *Herald* offered seven hundred and fifty dollars for a short Christmas story, he signed a contract with *Cosmopolitan* to supply them with a series of stories at seven hundred and fifty dollars apiece about a character whom he called Smoke Bellew. Macmillan released *Lost Face,* a collection of short stories, *Revolution,* a collection of essays, and *Burning Daylight. Lost Face* earned him a deservedly warm press, for 'Lost Face,' 'Trust,' 'That Spot,' and 'The Passing of Marcus O'Brien' are successful humorous Alaskan tales, while *Flush of Gold* and *To Build a Fire* are intensely wrought dramatic tales. Not since *Son of the Wolf* and *God of His Fathers,* his first two volumes of short stories, had he maintained such a high standard of excellence. *Revolution,* a heterogeneous and uneven collection of essays, was received apathetically, but *Burning Daylight* received the exciting reception everyone had anticipated.

By a combination of force, driving power, concentration, and sheer talent he had accomplished what only giants can accomplish: in less than a year he had catapulted himself from the frightening abyss of death and destruction to the greatest heights ever enjoyed by an American author.

In June of 1911, heartily sick of living in makeshift accommodations at Wake Robin, and seeing that the Wolf House would not be completed for at least another two years, he made a move that brought him the happiest and richest years of his life: he bought the ten acres in the middle of the Kohler vineyards upon which stood an abandoned winery, a broken-down ranch house, and some barns. He put stonemasons and carpenters to work adding a comfortable dining-room with a huge fireplace, and a broad lounging verandah, then enlarged the kitchen and renewed the bedrooms and sleeping porches. One of the bedrooms he converted into a workshop, lining the walls with shelves for his books and papers and cardboard reference boxes. His small, screened sleeping porch overlooked a secluded tropical garden in front of the house, the rear lounging verandah overlooked a spacious yard and huge barn, part of which he turned into nine comfortable guest rooms for his friends. Nakata became general manager, employing two more Japanese to cook and keep the house clean.

The ranch house was a success from the beginning; it was informal and people could have fun in it. When living at

Wake Robin he had filled the cabins, tents, and every spare
cot with his friends and intimates: George Sterling, Cloudesley Johns, James Hopper, his socialist and anarchist friends,
newspapermen, sailors, tramps, and comrades that fitted into
no apparent category. Now that he had adequate accommodations he began inviting the wide world; every day became
Jack's Wednesday night open house. Nearly everyone in the
artistic, professional, or thinking world that came West spent
a few days at what he called his Beauty Ranch. In all the tens
of thousands of letters he sent out from the ranch, and a
goodly portion were to people who were quarreling with him,
attacking, or abusing him, he never failed to put at the end,
'The latchstring is always on the outside at the Beauty Ranch,
and there are always blankets and grub for our friends. Come
visit us, and stay as long as you like.' So many accepted that
he had to have circulars printed giving directions to Glen
Ellen from San Francisco and Oakland. Rarely were there
fewer than ten guests around the elastic dinner table; often
there were twenty and more. One dinner party included
Hyhar Dyall, founder of the Dyallist movement in India
against the British, an American novelist, a Stanford University professor of mathematics, a neighboring farmer, an engineer, Luther Burbank, a sailor just back from Penang, Princess Ula Humphrey, an actress who had been in the Sultan's
harem, three tramps, and a lunatic who was going to build a
house from San Franciso to New York. No matter from
what walk of life they came, visitors were stunned by their
fellow guests. Some of his brilliant non-working friends who
lived on the ranch for months at a time smelled so badly
from hardly ever taking a bath that he built a special house
for them in the woods; however, everyone ate at the same big
table in the stone dining-room. Writers, artists, politicians,
European statesmen and philosophers, churchmen, convicts,
business magnates, engineers, housewives, thousands of people were to be his guests during the following five years.
Tired of traveling, he now let the world come to him. Never
a train pulled into Glen Ellen station but was met with a
wagon from the Beauty Ranch to haul the visitors up the
winding dirt road over which so many tons of grapes had been
hauled before them.

He thrived and gloried in being the host, the benevolent
patriarch, the squire, in seeing his friends and associates
enjoy themselves as they ate at his table, rode his horses
across his mountains, slept in his beds. But best of all he
liked to probe the people who came to his ranch, to find out
'what made them tick,' to derive sustenance from the color of

their character, the wisdom of their mind, the foibles of their weaknesses, the flavor of their dialogue and the yarns of their background. What astounded and delighted his visitors, as hundreds of them have testified, was the clarity of his mind, the speed and accuracy of his thinking, the depth and range of his knowledge, and above all, the celerity with which he extracted and then absorbed the knowledge the world-renowned specialists brought to his table. No matter how small a fund of information a guest brought with him, by the time he left the ranch Jack was in possession of that knowledge. Always he talked the other man's subject, asking adroit questions, discussing heatedly, challenging fundamental concepts, correcting his own impressions, information, concepts, thinking methods, sometimes besting his opponent in intellectual dispute even though he might be disputing the other man's specialty. He relished a battle of wits; one of his favorite exclamations was, 'I'll take either side!'

He had the profound intellectual curiosity of the true scholar; he had amassed one of the finest collections of socialist books, pamphlets, reports, magazine and newspaper articles in America; the walls of his workroom were lined to the ceiling with the books he ordered constantly from New York and England. 'I for one can never have too many books, nor can my books cover too many subjects. I may never read them all, but they are always there, and I never know what strange coast I am going to pick up in sailing the world of knowledge.' The consistency with which topnotchers glowingly attested that Jack London had the richest brain they ever encountered is a tribute to the boy who had to go to work in a cannery at the age of thirteen because he could not afford to attend high school.

Alexander Irvine says that Jack talked softly, that he had the mellifluous, whispering voice of a gentle lady. He practised unfailing courtesy, even in the face of bigotry, ignorance, and foolishness, and since he was inviting hordes of absolute strangers to be his guests, he encountered these qualities, too. Men and women whose philosophies he despised, whom he regarded as enemies of civilization, would come to his ranch, sleep in his beds, ride his horses, eat at his table; no matter how long they stayed they never suspected that he harbored such sentiments about them. Human beings from every school, standard, income group, and background passed through his house . . . and into the texture of his work he wove their variegated richness of character. He took from his guests all they had to give, of wisdom and ignorance, of character and weakness, of viciousness and fun. Never trying to shout down his opponent, to beat him by brute strength, he was interested in the meat of the discussion, not the victory.

Everyone speaks of the force of his dynamic personality. Janet Winship, daughter of his friends from Napa, says that when he entered a room where a group of visitors would be sitting slumped in their chairs, silent, dull, uninterested, an electric current would shoot through them and they would come instantly to life, not only their bodies, but their minds and spirits. His tremendous vitality was only part of the cause; he had such a warm, vibrant, glowing quality of being alive that he invested everyone he met with a radiance, a spirit of well-being. Irvine summed it up for many of Jack's friends when he said, 'Jack London was a mountain in life.'

Before Jack retired at night, usually at eleven o'clock, Nakata fixed his night table with notepaper, pencils, galley proof, the books and pamphlets he was reading, manuscripts from aspiring authors sent to him for correction and criticism, some light food to nibble on to fight off sleep, a box of cigarettes and pitchers of an iced drink which he kept sipping to hydrize his mouth, parched from incessant smoking. The lamp burned deep into the humming silence while the man alone on the sleeping porch studied, made notes, smoked, sipped his iced drink, pored over printed words, words of wisdom and falsity, words of justice and man's inhumanity to man . . . until fatigue gathered like specks of dust under his burning eyelids. He drove himself continuously to acquire knowledge, not only because he loved knowledge, but for fear he might be missing something new or important in the world. And always on that night table, never to be moved until after his death, was a two-volume work by Paul du Chaillu, whose *African Travels* had been the first adventure book to fall into his hands when he had been eight years old, living on the ranch in Livermore. The two-volume work was called *The Viking Age*.

About one o'clock in the morning he would place a match in his book to mark his place, then set the hand on the cardboard time-dial hanging outside his door to show Nakata at what hour he wished to be awakened. He rarely allowed himself more than five hours of sleep; the latest time indicated on the dial is six o'clock. Generally at five Nakata would awaken him with his coffee, after which he would lie abed revising the previous day's manuscript, which Charmian had typed, reading the various government reports and technical studies for which he had sent, correcting the latest batch of galley proofs from his publishers, making notes for the day's work or future stories. By eight he was at his desk composing his original thousand words, glancing occasionally at the poem tacked on the wall:

> Now I get me up to work,
>   I pray the Lord I may not shirk;
> If I should die before the night,
>   I pray the Lord my work's all right.

His stint of the thousand words completed by eleven o'clock, he dug into his staggering piles of business and personal mail. He was now averaging ten thousand letters a year, the very least of which he answered fully and courteously. Many days he read and dictated replies to a round hundred letters.

All guests were notified that the mornings were reserved for quiet and work. At one o'clock, having already turned in an eight-hour day, he would wander onto the back porch, his hair mussed, his white shirt open at the throat, a green eyeshade slanted across his forehead, a cigarette between his lips, and a sheaf of papers in his hand. With a broad smile he would exclaim, 'Hello, folks!' and the room was full of him, full of his magnetic warmth, his clean-cut, boyish lovability, his richly alive and contagious humanness. His entrance marked the beginning of the day's fun.

After lunch, which lasted a couple of hours if the conversation was good and the banter amusing, saddle-horses were brought to the yard between the ranch house and the barn. When the party was mounted he led the way to the top of Sonoma Mountain and across the crest of the range overlooking San Francisco Bay; if the sun was out he galloped them up the lake, which he had formed for irrigation purposes by building a stone dam across a pond fed by running springs. Here in a bathhouse made of fresh-cut logs they changed into their bathing suits, swam, went boating in the warrior canoes he had brought back from the South Seas, sunned themselves on the dock, played leap frog and jousted, Indian-wrestled and boxed, dumped into the lake men who went boating in their street clothes. At dusk he led his party through the forest of redwood, spruce, and manzanita on the trail that ran past the Wolf House, dismounted, and guided it among the scaffoldings, telling how beautiful the Wolf House would be, pointing with pride to the flawless stone masonry, explaining that he did not need fire insurance because he was fireproofing his house with asbestos-covered pipes, fireproof paint over the woodwork, stone walls, and tile roofing.

Back at the ranch house they dressed, became acquainted

with the new arrivals, had a good dinner, discussed world
politics and philosophy. Cards were his favorite form of relaxation, and soon they were playing red dog or pedro for
twenty-five cents a hand. He was still inventing all sorts of
ridiculous practical jokes. Whenever anarchists such as
Emma Goldman visited the ranch, Jack set on their dinner
plate a book with the title *A Loud Noise* printed in bold letters across its cover. When the unsuspecting anarchist opened
the book it would explode in his hands from the firecracker
concealed in it. He always used their fright and consternation
to show them that they really wouldn't overthrow the world
by force even if they had the chance. The water glass with
the hole in the side was reserved for lay visitors who were so
stunned by the fact that they were actually sitting at the dinner table of the great Jack London that they could hardly
breathe, let alone eat.

Finn Frolich, a Norwegian sculptor and sailor with the
most tremendous, booming laugh ever vouchsafed to mortal,
whom Jack had made his court sculptor and jester, says:
'When I came up there I found they were playing like children, playing tricks and all kinds of funny games. When the
joke was on Jack he would laugh more than any of us.' A
favorite trick was to place a man against the dining-room
door to measure his height, and then hit the back of the door
at the head height with a mallet. The joke that got the best
laugh was practised on prissy people: holes were bored
through the floor of the guest's room, and rope interlaced between the holes and the bedposts. After the guest was asleep
the jokesters would begin heaving on the ropes, which would
rock the bed violently. The guest would tear out into the yard
in his nightclothes crying, 'Earthquake! Earthquake!' In Chop
and Stop the newcomer would be seated on the ground; as
water was poured between his spread legs it was his task to
keep chopping up mud to make embankments. When the victim had enough water collected, and was working frantically
to keep it from running over, his feet would be seized and he
would be pulled forward into the puddle of his own making.
'Jack was just an overgrown kid,' says Carrie Burlingame, a
neighbor from Sonoma. 'He did everything with full force;
even when he relaxed and had fun he did it with all his
might.' He would go so far for fun and laughter that one
night when his guests had scouted his story of eating raw fish
in the Solomons, he offered to eat a live goldfish from the
bowl in the center of the table if he chanced to pull the lowest card of the draw. The other men agreeing, the cards were
cut; the lowest fell to a visiting bridegroom. He thrust his

hand into the bowl, extracted a goldfish by the tail, and swallowed it . . . eliciting laughter and applause, and the cry from his bride that she would never kiss him again.

Jack enjoyed his ranch doubly because of the fun he could have on it with his guests. His most constant companion was George Sterling with his sharp Indian features and receding forehead that slanted back at an angle from his eyebrows, that he carefully kept hidden by combing his hair down in bangs; a magnificently ugly man with beauty in his sensitive, transparent face, and an intense feeling for the pain of life. Much of his poetry was brilliantly written, much of it was bombastic, loaded with biblical references and meaningless pageantry. Though his wife, Carrie, was a beautiful Junoesque woman in the Bessie Maddern tradition, though he was so gentle of nature he would not allow a spider caught in his house to be killed, he had no compunction over wounding his wife when his fancy was caught by another woman. Unlike Jack, he was protected by a wealthy uncle, knowing little of the proletarian base of life; a successful Don Juan and hard drinker, he was an almost perfect example of the vanishing Bohemian poet.

The story ran that every time George Sterling lost a hand at red dog or pedro he took a drink of Jack's liquor to make up the loss, and every time Jack lost he wrote a word to earn back the twenty-five cents. There was a sideboard in the dining-room with an array of bottles, the guests were invited to help themselves to as many drinks as they wanted, but for weeks at a time Jack did not join them even in a before-dinner cocktail. In Tokio, on the *Snark* trip, and in Reno he had drunk with his fellow correspondents; aside from an occasional drink for sociability in his hours of relaxation, he did no drinking on the ranch.

Glen Ellen was at that time a sporting village, its main street lined with saloons. Whenever he wanted to get away from his family, his heavy load of obligations and work, his ever-present friends, he harnessed four horses to his buggy, put his special bells on the horses' collars, and drove like mad down the winding dirt road to town. When Glen Ellen heard those bells, the village awakened from its hot torpor. 'Jack London's coming down the hill!' a native cried, and within an instant word had spread through the town, people thronged the streets wearing broad grins, bartenders got out bottles and polished glasses with new animation. As Jack drove down the main street everyone cried, 'Hi, Jack!' and when he saw someone he knew he would shout, 'Hello, Bill!' and wave his sombrero in the air. He tied his horses to the first hitching post and went into the nearest saloon, where, as in his sailor days, 'he called all hands to the bar.' No one else was allowed to show the color of his money. The crowd would kid him, laugh at his yarns, let him know what they thought of his latest publications, and tell him their new jokes, particularly the Jewish stories which he loved above all others. After a few minutes and a few drinks he would move on to the next saloon, where its particular clientèle was waiting to slap him on the back, wring his hand. Once again the drinks were on him, and there would be much loud masculine laughter and good fellowship. There were perhaps a dozen saloons in town; by nightfall he had visited them all, consumed a quart of whiskey, rubbed elbows, talked and bantered with a hundred men. Then he would walk back to his rig, untie the horses, and while Glen Ellen gathered to cry, 'So long, Jack! Come see us again soon!' he would drive his horses up the long dirt road through his orchards, vineyards, and rolling hills. Glen Ellen people tell that the brightest days in the year were the days when they heard those bells high up on the hillside, and Jack London, in a ranger's hat, bow tie, and white shirt, came dashing down the road behind his four spirited horses, a happy smile on his lips, a friendly salute for everybody.

One afternoon a week he would harness two of his fastest horses and drive at top speed the sixteen miles to Santa Rosa, the county seat and center for the hops, grapes, and wine industry; a hard-drinking town, but so reactionary in its politics that the residents did not think Jack merely mistaken to believe in socialism, they thought him insane. He would dash down the main street, his harness bells jingling, draw up in front of Ira Pyle's real estate office, shout, 'Hey, Puh-hyle! Let's go!' and the two men would ride over to the Hotel Overton bar, where Jack took up his leaning station in the last niche of the bar with his back to the rest of the room, and ordered a quart of Scotch. He drank his whiskey out of a twelve-ounce water tumbler; he always poured Pyle's first two drinks, after that Pyle could drink as much or as little as he wished.

Introduced as Jack's drinking partner, Pyle exclaimed, 'I could never claim that title! No one could. Jack stood in a class by himself. He was really two-fisted; he took four or five drinks to my one. Funny thing, though: eighty-five per cent of his conversation at the bar was about socialism. He came into Santa Rosa because he could get the best arguments there. People didn't like him because he would say things in the presence of judges, chamber of commerce executives and business men about how corrupt the capitalist system was. In all the years he came into Santa Rosa, I never heard anyone agree with him. When I asked him a stickler about the new socialist state, he would think for a moment, shake his head, say, "Wait until I get another drink under my belt, and then my mind will flow more freely." The next drink always did it, and he would be off on a discourse about how little commodities would cost the consumer when they were produced for use and not for profit.'

When he wasn't with Pyle he would walk into the Overton bar, take a quick look around, go to his nook, have a drink or two, then motion for somebody to come over and talk. He would start off with, 'Now, that point you made the other day about socialism destroying personal incentive, I've been thinking it over and I've got some new ideas. . . .' Friends who drank with him remember him discussing war, poverty as the cause of crime, biology, labor organization, Freud's psychoanalysis, judicial corruption, literature, travel, and the coming utopia. At six o'clock, having polished off a bottle of Scotch with whoever had joined him, he got into the buggy and drove home. He never had trouble with his horses, but when he had been drinking he liked to drive fast. Billy Hill, who was his bartender at the Overton bar, and later at Fetters and Boyes Springs, says, 'Jack could handle more liquor than any other man, but it never fazed him. He always stood up straight, always had his dignity on. When he pulled out of a place he pulled out like a gentleman. When he'd had enough, he'd had enough. I never saw him ugly or quarrelsome; he always remained jovial and pleasant, stayed out of arguments unless it was somebody who could really argue, but he was so much smarter than anybody he'd meet that he always won the argument.' Pyle says he never saw Jack drunk. He had the Irishman's capacity for absorbing whiskey. Drinking removed his fatigue and nerve strain, loosened his tongue, lubricated his brain, gave him a vacation, a change, and a rest.

Out of his drinking arose the idea for a book that was to win him more fame and infamy than any he published. *John Barleycorn* is an autobiographical novel; as far as it goes it tells the truth about his drinking, but like most autobiographical books, 'The only trouble about *John Barleycorn* is that I did not put in the whole truth. I did not dare put in the whole truth.' He omitted the fact that in certain periods of his life he suffered from despondency, that when he was low in spirits the knowledge of his illegitimacy, which he could forget or shrug off as unimportant when he was in good form, poisoned his mind and his thoughts, made him melancholy; that he often drank to drown that most indestructible of all bitter herbs. He exercised the utmost care to keep concealed from everyone these recurrent depressions. The attacks came too rarely, not more than five or six a year, to make him the manic depressive that is most every creative artist, yet when they gripped him he loathed his writing, his socialism, his ranch, his friends, his mechanistic philosophy, brilliantly defended man's right to suicide. At such times the load he was carrying seemed too heavy for his shoulders, he vowed he could carry it no further; at such times he drank heavily, became thick-jawed, insensitive, unsympathetic, quarrelsome. But the attacks passed, often in a single day.

The value of *John Barleycorn* as literature does not depend upon its conformity to the pattern of his life. *John Barleycorn* reads like a novel, is fresh, beautifully honest, simple and moving, contains magnificent writing about the White Logic, and remains as a classic on drinking. Were it wholly fiction it would still be convincing, first-rate fiction. Published in the *Saturday Evening Post,* and later in book form, it was read by millions of people. Ministers seized upon it as a moral lesson against drinking; temperance unions, prohibition organizations, anti-saloon leagues claimed the book as their own, reprinted material from it in pamphlets which they scattered by the hundreds of thousands. Educators, politicians, newspaper and magazine men, lecturers, organizations that would not be linked together for any other cause on earth, joined hands over *John Barleycorn* to fight the liquor interests. A motion picture was made of the book, which the distilleries offered huge sums to have suppressed. So tremendous was the tumult and shouting that hundreds of thousands who had not opened a book since they left grammar school avidly consumed *John Barleycorn.* Though he had portrayed his victory over alcohol, the public which garbles so much of what it reads set him down for a habitual drunkard.

John Barleycorn, because of the new and focused energy it released, was one of the leading factors in bringing Prohibition to the United States in 1919. The picture of a man who often drank to numb the cyclical pain of his illegitimacy, of a man who had had a great deal of fun, excitement, and comradeship from drinking, who had not the slightest intention of giving up liquor providing the ammunition with which the reformers brought upon the United States the horrors of the Prohibition Era, is one of the major ironies of a life crowded with mordant ironies.

The seasons passed, he watched his fields plowed and sowed with seed in the spring, grow green and then yellow in the late summer, a deep russet brown from the burning sun of the long dry autumn, then deluged with the winter rains. He took pride in his writings, in his newly cleared, revitalized land, in his countless friends. With everything in his life going well, 'the smile that won't come off' was never missing from his handsome Irish face. Finn Frolich says, 'I never saw a man with so much beautiful magnetism. If a preacher could have that much love in his make-up the whole world would go religious. When Jack talked he was marvelous; his eyes were big, and his mouth was just as sensitive and full of expression, and the words came out of him just rippling. It was something inside him, his brain ran sixty miles a minute, you couldn't keep up with him. No matter what he talked about his lips would go up, the humor would come out, you would have to laugh your head off.'

He was happy, everyone loved him, his work went forward with magnificent strides.

When he had first bought the Hill Ranch he had written to Cloudesley Johns, 'I am not going ranching; the only cleared ground on the place will be used for growing hay.' But he found that his interest in farming and ranching was growing apace, that every development led him into new operations. He subscribed to agricultural newspapers and magazines, wrote to the agricultural departments of the University of California and the state government for information and advice. With the passage of the months he realized that agriculture and ranching were exciting subjects, and that he was becoming fascinated. Tired of adventuring abroad, he now began to adventure at home; farming became his hobby. Giving himself to the new activity with his accustomed zeal, before long he found he had acquired sufficient knowledge to constitute himself something of an authority.

The more he studied agriculture in the State of California the more he found wrong with it, the more he decided that the entire agricultural system was a counterpart of the economic system, haphazard, wasteful, needing a sharp reconstruction with scientific methods. He had the land, he had the money, he had the knowledge and determination; he decided to put them together to rescue California farming. Slowly, as he continued with his studies and delved more deeply into his subject, there formed in his mind a vision of the type of model farm his foster father, John London, had wanted to build in Alameda and then Livermore. This model farm he would build through the years would point the way to a higher type of agriculture throughout the country, would enable the farmers to get a higher quality produce out of their land and stock.

He learned that the Kohler and Lamotte Ranches were worn out, useless because the former owners had tilled the land for forty years without feeding it fertilizer, without allowing it to lie fallow. He found the stock of the countryside had degenerated; scrub bulls without pedigree were being used for the mount; the horses, pigs, and goats were all of inferior breed. The fertile hills of California were being wasted; 'we must develop scientific methods to turn the slopes into productive areas.' He reasoned that if he rehabilitated the land and reinvigorated the stock, if he threw overboard the wasteful, destructive methods of the farmers who were failing all about him, if he farmed for only the highest-grade produce he could save that section of the state for agriculture. To achieve this end he and Eliza threw all their resources, energy, and capability into the task. Jack planned everything with Eliza, who then gave the orders and supervised the work.

'At the present moment I am the owner of six bankrupt ranches, united in my possession. The six bankrupt ranches represent at least eighteen bankruptcies; that is to say, at least eighteen farmers of the old school have lost their money, broken their hearts, lost their land. The challenge to me is this: by using my head, my judgment, and all the latest knowledge in the matter of farming, can I make a success where these eighteen men failed? I have pledged myself, my manhood, my fortune, my books, and all I possess to this undertaking.'

On his cleared fields he planted vetch and Canadian peas, for three years plowing under his crop to enrich the soil. Across from his ranch house were uncultivated hill slopes; he set men to work to clear and terrace them as he had seen hills terraced in Korea. He set twenty-two men to work in the vineyards to prune and sucker the vines. He told Eliza the grapes would have to begin to pay their own expenses, then rode Washoe Ban into Glen Ellen to vote for local prohibition because he believed the saloons were a menace to the families of workingmen. Convinced that national prohibition would come within a few years, and in addition learning that the soil in the vineyards was too exhausted to give him a good crop, he had his men tear out seven hundred acres of the vines, fertilize the fields, and replant them with eucalyptus trees because his studies had led him to the conviction that the eucalyptus tree, which produced what was called Circassian walnut, would be greatly in demand as hardwood for decoration and building. The first year he put in ten thousand trees, the second year twenty thousand more, until he had a hundred and forty thousand eucalyptus trees, at a planting cost of $46,862, growing on his land. 'I'll just plant them now, and twenty years from now they'll be worth a fortune, without my being forced to do anything with them.' He figured his investment was as safe as money in the bank, and in addition would be earning him thirty per cent interest.

In other fields he planted beets, carrots, red oats, grain, barley, hay, and alfalfa, on the raising of which Eliza had taken correspondence courses from the University of California; everything he felt he would need for the first-rate stock ranch he was in the process of creating. When Luther Burbank brought some of his new spineless cactus from his experimental gardens in Santa Rosa, Jack, game to try anything once, planted a field of it for feed.

As the foundation of his horse stock he bought a prize Shire stallion for twenty-five hundred dollars, then bought four pedigreed Shire mares for seven hundred dollars apiece. Because he believed that big workhorses were coming back he bought up all the mares used by the drayers in San Francisco that had developed sore feet on the cobblestones. When he needed more draft horses to clear and plow his fields, and couldn't find the kind of animal he wanted, he took a buying trip to Southern California. When he couldn't find the kinds of cows and heifers he wanted, he advertised in the agricultural journals, went to the stock show at Sacramento and purchased the blue-ribbon animals: a prize shorthorn bull for eight hundred dollars to sire his herd, and eight good heifers for three hundred and fifty dollars apiece. He went into the market and bought the finest pedigreed pigs and a herd of eighty-five angora goats. After a few seasons of scientific breeding he planned to sell some of his stock to the neighboring ranchers at low prices so the quality of their herds would be improved. He also planned to cull his beef and swine, just as John London had taught him to cull vegetables, selling only the very best meat to the San Francisco hotels. To accommodate his rapidly growing stock he built new barns, new pens, bought a complete blacksmith's shop in Glen Ellen and moved it up to the ranch. To accommodate his ever-growing list of laborers he built cottages and cabins to house the men and their families.

He wrote articles on the new agriculture, made notes for a 'back to the soil novel,' exchanged countless letters with agricultural societies and experimental farms, gave interviews to the curious newspaper reporters on his new activity. While on a stock-buying expedition to Los Angeles, where he stayed in the home of his old sculptor friend, Felix Piano, he told interviewers: 'I began studying the problem of why the fertility of this California land had been destroyed in forty or fifty years while land in China had been tilled for thousands of years, and is still fertile. I adopted the policy of taking nothing off the ranch. I raised stuff and fed it to the stock. I got the first manure-spreader ever seen up there. I set men to work clearing the brush and turning the brush land into tillable fields. Here is the desperate situation in this country which makes correct farming certain of good returns: in ten years the mouths to feed in the United States have increased by sixteen millions. In that ten years the number of hogs, sheep, dairy cows, and beef cattle have actually decreased on account of the breaking up of large ranches into small farms. The rancher who gets good stock and who conserves and builds up his soil is assured of success.'

By working his eleven hundred acres he was able to give men jobs, to enable them to earn a living. He instructed Eliza that on no condition was she to turn away any man looking for work until he had earned three or four days' wages, and eaten three or four days' square meals. If there was no work for the man, she was to make work, to set him clearing stones off the hillsides, or building fences between fields. To Forni, supervising the building of the Wolf House, he said, 'Forni, never let any man go away without three or four days' work, and if he's a good man, keep him.' Convicts in Folsom and San Quentin prisons who could be paroled if they had a job to go to wrote him asking to be hired. He nearly always advised the prison authorities that he would give the paroled man a job, refusing only when he had no bed or corner of a cottage to provide. One applying convict who was refused wrote back saying, 'You don't have to be afraid to let me work around the house. I wouldn't steal anything, I'm only a murderer.' Most of the time there were ten paroled convicts working and living on the ranch.

By the time his ranching activities reached their height in 1913, his payroll had reached the staggering figure of three thousand dollars a month. He was employing fifty-three men for farm work and thirty-five on the Wolf House, providing a living for nearly a hundred men and their families, or a round five hundred human souls. On payday he rode Washoe Ban across the fields and hills, paying the men in gold from money bags strapped around his waist, the same gold pouches he had carried in the Klondike. The knowledge that he was making work for men brought him profound and unending pleasure, as great as the pleasure he was deriving from his farming experiments and the thought that he was the savior of California agriculture.

The farmers of the neighborhood jeered at him for plowing three crops under, laughed at what they called the 'eight-hour socialists' working on the ranch. When he had been laughed at for building the *Snark,* just as he was being laughed at now for building a model ranch, he had complained, 'A man picks out a clean, wholesome way to make and spend money, and everybody jumps on him. If I went in for horse races or chorus girls, there'd be no end of indulgent comment.' To people who cautioned him against sinking such huge sums of money in experiments he answered, 'I earn my money honestly, and not off the backs of labor. If I want to spend it to give employment, to rehabilitate California ranching, why have I not the right to spend my money for my own peculiar kind of enjoyment?'

And enjoy himself he did. Each new guest was proudly escorted to the dairy barn to be shown the milking records being kept on each cow, the rich alfalfa and corn his fields were growing, the improved breeds of beef cattle, hogs, and goats he had started. When one of the animals won a blue ribbon at a stock show he was enormously set up. When away for a sailing trip on the *Roamer,* or on the four-horse driving trip with Charmian and Nakata, he wrote constant letters of advice and instruction to Eliza, who in turn wrote telling him every detail of what was happening on the ranch. He writes to her, 'See that the pigs in the pasture are fed. How did the barley fields get flooded? Don't forget to work the stallion. Are the engine and water hose shaded from the heat of the sun? I'm heartbroken that the pigs have cholera. Have the foundations of the twenty-stall barn repaired. Now is the time to see that every horse working, and every colt, is fed in addition to pasturage. In making the stone wall alongside the orchard, be sure the men haul only the large stones so they will make a beautiful stone wall.' Everything had to be the biggest and best: the Wolf House, the stone wall, the alfalfa and corn, the Shire horses, the cows, the hogs, the goats . . . always his vigorous and full-blooded Rex complex made him feel he must be a king among men (the last shall be first, the bastard shall be king); and his equally vigorous Messianic complex made it necessary for him to free American literature, American economics, and now American agriculture from destruction and decay.

He was earning seventy-five thousand dollars a year from his writing and spending a hundred thousand. Everything he owned was heavily mortgaged, including his future. On the first of each month he and Eliza sat at the desk in the corner of the dining-room, their heads glued together over the account book, sore beset to know how they were going to juggle their money to meet their obligations. At one time he was so broke Eliza had to put a five-hundred-dollar mortgage against her house in Oakland to buy feed for the stock. His letters East form a continuous wail for money. 'Please send the $2000 you owe for stories, as I am building the first stone silo in California. . . .' 'You must let me have another $5000 against book publication, as I have to build a new dairy barn.' . . . 'I need $1200 right away to buy a rock crusher.' . . . 'You must send me $1500 immediately as I have to put in a tile drainage system to keep my rich top soil from being washed away by floods.' . . . 'If you will contract in advance for this series of stories you will enable me to buy the adjoining Freund Ranch of four hundred acres for the reasonable price of $4500.' He gave his Eastern editors a liberal education in scientific ranching, but sometimes they would cry out in exasperation, 'Mr. London, we simply can't help it if you have to buy a new litter of pigs,' or 'We don't feel that the clearing of your new fields should be our responsibility!' One of them even had the temerity to tell him that 'it's all right for a writer to own a farm, providing he doesn't try to farm it!' There were delays, vexations, disputes, anxious and sometimes angry flurries of telegrams, but always he earned the money, always the thousands poured in with which to build not one stone silo to store his corn, but two; to build his dairy barn; to buy the rock crusher; to put in miles of irrigation pipes; to buy the Freund Ranch, which now brought his holdings to fifteen hundred acres; to put a twenty-five-hundred-dollar tile roof on the Wolf House, the cost of which, after three years of labor, had risen to seventy thousand dollars and much work remaining to be done. The faster the money came in, the faster it slipped through Eliza's often unwilling fingers, for more money meant to Jack that he could hire more men, clear more fields, add new stock, new irrigation and drainage systems. At no time was he less than twenty-five thousand dollars in debt; more often it was fifty thousand.

In addition to the workingmen for whose support he now was responsible, there was the ever-increasing coterie of relatives, relatives of his relatives, friends, friends of his friends, guests, charity cases, hangers-on, parasites of all descriptions. Generosity was as natural to him as breathing. Every tramp in America knew that the most illustrious of their former comrades was good for a meal, a drink, and a bed, and most of them included the Beauty Ranch in their itinerary. Jim Tully, who like Jack had risen to fame as a novelist after being a tramp on The Road, reports that one night in Los Angeles when a bum panhandled Jack for the price of a bed, Jack thrust a five-dollar gold piece into the man's hand. Johnny Heinhold reports him walking into the Last Chance saloon, taking one drink from a full bottle of whiskey, then leaving a five-dollar gold piece on the bar, saying, 'Johnny, tell the boys Jack London was in, and to have a drink on him.'

Convicts sent him handwoven bridles for which he had no use. He sent them twenty dollars apiece, unable to turn down an imprisoned man who was trying to earn a few dollars.

Nearly all his friends borrowed money, not once but continuously. Never was one dollar returned. He received thousands of requests for money through the mail, most of which he complied with. Writers, complete strangers, wrote asking to be subsidized while they completed a novel; he mailed them monthly checks. When socialist and labor newspapers were in financial trouble, which was almost always, he sent them subscriptions for all his friends, free articles and stories; when socialists or labor organizers were arrested, he sent money for their defense. When strikes were failing for lack of funds, he sent money for soup kitchens. When he heard of an Australian woman who had lost both sons in the World War, he sent her fifty dollars a month, unasked, as long as he lived. When an old woman from the mountains of New York wrote him tortured letters of poverty, and he had not one dollar in the bank, he sent Brett stricken letters imploring him to send the woman money and take it out of his future earnings. When San Francisco wanted to start a school of the opera, he pledged himself to pay so much a month. When a socialist comrade from Oregon, whom he did not know, wrote that he was bringing his pregnant wife and four children to stay on the ranch while he went to Arizona to cure his tuberculosis, Jack wired back that he had no cottage or beds in which to put them up. The family had already left Oregon; when they arrived on the ranch Jack said nothing about his wire, found them a cottage, fed and cared for the family, had the wife delivered of her fifth child, and gave the family back to the father when he returned from Arizona, six months later.

Socialist comrades wrote by the thousands for the chance to come and live on the ranch. 'Just give me one acre and some chickens and I'll make a go of it.'—'Couldn't you spare me a couple of acres, and a cow? That's all my family needs.'

He would order Eliza not to employ any more people, then a workingman with his wife and children would wander onto the ranch, having heard that a man could always find work there, and he would hire him himself. Eliza, who kept the books, says that half of all the money Jack earned was given to other people. If one adds the money he paid for labor for which he had no legitimate use, the figure would rise to nearly two thirds of his income. Anybody could touch him who told a good story, but half the time he sent money without being asked. Only once did he refuse to give help; the wife of Bob Fitzsimmons, the prize fighter, wired him that she needed a hundred dollars immediately but gave no explanation of what she needed the money for. Racking his brain to find three thousand dollars with which to pay his insurance and interest on mortgages, he wired back that he was broke. Two days later he read in the newspaper that Mrs. Fitzsimmons had been operated on in the charity clinic of a county hospital. He never forgave himself; after that when people asked him for money he didn't have, he went out and borrowed it.

He spent little on himself, eating and dressing simply. On his friends and hospitality he spent a fortune, rarely accepting hospitality in return. When he did go out for dinner he would eat half a pound of raw hamburger before leaving home because he did not care for other people's cooking. So fastidious was he about money matters that no guest was allowed to give another guest an I.O.U. over his card table. He took the I.O.U., paid out the money to the winner, then put the note of indebtedness into a cigar box. One day when Frolich was passing Jack's study a shower of white papers flew out the window. Picking up a few scraps, he saw that Jack had just torn up another box of the I.O.U.'s.

With his life he was painting a portrait of a native Californian, that unusual specimen of humanity indigenous to the soil of the state, to be found nowhere else in the same form. A modest megalomaniac, like most native Californians, he was simple, genuinely unpretentious with his friends and associates about his success and accomplishments, but to himself fiercely sure, positive. On the notes for the hundreds of short stories, articles, and novels he planned to write in the future one invariably finds scrawled: 'Great Short Story,' 'Tremendous Novel,' 'Terrific Idea,' 'Magnificent Labor Material,' 'Colossal Yarn.' Like most native Californians he was robust, hearty in manner, with strong physical appetites, worshipping the beauty, strength, skill and pleasures of the body, which in turn led him to admire the arts and the fruits of culture. He was childlike in his desire to play, to have fun. Above all he wanted to laugh, not gently or delicately, but uproariously. Like most native Californians he was informal, hated starchy people and starchy ideas and preconceived prejudices, was intolerant of the bonds of tradition, enjoyed being a vigorous iconoclast. Like California's Spanish predecessors' his home was a sanctuary, open to all wayfarers, high or humble; no man was turned away without a meal, a drink, a night's lodging. He was happiest when twenty guests sat down to partake of his food. Like these Spanish predecessors he wanted space about him, could not stand to be cramped, had to be lord of a domain so vast it took him days to ride across his holdings.

Like the gold miners who opened up California he despised money because it could be made so easily and in such large quantities, and squandered it to show the world how little he was its slave. He was prodigal with the riches of his land, his brain, his purse, his friendship. Like most Californians he wanted to do everything at the top of his might: work, play, laugh, love, relax, conquer, create. He was independent, self-willed, difficult to lead around by the nose; moody, volatile, often ornery, pig-headed, tempestuous, sadistic. Like most native Californians he despised mental and physical cowardice, had great personal courage. 'He had the guts of a bear,' said Ira Pyle; 'he would plow into anybody or anything.' Like most native Californians he thought himself a pioneer, a trail-blazer, a creator of a new and better civilization. Since everything around him was so strong and so vast and so rich, he had boundless confidence in himself, positive that everything that sprang from the California soil was the greatest on earth.

Living in so fertile and spontaneous a countryside he too was spontaneous, flaring quickly to new ideas, new enthusiasms, to love or anger. He worshipped beauty and nature because he was surrounded by such magnificent natural beauty. Impatient, reckless, charged with impetuosity, swagger, and exaggeration, he had in him a love for primitive crudity and emotion; but living in the midst of romantic scenery and opulence his red-blooded violence was crossed with an almost feminine sensitivity to beauty and to pain. Bluff, honest, often noisy and crude, he harbored no suspicion of his fellow man, believed every man honest until he proved himself otherwise. As a result he was often credulous, gullible, easily hoaxed. In his fearlessness, his toughness, his hardness to kill he resembled the grizzly bear which stood on the state flag as its emblem. Constant in his faiths and friendships, open-handedly generous, bitter only against human poverty and injustice, he was a true pagan, pantheistic in his worship of God in the natural beauty and forces that surrounded him. An unquenchable optimist, believing in human progress, he was willing to devote his life to bringing to mankind an intelligent civilization.

By the spring of 1913 he was the highest-paid, best-known, and most popular writer in the world, filling the position Kipling had occupied at the opening of the century. His stories and novels were translated into Russian, French, German, Swedish, Norwegian, Danish, Dutch, Polish, Spanish, Italian, Hebrew. His photographs were reproduced so constantly that his youngish, handsome, clean-cut face was known and loved by millions.

Rumors and anecdotes about him spread as far as the wilds of Tartary. Every word he uttered, every move he made was rehearsed in the newspapers; when he did nothing that produced copy, the reporters made up news. 'I remember that on a single day three news dispatches went out concerning me: The first dispatch stated that my wife had quarreled with me in the city of Portland, Oregon, had packed her Saratoga trunk, and departed on a steamer for San Francisco, going to her mother. The second lie was that in the town of Eureka, California, I had been beaten up in a saloon row by a millionaire lumber man. The third lie was that in a mountain resort in the State of Washington, I had won a $100 bet by catching a perfectly uncatchable variety of lake trout. On the day in question my wife and I were deep in a forest reserve in southwestern Oregon, far from railroads, automobile roads, telegraph wires, and telephone lines.'

Though he never answered or defended himself against these journalistic fictions, he was often hurt and disgruntled. 'Do you know that when a university girl wandered into the hills in back of Berkeley and was attacked by a tramp the papers said it must have been Jack London?' Never once had he been invited to the Press Club of San Francisco, but when its members decided to build a clubhouse, they asked him to contribute two thousand dollars; it is the only time he derived pleasure from refusing a request.

Worse than these false and usually slanderous stories printed about him were the articles and pamphlets distributed with his name as the author. A single printed sheet called *The Military Ideal* caused him the most trouble. 'Young Man: the lowest aim in your life is to be a good soldier. The "good soldier" never tries to distinguish between right and wrong. If he is ordered to fire on his fellow citizens, on his friends, on his neighbors, he obeys without hesitation. If he is ordered to fire down a crowded street where the poor are clamoring for bread, he obeys and sees the gray hairs of age stained with red and the life tide gushing from the breast of woman, feels neither remorse nor sympathy. A good soldier is a blind, heartless, soulless, murderous machine.'

The article is cleverly concocted, for in both sentiment and language it sounds startlingly like Jack. The United States Army officers raised an uproar at the insult to its enlisted men. Protests were lodged with Congress. The Post Office Department decided they had a criminal case against him for distributing the circulars through the mails. Jack's vehement denial of authorship stopped the prosecution, but attacks against him because of the 'military canard' hounded him until his death.

Doubles sprang up all over America, wearing his well-known ranger's hat, bow tie, and sack coat, doubtless giving rise to many of the newspaper yarns. They lectured in his name, sold manuscripts purported to have been written by him, led revolutionary forces against Diaz in Mexico, signed his name to spurious checks, and lastly, made love to women as the red-blooded, primitive Jack London. Letters came in constantly from people who told about meeting him in places he had never been. All of this amused him until a double turned up in San Francisco who began to make love to a lady by the name of Babe. Babe sent open-faced postcards to Glen Ellen asking, 'Don't you love me any more?' signing them, 'Your sweetheart.' Because of the uncertainty of his antecedents, strangers claimed him as their son, brother, uncle, cousin. One story emerged from a family in Oswego, New York, that Jack London was in reality Harry Sands, who had run away from home at the age of fourteen. Newspapers printed the pictures of Harry Sands and Jack London side by side so the public might be given an opportunity to detect a resemblance.

Mingled with his good reviews and favorable stories were frequent literary attacks against him. There was the accusation of falsifying life in Alaska, of not knowing about what he was writing. Fred Thompson, with whom Jack had packed into the Yukon, and who remained in Alaska for twenty years, chuckled at these reports as he remembered the sourdoughs of Alaska waiting impatiently for Jack's tales of the Klondike, considering them the most authentic material written about them.

Plagiarism suits were so frequent he was almost never

without one. As far back as 1902 he had been accused of stealing a short story from one Frank Norris had published. When it was learned that still a third man had published a story on the identical subject, the matter was investigated and it was found that the three writers had been stirred by the same report of an occurrence in Seattle. Stanley Waterloo, upon whose *Story of Ab* Jack had based his *Before Adam,* caused an international scandal after the publication of the book. Jack replied by acknowledging his debt to Waterloo, then insisted that primitive man was in the realm of public domain. Frank Harris, erratic writer and editor, from one of whose articles Jack had lifted for *The Iron Heel* a speech purportedly made by the Bishop of London, now earned publicity for himself by quoting his article side by side with Jack's, showing Jack to be a literary thief. To quiet the uproar Jack could only answer, 'I am a sucker, not a plagiarist; I thought Harris was quoting from an historical document.'

To keep up with his expenditures, as well as the vast operating costs of the ranch and the Wolf House, he had to turn out an unending stream of stories that would sell. If he had dared to stop for a breather his whole superstructure of obligation and indebtedness would have come crashing down over his head. His surest sale was for Alaskan tales; he kept grinding them out, groaning, 'I'm still trying to dig myself out of the Klondike.' His mind was alert, rich, vigorous, and in spite of the strain on him to make everything salable, many of the Alaskan stories are well done, as are such South Seas yarns as 'The Seed of McCoy' and 'The Inevitable White Man' in *South Seas Tales,* and 'The House of Pride' and 'The Sheriff of Kona' in *The House of Pride.* Only the Smoke Bellew stories were fabricated so they would earn him money. The tales he had put on paper had been clamoring in his mind for expression; the need for money was the immediate incentive required to get them down. Aside from his early pot-boiling articles, the Smoke Bellew stories were his first hack work, of no literary value; they provided cement and lumber and copper for his home. For these commodities he gave honest, solid commodities in return. 'I didn't like the job of writing the thirteen Smoke Bellew stories, but I never hedged from my best in writing them.'

His short stories began to fall off in excellence, partly because he was tired of the short form, found it too limiting in scope. He wanted to write only novels. The two he created during this period, *John Barleycorn* and *Valley of the Moon,* are not only among the best he has done but stand shoulder to shoulder with the finest novels written in America. Aside from the third section, which deals with his agricultural observations and which should have been made into a separate book, *Valley of the Moon* contains the greatest thinking and writing to be found in the heart and brain of Jack London. His portraits of Saxon, the laundry girl, and Billy, the teamster, are done with utter conviction; the description of the Bricklayers Union free-for-all at their picnic in Weasel Park, where as a boy Jack had swept out the saloon on Sunday afternoons, is a classic of Irish-American folklore; and the drama and tragedy of the railroad strike in Oakland remains twenty-five years later the model for strike literature in the United States.

Sometimes he had to cast about in desperation for suitable plots for the magazines. It was in one of these periods of pressure that he received a letter from Sinclair Lewis, the gangling, red-headed chap who had wanted an interview for the *Yale News*, and who was now trying to become a writer. Lewis sent him the outlines of several plots which he suggested Jack might be able to use . . . at seven dollars and a half apiece. After studying them, he selected 'The Garden of Terror' and one other, sending Lewis a check for fifteen dollars. Lewis replied post-haste, thanking Jack and telling him that the fifteen dollars was now part of an overcoat against the wintry New York winds.

Later, while working on *The Volta Review* of the American Association to Promote the Teaching of Speech to the Deaf, Lewis sent him another group of twenty-three plot outlines on what he called 'a very businesslike INVOICE OF GOODS shipped as per yrs. of the steenth with prices of same,' signing himself 'Sinclair Lewis, otherwise Hal, alias Red.' In the accompanying letter he hoped Jack would be able to take a considerable part of the plots, for if he did, it would finally give Lewis the chance to get back to his freelance writing, claiming that what writing he had been doing had been done only at the cost of sleep—which was too cheap and instructive an amusement, was sleep, to be wasted. Jack bought Lewis's 'House of Illusion' idea for two-fifty, the list price, the 'Prodigal Father,' 'Guilt of John Avery,' 'Explanations,' 'Recommendations,' 'The Gallant Gentleman,' and 'Woman Who Gave Soul to Man' for five dollars each; 'The Dress Suit Pugilist,' and 'The Common Sense Jail' for seven-fifty each; and 'Mr. Cincinnatus' for ten dollars, sending Lewis a check for fifty-two dollars and fifty cents. Whatever else Lewis may have used the money for, he proudly wrote Jack that he was keeping up his Red, or Socialist, card. From these plot ideas Jack wrote the short story 'When All the World Was Young,' which he sold to the *Post*, and the short novel, *The Abysmal*

Brute, serialized in the *Popular Magazine.* When he wrote
Lewis that for the first time in his life he was disgusted with
a story, and didn't know what to do with Lewis's 'Assassination Bureau,' Lewis, his professional pride aroused, sent Jack
at no extra charge a long synopsis of how the plot should be
reconstructed.

His greatest generosity was to the aspiring writers who descended upon him in staggering numbers, their manuscripts
darkening his sky like a locust plague. Not a day of his life
passed without his receiving a manuscript from a hopeful author, asking him to criticize, rewrite, sell it. These manuscripts, which ranged from a one-page poem to eight-hun-
dred-page novels and treatises, he read with the utmost care,
then sent the authors long criticisms embodying the literary
technique he had worked out over a period of years. To these
strangers he gave the best he had in him, sparing himself neither time nor energy. If he thought the work was good he
tried to sell it to a magazine or publisher; if he thought it
bad, he told the author why he thought so. Often his honest
criticisms brought forth violent recriminations; the knowledge
that he almost certainly would be called unpleasant names
did not deter him from pointing out to these writers just
where their work was bad, and how it could be improved.
One author, to whom he had sent a trenchant criticism when
returning the unsolicited manuscript, wrote back a particularly vilifying letter. Jack sat up the better part of the night,
allowing himself only three hours of the sleep for which his
brain was crying, in order to write a brilliant and patient letter to the aspiring author, a letter of seven pages, the length
of a short story that could have fetched him five hundred
dollars, in which he pleaded with the man to learn how to
take criticism so that he might better his work.

The only writers with whom he grew angry were those
who wanted him to provide them with short cuts to literary
success. To these writers Jack said, 'The man who dreams of
artistry, and yet thinks it necessary for somebody else to lick
him into shape, is a man whose art is doomed to mediocrity.
If you're going to deliver the real goods, you've got to do
your own licking into shape. Buck up! Kick in! Get onto
yourself! Don't squeal. Don't tell me, or any man how good
you consider anything you've done, and that you think it is as
good as somebody else's. Make your work so damned well
better that you won't have time or thought to compare it with
another's mediocrity.'

In his files are letters from nearly every successful writer of
his time, telling him of their needs, their troubles, their men-

tal and spiritual anguish. To them all he gave of his sympathy, his encouragement, his love and understanding of their work, steeling them to believe in themselves, in literature, in the world they were trying to comprehend. When a publishing house had a book with social significance they sent him a copy; he read it faithfully and telegraphed back the praise needed to launch it.

In his business dealings with editors and publishers he was equally generous and honest. He always liked to play things 'the big way' and was constantly distressed at the business men at the other end 'playing things the small way.' He was gentle, courteous, and easy to get along with—until he decided that someone was cheating him or injuring his work. Then he descended upon the offender with the ferocity of an enraged grizzly.

Since 1910, the year in which *Burning Daylight* had been released, he had given Macmillan a play called *Theft*, the collection of South Seas articles called *The Cruise of the Snark*, and four volumes of short stories, none of which was selling well. Now Brett informed him that the market for collections of short stories was being wiped out by the pulp paper magazines appearing by the dozens and carrying good imitations of the action stories that had made Jack famous; that he felt himself unable to meet his constant demands for advances, few of which were under five thousand dollars. After ten years of successful association he parted company with Brett and Macmillan in 1912. He then signed a contract with the Century Company, which published *Smoke Bellew Tales, The Night Born,* and *The Abysmal Brute,* but refused to finance the writing of *John Barleycorn* at one thousand dollars a month for three months. Never having been happy at Century, and with *John Barleycorn* headed for his first brilliant success in three years, he sent them a series of sizzling telegrams in an effort to be released from his contract in order to return to Macmillan.

'All publishers agree that you can transfer Barleycorn. The only thing that can prevent you is the hope of big profits. You would sell yourself and your company's good name for a handful of silver. Please remember that I am not a money scavenger, and that the millions who read Barleycorn will later on read about you. The echoes of this will make you apologetic to the world for many a day, and when you are dust in your graves, the echoes in the brains of those yet unborn will stir your dust. I want your answer that you would rather be men than money grubbers. . . . I have sweated through hells you fellows never dreamed existed; I am possessed of a patience of which you fellows are incapable. I have a careless scorn of personal welfare and financial self-advantage that is beyond your shrinking comprehension. At any moment I will be able to look at my face in the mirror and be better pleased with myself than you fellows will be when you look at your faces in the mirror. . . . I raise my eyes and look at my bookshelf on which are the thirty-four books I have written which have already been published. In the whole row of thirty-four books there is only one scrubby volume *The Abysmal Brute,* published by you just now. Again it is a two-by-four publisher trying to publish the stuff of an eight-by-ten author. . . . Still awaiting reply to my long telegram of May 10, 1913. You have had several days in which to eat Sunday dinner and see your wives and children and be genial and human. Come on, then, and be genial and human with me and let go of me. You know that the one asset I can carry to a new publisher is Barleycorn. Let go the few dollars profit and let me go out from you not entirely naked.' When the Century Company does not reply, he sends one last desperate telegram: 'I can understand anger in any man, but sullenness is so abysmally primitive, so like the balky stupid horse, that I cannot comprehend such an attitude on the part of men who claim to be modern and fairly civilized.'

When Century finally refused to give up *John Barleycorn* he wrote, 'I have been whipped too many times in my life to hold grudges or bad feeling on account of my being whipped,' and co-operated with them fully. However, after *John Barleycorn* was released he went back to Macmillan and ventured forth no more. He admitted to Brett that he had been something of a brute, himself, in trying to get clear of the Century contract.

During the summer of 1913 he and Charmian spent happy weeks visiting the Sterlings in Carmel, swimming in the surf and sun-bathing on the sand, hunting for abalones and eating abalone steaks cooked over a wood fire on the beach, adding a myriad of verses to the humorous poem for which Sterling, ironically enough, is best remembered:

> *Oh! Some folks boast of quail on toast,*
> *Because they think it's tony;*
> *But I'm content to owe my rent*
> *And live on abalone.*

On his Beauty Ranch in the cool of the early morning he continued work on his series of long novels, writing *The Mu-*

tiny on the Elsinore, which *Cosmopolitan* serialized under the title of *The Sea Gangsters.* The half of the book that contains the straight line of action is well done, particularly the sea material for which he had been called the American Conrad; the other half, in which the main character talks about the action, is poorly done and injures the book so severely that *The Mutiny on the Elsinore* died a deserved death.

In the afternoons he rode the trails along the fertile fields ripening under the powerful sun, ending the day at the pool in Boyes Springs where he swam with his friends. On the way home he stopped at each of the bars for a drink, a story, a laugh. At dusk he rode to the Wolf House to talk to Forni and the workmen. By August, 1913, he had spent eighty thousand dollars on his almost completed home. The newspapers lashed him unmercifully as an apostate socialist building a castle; the socialists were angry, feeling they had been betrayed. Pyle reports that Jack would 'back and fill' when twitted about the magnificence of his home. To newspaper reporters he insisted that no matter how big his Wolf House, he was not a capitalist because he was building it with his own wages; when everyone referred to the Wolf House as a castle, he replied that the magnificent redwoods and red stone had belonged to him, that if the place resembled a palace of Justinian or Caesar, it was a fortunate accident costing him nothing in addition. When Harrison Fisher told him that he had the most beautiful home in America, he knew that all the money and effort spent on his Wolf House was justified.

At last, on August 18, clean-up day arrived. The electricians had completed their wiring, the carpenters and plumbers were finished, Forni's men went about gathering the waste which they had soaked in turpentine to wipe down the woodwork. On the following morning a crew of men would begin moving Jack and Charmian into their new house. That night Forni worked with Jack at the ranch house until eleven, then tramped past the Wolf House to his own cabin. Just before two in the morning he was awakened by a farmer dashing in and crying, 'Forni, it's burning! The Wolf House is burning!' When Forni reached the canyon the Wolf House was a mass of flames.

Within a few minutes Jack came running, out of breath, his hair flying. He stopped abruptly on the knoll where he had sat with the Italian workmen singing and drinking wine. Before him was a roaring inferno, every part of the house burning at once. It was mid-August, there was no water. He could do nothing but stand with tears running down his cheeks and watch one of his greatest life dreams be destroyed.

Every piece of woodwork was burning; even the window sills were burning with an unnatural blue flame. Lying out beyond the ring of redwoods that surrounded the house was a pile of finished redwood with which Jack's sleeping quarters were to have been trimmed. The ring of redwoods had not caught fire, but the pile of wood beyond them was ablaze. Many people were accused of the firing, a good part of them in anonymous letters sent to Jack. Shepard, whom Eliza was divorcing, had quarreled with Jack that very day; he was accused. A workman whom Jack had thrown off the ranch for beating his wife was seen in the vicinity; he was accused. An ill-tempered foreman was accused. Forni was accused, jealous socialists were accused, disgruntled tramps were accused. Forni feels the fire was a result of spontaneous combustion; the turpentine-saturated waste with which the woodwork had been rubbed down might have burst into flame. This would not explain the entire house burning at once. If the fire had started in any one room it could not have spread through the stone walls. Defective electrical wiring, if the current had been turned on, might have fired all the rooms simultaneously . . . but no wires extended to the pile of redwood outside the house, beyond the redwood ring . . .

Jack was convinced that the house had been fired, if not by the hand of man, then by the hand of a fate that did not want him to enjoy the fruits of his labor, that did not consider it meet for a socialist to dwell in a castle. During the long, bitter night he spoke only twice. While the flames were at their height he murmured, 'I would rather be the man whose house was burned, than the man who burned it.' At dawn, when only the outer stone shell that had been put together for the centuries was left standing, he said quietly, 'Forni, tomorrow we will start to rebuild.'

He never did rebuild the Wolf House. Something in his heart burned out that night and was destroyed forever.

10

FOR FOUR DAYS he lay in bed on the screened sleeping porch overlooking the tropical garden. Every illness he had contracted, from the earliest days of The Road and the Klondike through Korea and the Solomon Islands, rose up to smite him. Convinced that the Wolf House had been fired by someone he had befriended, he wrestled with a searing disgust. It was not merely the gutting of his house that crushed him; it was the loss of the love and faith in humanity that had dominated his hours and his character. His eyes were suddenly opened to much that he had not seen before, or, having seen, had passed as unimportant. The burning of the Wolf House appeared symbolic of the manner in which everything he had tried to do for socialism and literature would be destroyed. He aged considerably during those four days.

His first move when he climbed out of bed was to ride Washoe Ban across the fields to the Wolf House. Gazing forlornly at the skeleton of magnificent red stone jutting its nude towers into the blue Sonoma sky, he named it The Ruins. Though he could have declared himself bankrupt, he paid the contractors in full. Seventy thousand dollars was dead loss, as was the time and energy he had spent writing the Smoke Bellew stories . . . which again led him to wonder if there might be a moral hidden somewhere in the ashes. He wrote that he was now one hundred thousand dollars in debt; the weight of the money was not heavy upon his shoulders; but the thought of the creative work he was going to have to produce to earn it sat like a stone on his brain.

He repeated to Forni and Eliza that he was going to rebuild the Wolf House; he had Forni clear the débris from the ruins, and had Eliza cut down more redwoods to season. But deep in his mind he was discouraged . . . the house would only be burned again. When *Cosmopolitan* sportingly sent his monthly two thousand dollars ahead of time because of his loss, he built an extension to his overcrowded study, and here, under a cool, spreading oak, he moved his roll-top desk, his wire baskets loaded with papers and mail, his steel files with their records of accomplishment, his cardboard reference boxes with the notes for hundreds of stories, and his writing supplies. Here he spent the working hours of the last three years of his life.

He slipped back into his routine; everything was the same as it had always been, yet everything appeared different. When he rode about the ranch he could no longer fail to note that the laborers were soldiering on the job, putting out as little as they could for their wages. By a little discreet inquiry he learned that they considered the ranch a rich man's hobby, no more to be taken seriously than the workmen had taken the *Snark* seriously. His mechanics too were indifferent to the quality of the work they were turning out; when he jumped off Washoe Ban in front of the blacksmith shop and inspected a shoeing job the smithy had just completed, he saw that the man had rasped off half an inch of the toe of the hoof to make the shoe fit. Studying the ranch bills and feeling they were too high, he rode into town to consult with the merchants. They told him that his foremen demanded a twenty per cent kickback on every dollar of merchandise purchased, and that there was no alternative but to add it to the bills.

In 1900 he had written to Anna Strunsky, 'I do not feel that because I condemn the deficiencies of my friends is any reason why I should not love them.' Love and tolerance and generosity were the wellsprings of his nature; yet they were growing increasingly difficult to maintain. He asked his friend Ernest, who was in Oakland, to buy him some heavy draft horses. Ernest charged him a commission, added a bill for expenses, then shipped two sick horses and two below the specified weight. When he wrote Ernest that the horses were unsatisfactory, Ernest answered with an angry, insulted letter. Jack replied, 'You go bleating around about your hurt feelings, but what about me? Because I have the presumption to dare to tell you that the two work horses, instead of weighing the fifteen hundred pounds you said they did, weighed thirteen hundred and fifty, and the other two were sick and decrepit enough for chicken feed, you go up in the air, raise a roar about being called a grafter. You have stuck my money in a hole, and now you tell me to come and get it out. You feel sore! How many hundreds of dollars sore do you think I feel? Here I am with the only available horse money tied up, and not enough horses to work the ranch with.'

As far back as 1904 when his newspaper friend Noel had been out of work, Jack had given him the right to dramatize *The Sea Wolf*, and to keep two thirds of the royalties he might earn from the dramatization. Instead Noel had sold the dramatic rights to someone else and retained the thirty-five-hundred-dollar purchase price. Contracting with Hobart Bosworth to make a motion picture of the book, Jack had to plead among his publishers for the thirty-five hundred dollars needed to buy back those rights. And here was Noel urging him to put money into the Millergraph Company he was organizing to market an improved lithographing process. Resolving not to be changed or made hard by his newly awakened cynicism, he ordered Brett to pay Noel a thousand dollars; when the Millergraph Company needed more funds he again mortgaged Flora's house for four thousand dollars, writing to Noel, 'I play with my cards on the table, and put myself absolutely in the trust of my friends.' The stock he was supposed to receive was juggled, the company went into bankruptcy.

Charmian told him she had to have three hundred dollars immediately; he sent out pleas to the hundreds of men and women who had borrowed from him an aggregate of more than fifty thousand dollars, vowing they would return every cent. He could collect only fifty dollars. For the first time he wondered if his friends were laughing at him. Had he been marked early for a fall guy, a wild Irishman who spent his money like a drunken sailor? Always it had been a case of one-way traffic: he gave and gave, others took and took. His former bouts of despondence had been self-generated; because of their cyclical nature they had soon passed. Now his thoughts, steeping like tea, became increasingly black and bitter.

For several years he had been urging Bessie to bring the two girls to Glen Ellen during their summer vacations so they would come to love his Beauty Ranch. Only once had Bessie accepted his offer; she had brought Joan and Bess and a group of friends to the ranch for a picnic. No sooner had the lunch been spread than Charmian came galloping by in a cap and red shirt, spreading a fine layer of dust over the food.—Jack vowed fervently that if Bessie would allow him to build her a cottage on the ranch he would keep Charmian away from her. Bessie declined. Having lost her husband to Charmian, she feared she might also lose her daughters. She told him she did not consider the second Mrs. London a fit moral example to which to expose her growing girls.

His efforts to get a friendly word or gesture from Joan, who was now thirteen, failed. He had hoped she would be old enough to become his companion and friend. On August 24, four days after the burning of the Wolf House, he pleads with her to remember that he is her father, that he has fed her, clothed her, housed her, and loved her since the first moment she drew breath, and then asks, 'What do you feel for me? Am I a fool who gives much and receives nothing? I send you letters and telegrams, and I receive no word from you. Am I beneath your contempt in every way save as a meal ticket? Do you love me at all? What do I mean to you? I am sick—you are silent. My home is destroyed—you have no word to say. The world does not belong to the ones who remain silent, who by their very silence lie and cheat and make a mock of love and a meal ticket of their father. Don't you think it is about time I heard from you? Or do you want me to cease forever from caring to hear from you?'

What hurt most in his awakening was the cruel realization that Charmian, at the age of forty-three, was still a child, preoccupied with infantile details. Her neighbors report that 'she told interminable stories about childlike things, trivial things, about her jewels, her antique clothes, her little caps. She wanted to be eternally feminine, to use her wiles and charms.' He suffered acutely as he saw his guests try to conceal their embarrassment at her posing and acting, at her coyness, her attempts to play the young and beautiful girl she forever thought herself, at her bizarre, jeweled, red costume-clothing and frilly lace caps dating back to the past century. Charmian's stepsister says that when Charmian was young it was her habit to stick her head around a corner, make a face or say something cute, and then run, expecting to be chased. She was still sticking her head around corners, saying something cute, expecting to be chased. One evening as Jack sat with Eliza at the ranch desk in the dining-room, worried sick over how he was to meet his obligations, Charmian bounced in with an unwrapped bolt of velvet goods draped across her, strutted up and down as she cried, 'Look, Mate, won't this make a gorgeous outfit? I've just bought two bolts.' There was a long, sad silence after she left the room; then he turned to Eliza and said quietly, 'She is our little child. We must always take care of her.'

If he could have started out on another South Seas voyage or four-horse driving trip, or any adventure, Charmian would still have been the ideal companion. But he was living at home now, he had grown tired and disenchanted, he wanted a mature woman 'to stand flat-footed by his side' in a mature world. He needed a wife who would share his broad bed, whom he could touch with his hand when he awoke in the deep of night, troubled.

Surrounded by friends and relatives, with hundreds of thousands of admirers spread throughout the western world, he felt unutterably alone. He ached as only a man who has started on the down grade toward death can ache for his own flesh and blood, for that son who could be trusted, on whose strong and devoted shoulder he could lean in his older years, who would carry on his name and tradition.

In spite of the burning of the Wolf House and the burning up of his crops in the long drouth of the summer, the year 1913 proved to be his most fruitful; in it he reached the climax of his career. Four of his novels were serialized in magazines, among which was *The Scarlet Plague*, which showed how mankind reverted to primitive life when a plague wiped out civilization. In book form there were published *The Night Born*, which contains the stirring tales 'The Mexican,' 'To Kill a Man,' and 'When the World Was Young'; a short prize-fight novel, *The Abysmal Brute*, based on a Sinclair Lewis plot; and, within sixty days of each other, his two great novels, *John Barleycorn* and *Valley of the Moon*. This record of accomplishment made the publishing world regard him not so much as a man, as a natural force.

Fate, which could deliver shattering blows, could still treat him as its favorite. Toward the end of the year, having completed the exhausting *Mutiny of the Elsinore* and needing a big idea to revitalize him, his friend Ed Morrell was released from San Quentin. After having spent five years in solitary confinement Morrell had been taken out of the disciplinary strait-jacket and black hole to be made head trusty of the prison. For many years Jack had been working to have him pardoned, and at last succeeding, wired Morrell 'Congratulations and welcome home.' The two men met at the Saddle Rock restaurant in Oakland, where they made fast a friendship that had been begun through correspondence, as so many of Jack's friendships had begun. Morrell spent much of his time on the Beauty Ranch feeding Jack's lifelong interest in criminology and penology, subjects on which Professor Chaney had been writing with intelligence before Jack was born. Before long he had plunged into his eighth and last great novel, *The Star Rover*, powerful in emotional impact when describing the sufferings of the men lashed into canvas strait-jackets, tender in feeling when describing the friendships between the prisoners in their airless cells, bold in imagination when projecting their backward flights into the realm of time. For pure death-appeal, breathlessness of suspense, musical lyricism of writing, and profound human sympathy, *The Star Rover* is a magnificent literary accomplishment.

The work served as a catharsis; such gratification did the writing bring him that his mental and physical illnesses were shoved into the background. As in the early days of Piedmont, he derived pleasure from reading to his guests each new chapter as he completed it. To a young boy who wrote for encouragement he answered, 'I have been through the ennui of sixteen as well as twenty; and the boredom, and the blaséness and utter wretchedness of the ennui of twenty-five and thirty. And yet I live, am growing fat, and laugh a large portion of my waking hours.' Morrell says of this period, 'No matter what he said or did his ever-present kindness held you. He could say the rashest and brashest things, hurt your feelings and make you like it . . . because there was no personal sting. He was one of the most lovable characters of his age.'

As a man with a long and successful business career, an increasing portion of his time had to be devoted to promoting and protecting his interests. He had agreed with Hobart Bosworth, the actor, to take a portion of the profits in return for the right to make his books into motion pictures. Bosworth had no sooner begun work than other film companies pirated his stories and made pictures of them, two versions of *The Sea Wolf* playing in theaters on opposite sides of the street. The copyright laws were not only in confusion, but court decisions had been against the author, who found that when he sold material for serialization to a magazine the magazine automatically acquired all rights to that material. Jack learned that any of his work which had first appeared in a magazine belonged to the magazine rather than to him; that the pirating film companies were buying up these copyrights for insignificant sums.

He joined with Arthur Train and the newly formed Authors' League in a fight to have the law revised so that when an author sold a story to a magazine he retained his rights. Into this legal battle, which lasted for several years, he threw his strength, energy, and resources, making trips to New York and Hollywood, retaining lawyers, arguing cases in court, sending out hundreds of impassioned letters and telegrams. If the long and complicated battle was waged at the expense of the literature he might have been creating, he helped make it possible for future generations of American writers to derive the full benefit of their work.

By May of 1914, shortly after he had completed *The Star Rover*, the United States Government took a hand in the Villa-Carranza revolution in Mexico, sending battleships and troops to occupy Vera Cruz. Ever since he had been thwarted in his desire to report the Russian-Japanese War of 1904, Jack had looked forward to the day when he would be able to vindicate himself. Offered eleven hundred dollars a week and expenses by *Collier's*, he departed for Galveston within twenty-four hours, then shipped for Vera Cruz.

Once again he was unable to report the war . . . this time because there was no war to report; having no intention of conquering Mexico and establishing a protectorate, the United States contented itself with the show of arms in Vera Cruz. Once again he hammered out virile articles on 'The Red Game of War' and 'The Mexican Army,' described the United States Army clearing up the pestilence of Vera Cruz, and the revolutionists attacking the foreign oil interests in Tampico. For nearly two months he pursued war news, but all he was able to take out of Mexico was a severe case of amoebic dysentery; the memory of a crap game in which he cleaned out the newspaper correspondents and the ambassadors from France and Spain; and the material for a series of short stories about Mexico which excited him considerably. When the editor of *Cosmopolitan* expressed interest, he began outlining and annotating the stories.

He returned to Glen Ellen ravaged by the dysentery, pale and weak. In an effort to regain his strength he took the *Roamer* for a several weeks' cruise on San Francisco Bay. His recovery was slow, pain-fraught. When the editor of *Cosmopolit*an changed his mind about the newly projected group of stories, deciding that the American public was fed up with Mexico, Jack discarded the material without writing another word. In his fighting days he would have written his Mexican tales and made the magazines like them. If the planned stories would have been the equal of the only one he did write, 'The Mexican,' he robbed both himself and the world of a superb volume.

Ill health was attacking him more steadily; what Cloudesley Johns called his 'periods of mental depression when his splendid will to live almost left him' were becoming more frequent; the cycle had begun to accelerate. It was becoming increasingly difficult for him to squeeze out his thousand words daily . . . yet in the fall of 1914 he informed his editor that he had jumped into a new novel that was going to be the biggest, most tremendous thing he had ever written '. . . in a setting that never before in the history of all the literature of the world was ever put into print. A mighty trio in a mighty situation. As I go over this novel I am almost led to believe that it is what I have been working toward all my writing life. It will be utterly fresh, utterly unlike anything I have ever done.'

Starting with this apparently genuine conviction and enthusiasm—though in his fatigue and despair he may only have been trying to whip up his own interest as well as that of the editor—he began work on his back-to-the-land novel, *The Little Lady of the Big House*. Ostensibly an agricultural novel based on his ideas for a model ranch and the rehabilitation of California agriculture, it developed into a love triangle written with all the flowery sentimental hyperbole of the nineteenth century, a book so artificial, strained, and exaggerated that the reader is stunned, at a loss to understand how much spurious thinking could have emanated from Jack London.

Only a few months before he had completed *The Star Rover* and such first-rate stories as *Told in the Drooling Ward*, the scene of which was laid in the asylum which adjoined the Hill Ranch, and *South of the Slot*, a proletarian story of power and conviction. His confidence had not run down, his concentration and discipline had not run down, his eagerness to create had not run down, but the powerful machine that was the brain of Jack London, after having produced forty-one books in fourteen years, was at last beginning to tire, to lose its grip.

Deeply as he had been hurt by Joan the year before, he made another determined effort to win his daughters' allegiance. When Joan, who had just entered high school, sent him a play she had written he was as delighted with it as with anything he had turned out himself. 'I like it tremendously, and can hardly believe that I am the father of a girl who is so big that she can write such a play.' His business and personal letters of the next few months proudly tell that he is the father of a girl already in high school.

Having formulated his plans, he went humbly to the house

in Piedmont, where he laid his proposition before Bessie. If she would permit the children to visit him at the ranch, to become acquainted with their father all over again, and to love the ranch as they rode over its trails with him, he would change his will, which now deeded everything to Charmian, and leave the estate to the two girls. He would build Bessie a home in a protected corner of the ranch, so she could be with them. She could come with them at all times to be sure that Charmian would not intrude. . . . He would do anything she asked, anything, if only she would let him have back his two daughters. Bessie was not tempted.

A few days later he wrote directly to Joan. 'Now, Joan, it is a hard proposition to put up to you at your age, and the chances are that in deciding on this proposition I put up to you on Sunday night you will make the mistake of deciding to be a little person in a little world. You will make that mistake because you listened to your mother, who is a little person in a little place in a little part of the world, and who, out of her female sex jealousy against another woman, has sacrificed your future for you. I offer you the big things of the world, the big things that big people live and know and think and act.'

Many anxiously pleading letters followed. For a long time Joan remained silent. At last, at his insistence, she wrote him a one-page letter in which she told him that she was perfectly satisfied with her surroundings, that she had no wish to change them, that she would stay with her mother always, that she resented his opinions of Bessie, whom she loved as a good mother. She begged him to let her feel that this would be the last of the awful letters he would force her to write—a closing which Charmian was in reality a farewell.

When Charmian tried to take away from him the 'philosophic tramps' he kept permanently on the ranch, he said to her in a cry wrung from within, 'I get more sheer pleasure out of an hour's talk with Strawn-Hamilton than all of my inefficient Italian laborers have ever given me. He *pays* his way. My God, the laborers *never* have. Please remember that the ranch is *my* problem. What all the various ones who have worked on it have lost for me in cash is a thousand times more than the few meals and beds I've given my bums. I give these paltry things of paltry value out of my heart. I've not much heartthrob left for my fellow beings. Shall I cut this out, too?'

Charmian had developed sullen and moody spells, interfered with his management of the ranch, told him what trees he could or could not cut down, hampered the progress of the work by complaining that insomnia kept her awake all night and that the workmen, who reported at seven, were not to be allowed near the ranch house until nine because they might awaken her. When he insisted that they had work to do she picked up her bedding and slept in the barn. Defeated, Jack ordered the workmen to keep away from the house even if they had to stand idle . . . until one morning, when he was crossing his fields at five o'clock, he found her in a haystack with a young guest, watching the sunrise.

The criticisms he had made of Bessie London were that she dressed badly, that she was not a good hostess, and that she was jealous. By a twist of fate he found these same attributes in Charmian. She made no attempt to be a hostess or to manage the house; the Japanese servants ran everything, and she was simply another guest in his home. When friends arrived; Jack or Nakata showed them to their rooms; one woman guest tells of Jack's embarrassment because Charmian never troubled with the new arrivals, that he had even to show the women where the toilet was. Where Bessie had paid little attention to women unless they threw themselves upon his neck, Charmian was actively jealous of every other female. He was rarely permitted to go anywhere without her; when they were out she played a game which women who witnessed it called 'breaking it up.' For only two minutes was he allowed to talk to another woman, even though they might be discussing the coming election; at the end of that time she interrupted with a gushing monologue.

Once when his secretary, Jack Byrne, was sending him a telegram to Los Angeles, he added to it the information that a woman whose entire family Jack had known and loved for years would like to see him. Charmian told Byrne to omit this part of the message, as she would be wiring Jack later and would tell him about it. Her wire was never sent. Even at the cost of working herself half to death, she had never permitted Jack to employ a woman secretary. 'I wouldn't let anyone else in,' she said, 'I mustn't take my finger out of it.' It was not until Johnny Miller's mother died, and her second husband, Jack Byrne, was out of a job that he was allowed to have the full-time secretary he greatly needed.

From New York she received a telegraphic report that 'Jack is spending all his time with a woman who lives in the Van Cortlandt Hotel on Forty-Eighth Street. Amy.' Feeling unhappy, restless, he was having affairs with other women. Years before he had written to Charmian, 'Let me tell you a little affair which will indicate the ease with which I let loose the sexual man.' Yet his promiscuity seems to have resulted from a break-up of the marriage ties rather than any inherent license. He was faithful to Bessie until their marriage, physically, had been disrupted. He was faithful to Charmian for nine years, until their marriage, spiritually, was destroyed.

Though he had sometimes drunk to defeat his cyclical depressions, most of his drinking had been for companionship, pleasure, and relaxation. He now began drinking heavily, not to incur pleasure but to ease pain. He had rarely done any drinking on the ranch; now he drank there a good deal. He harnessed his horses and drove to Santa Rosa, not one afternoon a week, but three and four. Ira Pyle reports that he no longer argued for the fun of it; he grew angry, banged his fist on the bar, showed his disgust with people who reasoned from self-interest rather than logic. Except for his wild bouts as a young oyster pirate, he had been able to take his liquor or leave it alone. Only the year before, returning on the *S.S. Dirigo* around Cape Horn from a business trip in the East, he had put aboard at Baltimore one thousand books and pamphlets he wished to study, and forty gallons of whiskey. 'When we dock at Seattle either my thousand books will have been studied, or the forty gallons of whiskey will be gone.' He left the ship with the thousand volumes annotated, the whiskey untouched. But all this was changed; he had to have whiskey to deaden the long hours, to make them tolerable. His illnesses made him drink, his drinking made him ill. His mental fatigue and depression made him drink, his drinking fatigued and depressed him. No longer well, no longer young, no longer fresh, happy, and working vigorously, he could not handle his quart of Scotch a day. Before, people had seen him drink; now they saw him become drunk.

His disillusionment at the hands of his friends and business associates continued apace. Two friends tasting the grape juice he made from his grapes suggested they form a company to market it. They were to supply the money, Jack his name and the grapes. Before long he had been haled into court, where they were suing him for thirty-one thousand dollars. After spending thirty-five hundred dollars to get back the dramatic rights to *The Sea Wolf*, and giving the film companies his best stories, he was informed by the producers that there were no profits for him to share. He bought a half interest in an Arizona gold mine which he was never able to locate, a block of stock in the new Oakland Fidelity Loan and Mortgage Company, which kept him in the law courts for two years. Always 'a flyer, a white chip on the table, a lottery ticket' brought him grief.

His bitterest blow was the trouble Ninetta and Edward Payne, to whose support he was even yet contributing, stirred up among his neighbors, getting them to sign a petition preventing him from using the water from a second dam he had built high up on his land to control the winter rains, on the grounds that it would divert water from the creek which ran alongside their home. While few of the other neighbors seemed exercised or frightened at the possibility of losing their water, Ninetta and Edward Payne carried through, securing an injunction against him.

He learned that some of his friends who were constantly asking for money were saying that he made it so easily they would be fools not to help him spend it. Even George Sterling, to whom he had just sent one hundred dollars for a plot he did not want, because he knew Sterling was broke, was criticizing him for writing for 'Hearst's gold.' In his earlier years money had been easier to make, had given him more joy in the making. He had accepted avarice, sloth, and hypocrisy with the cheerful resignation of the man who knows the worst about humanity and goes on from there. Becoming increasingly ill and despondent, he now viewed this abuse of his generosity with bitterness as he beat out his brain to help support those who abused him.

In February of 1915, after a number of cold and bleak months, he left with Charmian for Hawaii to finish out the winter. Here in the warm sunlight, with daily swimming and horseback riding, his health improved sufficiently to enable him to begin a new novel, *Jerry of the Islands*, with the last remaining flare of the Jack London spirit. 'I assure you in advance that Jerry is uniquely new and different from anything that has appeared in fiction, not only under the classification of dog stories, but under the general classification of fiction. I am making fresh, vivid, new stuff, and dog psychology that will warm the hearts of dog lovers and the heads of psychologists.' *Jerry of the Islands* is a delightful story of dog adventure in the New Hebrides. Sitting in a loose kimona at his desk on an open verandah facing the palm-fringed lagoon, his mind journeyed back to snow-covered Alaska, back to Buck of *The Call of the Wild*, the dog that had sent him skyrocketing to fame. It was pleasant to think about dogs and to write about them; they were a loyal species.

By summer he had completed *Jerry of the Islands*, and returned to Glen Ellen. He went to the Bohemian Grove on the

Russian River for the High Jinks of the Bohemian Club, where he met a number of his artist friends, argued socialism versus defeatism, swam in the river, and drank heavily. After the Jinks he brought Sterling, Martinez, and a few others bank to the ranch; the drinking continued. His uremia became acute, but he was not willing to stop drinking long enough to cure the infection. He worked only on the movie story *Hearts of Three* for which entertainment nonsense the *Cosmopolitan* had offered him twenty-five thousand dollars. Glad of the opportunity to escape serious thinking, he tossed off his daily thousand words in an hour and a half.

He still liked to laugh, but his sporadic gaiety was forced. Finn Frolich says, 'He didn't do the sporting things he used to do, wrestle, play, didn't want to go up into the mountains riding horseback any more. The gleam was gone from his eye.' He no longer discussed to obtain information, to enjoy a battle of wits. He argued to win, sometimes grew quarrelsome. George Sterling advised Upton Sinclair not to visit the Beauty Ranch, as Jack had changed.

His only peace and pleasure was derived from the ranch itself. Though he was disgusted with a large part of the men who were working for him, he never lost his confidence in the land. 'I am that sort of farmer who, after delving in all the books to satisfy his quest for economic values, returns to the soil as the source and foundation of all economics.' He continued to clear new fields, to plant new crops, to extend his irrigation systems, to put up new stone buildings for his stock. To Joe King, the printing bill for whose appeal he had paid six years before, and whom he was still trying to get pardoned from San Quentin, he wrote, 'I have just completed a pig pen that will make anyone in the United States who is interested in the manufacture of pork sit up and take notice. There is nothing like it in the way of piggeries ever built. It cost three thousand dollars to build and will pay twelve per cent in the mere cost of labor. I am running nothing but registered pigs on the Ranch. I plan shortly to build a slaughterhouse and install a refrigerating plant.'

He was not exaggerating about his Pig Palace, as the piggery was soon named. There was a private indoor and outdoor suite for each pig family, with two taps of running water. Built by Forni in a perfect circle with a stone house in the center in which to store the feed, it is a work of art, architecturally flawless. He also planned with Forni to build a circular stone barn for his cows which would be equally labor-saving and permanent. To the editor of *Cosmopolitan* he wrote, 'Please remember that my Ranch is the apple of my eye. I am working for results and I am going to get results that will take their place in books some of these days.'

In his mind he was slowly developing a new idea, an extension of his plan for a model farm. He would establish a select rural community. Weeding out the undesirable laborers, he would employ only those men who had a personal integrity and a love for the land. For each of these men he would build a cottage; there would be a general store at which commodities would be sold for cost; and a little school for the laborers' children. The number of families he would include in his model community would depend solely on the number the land could support. 'My fondest hope is that somewhere in the next six or seven years I shall be able to break even on the Ranch.' He wanted no profit, no return on his investment of a quarter of a million dollars; he wanted only to break even, to maintain a real community of workers, bound by their common love of the soil.

Misfortune struck his plans almost at once. Though he had gone to the Agriculture Department of the University of California for advice about his piggery, the entire collection of registered pigs caught pneumonia on the stone floors, and died. His prize shorthorn bull, the foundation of his stock, slipped in its pen, dug a horn into the earth, fell over it, and broke its neck. The herd of Angora goats was wiped out by disease. The Shire stallion which had won him several blue ribbons, and whom he loved as though it were human, was found dead in the fields. His entire investment in Shire horses proved to be a mistake, for the hair on their legs made it impossible to keep them clean and in working shape during the winter months. His heavy draft horses, too, had been an error in judgment; they were being replaced by lighter equipment, which lighter horses could pull, and by tractors. His one hundred and forty thousand eucalyptus trees, which were to grow by themselves and net him a fortune after twenty years, were suddenly useless for anything but firewood; all interest in Circassian walnut had disappeared.

He was whipped, he knew he was whipped, but he would not admit it. If anyone had come to him and said, 'Jack, the ranch is an expensive failure, for your own sake you had better abandon it,' he would have cried, as he had cried when he had been urged to give up the *Snark*, 'I can't quit!' In order to earn money to keep the ranch going he eked out his thousand words a day. The act of writing, which had been blood in his veins and air in his lungs, was now poison to him. 'The only reason I keep on writing is that I have to. If I did not have to, I'd never write another line. Take that straight.'

He was not the only one tiring of his work. The critics and public were also tiring, choked by a plethora. When he finished *Hearts of Three* he wrote, 'This yarn is a celebration. By its completion I celebrate my fortieth birthday, my fiftieth book, my sixteenth year in the writing game.' A few days later he groused, 'I have not seen a best seller of my own for a weary time. Is the work of other authors better than mine? Is the public souring on me?' *The Valley of the Moon* had been his last book to be favorably received; though *The Strength of the Strong* contains his best proletarian and prophetic stories, and represents the finest cross-cut of his variegated genius, it passed as just another collection of Jack London tales. To a lone friendly reviewer he wrote, 'You are the only man in the United States who has cared a whoop in hell for *The Star Rover*. The rest of the reviewers have said that *The Star Rover* is my regular red-blood, up-to-the-neck, primeval gore sort of stuff, too horrible for women to read, and too horrible for men to read, except degenerates. If my stories are fierce, then life is fierce. I think life is strong, not fierce, and I try to make my stories as strong as life is strong.'

He had his five-year contract with *Cosmopolitan* to provide them with two novels a year, but the failing giant was now so completely enchained that his secretary Byrne wrote to a man who wanted Jack to collaborate on a new idea, 'The class of work he must turn out is indicated to him by his publishers, to whom he is under contract for several years to come.' At the age of twenty-four he had revitalized the magazine world, made his own rules. Now he replied to an aspiring author, 'If you want to write for the magazines you must write what the magazines want. Magazines have their own game. If you want to play their game you must play it their way!'

No longer could he awaken himself to combat. To a woman high-school teacher in a small town in California who wrote to him for help against a corrupt political machine, he answered, 'It is a good many years since I jumped into the battle to right political affairs, to give all men and women a square deal. Really, I feel a sort of veteran when I think over the long years of the fight. I am not exactly a beaten veteran, but unlike the raw recruit I do not expect to storm and capture the enemy's position by the next sunrise. I am the veteran who neither hopes to see the end of the campaign, nor any longer forecasts the date of the end of the campaign.' To

another friend who wanted him to join in a concerted attack
on religion, he wrote that 'the battle over religion seems so
far away, a little and forgotten battle still being waged off
somewhere in a secret corner of the world. I think you are
fighting an antagonist already, intellectually, beaten.' To
Mary Austin, who complained to him that her finest writings
were being misunderstood, he replied, wearily, 'The best
efforts of my heart and head have missed fire with practically
everybody in the world who reads, and I do not worry about
it. I go ahead content to be admired for my red-blood brutal-
ity, and for a number of other nice little things that are not
true of my work at all. Those who sit alone must sit alone.
As I remember it, the prophets and seers of all times have
been compelled to sit alone except at such times as they were
stoned or burned at the stake.'

He retired to his study like an injured grizzly bear into a
cave to lick its wounds. When he received hurt, angry, and
disillusioned letters from his followers about *The Little Lady
of the Big House*—for they were flinging copies of the magazine into the fire, begging him to come down to earth again
—he lashed out at them, sensitive and stung. 'Let me tell you
right now that I am damned proud of The Little Lady.'

What no one except Eliza knew was that he was torturing
himself with the fear of going insane. His brain was too exhausted to work, to create, and yet he had to write every day
of his life. He was afraid that his mind would break under
the constant and heavy pressure, a fear intensified by his conviction that his mother was not rational. Time and again he
begged, 'Eliza, if I go insane, promise that you won't put me
in an institution. Promise!' Nor could Eliza minimize his
fears. Each time she had to assure him solemnly that she
would not put him in a public institution, that she would take
care of him.

He held out only one hope for himself: that he would find
a mature, genuine woman whom he could love, who would
love him, and give him a son. He knew Charmian would
never give him the son for whom he hungered. So grieved
was he that he would go childless to his death, he who had
been so fruitful in creating human beings on the printed
page, that he vowed 'he was going to have a son, and he
didn't care how he got one. He was going out to find a
woman who would give him a son, and bring her to the
Ranch.' There is ample evidence that he found the woman he
was looking for, that he loved her deeply, and that she loved
him. But he never carried out his determination. He could

not bring himself to hurt Charmian. He was gentle with her as one is gentle with a child, continued to write glowing inscriptions into her copy of his books . . . for she had given him years of companionship, and he was grateful.

Charmian was greatly upset, nervous; she knew that he was being unfaithful to her, that she was in grave danger of losing him. Rumors of divorce flew about Oakland. She suffered constantly from insomnia, told everyone at the ranch that the night after Jack's death she enjoyed her first sleep in many months.

He knew himself to be caught in an impasse. With his various distresses tearing at his mind, he drank constantly. His writing had by now become little more than the reflex of a once powerful organism. In 1915, beside *The Little Lady of the Big House*, he had published only one short story, 'A Hyperborean Brew,' both of which had been written the year before. On December 1, 1914, he had written, 'Yesterday I finished my last novel, *The Little Lady of the Big House;* tomorrow I begin to frame up my next novel, which I think will be entitled "The Box Without a Lid." ' This book was never written. 'The Assassination Bureau' he abandoned in the middle as hopeless.

In January of 1916, hoping the sun would once again cure his illnesses, he and Charmian sailed for Hawaii. At the very beginning of his career he had cried out exultantly, 'Socialism is the greatest thing in the world!' Only a month before he had been heading his letters 'Dear Comrade' and ending them with 'Yours for the Revolution.' Only a few months before he had written a fervent introduction to Upton Sinclair's anthology, *The Cry for Justice*, that was an indictment of the 'unfairness, cruelty, and suffering' that existed in the world. He had not allowed the betrayals of his friends or untrustworthy laborers to injure his belief in the socialized state; more militantly than ever he believed in the economic philosophy and human logic of socialism. But he was embittered with mankind for its lethargy in throwing off its shackles. Sitting in his stateroom he wrote, 'I am resigning from the Socialist Party because of its lack of fire and fight, and its loss of emphasis on the class struggle. I was originally a member of the old, revolutionary, up-on-its-hind-legs, fighting Socialist Labor Party. Trained in the class struggle, I believe that the working class, by fighting, by never fusing, by never making terms with the enemy, could emancipate itself. Since the whole trend of socialism in the United States of recent years has been one of peaceableness and compromise, I find that my mind refuses further sanction of my remaining a party member. Hence my resignation.'

He had done a great deal for the Cause, and the Cause had done a great deal for him. It made no difference that he thought he was quitting to go farther Left; by his resignation after fifteen years of loyal service he dealt the party a severe blow, and himself a death blow. In *Martin Eden* he had had Brissenden warn Martin that he had better tie himself to socialism, or when success came he would have no reason to continue living. In December, 1912, he had replied to an admirer, 'As I said in *John Barleycorn,* I am Martin Eden. Martin Eden died because he was an individualist, I live because I am a socialist and have social consciousness.'

This time Hawaii healed neither his mind nor his body. He wrote 'Michael, Brother of Jerry,' a few feeble Hawaiian stories, and began work on a novel about an Eurasian girl named Cherry which he never completed. He drank hard to drown his uncertainty and unhappiness . . . but they would not drown. When he returned to Glen Ellen his friends hardly knew him. Eliza said he was not the same man. He had grown fat, his ankles were swollen, his face bloated, his eyes lack-luster. He who had always looked so boyish now looked many years past his age. He was morose, despondent, in pain. Only occasionally did he invite his cronies up to the ranch for a pressed duck dinner. Drifting, completely off balance, he was seen drunk in Oakland, caused scenes in public places.

Shortly after his return he went to Bessie's home in Piedmont, for he at last realized that he had been cruel, that the loss of his children had been his own fault. In return for two small endowment policies which would not fall due for several years, he offered to double her allowance. Bessie accepted. The former husband and wife had a tender meeting in which he said, 'If you ever need me, and I am at the end of the earth, I will come back to you.' Bessie answered, 'I don't think I will ever need you, Jack, but if I ever do, I will send for you.'

Aside from Eliza there was only one human being he loved and trusted completely: 'Nakata, for six or seven years you have been with me night and day. You have been with me through every danger over the whole world. Storm and violent death have been common in your and my experience. I remember the times in storms when you stood nobly by. I remember the hours of sickness when you nursed me. I remember the hours of fun when you laughed with me and I laughed with you.' Nakata, leaving 'Master' to study dentistry in Honolulu, replied, 'You sheltered me and fed me, you have stayed up all night to save me when I was helpless with fish poisoning. You took your valuable time and taught me how to write and read. You have introduced me to your guests and friends as your friend and son. You have treated me as your son. This beautiful relationship was made by "your big heart." ' And so, with Nakata, his Japanese servant, Jack found the only son, the only son's love he was to know. When Eliza said to him, 'Jack, you are the loneliest man in the world. The things your heart wanted, you've never had,' he demanded, 'How the devil did you know?'

He had always said he wanted a short life and a merry one. He had wanted to blaze across the firmament of his age like a white streak of fire, searing the image of his thoughts into every last human mind. He had wanted to burn hard and bright and burn himself out for fear death might catch him unawares with a dollar unspent or an idea uncommunicated. He and George Sterling had always agreed they would never sit up with the corpse; when their work was done, their life spent, they would bow themselves out.

There were books he would still like to write, his 'Christ' novel, his *Sailor on Horseback* autobiography, *The Farthest Distant*, a story of the days when the planet was growing cold. When he had been going strong no book had been big enough to hold everything he had had to say on the subject; nor had his fifty books been big enough to hold the force he felt within him. But he was tired. When he passed the rows of white boxes in his workroom in which he had notes for many, many more stories, he once again said to himself that he was no longer the raw recruit, he was the veteran who knew that the enemy's position would not be captured by sunrise, nor a century of sunrises.

He had fought his fight; he had done his share; he had had his say; he had earned his rest. He had made many mistakes and committed innumerable follies, but at least he had the satisfaction of knowing that they had been big ones. He had never played life 'the little way.' Time now to make room for the younger men who were fighting upward. Like the prize fighters he had written about, his legs were weakening, his wind was gone, he had to give way to what he had so often called 'youth unquenchable and irresistible—youth that must have its will, and that will never die.'

It was funny, he mused, how people became known for something they did not stand for. The critics charged his work with a lack of spirituality—he whose writing had been permeated with philosophy and the love of mankind. He had always written with two motifs—the superficial running motif, and the deep underlying motif, which only a few had ever glimpsed. When reporting the Russian-Japanese War, an official had come to his hotel and told him the entire population was gathered in the square below to see him. He had felt enormously set up to think his fame had spread to the wilds of Korea. But when he mounted the platform that had been erected for him, the official asked if he wouldn't take out his bridge of artificial teeth. For half an hour he had stood there taking out his teeth and putting them back again to the applause of the multitude; it was then that he had had his first glimpse of the fact that men rarely become famous for the things for which they strive and die.

To a young girl writing for encouragement he answered, 'At my present mature age I am convinced that the game is worth the candle. I have had a very fortunate life, I have been luckier than many hundreds of millions of men of my generation have been lucky, and, while I have suffered much, I have lived much, seen much, and felt much that has been denied to the average man. Yes, indeed, the game is worth the candle. As a proof of it, my friends all tell me I am getting stout. That, in itself, is the advertisement of spiritual victory.'

The long battle had been even more enjoyable than the victory; sunk by his mother's irresponsibility in the very abyss of poverty, he had fought his way upward, unaided. It had been a good brain Professor Chaney had bequeathed him, and though he had often been miserable over his illegitimacy, it had provided him with an important part of his driving power. He had a feeling that Professor Chaney would be proud of his son.

It seemed to him that the world, too, was growing old. 'The world of adventure is almost over now. Even the purple ports of the seven seas have passed away, and have become prosaic.' Long ago he had said, 'I am an idealist who believes in reality, and who therefore, in all I write strive to be real, to keep my own feet and the feet of the readers on the ground, so that no matter how high we dream our dreams will be based on reality.' He had dreamed his dreams, and they had been high dreams; and now he would face the reality that his dreams and his life were over.

Before the end the dying organism reared up for one last show of strength. He wrote 'Like Argus of the Ancient

Times,' one of his most delightful Alaskan stories, and 'The Princess,' one of his best stories of The Road, flashing back to the wild adventurous days of his youth and his first success. He ordered Forni to begin work on the circular stone dairy barn, and had the sacks of cement hauled up the long road. He would send to San Francisco the very finest J.L. milk, butter, and cheese . . . and old John London too would be proud of his son. He went with Eliza to Sacramento to attend the state fair, told her they would go forward with all their plans for the ranch, that they had three of their fences built and soon they would have the fourth one built and would be self-supporting. From three different catalogues he sent to New York and England for copies of *The Siege of Rochelle, Racial Decay, Conjugal Happiness*, a copy of Dreiser's *The Genius*, Stanley's *The Congo*, and a half dozen other books on botany, evolution, California plants, monkeys, the Dutch founding of New York.

He planned to go to the Orient, reserved his steamship tickets, then canceled them. He planned to go to New York, alone, but Ninetta Payne organized the water suit against him, and he had to remain in Glen Ellen. Nearly everyone agreed he had a right to the water. On the concluding day of the trial he testified for four hours, then left the courtroom with Forni, who reports that he was ill with uremia and in great pain. A few days later he invited to luncheon all the neighbors who had signed the petition for the suit; over the friendly table they assured him they had never wanted the injunction put against him.

On Tuesday, November 21, 1916, he completed his plans to leave for New York the following day, talked quietly and alone with Eliza until nine o'clock. He said he would stop over at the Chicago stock fair, buy some good stock and ship it home. Eliza agreed to go to the fair at Pendleton, Oregon, to see if she could find some shorthorn beef cattle. He told her to put an acre of ground at every laborer's family's disposal, and to build a house on it; to select a site for the community school and to apply for a teacher. She was also to pick a site for the community store. It was his ambition to raise everything on the ranch, to make it self-sufficient, to haul nothing up the hill except flour and sugar.

Ready to retire for the night, they walked together down the long hall to his study. Eliza said, 'By the time you come back I'll have the store all built and stocked, and the school all built and the teacher applied for. We'll apply to the government for a post office, and I'll put up a flagpole and we'll

have a little town of our own up here, and we'll call it Independence.' He put his arm about her shoulder, gave it a
rough squeeze, said in deadly earnest, 'I go you, old girl,'
walked through his study and onto his sleeping porch. Eliza
went to bed.

At seven o'clock the next morning Sekine, the Japanese
servant who had replaced Nakata, came running into Eliza's
room with terror on his face, crying, 'Missie, come quick.
Master act funny, like he drunk.' Eliza ran to the sleeping
porch, saw at once that Jack was unconscious, telephoned to
Sonoma for Doctor Allan Thomson. Doctor Thomson found
Jack in a state of narcosis; he had apparently been unconscious for some time. On the floor of the room he found two
empty vials labeled morphine sulphate and atropine sulphate;
on the night table he found a pad with some figures on it
which represented a calculation of the lethal dose of the
drug. He then telephoned the druggist in Sonoma to prepare
an antidote for morphine poisoning, and asked his assistant,
Doctor Hayes, to bring it up with him. The two doctors
washed out Jack's stomach, administered stimulants, mas-
saged his limbs. Only once during these treatments did he
seem to respond. His eyes opened slowly, his lips muttered
what might have been 'Hello.' He then again relaxed into unconsciousness.

Doctor Thomson reports that grief-stricken Eliza worked
with him as a nurse; that 'in a conversation with me during
the day Mrs. Charmian London [to whom Jack's 1911 will
left his entire estate] said it was very important that the now
probable death of Jack London should not be ascribed to
anything but uremic poisoning. I told her it would be difficult
to ascribe it to that alone, as any of the telephone conversa-
tions overheard that morning, or any information supplied by
the druggist who prepared the antidote, would tend to ascribe
his death to morphine poisoning.'

Jack died at a little after seven that evening. The following
day his body was taken to Oakland, where Flora, Bessie, and
his two daughters held services. The whole world mourned
his passing. In Europe his death was given more space than
that of the Emperor Franz Joseph of Austria, who had died
the day before him. The grief of America is best pictured by
Mrs. Luther Burbank, who picked up a newspaper and cried
out to a frolicking group of young friends leaving for the
University campus, 'Don't laugh! Jack London is dead.'
Edwin Markham had called him part of the youth and heroic

courage of the world; with his passing the world was bereft of a flame.

That night his body was cremated, and the ashes returned to his Beauty Ranch. Only two weeks before, while riding over a majestic knoll with Eliza, Jack had reined in his horse and said, 'Eliza, when I die I want you to bury my ashes on this hill.' She put his ashes in a box, dug a hole on the very top of the knoll that was shaded from the hot sun by madrone and manzanita, buried them, and cemented over the top. There she placed the huge red stone that he had named, 'The stone the builders rejected.'

ACKNOWLEGMENTS

MY GREATEST DEBT is to Mrs. Charmian Kittredge London and Mrs. Eliza London Shepard, who turned over to me Jack London's private files, library, account books, papers, correspondence, notes, manuscripts, and family documents; who revoked their order to the Huntington Library that the business correspondence in their possession was not to be shown during their lifetime; and who agreed that I might write and publish about them, in relation to Jack London, anything which in my opinion seemed necessary.

Mrs. Bessie London was at all times sympathetic and helpful. Irving and Mildred Shepard have been unflagging in their efforts to aid me in documenting the life of their uncle.

I wish to express my gratitude to the host of Jack London's friends who gave unstintingly of their time, their material, and their memories: Anna Strunsky, Frank Atherton, Cloudesley Johns, Edward Applegarth, Mr. and Mrs. Johnny Miller, Fred Thompson, James Hopper, Xaviar Martinez, Upton Sinclair, Finn Frolich, Ed Morrell, Janet Winship, Austin Lewis, J. Stitt Wilson, Doctor Jessica Peixotto, Alexander Irvine, Mrs. Robert Hill, Mrs. Carrie Burlingame, Forni, Billy Hill, Ira Pyle, Blanche Partington, Mira Mac-Clay, Thomas Hill, Doctor and Mrs. Allan Thomson.

Thanks are due to Mrs. Charmian Kittredge London's relatives for their courtesy: Mrs. Ninetta Eames-Payne, Mrs. Growell, Beth Wiley and Mrs. Wiley.

It is a pleasure to be able to express my appreciation to the people of Santa Rosa and Sonoma for their co-operation: Ang and Gertrude Franchetti, godparents of this project; Mrs. Byrd Weyler Kellogg and Senator Herbert Slater of the Santa Rosa *Press Democrat;* R. M. Barrett, Mrs. Luther Burbank, Glen Murdock, Fred Kellogg, Mrs. Paramore, and

Mrs. Celeste Murphey. To Robert Pickering for his scout work.

To the efficient and courteous staffs of the Bancroft Library of the University of California and the Huntington Library of San Marino, my salutations for making research work a joy; to the public libraries of Massillon, Ohio, and Van Nuys, California, my appreciation for their helpfulness; and to the Huntington Library for turning over to me their Jack London material, my heartfelt thanks.

IRVING STONE

ENCINO, CALIFORNIA

INDEX

⊘ SIGNET   (0451)

LIVES OF GENIUS AND PASSION

☐ **ELEANOR AND FRANKLIN by Joseph P. Lash.** Based on Eleanor Roosevelt's private papers, this is an intimate chronicle of an extraordinary woman's life, from her childhood through the death of her husband, FDR.
(140761—$5.95)*

☐ **KATE: THE LIFE OF KATHARINE HEPBURN by Charles Wigham.** In exclusive interviews and in her own words, here is a vivid portrait of the most elegant, independent, and tempestuous superstar of them all. With 8 pages of rare and fascinating photos. (112121—$2.95)*

☐ **THE ROCKEFELLERS by Peter Collier and David Horowitz.** Here are the myths, the rumors, the scandals, and, above all, the endlessly enthralling, often shocking truth about the most powerful family in America. "Remarkable!"—*The New York Times Book Review* (141075—$5.95)*

☐ **JENNIE: The Life of Lady Randolph Churchill, Volume I 1845-1895 by Ralph G. Martin.** The nationwide bestseller about the scandalous American beauty who ruled an age and raised her son Winston Churchill to shape history. (136942—$4.95)

☐ **JENNIE: The Life of Lady Randolph Churchill, Volume II 1895-1921 by Ralph G. Martin.** Wife to three men and mistress to many more, here are the climactic years of scandalous passion and immortal greatness of an extraordinary American beauty. (136934—$4.95)

*Prices slightly higher in Canada

Buy them at your local bookstore or use this convenient coupon for ordering.

NEW AMERICAN LIBRARY
P.O. Box 999, Bergenfield, New Jersey 07621

Please send me the books I have checked above. I am enclosing $_____
(please add $1.00 to this order to cover postage and handling). Send check or money order—no cash or C.O.D.'s. Prices and numbers are subject to change without notice.

Name _____

Address _____

City_____ State_____ Zip Code_____
Allow 4-6 weeks for delivery.
This offer is subject to withdrawal without notice.